The Man

City of Halos: Book 1
The Man

Kesava Anderson

VULPINE
PRESS

Published by Vulpine Press in the United Kingdom in 2025

ISBN: 978-1-83919-638-6

www.vulpine-press.com

To all of those who fight with their own demons of addiction and mental health. May you win the battles and the war.

Prologue

"Good morning New Justice Coalition and welcome to SafeCity Day, a nationwide celebration commemorating thirty years since the last gunshot death in our beloved Union State. Today, we reflect on the remarkable journey that led us here, to a realm where bullets are nothing more than a distant memory, thanks to the visionary efforts of one man: Ezekial Young," said the spry voice from the fake smile of a news correspondent with more make-up on than fillers and plastic surgery, which was saying something for sure. She turned to her cohost and there was an obvious rehearsed handoff, then he began to speak as he smoldered fiercely at the camera.

"In 2025, tragedy struck Ezekial's life when his daughter became a victim of senseless gun violence. Fueled by grief and propelled by an unwavering determination, Zeke embarked on a quest to render guns obsolete. Through tireless research and boundless creativity, he unveiled the groundbreaking Personal Defense System, a technology that neutralized the destructive potential of bullets with a gravitational pulse. Despite facing initial skepticism and resistance, Zeke's invention soon gained traction, spreading from homes and schools to entire cities. The concept of SafeCities was born, where bullets ceased to be a threat, and communities flourished in newfound safety.

"However, not everyone embraced this paradigm shift. Dissenters, including groups like the Southern Patriots, clung to their weapons and seceded to form the Liberty States. Yet, the SafeCities thrived, fortified by advanced technologies like Halospheres, which shielded them from external threats."

A gentle head nod and the camera angle changed, and the female anchor was ready to pick her spot on que. She smiled big and took a deep breath and launched into her transitioning statement.

"As we celebrate three decades of peace and prosperity, we must also acknowledge the challenges that lie ahead. The deep civil divide of North America and the rise of alternative threats remind us that the journey to lasting peace is ongoing. But on this SafeCity Day, let us honor Ezekial Young's legacy and reaffirm our commitment to a future where violence is but a distant memory."

As she concluded her speech, the two hosts rose from behind the reporter's desk, their posture exuding confidence and pride. In unison, they proclaimed, "Today, I celebrate my Safety!" With hands clasped together, they stepped out from behind the desk and made their way toward a waiting stage, where an eager audience awaited, surrounded by festive decorations.

The stage was set with a sleek, modern backdrop adorned with decorative shades of blue and silver, embodying the spirit of the holiday. Standing at the center were the charismatic hosts: a tall, black man with a winning smile and a white woman radiating warmth and enthusiasm, both thinner and more athletic than the average person.

As the camera panned to them, the audience erupted into applause, eager to hear their banter. The host, impeccably dressed in a sharp suit, flashed a charming grin as he addressed the viewers.

"Good morning, folks, and welcome to SafeCity Day celebrations! Today is June 21, 2055, and we are SAFE!" he began, his voice smooth and confident. "I'm Marcus, your guide through today's festivities, and joining me is the lovely Emily."

Emily, equally stylish in her attire, grinned in response. "Thanks, Marcus! It's great to be here on such a special occasion."

Marcus nodded, his expression turning serious for a moment. "Absolutely, Emily. SafeCity Day is more than just a holiday—it's a testament to the progress we've made in ensuring the safety and security of our communities."

Emily nodded in agreement. "That's right, Marcus. Thanks to the vision and ingenuity of people like Ezekial Young, we've been able to create environments where families can live without fear of gun violence."

Marcus leaned in, his tone becoming more animated. "And let's not forget the incredible advancements in technology that have made SafeCities possible. From the revolutionary Personal Defense System to the innovative Halospheres, we've truly transformed the way we think about safety."

Emily nodded, her eyes alight with enthusiasm. "Exactly, Marcus! But it's also important to remember that our work is far from over. We still face challenges, both within our communities and beyond. SafeCity Day serves as a reminder of the progress we've made and the work that lies ahead."

Marcus nodded in agreement. "Well said, Emily. So let's celebrate today, but let's also recommit ourselves to building a future where safety and security are not just ideals, but realities for all."

With that, the hosts exchanged a warm smile, their camaraderie evident as they prepared to guide viewers through a day filled with festivities and reflection.

"But first a word from our sponsor," Marcus said with a fake and dry smile

[The commercial began with a wide shot of a futuristic stadium bathed in neon lights, its sleek design hinting at the high-octane action within. The Deathball logo pulsated on the screen, accompanied by an intense soundtrack that set the tone for the adrenaline-fueled spectacle about to unfold.]

Narrator: "Welcome, sports enthusiasts, to the heart-pounding world of Deathball!"

[The camera zoomed in on the arena floor, where armored athletes are seen gearing up for battle. Their faces are a mix of determination and anticipation, signaling the fierce competition ahead.]

Narrator: "Get ready to witness the ultimate test of skill, speed, and strategy as elite teams clash in the arena!"

The scene transitioned to a tall, towering behemoth of a man staring at the screen intently.

Narrator: "From bone-crushing collisions to jaw-dropping maneuvers, Deathball delivers non-stop action and excitement!"

[The scene transitioned to the roaring crowds filling the stands, their energy palpable as they cheered on their favorite teams with unbridled enthusiasm.]

Narrator: "Join us for the most electrifying event of the season and experience the thrill of victory and the agony of defeat!"

[As the Deathball logo flashed on the screen one last time, the narrator delivered a final call to action.]

Narrator: "Don't miss out on the adrenaline rush of a lifetime! Get your tickets now and be part of the Deathball revolution June 23!

The screen faded to black.

"And we're back!" Emily said as they sat together and smiled. A somber moment overtook the studio and the lights began to fade, soft music began to play and a photo of Zeke's daughter faded onto the screen. A baritone voice began to speak.

"In 2025 a tragedy shook the very foundation of Ezekial Young's existence when his nine-year-old daughter fell victim to a school shooting.

"Zeke, not bound by extraordinary intelligence but rather an insatiable hunger for knowledge, channeled his grief into a singular mission: to render guns obsolete. He was a man of boundless creativity and unwavering focus, possessing the ability to master complex concepts swiftly. His relentless pursuit was born of love, driven by the agony of losing Mariah. Zeke joined the chorus of grieving parents who protested and lobbied for change, but their pleas fell upon deaf ears. Even his impassioned plea before Congress, just two months after his daughter's tragic death, couldn't secure a single vote across the aisle. Zeke was defeated, but within his despair, an idea stirred.

"For thirteen months, Zeke poured every ounce of his being into research and experimentation, emptying his pockets and selling his home and belongings to fund his quest. In December of 2026, he summoned the media to unveil his invention. Yet, the world had moved on, indifferent to a grieving father's plight. Twelve more school shootings in as many months had drowned out his voice. On Christmas morning, amid the pomp of politicians, Zeke approached the state Capitol, press pass in one hand, the other concealing a small but menacing semi-automatic rifle.

"Zeke's actions prompted a swift response from the Secret Service, their shots expertly aimed. Fifty-six rounds fired from within ten feet, yet not a single one found its mark; each bullet hung motionless in mid-air. Zeke cried out, 'the plans for the PDS are on my social pages, they are public. No one has to die from gun violence again.'

"The Personal Defense System (PDS) began as a quest to nullify the destructive potential of bullets, an intersection of gravity and velocity. Zeke's groundbreaking discovery allowed the velocity of projectiles to be neutralized through a gravitational pulse. Soon, others replicated his device, some with noble intentions, others with sinister motives. Within a year, the PDS expanded from homes and schools to entire cities, birthing the concept of SafeCities where bullets became obsolete."

The monitor cut off and I could see myself in the dark reflection. The stark adjustment from overly done news personalities to a hairy belly made me a little self-conscious, but only a little. I sat on the end of the bed and pondered about just how the world changed in my lifetime.

There was something oddly comforting about remembering that people who lived in the early 1900's once went from never seeing an airplane to watching men land on the moon. It made my mental gymnastics feel almost reasonable as I tried to make sense of two revolutions unfolding back-to-back—and a third drawing near a little over a 100 years later.

The first was the end of traditional warfare and it did not go with a bang, but with a slow, suffocating chokehold on those who resisted change. When the PDS was first introduced, the world did not celebrate its arrival. It recoiled. Governments saw it as a tool of disruption—an invention that could destabilize global power structures overnight. Criminals saw it as a death sentence to their underground empires. The general public was left torn, staring at a future where guns no longer dictated survival.

Ezekial Young didn't build the PDS to create division, but division followed it like a shadow at dusk.

The news shocked the world. News outlets ran headlines like "Firearms are extinct," "Here today, Gun tomorrow," and my personal favorite, "Here lies 2A."

The spectacle surrounding the PDS rivaled the technology itself. Massive marches flooded Washington, gun advocates taking to the streets in protest. The blame shifted between both sides of the aisle, yet neither took responsibility.

Blueprints for the PDS were all over thanks to Reddit and Ezekial, and before states could officially adopt them, armed civilians had already begun constructing their own. Violent protests erupted, resulting in casualties, including officers—events that solidified the immediate deployment of PDS technology for law enforcement.

Congress acted swiftly after an unprecedented attack—one man single-handedly eliminated a high-ranking official along with their entire Secret Service detail. In response, sweeping PDS legislation passed without hesitation.

Then came the larger versions.

The first major test came in San Diego in 2027, when the city deployed PDS towers at every major intersection, creating the first true SafeCity. Yeah, there was still poop on the streets, but at least you weren't going to be shot. The results were instant—gun-related crimes dropped to near-zero overnight. Bulletproof glass became obsolete, armored trucks unnecessary, and for the first time in decades, children played in the streets without fear.

The news ran endless loops of interviews with relieved parents and reformed criminals alike, but beneath the surface, opposition was boiling. The firearms industry, one of the most powerful lobbies in the nation, waged an all-out war on the system. Politicians took to the airwaves, claiming the technology was a step toward "globalist tyranny," comparing it to mass surveillance and arguing that once the government-controlled guns, they controlled everything.

The divide wasn't just political. It was cultural.

In the Midwest and South, armed militias flourished in backwoods towns and sprawling rural landscapes, vowing never to surrender their weapons. In California, New York, and other progressive strongholds,

SafeCities became a symbol of enlightenment and progress. The nation fractured before it even realized what was happening.

Extremely liberal territories proposed turning over gun violence convictions, which was actually met with support. It failed miserably in court, and according to Jim Carey, "Bleeding hearts of the world unite."

When Florida and Texas formally seceded in 2029, they weren't the first, but they were the loudest. Governors stood on statehouse steps, flanked by military generals and corporate allies, announcing their withdrawal from what they called a "technocratic dictatorship." Texas absorbed Oklahoma, parts of New Mexico, and Arizona, forming the first Liberty State. Florida, Georgia, Alabama, and Mississippi followed suit.

They claimed their independence in the name of "freedom," but freedom was a fragile illusion.

Out of the gate, SafeCities thrived, but the Liberty States struggled. Without access to advanced technology, they relied on outdated infrastructure, fossil fuels, and barter economies. Electricity became inconsistent. Food supply chains dwindled. Their newfound allies, Russia and China, flooded them with aid—at a price. The Liberty States traded autonomy for survival, allowing foreign nations to establish "trade zones" that were little more than militarized strongholds.

The United States—now calling itself the Union States—didn't retaliate with war. They retaliated with time.

By 2035 SafeCities covered 82% of the Union States' population and held 94% of the wealth. The remaining 18%—those in outposts, rural towns, or the secessionist states—became relics of the past, their ways of life preserved only by sheer stubbornness and the will to survive in a crumbling world.

For those still within the Union, the term "American" ceased to exist. You were either a SafeCity citizen, an Outposter, or a Libertarian—each group as foreign to the other as night and day.

But peace never lasts.

The Liberty States, backed by foreign powers, began an attempt to develop PDS disruptors. By 2040 sabotage attacks to the power grids were frequent, and it became clear that the divide was no longer ideological—it was existential. The world had fractured into those who embraced control and those who sought chaos. The disruptor attempt led to a breakthrough in Halosphere technology that was the be-all and end-all of the advances keeping SafeCities in their namesake. Halosphere independence from government regulation kicked in, and another overnight revolution was born. The governmental control of each state was now a four-branch entity. Executive, Legislative, Judicial, and now Corporate. It had always been like that, but now it was official. Most residents didn't mind it. Citizens voiced their dissatisfaction through their spending, favoring companies that reflected their values and priorities while avoiding—even boycotting—those that didn't.

The fervor for the Second Amendment led to the formation of groups like the Southern Patriots, The Reckoning, The 2A Knights, and several other militias, determined to hold onto their weapons. These dissenters abandoned the SafeCities in favor of building their own territories known as "Liberty States." Texas and Florida spoke out first against the US Government after the ban on alternative ammunition, sonic rounds, and explosive shots that would cause concussive damage.

Zeke met his end in a jail cell. Rumors swirled about the circumstances—some suggested foul play, others believed he had finally found peace. Regardless, he knew his invention would reshape the world. Warfare shifted to a battle of bullet-stopping capabilities.

Chemical and biological threats became prevalent, leading SafeCities to construct Halospheres of magnanimous proportion, enhanced PDS technology encasing them in protective shields. The thin layer of metallic dust formed an impenetrable barrier, guarding against external attacks. Huge purple glowing domes over some of America's largest cities were no longer science fiction. It was daily life.

And in the middle, caught between a war of old and new, were people like me.

Those too skilled to be ignored.

Too valuable to be free.

Chapter 1
A World Transformed

Waking up to these two yahoos on the TV was my least favorite alarm. I could have sworn I was watching something else the night before. "Ughhh," I groaned, as my eyes locked onto the clock as 5:59 magically ticked over to 6:00, and the tiniest smile flittered onto my face, then a premonition that the phone would soon ring, especially after a dream like that. I've had these dreams before. Clear and crisp as reality right after waking but fleeting with every moment that passed. I could remember every gory and frightening detail of my nightmare until I focused in on it and tried to rationalize it. Grasping at the details in the dream after I awoke was like trying to catch fireflies in a moonlit field—you'd see only the light, a remnant but long gone by the time you got there. I knew something had been there though, so real, but it was fleeting at best. Rest had been a precious commodity in my life actually, especially lately, where a mere six hours of sleep hardly sufficed.

My phone rang, just as I predicted. A nostalgic tethered phone with a dial tone. More common than anyone would expect for the year. Someone in 1999 wouldn't have thought in the year 2055 a hot commodity would be a see-through acrylic phone, but I was a sucker for antiques. After losing all microchips, computers, and advanced technology for 5 years, many of us embraced it. When the chip embargo was lifted, some of held on to the things that wouldn't die on us in case of another EMP attack.

I picked up my phone, and it was my therapist, an upbeat female voice who asked me to tell her about my dream immediately. She didn't even ask me how my previous day had gone. I tried to tell her about my dream, but trying to remember it was like trying to catch a butterfly. It was close and clumsy but impossible to clinch. The closer I got, the further away the details seemed.

"Garlands BBQ, do you want a 5-piece tender and sauce on your fries?"

"You're doing it again," my therapist admonished, her voice breaking my reverie.

"What?" I replied, feigning nonchalance knowing that I was pulling random details from previous dreams that I actually remembered and piecing them together.

"Please, take this seriously," she said with annoyance in her voice.

"I am calling because there was a ping from your Synaptic Augmented Enhanced Implant activated last night at 2:07 a.m. for 0.7 milliseconds," she explained patiently.

"Every other implant gets removed after service; why can't you remove this one and give me my life back?" I grumbled in frustration.

"Mark, tell me about your implant," the voice on the other end replied.

"Sixty-seven sessions, and you ask me the same thing every time," I countered in frustration.

Her response was almost robotic, sharply edged with rehearsed precision. "You are required to explain the purpose of your implant during each session to maintain congruence. It must match your previous explanations for the system to compare your mental recall status. Your mental coherence and stability are essential for discharge consideration.

Data and information recall are vital for assessment. Memory failure is a primary symptom of Implant Malfunction Syndrome."

"Oh, that didn't sound recorded at all," I teased, my frustration now only thinly veiled.

"Mark, tell me about your implant," the voice reiterated.

I sighed deeply before launching into an explanation. "There are two types of implants. The first, given to army infantry, is the basic BattleSync implant. It assists with aiming, provides feedback to the base, and enables team communication. It's a simple but invaluable tool on the battlefield. The second type is more complex, incorporating cognitive functions. It operates in the subconscious, allowing a nano-computer, the Synaptic Augmented Enhanced Implant (SAI), to take control of our reflexes. It enhances endurance, resistance to pain, and the ability to focus on a single sense amidst chaos."

I continued, "The SAI can release adrenaline, slow our heart rate, or even eliminate our fight-or-flight response if necessary. It's designed to reduce battlefield fatigue and prevent PTSD by filtering out traumatic experiences before they become permanent memories. Out of 2,600 SAI implants attempted, only ten survived. Implant Malfunction Syndrome claimed most upon activation, and drove others into madness. They heard voices only they could perceive, reported strange occurrences, and became violent. They had to be remotely deactivated.

"My value to this nation lies in being one of those ten survivors. I need my retirement benefits; my family needs them. But to retire, I need a full deactivation," I asserted.

"We cannot fully deactivate you until we're certain you're cognitively separated from your SAI. Disabling your SAI without certainty would result in Implant Sickness, leading to IMS—agitation, sleep loss, and memory lapses. I need to know if you're experiencing any of these symptoms," the voice explained.

"How many have you worked with? Out of the 2,600, how many have you had to decommission remotely? You have that button in front of you, just in case. How many disclosed their symptoms before you sent the command to their SAI?" I pressed, a burning determination to unravel the enigmatic process in my voice.

"How many of us would want you to know if we are falling apart from the inside?" I continued in a hushed and concerned tone, peering for answers.

Her response was measured, revealing just enough without revealing everything. "There were a few who confided, not many, but none as significant as you. You're the only Augmented Neurological Guardian Link (ANGL) seeking deactivation. Once it's off, we can't turn you back on, and..." She trailed off, leaving the unspoken consequence hanging in the air.

I picked up where she left off, stating a harsh truth. "And you will have to decommission and kill 250 perfectly good soldiers for the odds of getting just one other ANGL. It's a tough call for you but a far tougher ordeal for them. Isn't it? All of the lies you'll have to tell and families you'll need to deceive, including my personal favorite: 'Your family will get full access to New Justice Coalition...'"

We called it New Jack Chicago as a snarky nickname, but I kept that to myself. Not the time or place, despite crime not going away, just changing.

She interrupted with a firm reminder, "They will, Mark, but only after you're fully deactivated. I cannot deactivate you until I am certain that the SAI psy-link is completely severed. Until then, your family will remain in an Outpost, where they are well protected and have the ability to make a living outside of The Waste."

"Can we wrap this up? I've got work soon," I grumbled, trying to keep the situation from growing any sadder. Both she and I knew that my restless nights might be a potential symptom of Implant Sickness.

While I hadn't lost time, memories, or grown overly agitated over triv-ial matters, there was still a chance. I was willing to take that risk if it meant securing a better future for my family—my mom, brother, sis-ter, and uncle—by getting them into New Justice Coalition (NJC) sooner rather than later.

She shifted back into her all-business tone, requesting, "State your designation, rank, and status."

"Mark Romero Andeya, 0010, Captain, Active-Pending," I replied in kind.

"Please answer the following questions," she continued, her voice now sounding extra official.

Her: What year is it?
Me: 2055
Tone: True

Her: Where are you located?
Me: In my apartment
Tone: Specified Response Required

Her: What location?
Me: New Justice Coalition, Formerly Chicago "Where Progress Meets Protection: Your Sanctuary in the Future."
Tone: True

Her: Who's the President of your State?
Me: Jeremiah Mason
Tone: False

"Now's not the time to try to game the system, Mark," said the voice over the phone.

"I'm not," I defended, "Jeremiah Mason is the President," I said genuinely confused.

Tone: False

"Moving on," she retorted with a slight agitation.

"Please answer truthfully and directly. Have you experienced any of the following symptoms in the past 24 hours?"

Her: Confusion?
Me: No
Tone: True

Her: Unprovoked Anger?
Me: No
Tone: True

Her: Voices in your head?
Me: No
Tone: True

Her: Memory loss?
Me: No
Tone: True

Her: BattleLink Residuals or Relived Combat Experiences?
Me: No
Tone: Processing
Tone: Processing
Tone: Processing
Tone: True

"Thank you for your time, Captain; one more session and passed polygraph and I can recommend your full deactivation and discharge," she concluded.

"I sharted myself last week after eating some questionable Mexican food."

Tone: True

There was a heavy sigh on her end, that I am confident escaped through a smile, accompanied by a palm to the face. A sound that seemed to escape despite her professional demeanor, and then the line went silent.

~

Lying on my back, I found myself fixating on the ceiling of my apartment, lost in contemplation, and fighting sleep. Questions swirled in my mind, each one probing deeper into the circumstances that had led me here. It was a moment of introspection, a chance to take stock of my reality and consider the best course of action to support my family back in the Outpost.

As I nestled, I did take note that I had a pretty decent bed. Or at least the best that an NJC trial officer's salary could afford. But then I realized I actually had two jobs. My first was to track down suspects and collect evidence, a job that my mother still gave me grief about. She called it too dangerous. I gave them a trial on the spot while a group of people, sitting in the safety of their home, would be given the evidence I collected, and they would decide if they were innocent or guilty. Some real Judge Dredd stuff if you ask me. I got paid based on the number of people I could successfully track down who were found guilty. Lawyers and prosecutors had fifteen minutes to plead their sides.

My second job was much more exciting; if and when found guilty, people often ran. When people ran, they weren't always easy to catch. I tracked down guilty parties for other trial officers. That's what I'm good at: catching people. I shook my head at my own ridiculousness and scoffed out loud.

I thought of that most nights while lying there in my bed, which was right in my kitchen. Yes, I had a bed and kitchen combo. Oh, the joys of a studio apartment. So many reasons to celebrate… or not. It took some adjusting to doze off next to my kitchen table. White walls, bare, save for the picture of my ex-girlfriend, who, by the way, was holding my dog in the photo. I left up the photo because she still had my dog, Ali, a Labrador and Pitbull mix. Mostly black with white paws, hence the name.

Though the standard twenty-by-twenty flats in my building were tiny and annoying, the quirky toilet-shower combo still stuck with me as most odd. I am going to shower one day while taking a dump, to defy societal norms. I am a loner Dottie, a rebel.

I kept trying to remember what I had on the TV last night that would make me wake up to NJC's most uniformly disliked morning show, then it hit me like most others: I had fallen asleep to a 2D classic: *The Fifth Element.* "Lilu Dallas Multipass" was a phrase I whispered out loud to entertain myself and had become almost a lullaby. Usually, it was the last thing I heard before falling into a sweet slumber. Although they created Neural Original Content (NOC) versions for such movies, I had a penchant for experiencing them in their original, unaltered glory. Streaming videos directly to smart lenses might be tempting, but I could still discern the difference. Besides, they were uncomfortable, vulnerable to hacking, and prohibitively expensive. Over two thousand crypto-credits last time I checked, and my Hololens resolution was terrible. Good enough for government work, but that was it. I owned a genuine television, pulled straight from The Waste. A 43-inch LCD 720p, Sanyo to be exact. Then how did Marcus and Emily grace my screen this morning?

"I must have rolled onto the remote at some point in the night," I thought to myself.

"I should be happy I have a screen to watch," was my next thought. I had lived through The Blackout.

In 2040 the world entered a five-year period known as The Blackout, a time when advanced circuitry and AI-controlled systems started a conflict. During this conflict, an electromagnetic pulse (EMP) event occurred, resulting in the shutdown of virtually all electronic devices and systems on Earth. Miraculously, the Halospheres, inscrutable structures that had always been a source of both wonder and mystery, remained untouched by the EMP. Although the technology housed within these colossal structures was wiped clean, the Halospheres themselves stood impervious to the devastating pulse. This peculiar phenomenon puzzled scientists and experts alike, and it remains a mystery to this day.

There was an unknown AI war in space. We found out later that our AI won. The singular AI's unexpected victory over the other AIs in orbit left Earth in a state of both relief and continued uncertainty. Society on Earth had no way of knowing about this silent, high-stakes battle unfolding in orbit, so we continued to live without advanced technology, relying on more primitive means of communication and entertainment.

That's how I fell in love with the 2D classics like *Die Hard* and *Lethal Weapon*. It's probably why I went into law enforcement after the corps, too. I watched them on repeat.

I walked over to my collection and thumbed through my retirement. I called it my retirement because some of these things are priceless scavenged from The Waste. My Sony Walkman CD Player in pristine condition along with an unscratched Backstreet Boys album, my perfect condition DVD collection featuring the likes of Lorezno Lamas, Michael Dudikoff and the hero himself, Richard Dean Anderson. I had other things, but this was my nest-egg.

In the absence of advanced technology, society was forced to adapt to a more analog way of life. People turned to manual labor, traditional methods, and age-old practices for their daily needs and survival. The Blackout era served as a sobering reminder of the potential dangers of unrestrained technological advancement. Nations around the world agreed to exercise caution and responsibility when developing new technology, as the looming threat of nuclear annihilation remained a constant reminder of the consequences of unchecked progress. The Blackout era left an indelible mark on humanity, shaping the course of technological development and instilling a collective commitment to safeguarding the future.

Books, radios, UHF/VHF signals, and VHS tapes became the primary modes of communication and entertainment for the people of Earth. Those with a stash of CDs and DVDs suddenly found themselves in possession of highly coveted items, as these became the new standard for audio and video entertainment. Remote pawn shops became treasure troves, and individuals with collections of tapes could practically write their own checks as they sold or traded their analog treasures. Gold and silver, as expected, became the standard in trade. Crypto, if you had a digital wallet that was still intact, became the new gold rush.

In this tech-deprived world, theaters experienced a resurgence in popularity as people sought out communal entertainment experiences. However, old-fashioned projectors were a rarity, making each visit to the cinema a unique and cherished event. The absence of advanced circuitry forced humanity to adapt and rediscover the simpler pleasures of life, all while unaware of the silent guardian AI watching over them from above. If you found a place to go, you stuck to it. Drive-ins made a killing. But a working TV in your possession made you a god amongst men.

Cassettes, the iconic relic of the 90's, became an unexpected lifeline for humanity in this tech-deprived era. With advanced circuitry off the table, people turned to these analog wonders for both nostalgia and practicality. Everything about the 90s, from the music to the fashion, became gospel and a source of inspiration for the survival of a society that had been forced to rediscover simpler ways of life. The familiar hiss and click of a cassette tape brought comfort and a sense of connection to a bygone era, reminding people of the resilience of the human spirit in the face of unexpected challenges.

Chapter 2
Outposts

I gazed out of my window, noticing that the usual filter for our vibrant purple sky had been temporarily disabled. The world outside took on a surreal quality, bathed in varying shades of blueish-purple. It was a stark reminder of the unique blend of tradition and innovation that defined life in the NJC, now an integral part of the vast city of Chicago.

The view from above showcased a fascinating juxtaposition. While the traditional architecture of Chicago's storied past still graced our streets, the unmistakable mark of NJC's technological prowess was impossible to miss. The gleaming towers of new construction stood as modern marvels, reaching skyward with an ambition that rivaled the highest skyscrapers. NJC's architecture seamlessly fused the city's historical charm with cutting-edge advancements, creating a distinctive urban landscape that was both nostalgic and forward-looking.

My eyes drifted from the architectural wonders to the sky itself. Its deep purple hue this particular morning hinted at a change in our daily routine. In NJC, our weather was meticulously controlled to provide the ideal living conditions, and the varying sky colors served as indicators. A deep purple sky, like the one above, signaled increased humidity. While it didn't rain every day, the air was perpetually saturated with moisture, lending an ever-present dampness to the environment. Occasionally, a gentle drizzle would descend upon the streets, a reminder of the unpredictable beauty of nature that persisted alongside our technological utopia.

As I took in the view, I couldn't help but appreciate the unique blend of past and future that defined life in NJC. Our city was a testament to human innovation and adaptability, where history and progress coexisted in harmony under the ever-watchful, purple-tinged sky.

Just by sight, my nose automatically prepared itself for the permanent petrichor of outside. After some time, you'd think you'd get used to it, but I didn't. Instead, it hit me like new each time I went out there.

NJC had its own peculiar brand of weather, a controlled and predictable symphony that played day after day. The temperature held steadfast at a balmy 63.7 degrees Fahrenheit, a climate meticulously maintained to ensure our comfort. Occasionally, it would dip to 58 degrees, prompting us to reach for our trusty sweaters or jackets. On other days, a slight rise to 67 degrees would inspire us to break out our summer attire, relishing in the fleeting warmth.

Yet, beyond the weather, it was the fashion choices that revealed the most about life in NJC. While sweaters and jackets were standard attire for most, the true fashion statement was worn on one's face. The ubiquitous Hololens served a dual purpose, filtering out the purple-hued light that bathed our city while also acting as our primary communication devices. Our video chats, data feeds, and entertainment all centered around our Hololens. Simple, but easy to use technology.

Hololens came in various styles, ranging from the sleek and discreet, barely noticeable thin lenses that resembled contact lenses, to the more conspicuous and bulky models reminiscent of 19th-century aviation goggles. The elites of NJC typically sported the former, while I found myself in possession of something closer to the latter.

As much as I admired the aesthetic of the Halospheres, the purple hue that shone on every surface made it difficult to discern subtle details in the world around me. So, I bore my clunky government-issued Hololens to filter it out. They were so big and obvious that they made me look like I was either a narc or completely destitute. They did wonders for my personal life.

I looked over to see 6:15 a.m. on the clock. In the solitude of that moment, I contemplated the idea that just fifteen more minutes of sleep could change my life, for the better of course. Ultimately, I gave in to the temptation, surrendering to the allure of my bed's sweet embrace. It wasn't a full-fledged commitment, merely a retreat to the sanctuary above the sheets and beneath the comforter's hefty weight. It felt like an act of rebellion, like making it to second base back in eighth grade—a bit taboo yet socially acceptable. But my aim wasn't sleep; it was rest.

The previous night's dream lingered in the corners of my mind, casting a shadow over my desire to fall back asleep. If I could just remember one thing about the dream, I would be happy, I thought to myself. It wasn't one of those BattleSync mirages; no, this was something entirely different. I did find one morsel that came back to me. My dreams usually involved me as an observer, watching myself from the third person—either over my shoulder or standing alongside myself. But this time, it was in the first person, and that was unusual. I couldn't help but wonder if the effects of Implant Sickness were manifesting themselves in a different way within me.

24

It had been over a decade since I'd received the implant. I still vividly remembered the recruiter who had come to my high school, perfectly dressed and fast-talking, spinning tales of hover-bikes and easy money. He had been relentless, refusing to leave me alone. Back then, my grades had been decent for a kid living in an Outpost town. But, not good enough to take a spot at the uni on scholarship. My grandmother often complained about how much school had changed; we no longer had physical classrooms or real teachers. Instead, we had giant Holoboards projecting lessons from teachers hundreds of miles away, instructing kids in SafeCities in person who were genuinely learning. In the Outpost towns, no hand raising or interaction was allowed unless it was with an AI, a restriction that stemmed from the limitations imposed since the AI war. Trades were the most important jobs unless you lived in a SafeCity.

Outpost towns were prime recruiting grounds in this post-war society. Each of these towns had a single, imposing DWAR (Disarmament Weaponry and Advanced Robotics) in the center, effectively eliminating firearms while allowing everything else. Growing up in these towns meant learning self-defense from a young age. After all, anything or anyone could find its way in from The Waste—a harsh and unpredictable realm. Most, if not all, residents of an Outpost town rarely ventured beyond its borders unless they never planned on returning.

Outposts were never meant to last.

When the first SafeCities came online, the world was supposed to be simple—you either lived inside the domes or you didn't. The government never planned for the in-between, never accounted for the millions who wouldn't fit into either category. And yet, Outposts persisted.

I grew up in one.

Most Outposts served as waiting rooms for SafeCity rejects—people who applied but didn't make the cut, either because they lacked the right skills, the right connections, or, more often than not, because the system was never designed to let everyone in. The government couldn't just abandon them outright, so they built these makeshift settlements just outside the domes, gave them minimal infrastructure, and dangled a promise in front of them: serve the SafeCity, and maybe—just maybe—you'll earn your way in.

It was a lie.

I watched people grind their whole lives away chasing that dream. Engineers worked double shifts maintaining SafeCity power grids, farmers kept the dome-fed populations alive, laborers hauled materials to build the city's expansions. Everyone contributed. But when NJC officials came through every few months to read the Lottery List, the names were always the same—executives, researchers, government loyalists. People who had never touched a wrench or tilled a field.

My mother always believed that if we worked hard enough, we'd get in. I never did.

Outposts became their own ecosystem, neither abandoned nor accepted. A limbo where people survived, but never thrived. The divide was obvious. Inside the domes, SafeCitizens lived in luxury, sheltered by tech and security. In the Liberty States, people fended for themselves, answering only to the warlords and foreign investors propping them up. And then there was us—Outposters. Forgotten. Disposable.

And every few months, we gathered for The Lottery.

The NJC claimed it was a fair system—prove yourself, and you'd be allowed to join SafeCity life. But no one who actually deserved it ever got chosen. The algorithm, if there even was one, always picked the ones already set up for success. Those of us doing the hard work? We were stuck. Indefinitely.

So people found other ways to survive.

Some, like me, became officers. Trial agents, bounty hunters, enforcers—whatever the NJC needed. Others turned to the black market, smuggling contraband in and out of SafeCities. Alcohol, unapproved stimulants, banned media—if the dome-dwellers wanted it, Outposts made sure they got it. The NJC took their cut, of course. Protection always comes at a price.

Then there were the bandits. The ones who gave up on the system entirely.

Some of them were exiles—people who had once lived inside a SafeCity and got thrown out for breaking the wrong rules. Others were just desperate, scavengers who roamed the outskirts, taking whatever they could. And beyond them, in the true wildlands, lurked The Reckoning.

The NJC called them terrorists. Outposters called them ghosts.

They didn't just hate SafeCities—they wanted to burn them to the ground.

I'd seen what they were capable of. I'd walked through the aftermath of their attacks—factories gutted, supply lines cut, entire townships wiped out in a single night. They didn't care who they killed. SafeCitizens, Outposters, even their own kind. If you weren't with them, you were against them.

I spent my whole life in an Outpost, knowing that no matter what I did, I would never be one of them. Never be one of the SafeCitizens who got to live in comfort, never be one of the rebels fighting to tear it all down.

But that didn't mean I wasn't useful.

People like me—the ones too skilled to be ignored, too valuable to be free—were always needed.

And in a place like this, usefulness was the only thing keeping you alive.

I remember being targeted and recruited in high school.

That morning in class felt like any other, the monotony of lectures and assignments stretching out before me like an endless expanse of boredom. But amidst the drudgery, there was one bright spot that never failed to catch my eye: Ms. Wang. We didn't have many teachers on Outpost, but out of the few we had, this was the woman of every teen boy's dream.

With her radiant smile and infectious enthusiasm, Ms. Wang was a beacon of light in an otherwise dreary high school experience. I found myself hanging on her every word, eagerly soaking up her wisdom and guidance like a parched desert traveler stumbling upon an oasis. Even as she scrolled quadratic equations across the old school chalk board. I could not take my eyes off her.

But it wasn't just her intellect or her beauty that drew me to her. There was something indefinable about Ms. Wang, a magnetic quality that made her stand out from the rest of the faculty. Maybe it was her genuine warmth, or the way she seemed to sincerely care about each and every one of her students. Whatever it was, I couldn't help but be drawn to her like a moth to a flame.

So when she told me that someone wanted to speak with me, my heart skipped a beat with excitement. For a brief moment, I allowed myself to entertain the possibility that maybe, just maybe, it was her who wanted to talk to me. The thought sent a thrill of anticipation coursing through my veins, filling me with a heady sense of possibility.

As I made my way to the designated meeting spot, my mind raced with possibilities. Could this be the moment that would change everything? Only time would tell, but one thing was for certain: I was ready for whatever the future had in store.

The school, mostly empty, buzzed with the chatter of students rushing to their Outpost assignments or a study room when I nearly ran into the recruiter as I walked into the room Ms. Wang directed me to. The man exuded confidence as he approached me, a hint of a knowing smile playing at the corner of his lips.

"Mark," the recruiter began, his voice firm yet persuasive.

"You're not Ms. Wang," I said with unintentional disgust.

"No, I'm Captain Robinson and I've been hearing some great things about you. You've got the grades and the skills. I think you've got what it takes to be something more."

"Oh, really?" I retorted, a smirk tugging at my lips. "And what's in it for me, besides the allure of free college and easy money?"

The recruiter chuckled, clearly accustomed to my brand of snark. "Well," he began, "there's more to it than just that. You see, the world out there is changing, and it's getting tougher by the day. We need individuals like you to protect our Outpost towns."

I couldn't resist a snide comment. "Protect them from what, exactly? Rampaging herds of mutant chipmunks?"

The recruiter laughed heartily. "Not quite, but you'd be trained to handle whatever challenges come your way. The real reward is the chance to make a difference, to be part of something bigger. You've seen how the world's transformed. We need people who can rise to the occasion."

My interest piqued, despite my best efforts. I leaned in a little closer. "Alright," I conceded, "let's say I'm intrigued. What's the catch, then?"

The recruiter leaned in as well, his voice dropping lower. "The catch, Mark, is commitment. This isn't just a job; it's a way of life. We need dedicated individuals who can put in the work, day-in and day-out. But in return, you'll have opportunities beyond your wildest imagination."

Young me nodded thoughtfully, the gears in my mind turning. "I'll give it some thought," I said, "but you'll have to do better than college tuition and easy money to seal the deal."

The recruiter smiled knowingly; his eyes fixed on me. "Mark, the more you learn about what we do, the more enticing it'll become. The world is changing fast. Opportunities like this don't come knocking twice."

I began to walk away, and when the recruiter yelled, "Five passes to NJC for your family," I didn't pass it up. I didn't even think about it. After the AI War and Restriction DWAR technology evolved, the world's militaries grew increasingly desperate to change and adapt their tactics. The books on warfare were rewritten overnight. Hand-to-hand combat, swordplay, and crossbows were once again a foundation of battle.

Even after fifteen years, my mind often drifted back to my school days—to a world that no longer existed. Back then, there were no Union States, no Liberty States—only the fragile unity we called America, now splintered beyond recognition.

In our new reality, the concept of "CityGuard" was introduced. The government mandated that all cities had to run CityGuard programs to ensure safety in order to receive government services. It was a response to the growing divide between those who wanted to retain their guns and those who craved safety.

Outposts acted as safe stops for people traveling between SafeCities. Air travel still existed, but it was a dangerous and costly affair. The partnership between Liberty States and China afforded some of them some amazingly advanced technology like drones and access to state sensitive information.

North America now had two competing governments operating on a precarious edge. Neither wanted to push things to an all-out civil war, which meant they avoided interfering with individual state issues.

Each state was almost independent, mobilizing its troops only when war was declared. This is where Outposts like mine came into play. There were conflicts, but no declarations of war.

SafeCities had population limits, and Outposts served as a kind of feeder system for them. If you signed up for a SafeCity but didn't make it, you were placed in an Outpost with specific duties and expectations. The reward for success was a spot in a SafeCity, if you were lucky.

These places just weren't just guarded by a DWAR in the center, which prevented the use of projectile weapons like guns. They also had physical barriers to protect against rocket, missile, and biological attacks. Domes created by immense energy pushed out by the heart of the DWAR. A self-sustaining Fusion engine. The domes created a closed weather ecosystem, allowing SafeCities to control climate patterns and regulate how much sunlight filtered through. The effort to keep the weather as consistent to each region was important.

Then there were "The Free Territories," or as we called them, "The Waste." They seemed to operate by their own rules, primarily caring about food, water, and liberty. Trade with them happened at the Outposts, and drones transported food daily into the SafeCities. They were the in-between lawless areas not protected but claimed by the Liberty States.

But not everyone liked this arrangement. As a result, domestic terror attacks became all too common. Some believed the SafeCities would crumble if cut off from their Outposts. This led to incidents like fire-bombings, diseased crops, knife attacks, and even arrows to the knee becoming part of daily life for those who lived life outside of the dome. Play-fighting as kids evolved into learning and understanding the foundations of self-defense and effective strikes.

And that's where I found myself when the military needed new cadets. Outposts like mine were prime recruiting grounds. Outposts were just smaller towns with agricultural significance whether it be conveyance or proximity. SafeCities would all but starve without their Outposts.

As I looked back on my years in school, it was clear that the world had drastically changed. The United States had changed, and we were now navigating a complex and divided landscape. Little did I know that I was about to become a part of something much bigger than myself in a world where survival was anything but certain.

People in SafeCities liked to tell themselves they were untouchable. As long as the Halospheres were up and the DWAR system was active, nothing from the outside could hurt them. No bullets, no bombs, no missile strikes.

They're not wrong. But war isn't just fought with bullets anymore. And The Reckoning figured that out a long time ago. They didn't need to bypass the PDS. They didn't need to fire a single shot. They just needed time, patience, and a little creativity.

I've seen their work firsthand. Not on the battlefields—there aren't many, not in the traditional sense—but in the aftermath.

The Burnings were the first real sign of what they could do. It started with food stores going up in flames. Not just in Outposts, but in SafeCity processing plants, the places that kept their precious automated supply chains running. No one saw it coming. No alarms tripped. By the time responders arrived, the entire shipment was nothing but cinders.

Then came the water crisis in St. Louis—except it wasn't a crisis. It was an attack.

The Reckoning didn't hack systems. They didn't have the resources or the interest. But what they did have were people willing to do the unthinkable. Someone—an NJC worker, a technician, maybe even a disgruntled citizen—dropped six liters of engineered bacteria into the main supply line. Bacteria that spread, multiplied, and sat unnoticed in the filtration systems for weeks.

It wasn't designed to kill. That wasn't the point. It was designed to make people sick. High fevers. Hallucinations. Chronic fatigue. A city full of people who couldn't think straight. Who became paranoid, who turned on each other in desperation.

That was The Reckoning's real weapon. They didn't break the system. They made the system break itself. They've used fear as a tool for years. Smoke Bombs in Transit Centers—not deadly, not even dangerous, but in a city where people have never known violence, it was enough to cause stampedes. Enough to make SafeCitizens afraid of their own streets.

The Charleston Sirens—a single night where every emergency alarm in the city blared for seven hours straight. No explanation, no reason. The entire city thought they were under attack. Some jumped from their apartments. Some locked themselves in their homes and refused to leave for weeks.

The Vanishing—seventeen NJC officers gone without a trace over the course of a year. No bodies, no signs of struggle. They just disappeared. The Reckoning never took credit, never made demands. They just let the rumors spread.

The SafeCities don't know how to fight an enemy they can't see. And that's why they're scared, some even wanting to leave to go live in The Waste as a last resort.

People in SafeCities had this idea that The Waste is nothing but a sun-bleached graveyard. They think it's all crumbling highways, skeletal buildings, and people so ragged they can barely be called human anymore. They think it's dead.

They're wrong.

The Waste isn't ugly. Not always.

Drive far enough past the SafeCity borders, and it still looks like America. Not the polished, sterilized version inside the domes, but something real—farmhouses with wide porches, rusted mailboxes leaning at an angle, two-lane roads stretching into the horizon. At a glance, you'd think life still goes on out there.

And sometimes, it does.

Until it doesn't.

Because The Waste is only peaceful until the moment it isn't.

One day, a town is alive—shops open, kids playing, people gathering for a makeshift market in the square. The next? It's gone. Burned to the ground by looters, swallowed by a flood, torn apart by an F5 tornado that had no business being in North Carolina.

Out there, nothing lasts.

Some towns survive so long because they pay for peace.

The NJC doesn't police The Waste. They don't have to. People figured out their own version of law and order, and it's simple. If you want safety, you buy it. And safety doesn't come cheap.

Different crime lords, mercenaries, and corporate remnants claim towns as their own. They call it protection. The people living there call it extortion.

Some towns pay in cash, funneling SafeCity crypto through black-market traders. Others pay in resources—food, water, working tech, whatever keeps their "protectors" happy. And then there are the places that pay in labor. And not all labor is voluntary.

But no one fights back.

Because if you don't pay, you don't stay.

And if you think you can resist? You don't understand how this world works.

The three names you hear the most in The Waste aren't politicians or presidents. They don't sit in clean offices, pushing papers and pretending they're in control. They walk among the ruins, owning whatever they can hold.

The Black Hands used to be military contractors before the world fell apart. They saw the collapse coming and did what soldiers always do—claimed their own territory.

Major Elias Rourke runs them like an army. Ex-Navy, ex-NJC, all predator. He doesn't care about SafeCities, The Reckoning, or Outpost politics. He just wants a kingdom to rule.

Under Black Hands' rule, there's no crime, no chaos, no war. But there's no freedom, either.

Curfews are strict. Disobedience is punished publicly. Loyalty isn't optional.

But the Black Hands keep their word.

If you live in a Black Hand town, you don't have to worry about looters, raiders, or Reckoning attacks. No one dares cross a settlement under their protection.

Because if you do?

They'll send a message. And the message will be written in blood.

Where the Black Hands rule through fear, the Ivory Sons rule through wealth.

Before the collapse, they were just another corporate dynasty. When everything fell apart, they bought up the ruins.

They don't need soldiers. They don't need force.

If you live in an Ivory-controlled town, you sign a deal. You work for them, owe them favors, or give them a cut of everything you make.

Refusing isn't an option.

They don't send goons to break your legs. They don't torch your home. They just erase you.

Your house gets repossessed. Your land gets transferred. Your ID stops working. No one will trade with you, no one will house you, no one will acknowledge you exist.

And if you still don't get the message?

You just disappear.

No one talks about it. They just adjust.

Because that's what you do when you live under the Ivory Sons.

The Stormborn don't own towns. They don't claim land. They move, with the weather, with the seasons, with the storms.

Some say they live in floating cities, old military airships refitted to ride the jet streams, dropping in only to trade, recruit, or warn of coming disasters. I think they just have really good vehicles.

They're not raiders. They're not warlords. They don't care about power.

They care about what's coming.

Because the world isn't done breaking.

And The Waste?

It's just the beginning.

The Waste isn't dead. It's alive and angry.

And the weather proves it. Summers hit 120 degrees plus for weeks at a time. If you don't have shade or water, you die. Winters stay mild—until they don't. Snowstorms blast through Texas and Alabama, dumping two feet of snow in four hours. Floods rip through valleys, drowning entire settlements overnight. Tornadoes don't stick to the Midwest anymore. I've seen F5s rip through Tennessee, flattening entire towns in seconds.

People don't die in The Waste because of war.

They die because they weren't fast enough.

Chapter 3
The Stolen Blade

Six thirty a.m. rudely announced its arrival with a cruel howl from my antique, brown, digital clock next to the bed. Then, the alarm clock nested within my Hololens started with a soft hum, escalating to the full-blown crescendo of NSYNC's "Rock Your Body." I didn't choose the songs; they were selected at random from my listening history, leaning toward the most frequently and recently played tunes. My Hololens somehow found its way to the bathroom counter. I racked my brain trying to figure out how they made it in there, but the morning fog was too thick to fight through.

I rolled out of bed with the grace of a tipsy baby panda grappling with an inner ear infection and stumbled into the bathroom, where I encountered the multifunctional marvel known as the toilet-shower combo.

The holomirror sprang to life the moment my face graced its surface. Olive skin, a scratchy short beard, curly head of hair, accented sleepy eyes, and a nose that my ex-called a "boop." Not many mixed-race kids come out of the Outposts, but there I was in all of my permanently tanned and ambiguously raced glory. Could I lose a few pounds? Yes. Will I? Nope. At 5'11 and 200lbs, I had a lot of leftover muscle from daily rucks across the world's most challenging environments. My genetics were holding, or maybe it's the SAI regulating my metabolism, I thought to myself.

A digital voice chimed in, "Today's to-do list, 243 days overdue."

"Skip," I muttered in response.

The mirror persisted, "Incoming call, NJCPD."

"Ignore," I groaned. My shift didn't start until 7 a.m., and whatever was calling could surely wait.

"Urgent message from NJCPD," the mirror insisted.

"Noooooo," I groaned begrudgingly.

I finally snapped, "Silence all notifications," as I swiped away the incessant intrusions.

Three briefs awaited my attention in my digital inbox. One appeared to be corrupt, and I decided never to open that spammy conundrum. The second was an executive priority case, offering substantial compensation but with the catch that the funds would go straight into my public account—taxes, retirement contributions, and fines would devour most of it. Plus, it likely involved some dreary security detail.

The third brief, though, piqued my interest. It was a crypto payment, a piece of Digital Fluid State Currency, barely seven minutes old, and it held the promise of being claimed by someone else at any moment. I accepted the task and opened the brief, revealing that I was the sole designated recipient.

Credits Transferred: 30,000/100,000

Known Location: 454º SE 23.2º W

Item: Honjo Masamune: The Honjo Masamune

"Wait a second," I muttered to myself, absorbing the gravity of the situation. "Someone stole the most revered sword known to humanity? Poor guys."

A note accompanied the brief: "Return blade, unscathed. Any damage to the blade will be considered dishonorable."

"Dishonorable?" I scoffed out loud to myself as it dawned on me that this could only be Tagadashi Hiroshi who is searching for his sword. Sure, he's the most notorious criminal I could think of, and yes, he's prepaid a deposit, but assisting a criminal syndicate leader that I've known since I was a child in recovering his stolen property? That's a moral tightrope. Hard pass. I'm broke but not stupid.

A system message interrupted my internal debate: "Error; Brief unreturnable."

Tagadashi would know I had received this brief, and he could connect the dots. I had two choices:

1. Retreat to the desolate wastes, dwelling on my past deeds. Live a life of hermit. Die alone and old.
2. Return the sword to Tagadashi.

The sword's location wasn't far, and the potential reward was enticing. My financial situation demanded my attention.

I dressed for the occasion. My base layer consisted of reactive Kevlar mesh, a body suit that adapted to impact and grounded shock. As an NJCPD trial officer stun weapons had become a weapon of choice for most as they were efficient and cheap. Over that, I wore the attire of a nostalgic soul: black cotton slacks, a slightly wrinkled and fitting button-up shirt, a loosely knotted black tie, and a black blazer, all picked up from a nostalgia shop I found outside the dome while tracking down a runner. Everything came from some place named J.C. Penny. Some throwback sneakers and I pulled it all together with my Hololens that fit snuggly on with an adjustable leather strap, courtesy of a repurposed belt from the same store.

As I swung open my front door, I was met with the sight of Tagadashi Jr., not his father. He went by his middle name, Michael, clad in all black—suit, shirt, and tie. He definitely had a bigger clothing budget than me.

"Mark-san, 10, brother," he greeted me respectfully, "we hoped you'd be willing to assist with this delicate matter."

"I grew up with your father, you, and your family. His kindness was instrumental to me as a child. As hard as it is to say no, I must decl…" I started to say no, then I was interrupted, abruptly.

"I knew you would accept. We know you need the gratuitous reward, and we're aware you're close to retirement," he continued. "My father still hopes that you would consider his offer of employment."

The Tagadashis specialized in crafting modern-age weapons, particularly knives and swords. In a world where handguns had become obsolete, a man's stature was determined by the size of his blade and his prowess with it. Tagadashi's blades were renowned, but they came at a cost—both in credits and in terms of allegiances and favors.

Buying a single Tagadashi blade wasn't just expensive, costing as much as a whole year's earnings. The real cost came after the purchase. The smiths expected favors in return, not just money. These weren't small favors either; they were big, often personal, and could end up costing you a lot more than cash ever would. You'd be caught up in a network of obligations that could take a lot to get out of. It was a debt of honor, a series of unspoken promises that wove the buyer into a complex web of service and reciprocity that, once entered, was not easily escaped.

Their forges remained a well-guarded secret in The Waste, forging self-healing, nanoparticle-charged steel. Describing their blades as "sharp" would be an understatement to say the least; they could cut through virtually any material.

"My father offers this as a token of his gratitude," Jr. said with a still-forced accent. "Please accept it. Refusal would be considered disrespectful. He makes this gesture because of your kinship with his son, my brother Jiro. And considers you family."

Tagadashi Jr. stood in front of me, his arms outstretched, and head slightly bowed. In his hands, palms up, he cradled a Japanese sword that gleamed with exquisite craftsmanship. The sheath of the sword was a canvas of intricate artistry, telling a vivid and captivating story.

On the sheath, an etched dragon breathed fire near the hilt, its flames gracefully curling upward into the shape of clouds. Below the fiery display, a traditional Japanese farmhouse, known as a Minka, overlooked a serene pond, its reflection captured with stunning detail. As the artwork continued down the sheath, it transformed into a profusion of vibrant flowers, each petal and stem meticulously rendered.

It wasn't until Tagadashi Jr. broke the silence, uttering the words "Japanese Dahlia," that the meaning of this intricate design became clear. The sheath was a visual representation of this concept, though some of its finer details remained a mystery to me.

The hilt of the sword was no less impressive. Crafted from nanoparticle-charged steel, the sheathe possessed a deadly elegance. While not as sharp as the blade itself, it was a testament to the sword's exceptional quality and the artistry that had gone into its creation.

This sword was a rare gem, a fusion of tradition and technology, and it spoke volumes about Tagadashi's deep connection to his Japanese heritage and his profound appreciation for the art of sword smithing. Its presence in his hands was a statement, a true representation of his reverence for craftsmanship and the rich history it embodied.

As my fingers brushed against the sword's surface, a subtle yet captivating transformation occurred. The once-static artwork on the sheath seemed to come to life, the colors shimmering with a radiant orange sheen. It began at the dragon's mouth, where the vivid flames seemed to dance and flicker, and then flowed gracefully down to the intricate petals of the flowers.

This mesmerizing display served as a symbolic transfer of ownership, a silent acknowledgment that the sword had found itself in new hands. It was a moment charged with significance, an unspoken bond between the blade and its new master.

As this connection between the sword and me was established, my Hololens seamlessly synced with the sword's interface, forming a digital bridge that would enhance my understanding of its capabilities and provide access to its hidden features. It was a fusion of traditional craftsmanship and cutting-edge technology, a harmonious blend that promised both beauty and functionality.

I accepted the sword, hoping that I could return it later without complications or offense. This sword was worth more than my life, and men would kill me, or at least try to, just by seeing it in my possession.

"You are now in my father's favor," he added, cementing our unspoken agreement.

Chapter 4
The Unlikely Rise of Tagadashi

Tagadashi's infamous reputation as a crime syndicate boss concealed a once-respected academic and scientist who thrived in pre-war Chicago. A polymath, he taught physics and made pioneering contributions to self-healing polymers for DARPA, drawing admiration from scholars and students alike. My adoptive father, who attended one of his challenging courses, often regaled me with stories of how it was one of the most demanding yet rewarding academic experiences he ever had.

As firearms became obsolete, the scientific community redirected its focus toward reviving medieval weaponry, and Tagadashi found himself at the forefront of this resurgence.

Tagadashi was a father to three sons: Han and Jiro, who were twins, and the younger Michael. Raised in an environment where swords were as familiar as household items and intelligence was prized above all, the twins displayed exceptional aptitude. They achieved a groundbreaking scientific breakthrough by integrating nanoparticle polymers into sword-making techniques, forever changing the landscape of blade craftsmanship. The swords they produced boasted edges formed from a super-heating self-healing polymer intricately interwoven with carbon steel. Their love for anime undoubtedly fueled their ambitions as they yearned to build upon their father's decades of research and step out from his imposing shadow.

The swords crafted by Han and Jiro Tagadashi were nothing short of revolutionary, evidence of their unparalleled skill and innovation. Infused with cutting-edge nanoparticle polymers, these blades shattered the limitations of traditional sword-making, forging a bridge between ancient artistry and advanced technology.

At first glance, they appeared as masterpieces—sleek, perfectly balanced, and exquisite in design. But upon closer examination, their true ingenuity became apparent. The edges gleamed with an almost ethereal brilliance, as if lit from within by an unseen fire. If lightsabers were real and you had to choose between the two, you'd pick the sword.

These were not mere weapons. They were the future of the blade, honed to perfection by two of the most gifted craftsmen of their time.

When activated, the swords would emit a radiant glow, casting a vivid red hue that pulsed only along the razor-sharp edge. This was no mere aesthetic feature; it was a testament to the power contained within. The red glow served as a visual indicator of the sword's activation, a warning to any who dared to stand against its wielder.

The swords didn't need a power source, either. The stored kinetic tension fueled the super-heating element. To charge it up, you practiced with it. The more you used it, the more energy was stored. The more energy stored, the hotter the edge got. What's cooler is that each sword is genetically coded to its owner. No one else could make a sword activate, but its original owner. Gripping the blade was the bonding process. These swords have been studied for years, but without the original owner, the blade sits dormant and the nano layers composing the sword degrade.

But perhaps the most remarkable aspect of these swords was their unparalleled durability. The edges would never dull, and were virtually indestructible, capable of slicing through even the toughest materials with ease. No matter how many battles they endured, the edges would remain sharp and pristine, a testament to the skill and ingenuity of their creators.

For Han and Jiro Tagadashi, these swords represented more than just weapons; they were a symbol of their ambition, their determination to push the boundaries of what was possible. With each swing of the blade, they sought to carve out a new legacy for themselves, one that would echo through the annals of history for generations to come.

The twins first learned about the ANGL project during its embryonic stages, thanks to their connections within DARPA. They volunteered against their father's cautious counsel, driven by a thirst for knowledge and adventure and maybe a desire to write their own future. Tragedy struck swiftly as Han succumbed to the ravages of IMS, or Implant Sickness, immediately upon implant activation.

Jiro, left heartbroken and silently driven, assumed the role of our ANGL leader. Also known as Number 1, his skills and abilities allowed him to engage entire brigades on his own. But that's a story for another day. He wields both his brother's sword and his own, emerging as the sole ANGL skilled in wielding two long blades with deadly precision.

The loss of Han sent Tagadashi Sr. on a different path. Fueled by grief and a desire for justice, he turned to politics, vying for the state presidency in a bid to enact change from within the system. Though he narrowly lost by a mere handful of votes in two successive elections, Tagadashi Sr. eventually abandoned the sanctuary of NJC. In The Waste, he built his forges, amassed wealth, and cultivated a reputation that morphed him from an innovator into an enemy of the state practically overnight. The Liberty States embraced him warmly, and he entrusted his son to oversee his "local interests" here.

These "local interests" mostly entailed the illegal trade of contraband goods smuggled into and out of The Waste. While much of it was innocuous—cosmetics, cigars, even pets—occasionally, newly developed combat technology found its way into their operations. Last year, a stun capacitor, compact but boasting a charge of 75 gigajoules, was detonated during a political rally for one of Tagadashi's former political rivals. Six people were electrocuted, and dozens more were hospitalized. Though suspicions abounded, Tagadashi distanced himself from any involvement or knowledge of the incident. I was assigned to investigate but found no evidence linking him to the attack. Tagadashi regarded my efforts as an olive branch and temporarily incorporated my family's Outpost duties into his operations for six months, a decision that brought unparalleled joy to my mother— it offered my family a rare sense of safety and stability, filling them with quiet relief. As for me, I garnered a reprimand on my record for accepting illicit gifts, a mark I couldn't care less about.

Behind Tagadashi Jr, I saw an armed escort of NJC officers offloading from the lift, approaching my door.

"Captain Andeya?" a voice emanated from the group of SWAT-armored agents. Their helmets remained firmly in place despite their words.

Tagadashi Jr. bowed respectfully and spoke without an accent, "Do not overlook our agreement," before slipping away from the small battalion that now stood at my doorstep.

"We need you to come with us," one of the agents declared.

"Who is 'Us,' and where are we going?" I demanded.

"We cannot divulge that information. Our orders are clear: Retrieve Captain Andeya immediately. Destination details are loaded directly into our navigation system. We remain unaware," retorted the voice.

"Let me go back in and get my…" I began, only to be swiftly interrupted by the cryptic voice, "You must come with us now, on an executive order. We cannot permit you back into your apartment."

"What about this?" I asked, raising my most recent acquisition to my shoulder—the sword so generously gifted to me.

They exchanged glances and shrugged. "Bring it along," came the electronically altered voice.

"Is that a Tagadashi Hono?" one of the officers marveled.

"That, unfortunately, it is," I admitted.

"Can I hold it?" an eager voice chimed in.

"No," I replied curtly, and I could have sworn I detected a note of electronic disappointment.

"Here, but hand it right back," I relented, extending the sword hesitantly.

"Why won't it come out of its scabbard, and what's that quote mean?" queried one of the voices.

"There's an inscription," another voice noted, proceeding to read it aloud, "Revelation 12:7: 'Then war broke out in heaven. Michael and his angels fought against the dragon, and the dragon and his angels fought back.'"

I looked down and smiled to myself, remembering where I'd heard this for the first time.

~

Jiro's grip on the wooden training sword tightened. Sweat clung to his brow as he circled our opponent, Tagadashi, the grizzled warrior who had trained a hundred swordsmen before us. Han and I mirrored his movements, each of us struggling to match the master's effortless foot-work.

"Again!" Tagadashi barked, his own sword moving like lightning.

I lunged, but before I could land a strike, the wooden blade was knocked from my hands with a sharp crack.

Han hesitated. Jiro didn't.

He feigned left before twisting his stance, bringing his sword up in a sweeping arc. It was the right move—but not fast enough. Tagadashi sidestepped and delivered a punishing blow to Jiro's ribs.

I gritted my teeth. I had to get faster. Stronger.

Tagadashi exhaled, nodding. "You three are not hopeless. But if you wish to master the blade, you must learn to read the battle before it unfolds. Now, again!"

Without warning, Tagadashi turned, walked to a weapons rack, and retrieved three real swords. He tossed one to each of us before donning a dragon Kobu mask. His voice was calm but firm as he spoke.

"The first to draw blood is the winner."

Jiro and Han attacked with ferocity. If their father had missed even a single block, they would have maimed him if not worse. But he was swift, efficient, making quick work of them. A flick of his wrist, a calculated strike, and both stumbled back, each clutching a fresh wound.

Jiro's left arm. Han's right.

Tagadashi chuckled, his voice muffled behind the mask. "Easier to tell you apart now."

Then, it was my turn.

I didn't charge like the others. I stood firm, waiting.

Tagadashi took slow, measured steps, testing me. The master struck, feigning left before closing in, his blade moving to give me my first scar.

I spoke before he could land the blow.

"You've already lost."

Tagadashi froze. He looked down.

Blood trickled from beneath his mask. The strap had been pulled too tight, cutting into his skin.

A silence hung between us before Tagadashi let out a deep, satisfied laugh.

"Clever boy. You win."

I lowered my blade. I had never needed to swing it. Then Tagadashi quoted the scripture. I wondered if I was an angel or the dragon then. I guess I know now.

~

I looked down at the man who asked about the inscription and responded, "If you have to ask, then you must learn on your own." To which another responded, "Yah Richard, you dumbass."

~

Michael sank deeper into the worn leather seat of his matte-black AeroGlide XR—a government-approved hovercar designed for rapid urban transit within NJC. The vehicle's Helio engine buzzed as it navigated the sleek, neon-lit avenues, its reflective surfaces mirroring the dazzling glow of the holographic billboards and towering skyscrapers.

Across from him, his partner Rae studied the luminous dashboard, which displayed the live traffic feeds and digital overlays of the cityscape. Despite the marvels of urban technology, Michael's thoughts churned with a growing resentment toward Mark—a recurring frustration born of Mark's cavalier attitude and habitual tendency to evade responsibility. He lamented internally how much he hated being called Tagadashi Jr. It stole from his independence and self-identity.

The comm unit buzzed, snapping Michael back to the present. He answered with a steady voice, though his tone betrayed a hint of the bitterness he felt.

Michael (into the comm): "Father, it's Michael. I just delivered the Hono to Mark. Shortly after the handoff, a unit of officers intercepted him and took him away."

He paused for a moment, watching the city blur past in the Aer-oGlide XR's window—a mosaic of light and ambition that contrasted sharply with the turmoil inside him.

Tagadashi (Michael's father, his voice measured yet expectant): "Michael, give me your status. Did everything go according to plan?"

Michael's gaze shifted to Rae, whose silent nod reminded him that despite his inner doubts, the mission was proceeding as expected. The urban route carried him smoothly through districts pulsing with energy and promise.

Michael: "Yes, Dad. The Hono was delivered without any issues. Mark accepted it, but you know how he is—his unpredictability never fails to get under my skin. As soon as the exchange was over, the officers swooped in and picked him up. So, on paper, everything's moving as planned."

A brief silence followed as Michael allowed himself a moment to stew over Mark's nonchalant smirk—the kind that made Michael feel like he was always left to pick up the pieces.

Tagadashi (after a measured pause, his tone turning steely): "Excellent. That means our timing is right."

Michael exhaled slowly, the hum of the hovercar and the vibrant cityscape outside offering little comfort from the weight of expectations and personal grievances. The bright urban lights seemed to underscore the duality of his mission: the polished efficiency of the city versus the murky undercurrents of their covert operations.

Michael (in a low, measured tone): "Understood, Dad. I'll keep you updated if anything changes."

After a moment of tense quiet, Tagadashi's final words crackled over the comm with an unmistakable resolve.

Tagadashi (firmly): "Good, I need that SAI."

Michael sat, contemplating as the NJC unfurled before him. The hovercar sliced through the urban arteries, and with every mile, memories and a relentless desire churned in his mind. The weight of his family's legacy pressed upon him—two brothers whose lives had become towering shadows over his own.

He remembered Han, the gentle soul whose brilliance was cruelly extinguished by implant sickness—a loss that transcended personal grief, symbolizing all that had spiraled out of control in this dangerous age. And then there was Jiro, the planet's most revered killing machine—the infamous ANGL #1, whose record was so heavily redacted that merely uttering his name could summon disaster. Jiro had grown into a living myth; his presence alone had ended countless lives, toppled world leaders, and sparked wars on a whim. The Corp's unwavering support for his ruthless methods had etched his reputation into both fear and reluctant admiration.

Michael's heart pounded with a volatile blend of envy and resolve as he recalled the day Jiro had burst into Tagadashi's office, demanding a sword—a blade from his father's legendary forge—promising to resurrect Han from the dead in exchange. Torn between pride and disapproval, Tagadashi had forged that very sword and entrusted it to Mark, an act meant to honor his sons' legacies but which only deepened Michael's sense of inadequacy. His father's eyes had always shone with quiet pride when speaking of Jiro's unstoppable force and the memory of Han, leaving Michael forever feeling overshadowed.

Now, as he navigated the bustling avenues of the city, Michael's thoughts oscillated between seething resentment and fierce determination. Every digital billboard and pulsating street sign reminded him that in a world of ambiguous loyalties and ruthless power plays, recognition was scarce and power was the ultimate prize. He longed to step out from under the colossal shadows of his brothers—not by emulating their brutal methods, but by forging his own path that might finally earn him the respect and love that seemed reserved only for Jiro and Han.

With a tightening grip on the Aerocar's joystick controls, Michael silently vowed that he would no longer be a mere footnote in his family's saga. He would transform his inner turmoil into more than just a raw emotion, daring to challenge the very system that had exalted his brothers to near-mythical status. Michael looked out the window and fought to hold back a tear, and for what, he did not know. Confusion and anger gripped him.

Chapter 5
Unforeseen Consequences

"Are we leaving or not?" I interrupted loudly as they passed the sword around, reveling in its craftsmanship, technology, and worth. I held my hand out as a reluctant hand extended from the crew to return the sword, which I indeed had no intention of keeping.

"Asset secure on the way to transport," muffled the first real voice I'd heard from this troop as they communicated through a radio.

"Asset?" I thought to myself. I am an employee. Sure, I outrank this peanut gallery, but I am not an "asset."

I had been called an "asset" once before, in the field during an intense four-day battle in the fight for Anchorage. We were losing, outnumbered. But why now? Why was I suddenly such a high-value commodity? And where were we going? The Aerodrones could have picked me up faster from my rooftop, but instead, we were headed away from the ports and toward the upscale part of town.

The SWAT team that picked me up turned the operation into an all-business affair once we boarded, and they remained silent, sitting at full attention. The Armored Troop Carrier (ATC) drove faster than I was comfortable with. We took a sharp turn, descending a steep hill, and darkness enveloped the world outside. Some heads began to nod, and eyes turned toward one another. My guess was that they were just as confused as I was. The Hono began to glow. Moments later, we came to an abrupt stop that almost sent me flying out of my seat. We all self-corrected and waited for the rear door to open. When it did, I expected to see the outdoors, but instead, we were in some kind of underground room or lower level of a building. The walls were concrete, and it seemed like a network of tunnels—a part of the city I wasn't very familiar with, which was saying something.

"Take the asset to Commander Robinson," one of the men who opened the transport door ordered.

"You won't need that," exclaimed one of the extraction agents, pointing at my sword.

"If you think I'm going to trust anyone else with this, you're an idiot," I replied calmly, tightening my grip on the weapon as they took a step toward me.

"If you try to take it from him, you'll only end up hurt," a low, raspy voice interrupted, and a man walked toward us with determination. He placed his arm on my shoulder. "Good to see you again, soldier. Today, the duck shat on its bread, and I hope you're ready for the crackers," he said, using one of his peculiar analogies.

Robinson had been our commanding officer for our missions from day one, not to mention the man who convinced me to join the corps. He knew everything there was to know about me and my battalion. When he left the service and set up shop in NJCPD, I couldn't pass up the opportunity to work for him. This was only my second year as a trial officer.

My job was to find the suspect, take stock of the scene, and decide whether they walked or didn't. Everything I saw streamed live to the jury through my Hololens—one hundred randomly selected citizens, all instant legal experts. They got fifteen minutes to poke at the evidence, ask their questions, and cast their vote. Fifty-one made a verdict. Quick. Simple. Not always right—but good enough for the people who mattered.

I was ushered into an elevator along with Robinson, and it was far too nice for the underground tunnel it connected to. "You ignored all of our calls, Mark?" Robinson grumbled.

"I was busy, finalizing a deal with Tagadashi Hiroshi," I retorted.

"I hope you're just saying that to get under my skin," Robinson said.

"Only if it's working," I quipped.

"Listen, Ten, what you're about to see is going to change your life, our world, everything. Now's not the time for jokes. And yes, it's working," said Robinson. "Take your lenses off," he said as the doors slid open after an uncharacteristically long elevator ride.

"We are locked out of every system. No security footage available. No eyewitnesses. Just this," Robinson said, pointing to something on the floor that looked like blood. I followed the trail, and there he was—President Mason, dead, a hole in his chest, lying next to what could only be the murder weapon, a loaded revolver.

The room felt cold and foreboding as we stood there, staring at the lifeless body of President Mason. My mind raced with questions, and the word "asset" continued to echo in my head. Robinson's somber expression told me that whatever had brought us here was far more serious than I had initially thought.

"Is this some kind of setup?" I finally asked, my voice low and full of suspicion. "Why are we here, Robinson?"

Robinson sighed deeply, his eyes fixed on the crime scene. "I wish I had all the answers, Mark," he replied, his tone grave. "But right now, we're facing a crisis of epic proportion. President Mason's murder threatens to plunge our already fragile society into chaos. The implications are staggering."

I took a step closer to the body, examining the scene carefully. The revolver lay next to him, its barrel cold, and a single bullet had found its mark in Mason's chest. It was a clear case of assassination.

"How did this happen?" I muttered, more to myself than anyone else.

Robinson nodded, his eyes never leaving the lifeless figure on the floor. "That's what we need to find out, and quickly. As an ANGL, you have access to information and resources that could be invaluable in solving this case."

I turned to face him, my curiosity mixed with a growing sense of unease. "But why me? Why not call in the NJCPD's best detectives?"

Robinson's gaze hardened. "Because, Mark, this goes far deeper than we can trust anyone else with at the moment. There are forces at play here that we can't fully comprehend. And you, with your unique abilities and connections, may be our only hope to unravel this mystery."

I couldn't deny the gravity of the situation, nor could I shake the feeling that I had just been thrust into something much larger than myself. The president's death had created a power vacuum, and the consequences of firearms being used again were potentially catastrophic.

"Fine," I said, resigning myself to the task ahead. "But I need access to all available information, and I need it now."

Robinson nodded in agreement. "You'll get everything you need, Mark. Just remember, this isn't just about solving a murder. It's about preserving what little order we have left in this city."

"This city?" I responded. "How about the world?" I asked incredulously. "Imagine if DWARs no longer worked. We finally found peace once guns and rockets didn't rain down on the innocent. Terrorism and genocide are more than just random uncoordinated attacks on an Outpost. That world should only live in our history, not our future."

I glanced at the Halos' field status to confirm its continued functionality. This field was an essential creation of the DWAR system, designed to ensure the safety and security of our cities. In larger urban centers, multiple DWAR units were deployed to provide comprehensive coverage. However, in areas where their coverage overlapped, interference sometimes occurred, resulting in ineffective areas.

There had been instances in early Halosphere development when individuals were transported to these overlapping zones and murdered to show that no system is perfect. The system's developers had promptly addressed these issues, rectified the bugs and implemented stringent testing procedures. Testers were strategically positioned in critical locations to assess the effectiveness of the Halos field.

As I reviewed the current status, the Halos field stood at 96% operational capacity. A field strength of 77% was sufficient to stop any projectiles fired from rifles or handguns.

As I began to process the enormity of the situation, I couldn't help but wonder how deep the rabbit hole went and what secrets lay hidden beneath the surface of NJC. Someone had figured out how to bring down Halos.

~

I began thinking about my first interaction with Mason and NJC secrets. The call came in at 14:00 a year ago. I was returning with a waste bounty and several out-of-print books. Books that had become illegal in some of the receding states, but still available in digital format in SafeCitys. I was just pulling them out of my rucksack when my visor flashed an urgent case.

Overdose. Male. Early thirties. SafeCity resident. No prior record of substance abuse. Substances had become more and more deadly as the synthetic components were more relied upon than the more natural routes. The Davis Brothers controlled Shrooms and Marijuana. A complete monopoly for pharmaceuticals, and given the lack of policing available in The Waste, they crushed any potential competition from large growers to a kid growing it in his closet. This made getting high either expensive and safe, or cheap and deadly. Pulling up to the house, I couldn't imagine this being a guy who would gamble with cheap and deadly. I turned off my 90's grunge feed and went in.

The general consensus was that people didn't overdose in SafeCities. Not unless they wanted to. The search for a reason was always my first priority. Depression hadn't gone anywhere in a SafeCity. In fact, suicide was just as prevalent here as in the outposts. Some would argue that the per-capita number made Outposts better for your mental health than a SafeCity. People not being able to put a gun to their temple inside of them skewed things a little. Overdoses tended to be the way to go.

The system was built to prevent just this. Every prescription was tracked, every refill monitored, every dosage controlled. No illicit trade, no unregistered substances. Every pill accounted for.

Yet here he was.

A dead man.

"Where's the note?" asked one of the other officers through chewing gum, who walked in with me with his hands on his hips and his Hololens scrolling through the last night's Deathball game's winners and losers.

"Dickhead," I murmured.

"Oh, it's okay, everyone. We've got an ANGL, everything's going to be okay, folks," he said with a theatrical bow. He turned his head and spit his gum into his hand before rolling it into a little ball and dropping it into a trashcan. Years ago, that would have left him with one less working clavicle, but I had grown some thick skin. I had found that I could sleep off most of my frustrations.

"This is an active crime scene, Durham," I sneered.

"An active crime scene?" He chuckled and held his hand palm up, gesturing toward the deceased.

He was sitting on his couch, lips blue, eyes frozen open. The glass-paneled apartment was sterile, spotless—a controlled environment where death wasn't supposed to happen. But nothing about this scene was controlled.

This was a Hype overdose. It was clear due to the way the eyes weren't closed. In fact, they were bugged out. Hype constricts the muscles and makes them tense, but decreases nerve feedback so most motions are far too overdone. More than just handshakes that are too tight, these are grips in a normal person that will crush a glass.

The empty pill bottle lay on the floor. I crouched, careful not to disturb anything, and turned it over in my palm. The name on the label stopped me cold. I closed my eyes and took a deep breath, exhaling loud and long.

"David Sinclair." I sighed.

I swore under my breath. I knew that name and everyone else did too, a little too well. He was more than a socialite, more than a media focus, he was President Mason's brother-in-law. He was a Waste Advocate and a known former Black Hand. He had come into it all after leaving The Waste and somehow making it through the lottery as a last-minute add. But his time in NJC was full of protest and ire. He'd been arrested many times, but nothing would stick. He claimed he wanted justice for The Waste.

I did not want this attention. I stood from my crouch and was in an empty room. I looked out the window to see the other NJC officers abandoning me loading into a hovercar.

"Couldn't have happened to a better officer," Durham shouted as the doors closed.

"Eat a bag of dicks you cunt waffles," I said without intending to. Even I was surprised by my choice of words.

The med scanner hummed as it processed its results. It beeped, taking my attention from my slip of words.

Prescription: Anti-anxiety medication. Standard dosage. No history of abuse.

Cause of Death: Respiratory failure due to stimulant toxicity.

That didn't track.

"He's not a Hype-head!" said a small voice from the doorway. It was his sixteen-year-old daughter, Katya, who had her own special treatment from the local media. She drew tons of attention when she had posted unsavory pictures of her new Mom. Pictures that Jen sent in confidence. Being a stepmom must be hard.

"Dad...David wasn't a junkie. He wasn't even on opioids," she continued. "I've never seen him take more than his meds and he didn't even like to take those," she said now through tears. She looked at her dad as her mom peeled her from the out of the doorway.

I picked up the bottle again, shaking a pill into my palm. Immediately, I knew something was wrong. Wrong shape. Wrong texture. A little too chalky, the edges a little too rough.

Either this wasn't what he was prescribed, or he was stuffing his Hype into this pill bottle.

If his daughter was right and his bottle was bad... how many others were? That's the way I felt most comfortable approaching this. If I kept looking at this as a suicide and not considering this a potential public health issue, then others could die. According to the date on the side of the bottle, he had just gotten his refill that day.

"Does he run out often?" I asked his wife.

"What?"

"Why was he taking medication that he just got? Was he out?"

Wiping away tears, she composed herself a little and spoke, "No, he's usually good about getting his meds on time. This one was delayed. He'd been out for a couple of days. He'd gotten real anxious and was there first thing in the morning, waiting."

I got this strong and strange feeling that more drugs were coming into NJC than we knew about. Somehow, I knew.

Mason showed up at the morgue the next morning while I was there getting the toxicology report. He was there in jeans and a T-shirt. He was there, but not as the President of NJC. Not as a politician. He came as a man who had just lost family. His sister was with him with a dark visor on to hide eyes that had been crying all night.

From the observation deck, I watched him stand over David's body, fists clenched at his sides, shoulders tight. He didn't say a word. Just stared at the cold, lifeless shell of the man he had once called his brother. I watched because these weren't the actions of a family who'd seen a man using or getting high on a regular basis. I'd seen those families before. A good number of times there was pain from guilt or anger from not intervening. This wasn't them.

I gave him a minute. Then I stepped inside, quietly, visor up and hands clasped behind my back. He didn't look at me when I spoke.

"I'm sorry," I said. And I meant it.

Mason exhaled sharply, his jaw working like he was trying to crush whatever grief or rage was rising inside him. "Tell me you have something. My sister is devastated. Our family is already stretched thin. I don't care about the lens of what happened, I just need to know."

I told him everything. The toxicology report had come back. Positive for Hype. But no anxiety meds were found in his system. He didn't have the serum levels consistent with someone who'd been using Hype on a regular basis. Somehow, he either decided to start a dangerous addiction, or it was a bad prescription. The fact was someone had either made a mistake—or deliberately tampered with the NJC's medication supply.

Mason was quiet for a long moment. Then he turned to me, eyes like sharpened glass.

"Find out who did this," he said. "And shut them down. You have the full range of the department's resources. I saw a video of the other NJC officers who vacated the scene. They are going to have to deal with me for now. And as for you, you deal with whoever you need to."

Tracking illicit drugs in a SafeCity wasn't hard because they weren't supposed to exist. After SafeCities watched their water turn lethal and thousands die from bacterial contamination, the response was predictable: clamp down hard on anything and everything trying to get through the gates.

Which meant whoever was moving them was careful. Connected. Untouchable. I had stepped in the biggest pile of trouble that was possible for a new NJC officer.

Whoever had done this was calculated and obviously experienced, but they'd made a mistake.

A logistics officer flagged an anomaly—a single shipment routed through an Outpost supply chain 50 clicks west before it made it into NJC. The Outpost review form had the signature of an import official who was off that day, Jeff Lewis. It wasn't a forgery, either. Forging someone's name took a skill that very few people had. You didn't just have to match the style and penmanship, but you had to do it with the same speed, angle, and flourish. Those are just as unique as a fingerprint. Fingerprints could be replicated through 3D skin prints, but signatures could not be.

That wasn't protocol. Import officials had to stay out on their days off in order for the rest of the team to do what was required of them and, as per statute, review anything that was out of the ordinary. This officer had made it to Indianapolis on a rail. Photos and videos gave him an alibi.

Which meant someone had tampered with it before it ever reached its destination and gave the wrong approval and Jeff's signature. And David and his family had been the ones to suffer for it.

Not a user. Not an addict. Just a man who'd taken his meds and died.

Mason sent me back to his sister's home that evening. I didn't want to go because there was nothing there. No note, no more clues. The crime scene unit had taken everything from there that would have meant anything. There was no real reason for me to go, but I did. Mason's wife, Claire, met me at the door. She had the same sharp eyes as Mason. She was there offering her company and condolences, but where he was steel, she was fire.

Her hands were shaking when she reached for mine, fingers curling around my wrist like she thought I could bring David back.

"He didn't overdose," she said. "David wasn't using."

I believed her.

But I needed proof. I had been to the pharmacy where he'd picked it up, and I tested the remaining meds of the same scripts. There'd been a long line for these meds when they arrived, and some people looked really agitated. I thought back to the conversation I had with his daughter. David was first in line as his shipment was late, and he was getting really anxious. Looking at the video, I could identify at least three people waiting in line behind him with bad sheets and expulsion notices.

None of the remaining meds were positive for Hype. But, there was a simple difference in their origination. A shipment from Outpost 47 to another SafeCity had been altered. Tampered with to match the shipment that was approved. With the same name as the official who was supposed to be off on the same day.

When I arrived to interview Jeff Lewis, he rolled his eyes, one of them blackened. "Oh shit, not this again. Look, I already told you, I was in Indianapolis." I didn't want to know which other NJC officers had tried to run down this lead, but I needed to hear it for myself. He told me that he had never heard or seen anything related to it.

Someone had been very, very careful to cover their tracks, but now it was clear. The first pack in distribution is used to fool the digital tracking. Then the next few packages were Hype. Then, after that, the remaining meds were safe.

I hadn't gone to Mason with my news yet. Because this was bigger than a single corrupt shipment. This was an operation, and losing a life to an OD was a big deal. At least, for me, it was. I had my own nagging feeling to solve this case. While everyone wanted me to write it off, I had a feeling from deep down inside.

A network.

A system that had been running for months—maybe years.

And I needed to be sure I could cut off each and every last head before I made a move.

So I set a trap. The next medication shipment was due in three days. I reviewed the shipment manifests from Outpost 47 with the same signature as Jeff and noticed one arriving.

I let it reach its destination. Only this time, I had every step monitored. Every handler. Every middleman. Every bastard who had his hands on that supply line.

By the time the shipment reached SafeCity, I had names. I had evidence. I had everything.

And when we moved in?

I got to the pharmacy early, the same way David did, and noticed the same men there to pick up a different prescription. I let them fill their prescriptions and followed them. One of them was none other than Jeff's brother, Clint. Clint had practiced his brother's signature for years, and if a signature was already provided, another was not needed. Clint was pumping in more drugs in one shipment than had been found in total for the past six months. Hype was in full swing, but we built a levee to slow the flood.

We took down every single one of them. Fifteen people in total. We sent most to The Waste as a sign of our lack of tolerance. And one, one was executed. Clint. His brother came to the execution, and so did President Mason. Mason minced no words that day and made many enemies at the price of his anger.

Mason called me to his office a week later.

I expected a handshake. Maybe a drink. What I got instead was a commendation.

A formal award that I didn't give jack shit about. I tossed it on the table and let it collect with random papers. One morning, I woke up with it on. I must have been drunk and wanted to show off. I couldn't remember. I read it for the first time, waking up as if I hadn't slept a wink. Recognition for "exemplary service in maintaining SafeCity integrity."

I didn't want it. I kept it anyway. Because, in the end, this wasn't about me. It was about David, and something lit up inside of me about this case.

About every person who'd taken the wrong pill, who trusted a system that was supposed to protect them, and had been failed. And if taking the commendation meant that no one else had to die like he did?

Then fine.

I'd take the damn thing.

"Anyone else would have given up on the case as soon as they learned who it was," Mason said while handing me a glass with brown liquid and ice. "The Black Hands are going to send another plant, you know."

"Not my problem until they break the law." I gestured at the plaque on the wall commemorating thirty years of peace.

Mason held out his glass and said, "The next time a law is broken, I know who to call."

That was a year ago and here I stood in the same place that I had been accepting the highest honor in NJC, over the body of a man who has been the first man shot in decades.

Chapter 6
The World Unwound

"Why me?" I demanded, my frustration simmering just beneath the surface.

"You're an ANGL, and I need—" Robinson began to explain.

"BULLSHIT!" I exploded, unable to contain my incredulity. "There are at least twenty more qualified investigators who can handle this better," I insisted, my voice laced with a hint of anger.

Robinson, seemingly unfazed by my outburst, maintained his composure. "There's something you need to see," he replied calmly.

He walked over to the table and picked up a piece of paper. On it were five names, written meticulously in almost perfect script.

President Mason
Dimitri Voynev
Kimberly Florres
Mark Andeya
Ryan Simmons

"Why is my name on this list?" I asked, a sense of unease creeping into my voice.

"I guess now you know why you're here," Robinson replied, his gaze steady.

"I need video footage, surveillance records, witnesses," I said urgently, a wave of determination washing over me.

Robinson's expression grew somber as he delivered the grim news. "All of the video has been wiped. Whoever did this had access to the archives. Everything is gone—door access times, fingerprints, even the voice data of the AI assistant. Everything except this paper. It's our only clue. It's as confusing as a first-grade math problem."

My mind raced as I contemplated the significance of the names on that list. I recognized each of them.

President Mason—dead from a gunshot wound, marking the first gun-related death in the state in thirty years.

Dimitri Voynev—ANGL number 7 and a contender in the upcoming presidential election.

Kimberly Florres—CEO of the Halos empire, responsible for DWAR systems and all Halospheres.

Mark Andeya—my name, inexplicably listed alongside the others.

Ryan Simmons—a city entertainer with a penchant for hosting dubious gatherings and facilitating covert dealings. If you needed to get someone in or out of the city discreetly, Ryan was the man to call, provided you had a substantial stash of crypto credits.

As I absorbed the weight of the situation, Robinson leaned in closer, his voice dropping to a hushed tone. "Mark, this isn't just a murder. It's a message—a warning."

I stared at the list of names, my mind racing to make sense of the connections. The victims were a diverse mix of political figures, corporate leaders, and even an entertainer. It was an eclectic group, and I struggled to find a common thread.

Robinson continued, "Each of these individuals represented a significant aspect of our society. Mason, as the President, was a symbol of our government's stability. Voynev was a rising star in politics, offering a fresh perspective and member of the elite 10 ANGLs.

Kimberly Florres controlled the very technology that sustains our Safe-Cities. And you, Mark, are a renowned investigator, someone who delves into the secrets of our world."

I nodded, starting to grasp the gravity of the situation. "But what's the message, and who's delivering it?"

Robinson's demeanor shifted, a look of concern etched across his face as he spoke. "The truth is, we're still in the dark about the full picture. But there are troubling indications, Mark. We need to tackle this head-on and not let it escalate any further." He emphasized his point by tapping the side of my Hololens, his other hand holding up the revolver by the barrel.

"Activate your UV function, soldier," he urged, the urgency evident in his voice. I complied, swiping a holographic command on my Hololens, and a faint half-thumbprint materialized before us. It was a tangible clue, a potential lead in the investigation.

We watched in tense silence as the partial print underwent analysis, the seconds stretching into minutes. Then, with a sense of grim finality, the result flashed across my vision—an unsettling match, me. The realization hit me like a brick, and my expression betrayed a mixture of shock and disbelief.

"Either you did it, or someone is setting you up for it," Robinson remarked, his voice measured but laced with concern. He leaned in closer, his gaze fixed on me. "Tell me, Mark. Where were you last night at 4:34 a.m.?"

My heart began to race, panic surging within me as I realized I had no alibi to offer other than the mundane truth of sleeping alone beneath the city's lights. My mind raced, desperately searching for any explanation or excuse that might cast doubt on the mounting suspicions. But before I could even attempt the feeble defense of "it was the one-armed man," Robinson intervened, sparing me the embarrassment of such a weak alibi.

In that moment, I couldn't help but appreciate Robinson's presence, even if he brought with him a disquieting revelation. His experience and sharp instincts were valuable assets in navigating the treacherous waters of this investigation. Yet, the weight of uncertainty and the ominous shadow of suspicion loomed over me, leaving me with a gnawing sense of dread.

"A group called 'The Reckoning' has a video detailing how they would frame someone for the president's murder, and what's worse is that I know you know how to wipe a scene better than this. I trained you how to do it. What do you know about this group?"

"The Reckoning?" I murmured quizzically. Then I thought about their last message sent out to broadcast on old UHF signals. They are a fringe group well known for controversial stances on sensitive subjects.

We were all being debriefed in the main training hall. The room was dark except for the flickering blue light of the old tube TV. The video played in fuzzy resolution, a masked figure standing before a symbol painted in stark red—a scale, one side tipped in blood. The voice was modulated, warped into something nearly inhuman.

"The world has become complacent, bound by the illusions of justice and order," the figure spoke, their gloved hands gesturing deliberately. "We are here to remind them that power unchecked is power undeserved. Those who sit on their gilded thrones, who make the rules to protect themselves, will be the first to fall."

The video cut to schematics, floor plans of the presidential estate, the security protocols mapped in eerie precision. The figure continued.

"A single moment, a single shot, and a single man takes the blame. The perfect crime. The perfect message. The Reckoning does not forgive. The Reckoning does not forget."

The screen flickered again, cutting to a grainy clip of a man being framed—false evidence planted, an escape route staged. The video ended abruptly, the silence in the room feeling heavier than before.

I clenched my fists, my mind racing. To an untrained eye, it looked like a terrorist threat. But on closer inspection, this was surgical. Precise. I knew the methods, the tricks they employed. And what was worse, the man across from me knew it too.

"The Reckoning," I said one more time, feeling the weight of the name settle over me like a dark cloud.

I met Robinson's gaze. He was waiting for my reaction, and I could already feel the storm brewing.

He nodded gravely. "Exactly. And it seems they have a broader agenda. They believe our reliance on PDS technology has made us vulnerable. They've made threats since the first day we turned on our DWAR. They want to shake the very foundation of our SafeCities."

Robinson's eyes bore into mine as he said, "Mark, I need you to find out who's behind this, why they're doing it, and how to stop them. We're standing on the precipice of a crisis that could fracture our world. I can keep this under wraps for three hours, Mark, maybe four. That's it. We have constructed a story about the president traveling to the capitol by Underground, but it won't hold sand for long. VP Baines is on board and, as a former operator, knows what it would take to pull off something like this."

"You mean *water*, not sand?" I interjected.

"I'm not thirsty son, focus," Robinson redirected.

I knew that uncovering answers wouldn't be easy. The deleted surveillance footage, the absence of witnesses, and the scarcity of leads left us with little to work with. Not to mention my partial on the murder weapon. It may not be enough to convict, but I was determined to get to the bottom of this mystery. Lives were at stake, and the future of our SafeCities hung in the balance.

As I began to gather my thoughts and plan my next steps, a growing sense of urgency gripped me. I needed to find out who had orchestrated this murder and why. The consequences of this act could have far-reaching effects, potentially destabilizing the fragile peace we'd enjoyed for decades.

I needed to delve deeper into the president's murder, following every lead, no matter where it might take me. The gravity of the situation weighed heavily on my shoulders; the urgency of my mission was clear in my mind. As I meticulously examined the crime scene, my trained eye sought out every detail, every clue that might shed light on this heinous act.

I began to tear the place apart in my hololense. It was a miracle, almost like a sixth sense that led me to the desk. There I stumbled upon something entirely unexpected—a small camera discreetly mounted in the ceiling vent of the president's office above the desk. It was a stark contrast to the high-tech security apparatus that blanketed our SafeCities. This camera was a rogue element, hidden away from official surveillance systems, and it immediately struck me as out of place.

I approached the camera, studying it closely. It was a sophisticated piece of technology, Tokyo Prime tech for sure. My fingers traced its contours, and my mind raced with questions. Who had installed it here, and why? What had this camera captured, and where was its live feed being sent?

As I examined the camera's intricate wiring, I discovered a data transmission cable that led to a concealed port behind the bookshelf with an array of wires. Without hesitation, I connected my Hololens to the port, hoping to trace the video feed's destination.

The display on my Hololens flickered to life, revealing a complex network of signals and data streams. I retrieved one image; it was garbled and encrypted. Some of the most intricate encryption I'd ever seen—end to end. Not in a million years would I be able to get this image to resolve without having the key to its locking mechanism.

It took only moments to decipher the camera's intended destination, though—an unknown location somewhere in The Waste. The realization sent a chill down my spine. The Waste was a vast, lawless expanse beyond the safety of our cities, a place where danger lurked around every corner.

The discovery of the camera's destination left me with a mix of intrigue and concern. It was undeniable proof that there was more to this murder than met the eye. The implications were far-reaching, and the questions it raised were daunting. Who had orchestrated this sophisticated surveillance? What secrets were they hiding, and why had they targeted the president's office?

As I disconnected my Hololens from the camera, I knew one thing for certain—I couldn't ignore this find. It was a potential thread in the intricate web of this case, a lead that begged to be pursued. My investigation had taken an unexpected turn, and I was determined to follow this new path, no matter where it might lead me. The president's murder was just the tip of the iceberg.

I had people to visit and connections to make, but where to start? The names on the list made sense, but the people who made the bold threats seemed the best option. Next stop, The Reckoning.

Chapter 7
Basement Bargains

"Where was his security?" I asked Robinson on the elevator back down.

"Sleeping. They heard the shot and struggled with the door for about five minutes before they gained entry," he replied.

"What time was that exactly?" I asked.

"4:34 a.m.," he replied.

I paused.

"You okay?" Robinson asked.

"Yeah, fine. I don't know, but that time just seems familiar to me for some reason," I told him. I said it because it did. It was like going into a grocery store for milk and getting everything else but milk, but that feeling you get when you're walking past the milk.

"I'm your escort," bleated a young, eager first-year officer who abruptly stepped in front of me as the elevator door opened, interrupting my precarious thoughts.

I couldn't help but roll my eyes at the notion. I had no desire for an escort, and frankly, I didn't need one. I tried to side-step him politely, saying, "I appreciate it, but I don't require an escort, thank you."

The young officer's face showed a mixture of determination and nervousness. "Commander Robinson insisted that I shadow you, or else…" His voice trailed off, leaving an air of uncertainty as he tried to make eye contact with me and Robinson for confirmation of his duties.

I raised an eyebrow, my patience wearing thin. "Or else what?" I asked, my tone laced with exasperation as I gestured toward him and scrunched my face at Robinson.

He fumbled for words, clearly unsure how to proceed. "Well, he mentioned something about Singapore and some really cute—"

I quickly cut him off, realizing that I wasn't going to win this battle. "Alright, alright, you're my escort, What's your name?" I conceded, though I couldn't help but wonder why Robinson would use a nuclear option against me for something as small as an escort.

"Patterson, sir," he replied. "I can hold that for you." He held out his hand hoping to help bear the load of me still carrying around my Tagadashi Hono Sword that I was unconsciously death gripping.

"I'm fine, can you get the transport?" I asked.

Robinson walked out behind me, and said just low enough for me to hear, "Four hours, Mark. After that, we will have to tell the world and I'll have to bring you in."

"How many people know?" I asked much later than I should have.

"Five, including you and me and VP Baines. His personal security who works overnight contacted me out of protocol before calling anyone else. I placed this on lockdown. Found the note and called you," he answered.

While waiting for Patterson, I connected to the States Interface to review everything I could on The Reckoning on my tablet. What I found made me think they couldn't be the masterminds behind a plot like this. Still, I had to follow every lead, no matter how ludicrous it seemed.

Hashtags of #donttreadonme #mybigblackrifle #pewpewsquad laced all their videos. Their videos cataloged them clearing rooms military style wearing full combat gear that fit oddly. These videos had a ton of views and looked extremely authentic, except for the size of the soldiers, who were at least two hundred pounds overweight. And, not to mention, their gear was fake. None of the guys in these videos had any real training, but the comments peppered throughout the thread had already pointed that out. Calling them "Meal Team 6," "Gravy Seals," "Banana Republicans," "Ya'll Queda," and my personal favorite, "The Roast Guard."

This didn't stop the posts from directly threatening the life of President Mason. Calling him a false winner and an illegitimate leader while calling for others to "take care of the Mason problem."

Based on the information fed to my hololense, a well known holobroadcast called the Daily Reckoning streamed from an apartment owned by a Gloria Bailey, fifty-seven years old, divorced, one child. Inherited resident of NJC. This wasn't the gotcha lead I wanted, but it was close and a place to start. I could start marking leads off the list, and the location of this place seemed familiar too. I'd seen this location on a map recently.

Patterson piloted the Aerodrone transport that was waiting for us at the street level. We lifted off without fanfare or sirens to keep the attention low. We made good time and landed near the edge of the dome within moments of taking off.

Patterson stayed in the drone transport at my command as I walked up to what The Reckoning called their headquarters—it was a far cry from what I expected. A dilapidated apartment building in a rundown part of the city with peeling paint and a flickering neon sign that read 'The Reckoning' in the lower floor window. Not very subtle, but criminals weren't known for their intelligence. I rolled my eyes as I saw one of the basement windows was blocked by a confederate flag.

I knocked on the door and was met by the largest bearded woman on wheels I had ever met. Although, I had never before met a bearded woman on wheels.

"It's about damn time," yelped the lady at me.

"I'm sorry, were you expecting me?" I said.

She said, "I've been sending 'anonymous' messages every damn day for the past year, and last night, they really screwed up."

Maybe this is the break that I need, I thought to myself. Surely it can't be this easy.

"Careful," she said as she rolled back beeping into the recesses of her own home, "he's got some tricks up his sleeves."

"How many are down there?" I asked as I walked by.

"Shit if I know, do I look like I can do *down the steps,* you dumbass?" she spat.

I charged my stun baton, walked to the door, and looked for the handle.

"How do I open it?" I inquired.

"What kind of reward do I get?" she asked.

"I won't arrest you as an accessory," I replied.

"30,000 crypto credits, and I will let you in," she bartered.

"Gloria? Is that your name?" I inquired slyly.

"You know it is," she said with the level of disdain only capable of someone who's living off the welfare of others.

"Your son is broadcasting materials in violation of the lawful media act of 2035 from this home. This home is now in full control of NJC's data enforcement department and the 32nd Amendment Review until further notice. Gloria, if I take ownership, I cannot give it back until the court finds that you were not involved in the distribution, which could take months or even years. You will be relocated to an Outpost, during which time you will be given a duty you are capable of carrying out. From the looks of it, recycling. Or you can give me the code, Gloriiaaaa."

"69420," she said with hesitation and embarrassment in the lowest of voices.

"See, it wasn't that hard," I said in mock victory.

I put the code in, smirked a little, and winced a little as the door to the basement opened and the smell hit me. Piss and body odor.

It was at this point it became quite obvious to me why Gloria was attempting to turn her own son in seemingly on a daily basis. I heard hushed whispers and arguments between three or four voices as I walked down the steps before I made it to the base of the first landing. I was an ANGL operating in a scenario to find and solve a case that could unravel the fabric of our democracy and peace and clear my name of wrongdoing. The scenario was not ideal. However, Basement Burger Boy should be an easy lead to follow up solo.

That is why when I heard someone yell "Syrian Decibel Grenade" my bootyhole puckered. If I'm being totally honest, at least a 6/10 pucker factor. A Syrian Decibel Grenade is a sound-based directional weapon that isn't as loud as it is disorienting. This grenade emits sound waves in different directions within a room, disrupting the balance and equilibrium of anyone within the range of effect. There's dizziness, vomiting, and loss of hearing, and that's just the beginning. So, I was quite amused when what looked exactly like a Syrian Decibel Grenade said, "Unable to connect to server, please check password and confirm," and rolled to the bottom of the steps. It was a fake. Real Syrian Decibel Grenades host their own technology onboard.

"I gave you four thousand crypto credits to buy that, Caleb!" yelled a voice from a dark corner.

"Well, the one from last night worked, Gene!" jabbed back a voice from the adjacent corner.

"What else we got, Rick?" yelled the first voice.

"Don't use my name, Gene!" complained Rick from behind a couch.

"What did you say, Richard Green of 1408 Arbor Avenue?" said Gene in full operational security defiance if that was a thing with these yahoos.

"I got a nuclear option, how about this pepper bomb, you bag of dicks!" hooted Rick as he stood from behind the couch, in a closed basement, no open windows and set off a federal-issued pepper bomb used for crowd control.

Years of advancements in pepper spray technology had turned most of these items into liquid fire. As a result, we were subjected to daily micro-doses of capsaicin, the active ingredient in pepper spray. It was a precautionary measure to ensure our tolerance remained high. I crept down the steps trying to gain a visual. That's when I saw them arming the pepper bomb. I decided not to stay as deploying these in an enclosed space was idiotic at best and negatively life-altering at worst. Options I didn't want fate to decide for me. Especially given my morning so far. I wasn't taking chances.

Among the group, Rick was the first to spot my hasty retreat and couldn't resist taunting, "Look, he's making a run for it!"

In the year 2040 the Philippines had introduced the Wondering Phantom Pepper, a synthetic pepper formulation that surpassed anything measurable on the Scoville scale. Merely one milliliter of this substance upon aerosolization caused immediate skin irritation, temporary blindness, and lung inflammation. Now, imagine a federal crowd dispersal bomb containing a hundred milliliters of this potent compound. While it might not have had a significant effect on me, it had been quite some time since my last encounter with such a substancial irritant.

I managed to reach the upper level just in time to close the doors behind me, allowing Custard's Last Stand Hot Dog to revel in their perceived victory over an ANGL. With the code in hand, I swiftly reset the password and positioned myself at the top of the stairs, preparing for what would undoubtedly be a tense negotiation.

Twenty seconds passed before a frantic pounding commenced. The cacophony of coughing, retching, arguing, and desperate pleas emanating from the door formed a grotesque symphony.

"Please!" He started to barf relentlessly.

"Open!" he managed to get out before more retching.

"The!" Followed by more coughing, crying, and retching.

"Door!" And more retching, this time accompanied by dry heaving.

Noticing a door wedge nearby, I promptly positioned it in front of the door. With a deep breath, I entered the code and allowed the door to swing open slightly, revealing three mouths, noses, and neckbeards desperately gasping for fresh air.

"Let me out!" Rick sputtered and gagged.

"Can I have some water?" Caleb begged.

"Shut up, you two! Please, man, I've got stuff to trade," pleaded Gene.

"I'm going to make this very easy. I have two questions," I said as I pulled out a Polysync, the standard issue portable and instant polygraph, 98% accurate. "Patterson, I need to detect any deviations in voice tone."

Patterson responded, "It's easier if I come and help in person."

"That's a negative, ghost rider, you will only slow me down," I said back.

Tone: True

I squatted at the entrance of the door and made myself as casual as possible, "Like I said, two questions."

"Screw you," spouted Caleb.

What I did next, I am not particularly proud of, but…

80

"You punched my teeth out!" Caleb cried.

"They weren't that nice to begin with," I retorted. "Back to my questions."

"Will you let us out if we answer?" Gene cried as he aligned his eyes to the opening in the doorway.

"As long as it's an honest response," I said calmly.

Tone: True

"We stole a sword from a merchant, it looks old. We used a Syrian Decibel Grenade that we bought from behind Ryan Simmon's club. We accidently set it off, and everyone started puking and falling over. If Rick wasn't prescribed Dramamine because of his ear infections, we would all still be there on the ground, flopping around. Caleb shat himself. Gene put earmuffs on us, grabbed the case, and we ran. We didn't know who we robbed and what we stole until we got home. We are so sorry. We had no idea they would send an ANGL."

Tone: True.

"Please don't kill us," cried Rick.

"Did you do anything else last night?" I asked openly with an assertive tone.

"No," said Caleb.

Tone: False.

I charged at the door with my baton, delivering electric shocks to the three men holding it. They jumped back in pain, allowing me to close and lock the door. Through the door, I reminded them, "I thought we had an arrangement."

Almost immediately, the barfing resumed.

"Please, open the door!" More Retching.

I slept with Gene's mom!" Caleb blurted out.

"Son of a bastard!" Gene yelled amidst the chaos and violence that erupted. I tried to intervene, but even Gloria chimed in, professing her undying love for Caleb from her hoverchair.

At this point, I gagged a little, and I wasn't sure if it wasn't solely from the pepper bomb or the mental image of Gloria and Caleb bumping chubbies.

I opened the door and let the basement air out before I headed downstairs and grabbed the stolen Honjo Masamune sword along with a large duffle bag filled with items, some cleverly fake, others potentially real, all of which should not be in the hands of the Delta Farce.

These items, whether fake or real, represented violations of numerous peacetime regulatory laws. I placed the men in restraints and initiated processing with the assistance of a mobile justice unit. The unit would collect evidence, start a trial, and provide sentencing through a virtual committee for charges and an online jury.

As the magcuffs locked into place with a sharp metallic snap, I spoke the words that activated the virtual court interface—an automated legal system that blurred the line between judicial process and digital arbitration.

"You are at the mercy of the Social Court by the law of NJCPD and Federal Jurisdiction. A Poly-Tribunal connection is being established. I, Officer Mark Andeya, do hereby arraign you on the following charges: Possession of stolen property, use of military grade arms in a SafeCity, and sex with your friend's mom, ewww."

I abruptly stopped myself.

Where the hell had that come from?

A beat of awkward silence. The men stared at me, confused.

I cleared my throat and continued. "I'm sorry. Possession of stolen property, use of military grade arms in a SafeCity. Guilty or not guilty?"

No one answered.

Not that it mattered.

Perched on my shoulder was a projector no bigger than a deck of cards, a seemingly innocuous piece of tech that just so happened to determine the fate of criminals in real-time.

The future hadn't gone full Judge Dredd, but for those in The Waste, this was too damn close for comfort.

The lumens on the projector were ridiculous, strong enough that looking directly into it was a fast-track to temporary blindness. It was always listening, but never recording—not until the command was given. *"You are at the mercy of Social Court."*

That phrase alone triggered the legal proceedings, initiating a live connection to the Tribunal system, which immediately processed the charges, analyzed the evidence, and issued a ruling—all within minutes.

Unlike the old-world justice system, which was bogged down by bureaucracy and endless appeals, this one operated with clinical efficiency. The AI didn't just make the ruling itself—it connected us with a real judge, a prosecutor, and a defense attorney, each of whom had only a few minutes to review the evidence before the case was deliberated.

If the data was complete—body cam footage, sensor logs, criminal records, or live testimony—the case moved forward at full speed. The prosecutor and defense could make brief arguments, and the defendant had a chance to speak, but there was no grandstanding, no theatrics, no drawn-out trials.

The verdict wasn't decided by a single judge, either. Instead, it was determined by a live tribunal of qualified citizens, selected at random from an approved pool. They reviewed the case, heard the defendant's statements, and voted.

If the evidence was airtight, the decision was swift.

And in this case?

There was no doubt.

Justice wasn't just efficient.

It was absolute.

Plenty of people claimed our hololenses were always recording. This led to accusations that the government was sitting on far more data and evidence than they admitted, keeping the pre-trial information locked away until it served their purposes.

There had been several cases that could have gone entirely differently if pre-recording had existed. But to believe that either the government was suppressing exonerating evidence, or that they were actively violating rights on a system-wide level, was the kind of conspiracy talk that got you expelled to the Outposts real quick.

The men stood together, shoulders squared, refusing to kneel or show even the slightest submission. One of them, a wiry man with a scar across his cheek, spoke for the rest.

"We are sovereign citizens. We do not recognize your jurisdiction."

I smiled.

Because that was the moment my job was done. In less than ten minutes, the verdict was delivered.

Guilty.

Their sentence? Outpost Duty.

A transport was already en route—a one-way trip into exile.

Soon, a new Outpost family would have the opportunity to replace them here in the NJC, taking their place in society as productive, law-abiding citizens.

The men didn't argue. Didn't fight.

They just stood there, the reality of their permanent removal settling in.

One of them muttered something under his breath.

I didn't care.

By the time the transport arrived, they wouldn't exist in SafeCity records anymore.

Because once the system had passed judgment—

There was no coming back.

The Poly-Tribunal AI didn't care about ideological nonsense.

The law was clear. The charges were processed. Evidence, undeniable.

Thinking about transport, I realized I could use the system's network to return the two swords to Tagadashi Jr., finally settling my debt. Even better, tapping into the transport logs might reveal where the data from the president's library had been streaming—giving me a much-needed lead.

I relayed the good and bad news to Robinson. He told me to keep on the trail of the camera and reminded me of my time remaining.

Chapter 8
Eyewitness Knows

Tagadashi Jr.'s residence was an unassuming building tucked away in one of the quieter corners of the city. I climbed a flight of stairs and reached his door, which bore no visible markings or signs of any kind. He preferred to keep a low profile, and it was evident in every aspect of his life.

I pressed the intercom button, and a voice crackled to life. "Who's there?"

"It's Mark, the adopted black one," I replied, keeping my tone neutral. "I need to speak with Tagadashi Jr."

There was a brief pause before the door buzzed, granting me access. I entered the dimly lit home, where the air was thick with the scent of incense. Tagadashi Jr. was kneeling on the floor, surrounded by a collection of holographic screens displaying various streams of data and hundreds of camera feeds.

It was 8:45 a.m., barely two hours after learning that his precious sword had been taken. Three hours remained until the news of the president's death would become national headlines and I would be formally charged. I walked in with both swords, one in either hand, with the intention of returning both, hopefully in exchange for information regarding the camera I found. The walls were lined with men.

"Mr. Andeya," he said in his best Agent Smith impression from the old *Matrix* movies as he grinned ear to ear, "I am afraid, I cannot accept either of these." He didn't look up from his screens.

I tilted my head in confusion like a lost puppy.

"What do you mean?" I asked.

"My father says that you must bring them to him since you broke his camera," Jr said in his own form of confused conveyance. He turned and disappeared into his home.

A feeling of excitement and nervousness peeled across my body. I had questions but could not ask them without compromising the investigation.

"People think that my father's empire is built on his swords, on fighting, on war." He smirked as he arose effortlessly. "People think my father makes money from selling trinkets of pain and suffering. Well, ANGL number ten, that is simply not true. My father is the information broker of the world and what you seek, he knows."

I looked upon Jr with curiosity to assess his involvement and level of knowledge.

"This room isn't secure, given its location inside the city, and…" He gave a quick gesture in my direction, more specifically my comically large hololenses. "Whatever that is, this isn't the place to talk about it."

He turned away from me and began to reengage with the screens, rapidly clicking and tapping at almost an inhuman speed. That's when I saw a small glint of metal at the base of his neck. An implant. I said nothing but took a mental note as it was not anything I'd ever seen before.

"How am I supposed to find him? Your father's location is the best kept secret in The Waste," I asked.

"You will reactivate your ANGL status, he will ping and meet you in The Waste," he replied with a prepared retort.

"I can't. I am one session…" I began and was interrupted.

"Yes, we know, one more session away from full deactivation. You know that's bullshit, Mark. Also, sorry you sharted yourself."

I didn't know how to respond. "Wait what?"

Jr scoffed and said, "Let me break it down for you, Barney style. There's no such thing as a full deactivation. My father has been working on the technology since my brother was killed by it, and my other brother…well it doesn't matter. There's no real deactivation. They are going to kill you, Mark. That's what deactivation is. They are mapping your neurotransmitters to get an accurate scan of your brain to be able to find the best next fit for your SAI. That's why they ask you the same questions every time. That's why you have to answer them the same way each time. That's why when you get a ping, they are worried because if you still have a strong connection and if they disconnect you from a working SAI, it will burn out the unit and lose the cerebral abilities that it's learned from being in your brain," he said all of this while still scanning feeds from cameras.

"Do you still have the list?" Tagadashi asked.

"What list?" I lied.

"My father will explain the list when you find him," Tagadashi Jr said as he raised his hand in a dismissive manner. In what sounded like a totally different voice, he then said with a strong Japanese accent, "Now go. I have no further information that I am permitted to share, and your time is growing scarcer. You have decisions to make."

Anytime Jr spoke of his brothers, there was an odd weight to it. He lived in the shadow of two of the most innovative minds and dastardly swordsmen. While they forged legendary weapons and tactics, Jr never had the chance to prove himself at their side. His father denied him entry into service, preventing him from demonstrating his physical prowess, and kept him away from The Waste, where artillery was engineered.

88

I spent more time with Han and Jiro than I ever did with Jr, and I think he resented me for it. I don't even know if Jr ever had the chance to hold a sword in true combat.

What unsettled me most was how Jr talked about Han as if he were still alive. I tried correcting him, reminding him that Han had died from implant sickness, but he would just ignore me and continue speaking as if nothing had changed.

Frustration boiled, and I turned my back to him, speaking the words I hoped he would hear.

"Your brother loved you."

I heard the subtle shift in his breath, the slight tilt in his voice as he responded, "Loves."

I hesitated, then nodded. "Yeah, that too."

His soldiers stepped away from the wall in perfect unison. They didn't turn their heads, but their message was clear: my welcome was overstayed. I stepped toward the door which was right behind me. As I made it to the door, a different but familiar voice came from Jr with a light Japanese accent.

"In case you need clarification, your report will say that you found a troop of men buying dangerous items while completing a merchant bounty. Upon investigation, you found incriminating evidence linking Tagadashi's empire to the illegal transfer of unauthorized weaponry into NJC."

Sometimes you meet smart people, but the amount of thought and manipulation just to get me this far was already at a level that would take months of planning.

"Just so you know, I was aware the three stooges having a working Syrian Decibel Grenade was your idea. There's no other illegal arms dealers with access to those weapons except you. I am just surprised you gave them more than one that worked. They were priced far too cheap," I poked in a light candor.

"My father fought it at every turn," Jr said and continued, "but, you can't argue with results. Now hurry. You heard what he said."

"WHAT?" I said in pure, unadulterated confusion.

I reentered the foyer, or was rather rushed there, my eyes scanning the mosaic of camera feeds displayed over Jr.'s shoulder as the doors were closed behind me. Among the feeds on the screen, one stood out. The label said it was the live stream from The ChiTown Echo Lounge, and it bore two names over the heads of two men on the screen speaking to each other over a desk. This coincidence, whether contrived or serendipitous, couldn't be ignored. On one side sat Dimitri Voynev, ANGL number 7, a formidable figure in the world of politics and war tactics. He could destabilize a nation by just meeting with their Prime Minister. I should know, I was the one who would find and retrieve the prime minister. Across from him was Ryan Simmons, the enigmatic night club owner known as "The Coyote" for his expertise in navigating people in and out of the treacherous Waste. I'd opened and closed several investigations against him unsuccessfully over the past year. What they were discussing I had no earthly idea.

Simmons had a reputation for scuttling people back and forth without official clearance, a shadowy operation shrouded in secrecy. Everyone who had been arrested that works for him did not have authorization to be in NJC. I could never get anyone to flip on him, though. Those who collaborated with him never divulged the details, regardless of the incentives offered by the authorities. It was a mystery that had confounded law enforcement for years.

Dimitri Voynev, on the other hand, was currently the frontrunner for the upcoming election, seizing the opportunity created by President Mason's untimely demise. Although he had never stood a chance against Mason in a fair race, the circumstances had changed dramatically. Why would an ANGL want to be president? The nation had experienced a period of relative peace and prosperity under Mason's leadership, with declining crime rates, robust job markets, and a flourishing economy.

My thoughts raced as I considered the implications of this meeting. Could Voynev have been driven to murder in his pursuit of the presidency? Was Ryan Simmons, with his connections to the murky world of The Waste, an accomplice in some nefarious scheme? Perhaps they had procured a unique piece of technology, smuggled from The Waste, essential for their murderous purposes. But why implicate me?

As I continued to analyze the situation, a multitude of questions swirled in my mind, each demanding answers. I retraced my steps toward my waiting transport, but not before pausing to admire a portrait hanging on the wall. It depicted a blissful family—painstakingly hand painted—the elder Tagadashi in a sharp black suit, two young twins, Han and Jiro in their short suits with jackets, with the innocence of childhood in their eyes and swords on their hips, and a radiant Mrs. Tagadashi cradling a baby Tagadashi Jr. As I looked closer saw that young Jiro's sword looked odd.

However, before my mind could process that, my revelation that Tagadashi Jr hadn't been born within the SafeCities was confirmed by this portrait. This painting was done by a Tokyo Prime savant named Oreko. Rumors that this painter was the sister of Tagadashi ran rampant. Her style was impeccable and unique. She'd never left Tokyo Prime and this was an original. I must have scrutinized the painting too intently, for the guards reacted swiftly, their body language conveying a clear warning, and I knew it was time to move on.

I marched to the car, tossing into a planter a wide-range data collection device for all unencrypted feeds to be intercepted. It was a long shot, but a chance I had to take.

Patterson was standing outside of the transport. "Where to now, sir?"

I walked past him and said, "Already loaded in the nav, best I don't say it out loud."

I stood there, mind still processing what I had just seen. Implants were standard issue for enlisted military personnel—a tool for increasing physical response times, coordination, and battlefield awareness. More than just a glorified tracking system, they were a direct neural interface, an extension of the soldier's mind, linking them to their unit and command in a way no army had ever achieved before.

But this? This was something else.

The problem with machine learning had always been intuition—an algorithm could predict, analyze, and optimize, but it couldn't feel. That was the beauty of the implants. By integrating a digital processor directly into the nervous system, the brain's executive functions were left unburdened, allowing soldiers to make split-second decisions while their implants handled the reflexes, the calculations, the minute adjustments that turned a trained fighter into a lethal machine.

There were illegal versions of these implants—off-market mods, black-market enhancements—but I never expected to see one here.

And definitely not on Michael.

Every implant I had ever encountered had been on the neck of a soldier heading on a mission or buried deep inside the skull of an elite special forces operative. Michael was neither.

My mind lingered on the small device at the base of his neck.

Right where the spine met the skull. There was nothing else it could have been.

If I was being pedantic—and let's face it, I was—he was never allowed to enter the corp. Maybe it was his way of rebelling against his dad. It sat just below the occipital lobe, where the nervous system was most vulnerable, most accessible. Tiny nanofibers stretched out from the implant, burrowing into the skin, too small to be detected by pain or pressure receptors. They slithered their way inward, a parasite wiring itself into the body.

I knew exactly where those fibers led.

First, the brainstem. The root of all reflexes, the subconscious commands that dictated movement before the conscious mind could even register an action. Soldiers with these implants could react faster than their own instincts.

Then, the occipital lobe. Processing visual input. There had been classified reports of real-time visual transmission—one soldier seeing through another's eyes, full battlefield integration. If that tech was real, then Michael wasn't just wearing an implant. He was part of something bigger.

The cerebellum was next. Balance, auditory processing, spatial awareness. It meant hearing wasn't just improved—it was rerouted, filtered, augmented.

But the real horror wasn't in what it connected to.

It was in what it replaced.

I read an after-action report once. A soldier had taken a bullet straight to the prefrontal cortex. Should have been dead on impact. Instead, the implant had kept him moving, kept him fighting, his body fully functional until swelling herniated the brainstem, shutting down base functions like breathing.

He had fought without a brain.

The implications were terrifying.

And yet, Michael had stood there. Alive. Coherent. Functional. With a black market implant.

And I had no idea why.

I thought about why. Michael had turned his head, spoke, and I had felt my stomach drop.

Two accents. Two distinct voices.

And the collective *we*.

"We do not understand your hesitation."

We.

I felt my pulse in my throat.

Implants weren't supposed to do that.

They didn't think for you. They didn't talk for you.

That was the whole point. The neural interface was meant to assist, not override.

Yet Michael had stood there, his voice splitting, his words shifting, something inside of him speaking that wasn't him.

I had a hundred questions.

Why was he using an illegal implant? Where did he get it? Why was it still active? And most importantly—who else was in there with him?

The list of mysteries kept getting longer and longer.

And for the first time in a long time…

I wasn't sure I wanted the answers.

⁓

Across town, in the dim glow of a streetlamp in an alleyway, two men stood facing each other. The night air was thick with unspoken tension. One very tall, the other standing almost two heads over the first.

The shorter of the two giants exhaled sharply, breaking the silence. "Mistakes like that aren't acceptable."

The other man adjusted the cuff of his perfectly pressed suit, his voice calm, almost amused. "Mistakes don't matter when the outcome is inevitable, comrade."

The first man's jaw tightened. "I'm not worried now, but if too much information slips, we'll have to establish a new timeline. And I doubt he would be pleased with that."

"Let me worry about him." The suited man smoothed an invisible crease from his sleeve, his tone carrying a quiet finality.

A silence stretched between them, heavy with consequence, before they parted ways, disappearing into the night like ghosts.

~

Inside his armored mobile command center—a roving hideout nestled in a prearranged safe zone on the outskirts of The Waste—Tagadashi activated the secure line. The low drone of the command center's machinery and the distant whistle of the winds from the plane formed the backdrop for his measured inquiry.

Tagadashi (through the comm, his voice resolute): "Michael, give me an update. Did Mark retrieve the clue?"

A pause, then Michael's voice came in, laced with restrained irritation.

Michael: "Father, he just left. Both swords in hand."

Tagadashi's gaze drifted to the reinforced viewport where the landscape shifted beneath a morning sky. He continued, his tone deliberate.

Tagadashi: "And does he suspect anything? Any indication of awareness that could jeopardize our timeline?"

Michael, sighing: "No, he seems as oblivious as ever. His usual unpredictability hasn't stirred any suspicions—for now, at least."

A heavy silence settled over the line as Tagadashi absorbed the information. His mind raced through contingencies and possibilities, all while the mobile command center rattled softly around him.

Tagadashi answered with quiet determination: "Good. That means our timeline remains intact. Michael, keep monitoring his actions closely. Soon, I will do my part. Keep an eye on him for now."

Michael's mind was a battlefield of conflicting impulses. He harbored a simmering resentment toward Mark—not merely for the sword he'd clutched like a trophy, but for the unspoken promise it carried, a legacy he'd always been forced to watch from the shadows.

In a rare moment of solitude, Michael absentmindedly rubbed the back of his head, his fingertips grazing the cool, steady pulse of his implanted SAI. That device, a hard-won relic from a near-fatal escapade in Tokyo Prime, was both his badge of survival and a scar of rebellion. It had nearly cost him his life, and his father's wrath had rained down on him like acid ever since he returned with it, his fury always circled back to his sons—Jiro, whose name alone could silence rooms, and Han, whose quiet genius had been stolen by the very technology meant to empower him.

Even as Jiro's spectral presence loomed large in every whispered conversation, Michael's heart ached for his father's elusive approval—a favor that seemed eternally reserved for his brothers. When Tagadashi laid out the plan to secure an SAI, Michael's emotions began to wax and wane like the phases of a distant moon. His anger bubbled beneath a veneer of reluctant compliance, a rebellion that was as much internal as it was outward.

Yet, as his hand brushed against the interface of his own SAI, a spark of certainty ignited within him. It was as if he'd discovered an ace up his sleeve—a trump card that could finally tip the scales in his favor. In that electric moment, every doubt and every resentful thought crystallized into resolve. Michael understood that to claim his father's respect, he might have to seize destiny with both hands, even if it meant challenging the order established by the titanic shadows of Jiro and Han.

Chapter 9
Just One of the Boys

Patterson glanced back at me, his expression filled with concern. "You can't tell me, can you?"

I realized that my poker face had deserted me. "No," I replied. "You wouldn't know what to do with any of this anyways."

The sheer magnitude of the information I had to process felt like trying to empty an entire swimming pool one teaspoon at a time. There were hidden cameras throughout NJC, my own life hung by a thread, the president was dead under mysterious circumstances, a list of potential victims or suspects loomed, and I'd thought I was one session away from retirement. *Lethal Weapon* would never be the same again after this, and somehow, I was in the middle of it all.

A faint smile formed on Patterson's face. "I have a master's degree in psychology, and I declined entry into a Psy D program. How about you give me a hypothetical and let me see if I can help? We have four minutes to reach our destination."

I hesitated for a moment, knowing that silence wasn't an option. "Let's say you have two dogs," I began, "and you come home to find the house in complete disarray. Trash is strewn everywhere, the couch is shredded, and curtains lie in tatters. The entire house is a disaster zone. When you walk in, both dogs look equally guilty. They won't make eye contact, their tails are tucked, and their behavior is bizarre.

97

If you punish the wrong one, the other will continue the destruction. If you punish both, they'll repeat the mayhem because they figure they'll be punished anyway. What would you do, Patterson? How do you choose the right dog?"

Patterson studied the scenario, his eyes scanning the horizon as he contemplated the situation. After a moment, he posed a crucial question, "Where's the cat?"

I was taken aback. "What?"

Patterson leaned in to elaborate further. "Think about it. Just because the dogs 'look' guilty doesn't necessarily mean they are guilty individually. They could be guilty by association until you prove otherwise. There might have been a cat involved that triggered all this chaos. Perhaps your dogs were chasing the cat or trying to protect it from some other threat. They're your dogs, they need you. Cats, on the other hand, can be real troublemakers. I love cats; my girl and I have two, Oreo and Sir Noiz. But they can really stir things up when they want to. It's in their nature. So yes, your dogs might have caused the mess, but find the cat before you assume you have the full story."

I squinted, contemplating the implications of Patterson's perspective and whether I had been misjudging the situation. Before I could respond, Patterson gestured toward the door. "The ChiTown Echo Lounge, sir."

Seven minutes had passed since I had observed those two men on a screen, seated across from each other, likely discussing the intricacies of horse husbandry, a topic that would undoubtedly be disturbing if explored too deeply. My mission was straightforward: determine why they were here and the nature of their conversation.

Entering the nightclub at nine in the morning was unusual, as only the kitchen staff would be active at this hour. To my surprise, I noticed an unmanned loading drone skiff transporting items into the freezer.

I ventured into the kitchen when I was abruptly confronted by someone.

"Hey buddy, hands up. I've got a taser arrow aimed at your head."

The voice was calm, level—the kind of voice that belonged to a
man who had no doubts about pulling the trigger.

I froze, every nerve in my body telling me to react, to counter, to
do something—but my training told me otherwise.

They stepped out of the shadows like ghosts, each moving with the
practiced ease of men who had spent a lifetime in combat zones. Not
SafeCity enforcers. Not NJC security. These were professionals. Six
against one wasn't a fight. It was an execution. For them. I knew that
if a confrontation began, each would fight to the death.

Mercenaries.

No, not just mercs. Killers.

They weren't uniformed, but I could still see their origins in the
way they stood, the way they held their weapons, the unspoken authority in their presence.

Each of them carried a past stamped into their bones, their eyes
sharp and unreadable. These were not the kind of men you met in a
bar.

They were the kind of men you hired when you wanted someone
dead and didn't want a body left behind.

I did a quick threat assessment.

- Australia—SASR. Special Air Service Regiment. Stealth.
  Close-quarters killing.
- United Kingdom—SAS. The best of the best. No hesitation.
  No mistakes.
- Iran—Quds Force. Black operations, wet work, untraceable.
- United States—SOCOM. A ghost among ghosts, trained to
  disappear before the shot even landed.

- South Africa—Recces. Ruthless, adaptable. A tracker who could hunt anything, anyone.
- Belgium—SFG. One of the deadliest urban warfare specialists on the planet.

Each of them represented a different battlefield. A different war. And now?

They were standing in a half-circle around me, weapons drawn, waiting for my next move.

I debated whether to attempt an escape, but it was clear that someone would be seriously injured if I tried. Security at this hour was surprisingly heavy, which raised more questions.

"That's ANGL 10," remarked the unmistakable Russian accent of Dimitri Voynev, ANGL 7, from behind me.

"Gentlemen, his name is Mark, and he is not armed. Treat him with respect," said Ryan, who had joined Dimitri.

"Some ANGL he is," a gruff voice with a southern accent chimed in. The speaker sported a Navy tattoo on his forearm and was nonchalantly smoking an illegal cigar. "Looks like a bit of a lightweight to me."

"He could take all of you down before the first body hits the floor," Dimitri interjected.

"Nahhhh, I'm out of practice, 7, and I haven't had much prep time," I replied jokingly, though with a hint of seriousness. "The one with the cigar seems like he'd drop too fast for me to maintain that reputation."

I lowered my arms and turned to offer a smile.

"How long has it been?" Dimitri asked, approaching me for a hug.

"At least two years since Sabrina…" I trailed off, realizing that the last time I had seen Dimitri was at his wife's funeral. She had been killed in an Outpost attack while doing some Outpost expansion, which had solidified Dimitri's determination to lead a place like this and increase its capacity to admit more Outposters.

"What brings you here?" Dimitri inquired.

"I'm following a case," I replied. "Some individuals purchased high-end gear in the alley behind here: Syrian Decibel Grenades, Federal Pepper Bombs…"

"Wait a minute," Ryan's deep baritone voice interrupted.

The mercenary's expression uniformly darkened as they watched Ryan, the Deathball legend, veer away from me instead of plowing into me as expected. Their disappointment was palpable, evident in the tight set of their jaws and the furrowed brows beneath the navy tattoos and other gear that set them apart from normal civies. It was clear that they had anticipated a different outcome, one that would have left me sprawled on the ground, defeated, and broken.

And who could blame them for expecting such a spectacle? After all, Deathball was no ordinary sport—it was a brutal, high-stakes game where victory often came at the expense of one's opponents. In Deathball, there were no rules, no mercy, only the relentless pursuit of glory and the crushing defeat of those who dared to stand in your way.

But for those unfamiliar with the blood-soaked arenas and bone-crushing battles of Deathball, allow me to enlighten you. Imagine a sport where the objective is not just to win, but to annihilate your enemies, where every collision is an opportunity to assert dominance and every victory is celebrated with a primal roar of triumph. That is Deathball in all its savage glory.

The man with the navy tattoo on his arm glanced at me with a mixture of disdain and frustration. He wanted a Deathball moment, and he was going to be disappointed.

Deathball was a savage, unforgiving sport played on a narrow battlefield—half the width of a football field but packed with violence. The objective is simple: carry the ball to the far end while surviving a gauntlet of escalating combat. Every ten yards brought a new opponent, each one stronger, faster, and deadlier than the last. Players enter empty-handed, forced to fight barehanded until they've defeated five challengers; only then can they claim a weapon. Every step forward demanded ruthless strategy and brutal efficiency—because every choice shaped the danger still ahead. Some players pushed their luck even further, attempting to run the field in reverse to raise their rank, battling all who stand in their way.

But Deathball's true brutality lay in its two merciless rules. The Gauntlet: survive the entire field unarmed, reach the end within two minutes, then defeat the final defender in under three—or die trying. And the territory itself: no nation claims it, no law governs it. The moment you step onto the field, you surrender all protection. If you lose, you either die where you stand or get thrown into The Waste—and if you're lucky, maybe you find your way back. Most don't.

Only one person has ever won the gauntlet. Ryan Simmons. He started in The Waste and bought his way into NJC.

My focus and goal had to be clear. Truth and justice would have to start falling into their places on this chessboard. I had to consider how to play this in order to get them.

"I am just looking for answers," I said as I looked up and into the eyes of the man who was taking this investigation personally. "I haven't made any connections to anyone here, and I don't think there's a reason for it," I said as I tried to smooth things over. He relaxed a bit, so I pressed into the forgiveness route. "I saw the door open and was hoping to find an office manager who can give me clearer surveillance footage from last night." And as I said that, all the rest of the tension seemed to clear the air, so I struck while it was still innocent. "And I ran into you all. 7, what are you doing here?" I asked for in a coy voice and for obfuscated reasons.

Faster than should be natural, he responded in a calm and even tone, "I just arrived, moments ago, securing a vote and donations."

This was a crossroads point for me that I was not ready for. I can either call him on the lie now and press him for the truth or play his game and see how deep the rabbit hole goes. The problem was I was not good at this game, nor did I know all of the rules. At this point I was an unknown variable, and if I played my cards right, I could call his bluff when I was ready.

I looked between the giant and the politician and asked the most appropriate question: "How far is Baker going to get on Deathball tonight? The going bets are at seventy yards."

Simmons looked at me in disbelief, adjusted his jacket lapels and said, "He won't make it past the sixty."

Dimitri released the tiniest breath. I had seen this man in combat, in his prime, and I knew his posture. It was a small change, but it was there, a sense of relief. I was now in the game.

"Are you going tomorrow?" I asked Dimitri. "The game tomorrow is expected to be epic. There hasn't been this much buzz since Ryan 'the Hammer' Simmons ran the gauntlet."

"And no one has done it since me," Ryan added with a hearty laugh.

I started in with the voice of someone who was on a late schedule, "Listen, I got to go, but before I do, can I look at your cameras? I need to see what's happening in these alleys."

"We will add your Hololens to the stream for camera archive," said Simmons with a confidence that was unmistakable. He truly believed I wouldn't find anything.

"Is that necessary?" asked Dimitri quickly. "This sounds like it has nothing to do with The Echo Lounge and more like the force needing to stick its nose where it doesn't belong. I am trying to create a place where state overreach is quelled," he said as he urged Simmons.

Simmons began to recant, when I interjected, "What are you hiding, Dimitri?" I decided to play a poor man's bluff. One that I know I'd lose in order to gain ground on my real investigation.

"How many illegally employed workers and security are you willing to overlook in order to get that campaign funding secured?"

Both men puffed up and took insult as I hoped they would. If they knew anything about the president's murder, it didn't show, and I needed to know why they would be on the list if they weren't the killers. Simmons began to cough and had trouble catching his breath.

The politician left his body, and ANGL 7 entered. "You and I haven't talked or seen each other since my wife died, and here you are, asking me about how am I funding my campaign? Last I heard, you wanted out. You couldn't do it anymore. That's a lot of nerve from you. Are you even an ANGL still? I could dismantle your career with one phone call. Why are you really here?"

I met him eye to eye and asked with concern and anger, "Who would want you dead?"

Dimitri allowed the politician to take him back. "Are you kidding me? That list would be a mile long. Is there a threat on my life? Wait, let me correct that, is there a credible threat against my life?"

"Don't know yet," I said genuinely.

"What about you, Simmons?" I turned to ask.

Simmons gestured at his formidable security detail. "These aren't for decoration. There's an attempt on my life at least once a month."

"Twice last month, boss," said a guy with a South American accent.

"Don't you have a Waste Bounty on your dick?" said Simmons as he looked at me with disdain.

"Aye, you're the dick bounty fella, are ya?" Chuckled a voice in an Aussie Accent. The dick bounty was a price put on my…second head after I was caught in bed with the wrong woman.

I put my hands up in protest, but before I could get a word in, Dimitri made his questions clear. "Where's this information coming from, 10?"

"I can't tell you, but it's real and I need to know if you've made any new enemies with substantial reach," I said in the most serious tone I'd taken since I strolled into the back of the club.

"How far deep of a reach are we talking about?" He looked into my eyes. No fear, no anger, just business.

"Far enough to reach you, that's for sure. Why did you come here today, and the truth this time?" I said, playing my hand.

Dimitri pulled me aside and placed his hands on my shoulders. He pulled out a device, pressed a button and all electronics beeped in confusion. "Four gave me this. We got twenty seconds; Simmons needs me in his pocket. I need Simmons to keep labor mixed. If I keep the labor costs low businesses thrive. Labor costs too high, businesses fail. It's a balance. Get me?"

I nodded in agreement. A few beats passed and all the electronics came back to life.

"Can that interfere with a Halosphere or DWAR?" I asked inquisitively.

"Yeah, if it was the size of a transport and was powered by the same amount of power," clipped back Dimitri. "Are you looking to make an unsanctioned Waste Run?"

I must have had a very confused look on my face.

"A device this size can only interfere with transmissions. Not turn anything off. There's a hole in our Halosphere somewhere. It's tiny. But big enough to get a small person through."

And that's when I noticed it. The entire crew of the kitchen, security, hell even the people unloading the skiff were small. How had I never noticed this before?

"I'll find it. Regulate it. And eventually fix it. But today, I need Simmons doing what Simmons does."

He firmed his hands on my shoulders, pulled me closer and whispered, "Don't Reactivate. If it's that bad, please don't Reactivate. They will come after you too!"

I know what that took. I don't know if he knew how close I was to saying goodbye to all of this. But, now knowing that I might die upon full deactivation, I wondered what would happen. He dropped the interference device in my pocket and patted my shoulder.

Simmons and Dimitri needed an eye on them, Jr would provide that. 7 was a master at manipulation. I am sure that he was trying to sow a seed of confusion and the best I could do was play along.

Dimitri laughed, a deep, guttural sound that made the whole situation feel more like a barroom joke than a deadly standoff. He turned, his massive frame shifting like a mountain in motion, and slapped his enormous hand against my chest.

"You'll be fine," he said, grinning, boisterous and loud.

"Not that fine," the Australian muttered, rolling his shoulders. "If we got the drop on you this time, you won't last a day."

Dimitri's grip tightened on my shoulder. Barely noticeable to anyone else. But I felt it. A warning. A shift in his demeanor so slight that only someone like me—someone trained to read the smallest tells—would catch it.

He didn't like that comment.

And neither did I.

The difference was, I wasn't about to say it out loud.

Dimitri didn't turn to face them. He kept his gaze locked on mine, as if assessing something deeper than just the words that had been spoken. Then, still looking at me, he spoke over his shoulder.

"You think you can take him?" Dimitri asked casually. Too casual.

The Aussie's cocky grin widened. "I could probably take him."

I leaned around Dimitri, eyeing the man who had just decided he was my problem.

"He could probably take me," I mused.

Dimitri's smirk sharpened, the kind of expression that made my stomach tighten in anticipation. Not fear. Not quite excitement either.

He was setting something up.

And I had the distinct feeling I wasn't going to like it.

"I have 50,000 crypto credits that says he can beat you," Dimitri said, voice smooth as glass. "With his hands tied behind his back. You? Any weapon you want."

The Aussie barked out a laugh. "You think he can take me with his hands tied behind his back?"

It started as a joke. A challenge meant to be brushed off.

Then the laughter stopped.

Dimitri finally broke his gaze from me and turned toward them, the weight of his confidence filling the space between us all like a loaded weapon.

"No," he said simply.

The air shifted.

"Not just you, little man," Dimitri continued, pointing at the Aussie. "You. And you. And you. And you. And you."

One by one, his finger leveled at each of them.

Their expressions blanked.

The humor? Gone.

The weight of what he was saying? Sinking in.

He wasn't saying I'd win. He was saying I'd beat them all.

I inhaled slowly, feeling the moment settle deep into my bones.

"Let's not get your man hurt," Rian, the Belgian, interjected, trying to redirect the conversation before it became something irreversible.

Dimitri didn't even glance at him.

"It's an easy 50,000 crypto."

"I don't have any crypto," the Iranian said, crossing his arms. "Only SLAVE coin."

That got my attention.

SLAVE coin. A different kind of currency. Used in Wasteland markets, black-market deals, and deep-tier corruption networks.

Dimitri turned his head slightly, his smirk widening just a fraction.

"Oh? You exchange SLAVE coin?" Dimitri mused. "I'll take it off your hands."

Then, flashing me a grin, he added, "That'll make Mark's job easier."

They all stiffened. Because now, it wasn't just a fight. Now it was a fight with meaning. A chance to prove something. A chance to humiliate me—or be humiliated themselves.

Ryan exhaled sharply. "Wait, you're not actually going to—"

Dimitri raised one finger. A silent command.

Ryan shut up.

"We are," Dimitri said.

And just like that, it was decided.

The circle formed fast. No hesitation. No more jokes. The moment Dimitri made it official, the operators fell into a rhythm—one they all knew well.

I stood in the center, my hands behind my back, as they removed jackets, loosened straps, checked their weapons. They were all relaxed, but alert. Professional.

They'd done this before. So had I.

"Mark," Dimitri said, stepping up beside me, voice low, "don't kill them."

I flicked my eyes toward him.

"Not making any promises."

Dimitri chuckled, clapped a hand on my shoulder, then turned back to the others.

"No headshots, no broken spines," he announced. "Other than that? Anything goes."

The Australian—Callum—cracked his knuckles. "This is gonna be quick."

The South African operator, Dane, rolled his shoulders. "Don't let him get behind you."

Callum scoffed. "Hands tied, mate. What's he gonna do? Dance on his knees?"

I said nothing. Instead, I rolled my wrists, flexed my shoulders, exhaled slow.

Not because I was worried. More for them than for me.

Callum lunged first. His moves predictable and rehearsed. Too confident, too eager to end it early. He threw a right hook, aimed at my temple—intended to rattle me, disorient me.

I didn't move. Not yet. I let the punch come. Let it get close enough that he thought he had me.

Then, at the last pico second, I twisted my body just enough, not to dodge, but to redirect.

His fist clipped my shoulder instead of my skull, but he had already committed too much force—his balance was off. And before he could adjust, I planted my foot, turned into him, and let him collapse over my leg. Fast. Brutal. Effective. His chest slammed against the floor, air punching out of his lungs in a wheezing gasp. "Ooooh, that look like it hurt. One down."

The others didn't hesitate.

Dane was next. He was smarter than Callum. Quicker. Didn't lunge blindly. Instead, he feigned left, waiting for me to react. I didn't. I just watched.

He dropped low, aiming for my legs—trying to sweep me off my feet.

"Sweep the leg? Are you serious, Cobra Kai?"

That was his mistake. Because I didn't need my hands to fight. I pivoted, snapped my knee up into his chin, and sent him staggering backward before he could complete the move. "You're going to need a dentist. Two down."

The SAS operative, Liam, didn't posture like the others. His movements were tight, efficient. No wasted energy. He knew better than to rush me like Callum or fall for games like Dane.

He circled, light on his feet, analyzing. Watching my breathing, my stance, calculating my range even with my hands tied.

"Smart," I said, nodding. "You might actually last ten seconds."

Liam didn't answer. He shot forward—fast. Low-line attack. He went for the knee, trying to hyperextend it with a quick inside kick, aiming to drop me clean before I could counter. Textbook SAS neutralization.

But I wasn't playing textbook. I shifted my weight mid-strike, letting his foot glance off my shin instead of locking into my joint. As his momentum carried him in close, I pivoted into him, driving my shoulder into his jaw with a sharp upward snap.

He stumbled, but to his credit, recovered quick—only for me to use his recovery against him. As he re-centered his balance, I dropped to one knee and swept his planted leg from behind. His body flipped awkwardly, crashing flat onto the floor. The wind left him in a hard grunt, teeth clacking.

"Three down," I said, standing over him. "Next?"

The others were already closing in and looked at each other, nodding their heads in agreement

Iranian, Belgian, American.

They adjusted fast. No more single strikes. They moved together—military precision.

Iranian went low, American went high, Belgian circled to cut off my movement.

Smart.

If I had let them surround me, it would have been over in seconds. But I didn't. Instead, I rushed them.

I went toward the Iranian first—not away. He wasn't expecting it.

In an instant, I was inside his reach, dropping my weight, slamming my shoulder into his chest. He stumbled back, and I used the momentum to turn, kick out one leg, and send the Belgian sprawling.

Now, it was just me and the American.

Roy.

He hesitated. Only for a second. But that second was enough.

I twisted, stepping in close, and drove my head into his sternum like a hammer. His body jerked backward, the force knocking him off balance, and before he could recover, I pivoted smoothly, launching a brutal roundhouse kick to the side of his skull.

The impact landed clean.

Roy hit the floor. Fast.

Silence stretched across the room, heavy and absolute.

Dimitri sighed, rubbing a hand down his face. "You really don't listen, do you?"

I rolled my shoulders, surveying the wreckage. "I left them alive."

Callum groaned from the floor, propping himself up on an elbow. "Barely."

Dane was still on his back, staring at the ceiling, blinking like a man who'd just been hit by a freight train. "How…the fuck…?"

Rian wasn't moving much, but at least he was breathing. Liam remained motionless but breathing.

I turned my head, catching sight of the Iranian and the Belgian, both of whom had yet to pick their jaws up off the floor.

"Did you bet against me?" I asked.

The Belgian gave a half-shrug. "I'll be honest. I don't know what I bet on anymore."

Dimitri laughed. Loud.

Shaking his head, he turned to the others. "Get up, idiots. You've been humbled."

One by one, they peeled themselves off the floor, still groggy, still processing what had just happened.

Rian groaned as he sat up, rubbing his head. "Fuck, man."

Dimitri slung an arm around my shoulders, shaking me slightly, still grinning. "Mark, my friend, you just made me a lot of money."

I exhaled through my nose, my gaze sweeping the room. The tension had shifted. Not gone. But changed.

They weren't just operators watching me anymore. Now? They were measuring me. And I could feel it.

The real game?

Had just started.

The air was thick with the aftermath of the fight, bodies shifting, slow groans filling the space as the men reeled from the reality of their defeat.

Dimitri stood off to the side, arms crossed, grinning like he'd just walked away from the easiest bet of his life. Then I heard him say, "You picked an odd day do die," directed at me from outside of my periphery.

I felt it before I saw it. A change in the air, a ripple of intent.

The telltale twitch of fingers reaching for a weapon as I heard the ruffle of clothing and the rubbing of fabric and the unmistakable sound of a something being unholstered.

And then—

The sharp crack of a taser discharge.

The bastard actually shot at me.

No words. No warning.

Just an arrow streaking toward my face.

The shot came without warning.

A sharp snap of electricity cracked through the air, the twin prongs of the taser arrow streaking toward my face with surgical precision. The Iranian operator Kahsim didn't hesitate, didn't second-guess—he wanted me on the ground, spasming, helpless.

I didn't think. I didn't need to.

My body moved before the impulse even reached my brain. My hand shot up, fingers outstretched—not to block, but to catch.

The taser struck my palm, the prongs biting into my skin.

And then…nothing.

Electricity should have surged through me, should have locked up my muscles, should have dropped me like a sack of bricks. Instead, the charge crawled across my skin like liquid fire, arcs of light twisting between my fingers. The current that should have ended the fight before it even began dispersed harmlessly through my body, like it had no idea what to do with me.

The wires strained, twitching like the muscles of a dying animal. I clenched my fist. The tines snapped.

The room went dead silent.

I moved. Fast. Too fast.

One second, I was across the room. The next? I was on him.

He didn't even have time to react before my arm locked around his throat. I drove my knee into his ribs, feeling the sharp exhale of breath against my forearm as I pinned him to the ground.

His body knew pain. But his eyes?

His eyes knew terror.

Not because of what I had done.

Because of what he had seen. The most telltale sign of an SAI activation is the pupil of the eye getting giant in order to take in as much of the surroundings as possible. If that wasn't weird enough, the fluid inside of the eye also glows a little due to the charge jumping from the optic nerve and macula to the edge of the cornea. It's seen by few and survived by fewer.

Something in me had unveiled itself in that moment, something that wasn't supposed to exist anymore. I was supposed to deactivate.

Something beyond human stirred. I smelled him, I took in a deep breath and smiled. "Mmmm, smells like teen spirit," I said without understanding why or what drove me to say something so lame.

Yet, for the first time, they all saw it.

They saw what I was.

What I had become.

Now?

They knew and then I heard the pitter patter of urine hitting the floor as Kahsim wet himself. He lost his SLAVE coin and his dignity.

I let the operator hang there for a second longer, just enough for him to feel the weight of his own stupidity pressing down on his lungs.

Then, without looking away, I let a small smile slip onto my face.

"I want my cut."

Dimitri exhaled a short chuckle, the same grin still plastered across his face. "Not the least bit surprised, comrade."

With a flick of his fingers, his holo-display materialized in midair through mine, glowing neon digits floating in the space between us along with an old-fashioned cash register sound. His fingers moved effortlessly across the interface, and within seconds, the credits began transferring.

A chunk from Callum.

From Roy.

From Dane.

From Liam.

From the Belgian.

A direct loss. A reminder. A statement.

But when the last transfer completed, Dimitri held out something else.

SLAVE coin from Kahsim.

I narrowed my eyes slightly, letting the weight of it settle between us.

Dimitri smirked, holding it up between two fingers before tossing it toward me.

"I know you want it gone," he said simply.

I caught it, turning the physical chip over in my palm. The metallic sheen reflected the dim light, its surface etched with encrypted codes, a relic of the deepest black-market trade networks in existence.

A currency tied to things that shouldn't exist.

Dimitri tapped the side of his head.

"Every little bit counts, eh?"

I said nothing.

Because he was right.

With a slow exhale, I let the last remnants of adrenaline drain from my system. My muscles uncoiled, my breathing steadied.

Then, with deliberate movements, I loosened my grip on the operator.

He stumbled back the second I let him go, hands shaking, his face pale. Not from exertion. From realization.

He wasn't afraid because he lost. He was afraid because he had seen something he didn't understand.

And that? That was more terrifying than any loss.

I pocketed the SLAVE coin, rolling my shoulders before turning away.

I walked out, leaving them with a new understanding. Because now? They weren't watching me to measure my skill.

They were watching me because they knew, deep down—I wasn't done yet. And neither were they.

At this point, there was one more name on the list, Kimberly Florres, daughter of the Halos magnate.

Chapter 10
The Purple Tower

I left Dimitri to what can be best described as "shady politics," and Simmons to his involvement with human trafficking. Unfortunately, another problem for another day. I knew their names were on the list, but at this point, they were both high-profile individuals, and there was someone out for them. With the security provided by Simmons and Dimitri being an ANGL, I wasn't as worried about their immediate safety. I had to follow this next lead before jumping to conclusions.

I met back with Patterson and immediately navigated to the center of the city, to Halos Inc.

"Cheap bastard!" I said under my breath as I checked the balance transfer. I got $10k and he kept $40k. Oh well.

A sense of déjà vu washed over me as I stepped into the top floor of Halos Tower. Opulence and exclusivity weren't just descriptors here—they were understatements.

Halos Inc. didn't just own wealth—it defined it. The company provided essential services to all Union States, controlling everything from energy and defense to communications and private security. They didn't just support governments, they replaced them.

The tower itself reflected that absolute dominance.

It stood as the tallest structure in the entire NJC skyline, a mono-lithic spire of glass, steel, and black-gold composite, stretching so high that its uppermost floors were often hidden by the clouds.

Even from the outside, Halos Tower didn't blend in—it stood apart. A titan among lesser giants.

The base of the tower was impenetrable, guarded by automated turrets, thermal scanners, and aerial drone patrols that monitored even the most subtle movements. The main entrance, located on the 200th floor skybridge, was only accessible through verified air routes, ensur-ing that no one entered without explicit clearance.

A massive gold-trimmed emblem of Halos Inc. adorned the pri-mary access gate, a reminder that this was not just a corporation.

This was an empire.

And the tower?

It was its throne.

Walking inside was like stepping into another reality.

The lower floors—levels 1 through 150—were occupied by corpo-rate offices, research labs, and military-grade security hubs. Employees who worked here rarely ever left the building, some even living on-site in tower-controlled apartments designed to keep them close to the machine they served.

But the real power wasn't in those lower floors.

It was here.

The top five floors were reserved for executives, government offi-cials, and the few people who actually ran the world. I received and reviewed the floors onto my Hololens.

Floor 205: The Executive Level.

It was a cavernous lobby of black marble and gold accents, stretch-ing four stories high, its walls lined with holo-displays that projected stock values, surveillance feeds, and international trade reports in real-time.

Everything in Halos Tower was data-driven. Information was currency, and nowhere was that more obvious than here.

The people who walked these halls weren't businessmen.

They were kingmakers.

Floor 206: The Vaults & Classified Archives.

Few people had access to Floor 206. It housed Halos' most sensitive records—documents older than most governments, evidence of the company's true influence, and classified technology far beyond what was known to the public.

This was where the secrets were kept.

And where history could be erased.

Floor 207: The Private Security Command Center.

I was taken back by what I saw. It was an entire military nerve center.

From here, Halos monitored SafeCities, Outposts, and The Waste.

Live drone feeds hovered across massive digital walls, capturing every riot, every conflict, every potential threat. The room was never empty—it operated 24/7, manned by some of the most highly trained security tacticians in the world.

The Halos Private Police Department was headquartered here. The very organization I worked for.

And we answered only to them.

Floor 208: The Luxury Level.

A place reserved for the untouchable elite—Union State leaders, foreign dignitaries, warlords from The Waste, and even the occasional rogue billionaire with the right connections.

This floor wasn't just wealth. It was decadence.

The penthouse suites dripped with opulence—furniture crafted from extinct wood, sculptures worth entire economies, liquor distilled before most modern nations even existed.

It was a world so detached from reality that even time seemed to move differently here.

And yet, even here, security was absolute.

Every guest was tracked. Every conversation recorded. Every indulgence monitored.

Floor 209: The Founder's Suite.

The final floor. No one entered without permission.

This was the personal residence of the Halos CEO. Some said she wasn't even human anymore because of how much she worked and how little she slept—that she had transcended into something else, more machine than flesh, a mind that operated beyond mortal comprehension. If you saw the pictures of her like I had, you'd understand that she was more angel than me. The heavenly kind, not the killer kind.

Either way, no one walked onto Floor 219 without being summoned there first.

Halos wasn't just another megacorporation.

Not even the old-world titans—Apple, Tesla, Amazon, the crumbling remnants of Silicon Valley—could compare.

They had played by the rules. Halos rewrote them. They controlled more than just commerce. They controlled war. They controlled law. They controlled people.

And as I stood there, taking in the sheer weight of the tower around me, I felt it.

That undeniable truth.

This wasn't a company.

This was a kingdom.

And we were all subjects.

However, what managed to set them apart was their discreet nature despite the evil villain lair in the middle of the city, trouncing the Sears Tower. They didn't engage in flashy social media posts; they simply conducted transactions. They made money and employed nearly half of the SafeCities they operated in. This was another reason to not suspect Dimitri; a gun-related incident in the city could potentially devastate Halos Inc., leading to skyrocketing unemployment as the DWAR system became defunct.

The Union States had access to the technology, but they licensed it from the Florres family due to corporate laws that prevented businesses and the government from fighting over control. Super PACs had bought the Supreme Court in the 2020s, leading to a chain of events culminating in a civil conflict and the formation of The Republic of Liberty, or what we call The Waste.

This environment was more than just a culture shock for me. Entering this building exceeded my comfort zone for luxury. I generally drew the line at associating with people I described as *"Human Money Trees."* The prevalence of illegal exotic pets here was astonishing.

As for the illegal designer DNA children, delving into that topic would open an entirely new can of worms. Right now, my priority was to speak with Kimberly Florres. I had one hour left before it became public knowledge that the president was dead, and I would be arrested for his murder. This was the last person on the list and my last chance at clearing my name.

I approached the front desk, expecting some protocol to follow, but instead, the guard waved me through. The facial recognition system must have been instantaneous. I made my way to the elevator, and without any screen prompts or requests for access, it whisked me away. Shooting into the air in front of me was the hypnotic look of the ornate door. A metallic sheet, hand made into a work of art. And behind me was a glass wall, overlooking the city. Through the towering glass behind me, the city stretched outward like a living tapestry of light and movement, a fusion of architectural marvels and engineered perfection. The skyline was a sea of illuminated spires, each structure reflecting a different era of ambition—sleek hyper-modern towers of glass and steel stood beside ancient stone facades, remnants of a time when craftsmanship mattered more than efficiency.

The streets far below pulsed with life, golden arteries weaving through the metropolis, vehicles gliding in silent, orderly streams, their motion synchronized like a symphony of progress. Elevated trams floated effortlessly between suspended walkways, while digital billboards cast neon halos onto the buildings, their shifting hues painting the day with ephemeral artistry.

Beyond the heart of the city, the SafeCity perimeter loomed—a vast, circular barrier of reinforced alloy and security grids, separating the controlled utopia from the chaos of the Outposts. Even from here, I could see the faint glow of distant lights beyond the walls, flickering remnants of a world that Halos had deemed obsolete.

Above it all, the sky stretched in infinite clouds, punctuated by the cold light of orbiting surveillance drones and the occasional streak of a high-speed aircraft cutting across the heavens.

A slow-moving tide of clouds drifted in, curling around the tallest spires like ghostly fingers, their edges illuminated by the city's glow. The world beneath me became fragmented, swallowed in shifting veils of mist and shadow, only to be revealed again in slivers and bursts of neon reflection.

Above, the Halosphere cast its eerie purple hue across the heavens, its presence both mesmerizing and ominous. The artificial ionization field—Halos Inc.'s crown jewel of atmospheric control—gave the sky an unearthly radiance, its soft violet glow stretching across the horizon, blurring the line between technology and the divine.

Through the breaks in the clouds, I caught glimpses of the sun beyond, and at night, tiny pinpricks of light barely visible past the Halosphere's interference. Stars flickered—distant, untouchable—

reminders of a world that once felt boundless, now caged beneath the hand of industry every night.

The air carried a charge, something almost electrified, as though the very atmosphere pulsed with Halos' influence. From up here, the city below felt like a dream, an illusion of order—but beyond the rolling mist and digital sky, something else lingered.

Something unseen. Something waiting.

And from where I stood, in the highest echelon of its ruling power, I could see it all—a kingdom of light built upon unseen shadows.

When the elevator doors opened, Kimberly stood at her desk, engrossed in work. She wore jeans, a jacket, white low-top tennis shoes, and a white tank top. Her office was enclosed by glass, and four Holos surrounded her. A large, imposing man stood by the door, and I couldn't help but notice his physical resemblance to Ryan Simmons.

Her back was to me, and I saw her long ponytail as she issued orders to other Halos Inc. directors. She seemed to have a strong grasp of what she was talking about, and nepotism was clearly not her guiding principle.

"There was a 0.7% flutter in Boston during the maintenance. Was this expected?" she asked sharply. Everyone at the meeting scrambled through their files, but her gaze eventually fixed on a short, pudgy man with red hair, casting a blameful glare.

The guard cleared his throat, drawing her attention to my presence. She turned toward me, and her almond-shaped eyes met mine. I was about to introduce myself when she surprised me with an unexpected statement.

"Dahlia, what are you doing back here so soon? Never mind, listen. The underground says that President Mason was murdered last night. We suspect that 7 is the murderer. The Sentinel Eye in the president's office went dark, and we have no idea who or what was responsible.

There were also multiple disruptions in the Halosphere last night near the North Gate."

The look of total and utter confusion covered my entire face gave her a pause. She stopped and peered into my eyes, took a deep breath and chewed her cheek for a moment then exhaled slowly and said, "Black Hole Sun…"

I just smiled in confusion, slightly shaking my head in disillusionment. "I think you have me mixed up with someone else. I mean I do love nineties grunge though."

"I do, but I don't," she said with a slight mixture of disappointment and curiosity. She walked around me and was around my height. I am 5'10 and we met nearly eye to eye as she stepped closer.

She held her arm out to the large bodyguard. "Baker, do you have the card Dahlia left last week?"

"Baker? Are you running the Deathball Gauntlet tomorrow night?" I asked in unexpected excitement.

"I sure am," he said with a confidence that only a man his size could have. He walked closer and his size became more impressive. He'd make Dimitri think a moment before trying any funny stuff.

"They've got you pegged to make it to the seventy-yard line," I said with a little challenge in my voice.

"It's all the way or no way, sir," he replied with his deep but cotton soft voice.

Kimberly smacked her lips. "Well, now that you have caught up your riveting excitements, you should read this." She handed me a slip of paper with my handwriting on it with one word: "Reactivate"

Latitude: 42.0970° N

Longitude: 88.6943° W

"This is my handwriting," I said as I waved the sheet of paper back and forth.

"That's interesting and probably because you wrote it," Kimberly said with a dry expression.

"Why did you call me Dahli?" I asked

"Dahlia," she corrected me, "and I don't have the time to explain that. But you wrote yourself that letter in case you came looking for me as you are."

"I don't understand any of this," I said sharply.

She looked at me deadpan, tilted her head, and spoke plainly and calmly, "I can't give you the answers you're looking for, but I can tell you that if you don't retrace where you've been, you and Halos and everyone inside of them are in danger. Now, you must go. This is what you told me to tell you. Now leave."

None of this was making sense, my mind was unraveling, and I could not put together any coherent thoughts, and who in the hell is this Dahlia!?

As I stepped back onto the elevator, Kimberly held the door. "I shouldn't tell you this, but 6 and 7 are not who you think they are, Dahlia told me they are chaos incarnate. Don't trust them."

Chapter 11
FU2

Conducting a mental inventory, I found myself ensnared in a perplexing labyrinth of enigmas. A figure, bearing an uncanny resemblance to myself, goes by the name Dahlia and shares an intricate connection with the heiress of Halos Corp. This heiress presides over an underground information network privy to the clandestine revelation of the president's untimely demise. She nurses profound distrust towards my own battalion, the very comrades with whom I have forged a decade-long bond through battles and hardship.

However, the plot thickened as I stumbled upon a disconcerting revelation. This heiress possesses a letter in my own handwriting—a cryptic message, originally conveyed to me covertly by 7, an individual I've been expressly cautioned against trusting. The missive implores "reactivation," yet harbors a sinister ultimatum: failure to comply will trigger the shutdown of my SAI, effectively extinguishing my consciousness and dooming me to have my battle-hardened knowledge moved to the next ANGL.

Adding to this interwoven cryptic case, an elusive camera network permeates NJC, its feeds secretly directed to Tagadashi. The chilling revelation of the president's murder, perpetrated with a firearm with my thumbprint, casts an ominous shroud entrenched within the

Halosphere. My Holohud ominously counts down the minutes until the president's death becomes my problem—a mere thirty-six minutes remain on the timer, increasing the urgency of this unfolding mystery.

Thirty-six minutes and I will be at the mercy of a system that is still jaded and unfair.

If Kimberly knows about Mason's death, the only person who's told her is Tagadashi, so that's where I am headed, to Tagadashi. I'd just made a conscious decision to become a fugitive. I requested a turbo jet. Well, not just any turbo jet, my hold over from the corp that synced to me when I acquired it. The formatting was so advanced that it could not be reassigned to any other ANGLs. Patterson can come, though I doubted I would need him, but being alone in The Waste is always a bad idea.

The scramdrone dropped silently out of the sky like a rock before slowing its decent precariously low to the ground. I didn't have many cool things in my life, but this was one. Harry Potter had his broom, Marty McFly had his DeLorean, James Bond had his Aston Martin and I, my Whisperwing. The scramdrone spun in a 180 descent and opened as I walked out of the tower and past the transport.

Unlike the roaring engines of conventional aircraft, it hovered silently, its sleek frame cutting through the air with barely a whisper. As it neared the ground, the warm, oxidized scent of metal filled the air, mingling with the faint hum of its smooth propulsion system.

The wind stirred around me, rustling through the leaves and sending ripples across the surface of nearby puddles. But amidst the gentle cacophony of nature's symphony, the scramdrone remained eerily silent, its advanced technology allowing it to blend seamlessly into the surroundings.

Even after ten thousand hours behind its yoke, Whisperwing still made my pulse quicken. Sleek, silent, impossible—a machine that shouldn't exist. At its core pulsed a miniature nuclear reactor, stabilized by its Halosphere, recycling radioactive waste into reusable elements in a closed, endless loop. Every surplus joule fed its Proton Engines, engines that inhaled atmospheric hydrogen and exhaled harmless helium. No fuel. No heat. No trail. It moved like a ghost through the sky, invisible to thermal, radar, or infrared—undetectable even to the satellites that scoured the globe.

But the real terror was the HaloCore—not just a failsafe, but total sensory erasure. No vibration. No noise. No whisper of motion. The Whisperwing didn't simply evade detection. It erased its own existence. It could push beyond Mach 10 when unmanned, store terrifying amounts of reserve energy, and—if triggered—unleash a speed no pilot had ever survived. The dual cockpit was built for those rare few willing to risk everything. But I didn't fly it. I *became* it. With the SAI link wired into my brain, every command was thought, every movement instinct. The Whisperwing responded faster than my own conscious mind, bending space and physics to keep me alive. In that machine, I wasn't a passenger. I was the weapon.

Relief was a rare luxury, but as the Whisperwing hovered in wait, I felt the closest thing to it.

Its soft, nearly imperceptible hum resonated through the air—a frequency only I could feel through the SAI link. It wasn't just a sound.

It was a presence. A pulse. Something almost alive.

Then, with a quiet hiss, the left cockpit bay slid open—my personal preference, acknowledged through nothing more than thought.

I stepped forward, feeling the connection strengthen the moment I approached, as if the Whisperwing itself was waiting for me.

It wasn't just my craft. It was me.

And the moment I strapped in? We were one.

~

Patterson ran after me. "Where are you going?" he asked nervously.

"We," I corrected.

"Huh?" he roused.

"Where are we going?" I said as turned toward him and continued. "We are going to The Waste."

"Sir, I am not authorized," he began to say to me, then I cut him off. I held up 5 fingers, then 4, then 3, then 2, then 1, and then his Hololens rang. He began to speak to someone who just called him. Then he spoke again, "Under no circumstances am I to leave your side per Commander Robinson."

"Yeah, and in thirty-three minutes, you're going to get another call and you're going to have to make a career decision," I said as I looked him square in the eye. "He's sending you with me for a very specific reason. He trusts you're going to do the right thing at the right time," I finished.

Patterson scurried beside me and hopped into the other seat and buckled in before speaking. "And what's what?" he asked in a desperate reach to find out what that could possibly be.

"You'll know it when it happens," I responded as I put in the coordinates from my unknown handwritten note.

The scramdrone roared to life in a spectacular display of power, its reactor flaring for the briefest moment before compressing the energy into a perfect, controlled launch sequence.

Reserved exclusively for high-stakes missions, these monstrosities of speed and maneuverability were engineered to launch us into the sky at a blistering 10gs, pressing me so hard into my seat that it felt like my ribs were moments from cracking.

It was the only way to survive the kind of missions we were sent on.

If you weren't moving at escape velocity the second you left the ground, you were dead before you knew it.

I felt the surge of force pull me back as the drone shot forward like a railgun slug, tearing through the urban corridors of the city. Within seconds, it executed a precise 90-degree turn, a move that would have pasted an unmodified human against the interior like a smear of red paint if we were going a smidge faster.

The drone knew what it was doing.

Every maneuver, every tilt of its adaptive vectoring engines, was calculated in nanoseconds.

Incoming lock? It adjusted before the missile even finished its targeting sequence.

Heat-seeking warheads? It deployed flares and decoy drones mid-drift, their forms breaking apart like falling stars.

Ballistic tracking? It ran an instant algorithmic recalibration, ensuring it was never where they thought it was.

Being an ANGL had a few perks. And one of those was having a scramdrone coded to my exact biometrics. No one else could pilot this machine. It was mine.

"Hell yeah," I said softly as we got to ascent altitude.

The scramdrone's HaloCore engaged, sealing us in an invisible cocoon of silence and light absorption. No heat signature. No sonic boom. No traceable footprint.

A ghost in the sky.

Fortunately, we wouldn't need its full stealth capabilities on this mission. Time was more valuable than silence. I charted a course through the city, threading us between skyscrapers, keeping our velocity razor-sharp. Whisperwing may have been an artful blend of man and machine, but this? This was a bullet in motion.

Even at near-supersonic speeds, decelerating felt like a sudden stop after leaping off a cliff with nothing but a bungee cord strapped to your waist.

The drone shuddered as we bled speed in the final stretch, but it held steady—perfect, calculating, deadly.

We dodged, weaved, and surged through the city's controlled airspace, reaching Mach 5 as we cut through the clouds, racing toward the Halosphere's edge.

The ascent that took less than three seconds now gave us a direct route to our destination.

I slowed and looked over at Patterson, smiled gently and asked him if he was okay. He was pale, shaking and sweating. So, I took off at ten percent launching us to Mach 1.2. Patterson's eyes grew wide and he gripped the 5-point harness with a hold so tight, white knuckle would be an understatement.

And in that time, we had already outrun the past, the present, and anyone foolish enough to try and follow.

~

Tagadashi Jr. had urged me to reactivate before embarking on this mission, but as I arrived here, this place felt hauntingly familiar. Memories rushed back, as vivid as the morning rain remembered in the afternoon. Tagadashi was here. I couldn't tell you exactly why I knew, but I knew.

In school we learned about the tipping point for climate change. What could have been saved was lost to corporate greed and personal selfish ideals. The sun now bore down mercilessly, a relentless orb in a cloudless sky. The air was thick, almost tangible in its heaviness, filled with the kind of humidity that immediately clung to your skin, seeping into your clothes and dampening your spirit. I could feel the sweat dripping down my sides.

I squinted against the brightness, my eyes taking in the expanse of fields stretching out, the cornstalks stunted and gasping for life in the parched earth. I had to immediately put my Hololens on just to be able to see.

The promise of a lush, green Midwest summer was a postcard from the past, now replaced by this drought-stricken picture. The nights offered no solace. I remembered the cool summer evenings of my youth, but now, they were as hot as the days, the darkness doing little to stifle the heat that radiated from the ground, releasing the sun's stored energy back into the atmosphere.

I heard the locals talk—the thunderstorms had become capricious, more violent. The gentle rains that used to nourish the crops were now torrential downpours that flooded the fields and swept away the soil. Small creeks had transformed into an unpredictable beasts, sometimes a trickle, other times a torrent.

From Illinois to the coasts, the entire country was a patchwork of climate-induced extremes. The Pacific Northwest's temperate clime was marred by the smoky season, where wildfires raged with increased ferocity. The Southwest was an inferno, cities like Phoenix and Las Vegas became symbols of resilience against the backdrop of brutal heatwaves. Hurricanes pounded the Southeast with greater force, their devastation more widespread, while the Northeast wilted under the strain of intensified urban heat islands.

For now, thankfully, the only enemy was the sun and the heat.

I stepped out of the scramdrone, the blast of dry, suffocating air hitting me like a wall the moment my boots touched the ground. The landscape stretched out in waves of shimmering distortion, the heat bending reality itself.

I grabbed a few things from the drone's compartment and turned toward Patterson, who was still strapped in.

"You wanna stay here?" I asked, already knowing the answer.

"Maybe I should come along—"

Before he could even unlatch his harness, Whisperwing shot into the sky, the canopy sealing shut in one fluid motion.

The sound that followed was something between a guttural scream and a dying animal.

"AHHHHHHHHHHHHHHHHhhhhhhhhhhhhhhh—"

The scream grew quieter and quieter, fading into the upper atmosphere as Whisperwing carried him higher and higher. I watched for a moment, hand on my hip, waiting until his voice became nothing more than a whisper on the wind.

"He'll be fine," I muttered to myself.

Not that he had a choice. Whisperwing wouldn't let him die. But he'd probably need a fresh pair of pants when he landed.

I accessed Whisperwing through my SAI link, setting it to hover at a safe altitude, ready to respond the moment I needed it. With the immediate chaos handled, I turned my attention to the old semi and trailer parked nearby.

It was ancient—a relic of a time before SafeCities, before automated logistics, before the world had fully handed itself over to machine efficiency. The faded paint and rusted edges suggested it had survived more than its fair share of roads long forgotten.

Beneath the shade of a large, sun-bleached umbrella, two figures stood.

One was young, tall, and rigid as a statue. Dressed entirely in black, he wore leather gloves and a chauffeur hat, his posture and expression giving away nothing. He exuded an air of precision, of control—a man who lived by strict codes of discipline.

But it was the older man who truly caught my attention.

133

His outfit was a disaster of contradictions—a worn-out Oxford jacket, light khaki pants, and a flannel shirt that had seen better days. On his feet were scuffed brown dress shoes, the kind that had either been cherished for decades or scavenged from a street vendor who had given up on life.

Everything about him screamed eccentricity—yet, somehow, it was intentional.

This man wasn't just some wandering relic of a bygone era.

No.

He wanted to be underestimated. And that made him far more dangerous than he looked.

I retrieved the Hono and Honjo Masamune from my back and approached the two men. As I drew nearer, I presented the swords with open palms, head bowed in a sign of deep respect. "Please accept these with my deepest respect, Tagadashi, sir. You honor my family by trusting me to retrieve them for you," I said, speaking slowly and clearly.

A faint smile graced Tagadashi's face. "You do honor your family, Mark-san, but not for these mere pieces of metal," he replied in a pleasant tone, bearing the trace of someone who had spent their formative years in Japan.

"Do not forget Mark-san." He paused to smile and make sure I was looking at him. "Our ancestors may be different, yet you are still family. You honor us all."

He took a step forward and reached for the Honjo Masamune in my hands, continuing to speak, "Do you know why the Honjo Masamune sword holds such significance, Mark-san?" Before I could offer an answer, he continued, "The Honjo Masamune is incredibly valuable due to its historical importance, exquisite craftsmanship, rarity, cultural significance, and high demand among collectors. This legendary Japanese sword is a true masterpiece, forged by the renowned swordsmith Goro Nyudo Masamune during the Kamakura period, which only adds to its worth. Furthermore, strict regulations, limited supply, and its illustrious provenance all contribute to its high value," he explained as he handed it over to his assistant.

Next, he reached for the Hono and smiled. "This is my own masterpiece, and one day, collectors will pursue it with the same fervor." He unsheathed the sword slightly, and it glowed, not orange but purple, allowing its blade to peek out from beneath the scabbard. "Both of these swords are for you. Take them and follow me."

He turned and began walking towards a rundown tractor-trailer. His taller companion strolled gracefully at his side, never once allowing the umbrella to expose Tagadashi.

"Genji, how much time do we have until 9 locates us?" Tagadashi inquired in a calm and direct manner.

"Twelve minutes, sir," the man in the chauffeur's hat promptly replied.

With a swift motion, Genji's fingers closed around my collar, extracting a concealed tracker. I jumped back, but I was not fast enough. It was all too evident that 7 had surreptitiously planted this tracking device on me during our conversation earlier. In that singular moment, a trio of realizations dawned upon me.

Firstly, it became glaringly clear that 7 had been tracking me for reasons unknown, casting a shadow of suspicion upon his actions. Secondly, Tagadashi appeared to possess an awareness of 7's motives for keeping tabs on me, suggesting a level of insight into the situation that eluded me. Lastly, I found myself standing at a precipice where I had to place my trust in Tagadashi, a man whose intentions and allegiances remained enigmatic, over my former platoon mate, 7. The circumstances demanded that I navigate this intricate web of intrigue with caution and discernment, for the stakes were higher than I could have ever imagined.

Before I could even utter a word, Tagadashi raised a hand. "You undoubtedly have many questions, Mark-san, but regrettably, we don't have the luxury of time to address them all. Allow me to elucidate the most critical aspects for you now. The rest, you'll have to discern on your own. Our timeline has been accelerated far more rapidly than anticipated."

As we reached the trailer, its rear opened, and I couldn't help but let out a chuckle of amusement. Both men turned to look at me in unison, and I shrugged. "Didn't you ever watch reruns of *Knight Rider?*"

Upon entering the trailer, it became evident that Tagadashi operated a mobile setup, rendering it virtually impossible to track him. It was nothing short of ingenious. He took a seat, and as the umbrella shifted position, I noticed it was more than just a sunshade—it was a scrambler, designed to interfere with satellite and geolocation systems. Any attempt to pinpoint his exact location in real-time would be met with alternative coordinates of his choosing. I recognized the technology, typically the size of a truck, cleverly condensed into an umbrella.

He noticed my curious gaze and commented, "Yes, my toy. I keep my most prized possessions to myself rather than yielding them to the Union States or the Liberty States."

Genji cleared his throat, redirecting our focus. "Mark-san, our foremost priority is to assist you in reactivation. You must be aware by now that deactivation amounts to certain death. I can offer my assistance with that, but you should be prepared to confront your inner demons as you transition back into battle mode. There are protocols in place to shield you from the horrors of war, and you won't be able to circumvent them. Do you understand?"

I weighed my options, which essentially boiled down to life or death. With a nod, I agreed, "Understood."

"Good," Tagadashi replied with a modest smile. He then settled into a chair with a cane, groaning slightly. "The president has been murdered, and your mission is to find the murderer, correct?"

"Yes," I answered eagerly.

"And, you have been trying to get your SAI removed for retirement?"

"Yes, but—" I was interrupted and Tagadashi put up a finger.

"They want your core. The core of your SAI and I do not have the time to tell you why. Even if I did tell you, the full story requires far more time than I have. For now, I will put you on the path." He reached into his shirt pocket and pulled out a Holocube—a compact, transparent data storage device used for high-security information transfers. Unlike standard digital files, Holocubes store data in a three-dimensional encrypted lattice, making them nearly impossible to alter or forge.

"This is an end-to-end universal encrypted file," he said, meaning that its security measures were built in from the moment the data was created until the moment it was accessed, ensuring that no one could intercept, tamper with, or manipulate the contents.

"Unbreakable, unfakeable," he emphasized, gripping the cube tightly before finally releasing it into my hand. It was more than a claim—it was a guarantee. The encryption was likely quantum-level, requiring either a specific key or an authorized neural signature to unlock.

"It will raise more questions," he warned, meaning the information inside was likely controversial, unsettling, or incomplete—something that would disrupt my understanding of the situation rather than immediately clarify it.

"But once they're answered, everything will fall into place."

In other words, the data inside wouldn't just provide answers—it would reveal a much larger truth, one that would only make sense after seeing the full picture.

"You do not have a doppelganger. After your reactivation, you will encounter Dahlia, but the two of you must return to the city. Find Kimberly and protect the Halos tower from 9, 8, and 7. They are attempting to shut it down, and we have yet to uncover their motives. You must discover why."

"Okay," I replied, my curiosity and determination fueled. "You mentioned that we still have eight minutes until 9 arrives."

Genji lowered his glasses, revealing fully black eyes, and addressed me directly. "Typically, the reactivation process spans 4 to 8 hours and is performed while the subject is unconscious. We will need to expedite it over the next few minutes while you're awake. Every second counts."

His movements, his speech, his eyes. They all told a story. A story connected all at once.

I blurted out a question without thinking, "You're an ArchSoul, aren't you?"

Genji confirmed, "I am indeed. A reanimated human."

Tagadashi looked at me, smiled the biggest smile and said, "Tell me what you know."

I beamed, the excitement barely contained as I spoke, talking to myself in wonderment and surprise from my revelation.

"Genji is a Reanimate. An ArchSoul."

The words felt heavy, weighted with meaning. A concept that shouldn't exist—yet here it was.

"And what does that mean to you? Mark-son," Tagadashi asked from behind raised eyebrows.

"It's a process that reanimates a human with an AI symbiote, nanomachines injecting themselves into the very fabric of life at the

precise moment of death. The instant the brain loses its base and cognitive functions, when the body should be beyond saving, but then…"
My eyes searched as I found the words. "But then the nanites ignite—a synthetic spark of life, an artificial resuscitation unlike anything nature ever intended."

I paused, letting that sink in, while my gaze fell upon Genji.

"How do you know all of this?" Tagadashi leaned in to ask while searching my expression.

"I…I don't know."

Tagadashi stood back in his original posture, throwing a look of skepticism. "Interesting."

"But I do know, this isn't just illegal. It's the most illegal thing on the planet."

Because it wasn't just medicine.

It wasn't just technology.

It was playing God.

"All the memories, the emotions, the cognitive functions—preserved. But what does that mean?" My voice softened, thoughts spiraling. "Is it still a person? Is it something else entirely? A perfect continuation, or just a machine wearing the ghost of a man?"

I exhaled. "It raises so many questions about existence." And yet, the only certainty was this Genji had crossed the threshold between life and death. And now, there was no going back. I took a breath, letting the weight of the revelation settle.

Tagadashi opened his mouth to speak, and I took a moment to gather my thoughts, racing as they were, then he asked, "Why is it wrong to save a life?"

"I mean it's not. Or it shouldn't be. Think about this—your body isn't the same body you were born with. Not even close."

I leaned forward, watching their expressions shift, their eyes met in a side glance to each other, then back on me.

"Cellular mitosis and apoptosis. The fundamental cycle of life. Every seven years, your body has replaced nearly every cell within it. Some live only hours, others months, but they all follow the same rule—they die so you can keep living."

I let the thought sink in before pushing further, looking back at the duo as they stared at me while I gave an explanation I had no idea that I had, then I continued.

"Your neurons? They last longer, sure, but they still degrade, still renew. So ask yourself—if every cell in your body is replaced over time, are you still the same person? Is the 'you' that existed seven years ago still here, or is it just a memory carried forward in a vessel that's constantly being rewritten?"

I could see the hesitation, the momentary discomfort in the realization.

Then I went deeper.

"Now take that same process—but digitize it."

I let the silence stretch for a moment before I continued, my voice steady.

"What if instead of biological mitosis, it was nanocellular mitosis? Instead of programmed apoptosis, targeted digital apoptosis? A system that rebuilds you, not with the randomness of biology, but with deliberate precision. Every dying cell seamlessly replaced, not with organic copies, but with synthetic perfection."

I could feel them trying to follow the logic. Trying to find a reason to dismiss it.

"Would that make you any less of yourself?" I pressed. "Would you even notice? If each replacement happened so gradually, so imperceptibly, would you ever feel different? Or would you wake up every day, same memories, same thoughts, never realizing you were becoming something else?"

A beat.

Then the final strike.

"If you are your memories, your consciousness, your perception of self...does it matter if the cells carrying those things are biological or synthetic?"

I leaned back, the question hanging in the air like a loaded gun. Because in the end, it wasn't really a question at all.

Tagadashi leaned in and met my eyes. "I'll ask again, why do you know so much?"

"I...I...I...I don't know," I stuttered.

"You will," he said.

"Five minutes," Genji interjected, and Tagadashi looked upon me with the same fatherly eyes as he had since the day we'd met.

Tagadashi leaned back on his heels. "Now you know why we cannot compromise our location and why we must keep our interaction brief. Our research must continue. There is more at stake than I can begin to explain."

"Do you wish to activate now?" Tagadashi inquired, raising an eyebrow as he locked eyes with me.

"Activate, affirmative," I agreed.

Genji leaned toward me closer, adjusting his angle to have direct access to my SAI—the artificial symbiote intelligence that had long since become an extension of myself.

For most, the SAI was an attachment, a piece of technology grafted onto the exterior of the body. The procedure was relatively simple: the head was shaved, and the apparatus was fitted directly to the base of the skull, just behind the ear. From there, the machine did the rest, its nanofilaments burrowing into the nervous system, seamlessly integrating with the user's motor and cognitive functions.

But for ANGLs, it was different. Ours wasn't an attachment. It was an implant. Installed directly into the hippocampus; the procedure was invasive, precise, and permanent. Mostly.

The process began with an incision between the upper teeth and the lip, an entry point designed to avoid external scars. A probe was carefully slid behind the sinus cavity, navigating the delicate network of tissue and bone before reaching the brain.

From there, a complex endoscopic procedure placed the implant—a series of microcomputers running on technology so advanced that its design was a highly guarded secret.

Two critical nodes were left behind:

One nestled deep in the hippocampus, the region of the brain responsible for memory, learning, and spatial awareness.

The other at the base of the brainstem—controlling reflexes, body regulation, and ensuring that the machine and mind were in constant synchronization.

The brain and implant weren't separate entities—they were partners, constantly adapting to one another, refining response times, optimizing efficiency. It wasn't just technology working alongside a person.

It was a system that was only as strong as the mind that wielded it. And if the brain failed—whether from injury, neural degradation, or trauma—then the implant was worthless. Attachment-based SAIs had a built-in failsafe: If anyone tried to remove them, or if the user died, they self-destructed.

The battlefield had been littered with the aftermath of such events—heads ruptured, cranial detonations turning soldiers into cautionary tales. The sight of it was something no amount of training could ever dull.

For ANGLs, the failsafe was even more severe.

If the implant lost connection for an unexpected period, or if the ANGL was captured, the implant was automatically deactivated. The SAI knew when it was being isolated, compromised, or tampered with. If it wasn't properly deactivated, the ANGL died.

If it was deactivated, there was a window of time before it could be safely removed through surgery, severing the ANGL's connection to their handlers and officially ending their service. It was the only way out. If you lived long enough.

I felt Genji snap the universal interface module onto my neck, the cold, metallic connection sending an instant shudder down my spine. Then it hit. A sensation I knew well but never fully adjusted to.

My body shivered with sudden goosebumps, my nervous system registering something foreign, something invasive. At the same time, I felt smaller than my own body, like I had just been compressed into something less human, something more digital.

The environment around me shifted, flickering between the tangible and the artificial, my perception caught between the real world and the network of data streams Genji had just tapped into.

I wasn't just in my body anymore. I was somewhere else. And wherever that was, it was far from comfortable.

The moment the process began, the haunting melody of "Black Hole Sun" by Soundgarden enveloped my senses, its eerie, melancholic tones weaving through the air like a spectral presence.

I wasn't sure if the music was emanating from my own mind, conjured up from the depths of my subconscious, or if it was somehow resonating through the walls of the cabin, an echo from another reality.

It felt like falling.

I had heard this song so many times before, but there was something different about it now. Something wrong. I felt a compulsion to turn it off, to break the spell it was casting over me.

But I couldn't.

Genji had attached the remote gate to my temples. A device typically used for brain scans—a harmless tool of diagnostics and neural mapping.

But this?

This was something more. Something deeper. Something that shouldn't be possible.

The music curled around me, its lyrics warping, stretching, twisting in ways that sent a chill down my spine.

"In my eyes, indisposed…in disguises no one knows…"

The words sank into my mind, not as sound, but as invasive thoughts, as if they were being played inside of me, rather than around me.

And then, the battle began.

I felt it before I saw it.

A pull—a sudden, unstoppable descent into a black abyss, as if my very existence was being ripped away from the physical world and plunged into the depths of my own psyche.

Darkness swallowed my vision, stretching infinitely in all directions, shifting and curling like a living thing. My breath caught in my throat, the sensation of freefall overwhelming every nerve, but my body never hit the ground.

Because there was no ground.

There was only the void. And within it, something stirred. The demons were waiting. They had always been waiting.

I clenched my fists, though I wasn't sure if I even still had a body here. Shapes moved in the distance, shadows within shadows, whispering in voices that belonged to me but also…didn't.

"Black hole sun…won't you come…wash away the rain…"

The melody twisted, distorting into something else, something ancient, something not meant to be understood.

I wasn't in control. Not here. Not yet. But I would be. I had to be.

The lyrics of the song and its haunting melody seemed to play in separate spaces within my mind, akin to different rooms within a small, mysterious house. My vision went black, and sand washed over the empty space, leaving behind solid objects as it flew past. I found myself sitting in my bedroom in my childhood home. It smelled the same, stale air, empty walls save for a calendar and a bed with sheets strewn about. I heard something coming through the door. A melody beckoning me through the door, so I left the room to see what it was. The sound turned to music, the music tuned to lyrics, and the lyrics echoed from a distant bedroom on the other side of the home, while the instrumental elements of the song reverberated from the living room. I heard a soft child's voice sing the words in melody:

"In my eyes
Indisposed
In disguises, no one knows
Hides the face
Lies the snake
And the sun in my disgrace"

My vision went black, an all-consuming void swallowing me whole. Then, with the sharpness of a needle pulling free from numbness, it clarified—and I was no longer in the cabin, no longer in control of my body, my senses, or my mind.

I found myself standing in the middle of a desolate, flat, rocky expanse, the ground beneath me cracked and dry, scarred by the scorched remnants of a world ravaged by violence and decay. The horizon stretched endlessly in every direction, broken only by jagged rocks and the haze of something far more sinister in the air.

But it was the scene in front of me that paralyzed my thoughts.

A mass grave.

A pit of death so deep that it seemed to swallow the earth itself. The remains of countless individuals, tangled in their final, desperate embrace, lay strewn across the sand like discarded objects, their faces frozen in horror. Bodies of every size, shape, and color—undistinguishable in death, yet eerily familiar in their shared fate.

The stench hit me before I could comprehend it—the heavy, cloying scent of rotting flesh mingled with something darker, something that spoke of humanity's desperate final breath. It hit me so hard I rocked back on my heels, gagging, my throat burning with the taste of bile. The wind whipped across my face, carrying the gritty sand with it, making every breath feel like I was choking on the very world around me.

I closed my eyes for a second, trying to steady myself against the overwhelming wave of emotion that threatened to drown me. Sorrow. Guilt. A sense of loss so deep it pierced the core of my being.

But there was no time to linger in that moment. 7 stood beside me.

A fellow participant, though I wasn't sure if that word even had meaning here. His presence was as cold as the grave itself, a figure clad in shadow. His Russian accent cut through the silence, chilling me to the bone.

"What a shame," he said, his voice devoid of remorse. "But it's a price the world has to pay for peace."

The words hit harder than any weapon could.

I looked down and things looked more like reality now. I was in a memory. A tangible memory. I could smell the mixture of burning and concrete. This was the hospital we were assigned to destroy and leave no survivors. The place was supposed to be a Hamas stronghold, but it wasn't. And those that were lost were innocent.

In that moment, I understood. Thinking this was a grave was an understatement. This was the price of something far bigger. Something that had been bought with the lives of all these people—and countless others.

"Peace at any cost," 7 said as he walked away. A cost I had been complicit in.

As dusk settled over the Middle Eastern city, 9 slipped away from our unit, the trigger detonator secure in his grip. It was a small device, but its potential for destruction was immense. We had planned this, meticulously plotted every detail to make it look like both sides were equally barbaric, hoping the world would force a ceasefire to stop the senseless killing.

9 was in charge of demolition and anything explosive-related. He could make a bomb from pretty much anything.

7, the squad leader, had coldly argued that this was the only way to bring peace. I went further back into the memory and saw how I had played my part, rounding up local leaders for what they thought was a crisis meeting at the hospital, not knowing we had marked it for destruction.

I watched the memory as 9 positioned the squad out of the blast radius, and I was left alone with the echo of my conscience. I saw myself standing back. Why hadn't I stopped it? Why had I let this madness go on? The questions were relentless, but they were nothing compared to the coming storm. Soon, the detonator would be pressed, and the world would watch in horror as the hospital turned to rubble. And I, who had done nothing to prevent it, would have to live with the screams that would surely follow.

Once again, my vision plunged into darkness, and I found myself back within the perplexing house. The music shifted from one room to another, its discordant elements disorienting yet compelling. I could feel the doorways and halls. The picture frames shifting, falling and breaking as I tried to walk blindly through unknown home. The lyrics emanated from the kitchen, while the instrumental components seemed to resonate from the basement below. A relentless urge drove me to seek the source of this haunting melody, as if it held the key to understanding my own tormented past.

"Boiling heat
Summer stench
Neath the black, the sky looks dead
Call my name
Through the cream
And I'll hear you scream again."

Inexplicably, I felt the searing heat of flames against my skin, and I bore witness to a harrowing scene—a fiery conflagration consuming countless bodies. It felt like a memory, yet it also possessed an unsettling familiarity, like a recurring nightmare. I could recount the events that unfolded next, but it felt as though I were a mere observer, detached from the horrifying reality. We executed three more targets on this mission—two sanctuaries for the vulnerable and even a sacred church. 9 meticulously erased all traces of our intrusion, leaving behind only destruction and chaos. Our sinister objective was clear: perpetuate a cycle of division and conflict in the world, a calculated and malicious effort orchestrated by our enigmatic group of ten. But why did my memories remain fragmented, withholding the rest of this sinister puzzle?

Once more, the world plunged into darkness, and I was left grappling with the tormenting fragments of my own history.

I found the voice: It was mine. Quietly and singing and crying.

"Black hole sun, won't you come, and wash away the rain."

A light came and I realized that it was in real time and I heard a buzzing.

"Incoming ordinance," alerted a digital voice.

A male digital voice blurted out, "Battlesync incomplete, Battlesync 66.8% effective."

"Ooooh shit, that's not good," said Tagadashi in an uncharacteristically disappointed and worried tone.

As Genji unstrapped me from the chair, an unsettling sensation washed over me, one I hadn't experienced in a very long time—an encounter with Halos encapsulation during a high yield attack. The Halos DWAR2 initiated a disorienting quantum fracture, a brief moment where we existed simultaneously in two separate locations, thanks to the rocket's explosion that unleashed its devastating force in a mere picosecond. The DWAR's capacity to absorb energy was directly tied to its power supply, meaning that if 9 continued his relentless assault, he would eventually break through our defenses. We weren't tied to a mini nuke reactor…that I knew of.

It was as though Genji had tapped directly into my thoughts, his voice cutting through the urgency of the moment with an eerie clarity that blurred the line between reality and transmission.

His words weren't spoken aloud in the traditional sense—they existed somewhere between telepathy and radio static, fading in and out like an old frequency struggling against interference.

"We can withstand two more similar yield impacts. Three more incoming rockets. Thirty-two seconds remaining."

The cadence was unnatural, a mix of mechanical precision and human urgency, his voice fluctuating between sounding as if he were right beside me and as if he were transmitting from another plane entirely.

At one point it felt like he was inside my skull, bypassing my ears altogether. Then, his words came through with the distorted quality of a distant radio playing loudly enough to hear clearly, but far enough away to know that he was at a distance—like reality itself was fighting to stabilize the connection. I could almost hear two voices overlapping, the subtle compression of sound that made it clear this was more complex than speech—this was data being relayed.

Genji wasn't just speaking to me. He was merging with my perception.

And with each passing second, the line between his awareness and mine was growing thinner. Then everything snapped back. Reality came rushing back at me in an instant. "I repeat, we can withstand two more similar yield impacts. Three more incoming rockets. Thirty seconds remaining," he said looking at me in annoyance as if his first transmission should have been enough for me to understand. I jumped up at his second statement.

With no time to waste, we hurried toward the autonomous cab at the front, which was towing the trailer we were in behind it. Genji swiftly operated a sequence of buttons without even looking, either rehearsed or an extension of his mind. He was an ArchSoul and from what I could tell, the only one of his kind. His button pressing initiated a detachment process that separated the trailer from the rig. We could see it through the small window of the door that separated the cab from the rear. As the trailer distanced itself, a massive umbrella-like structure unfurled over our cab, providing additional protection.

Genji carefully placed the tracker into a small receptacle that lit up when the penny sized disc made contact. From there, it showed the bidirectional primary transmission route. Where we were and where the data was being transmitted. It wasn't far. Genji proceeded to input fabricated coordinates, a ruse to mislead pursuers, which had to be 8 and 9 due to the missile strike. Wherever there was 9, 8 was close behind. Then, just in that moment, our survival hinged on calculated maneuvers and the precious seconds we could gain by outsmarting the relentless two ANGLs coming after us.

They knew where we were and what yield to tie into the ordinance to disable the defenses in order to knock me out or worse. I began to ponder if I had to be alive in order for them to harvest my SAI core.

Tagadashi sat in the passenger seat, and looked at me and bowed slightly before speaking, "I'm afraid our time is coming to an end for now, Mark-San. Genji will"—four hundred meters behind us an explosion rocked us and the self-driving hull corrected—"as I was saying, our time is over for now. You are reactivated as closely as we can, and soon, even my umbrella will not shield us from visual identification. My location must remain unknown. Call your Whisperwing down; it is geo-locked to you."

I opened the interface on my Hololens and began its descent. Genji touched the side of the Hololenses and the interface that fed me visual data glitched and I pulled my face away. The truck slowed and pulled over, and we stepped out. I looked up and the umbrella even provided a real time LCD camo.

I looked him in the eye. I had so many questions.

"Your son, number one, Jiro. He's trying to kill me too?" I asked with hesitation.

"Yes," he said sadly as he held his head down. "That is a story that I truly wish we had the time to tell, but Dahlia I am sure will fill you in."

Genji approached the hull of the Whisperwing, his palm touching it reverently, his chin tilting towards the heavens. My Hololens interface glitched momentarily again, and as Genji withdrew his hand, a striking black handprint remained, reminiscent of a scene from the old *Lord of the Rings* films.

"What did you do?" I demanded, irritation clear in my voice as I attempted to wipe away the unusual mark.

"You are on a private satellite, a secure communications relay. And now it's genuinely speedy," Genji replied, finally sporting an honest smile as he adjusted his glasses.

"Gen…gen…genuinely speedy? What…arg! You better not have broken this," I complained.

"I assure you, he has made it better!" Tagadashi yelled from the truck.

He turned and walked away, his posture immaculate, his stride confident. The most illegal thing in the world. As he stepped back onto the rig, it immediately began to move. I rushed to the navigation seat, realizing with a start that I had completely forgotten about my time to solve this crime because of these chaotic events.

"AHHHHHH!" I shouted as I dropped into the cockpit.

"AHHHHHHHH!" Patterson screamed, flailing in his seat.

"AHHHHHH!"

"OH MY GOD!" Patterson gasped, clutching his chest. "WHO WAS THAT?! WHO'S FIRING ROCKETS?!"

"I CAN'T TELL YOU!" I said, trying not to laugh. "AND WHY ARE WE YELLING?"

"I DON'T KNOW!" Patterson barked back. "YOU STARTED IT!"

We both sat there for a second, breathing hard.

"Seriously," he panted, "don't ever do that again."

I smirked. "Noted."

After moments of breathing heavily to calm down, I spoke. "Patterson, I've got to get to a cubeport," I told him urgently.

After some convincing, I persuaded Patterson to head to the nearest Outpost instead of returning to the city and to ignore the call from Robinson. The timer on my fugitive countdown was seven minutes. I fabricated a story about investigating the rocket attacks' origin. Once we reached the Outpost, I found a local bounty post with a cubeport, set it as our destination, the perfect place to finally uncover the truth behind the president's murder, and exonerate my name. I sent Robinson a message and ignored the incoming messages and calls.

Inside the armored confines of the remains of his roving hideout—the mobile command center found its way to a prearranged safe zone on deep in the Waste—Tagadashi's gloved fingers danced over the holographic interface. Having just unlocked Mark's SAI for the sync, he keyed in the secure line and waited for his contact to pick up.

Tagadashi: "This is Tagadashi. I've successfully unlocked, partially Mark's SAI for the sync. Data indicates his next destination is Sgt. Hammocks."

A crackle of static then gave way to a measured voice on the other end.

Contact: "Partially? This only works if he is fully activated!"

A brief pause, heavy with the unspoken risks of their operation.

Contact (continuing): "And Tagadashi, you also know the extraction process for the SAI is 100% deadly if anything goes wrong. Are you absolutely sure about this move?"

Tagadashi's eyes narrowed as he scanned the live data feed, the low whirr of machinery punctuating his words.

Tagadashi: "I'm aware of the risks. I've run every simulation and cross-checked the protocol. The removal might be lethal—but it's the only way. We have no alternative. Trust me, I wish we could do it differently."

Contact: "One misstep, and it's not just a protocol breach; it's a fatal outcome, for all of us. You're certain that all variables have been accounted for?"

Tagadashi's voice remained unflinching, resolute despite the gravity of the task.

Tagadashi: "I'm certain. The data doesn't lie. The trajectory is clear, and the extraction window is optimal. It's Mark or no one. Our success hinges on this."

A silence fell over the line as the contact considered the implications. Contact (finally): "Thank you for the handoff, Tagadashi. I'll take it from here."

The call ended, leaving Tagadashi alone with the persistent whine of his hideout and the weight of a decision that teetered on the edge of lethal precision and revolutionary ambition.

~

The central business district was always bustling, even on a Monday afternoon, as locals went about their errands and business. The buildings were a tapestry of architectural history: sturdy turn-of-the-century brick structures stood shoulder-to-shoulder with sleek, modern storefronts. The grain silo near the railway station leading to NJC loomed large, a metallic guardian that stood as a testament to the town's agricultural heritage.

The main street's diner, with its buzzing retro neon sign, was a magnet for farmers and townsfolk alike, offering a hot meal or a strong cup of coffee. Pickup trucks and utility vehicles had been parked in the angled spots, interspersed with the occasional electric car or truck.

Sidewalks had been sprinkled with people of all ages, from the seasoned farmers whose smile lines were a roadmap of a life spent under the sun, to the energetic youths who had brought new ideas back home after college. Their attire was a mix of practical and professional, denoting their various roles within the community.

The scent of fresh earth lingered in the air, but it was still musty, not letting you forget you were under the protection of a dome. The local hardware store had buzzed with activity, a meeting place for farmers to stock up on supplies and exchange stories. Many of these spots were vintage exchange locations. Areas and homes abandoned in

The Waste near the coast that were scoured and pilfered and brought here to be traded to for food.

Schools had released children for lunch, and they had burst into the parks and along the sidewalks, their carefree laughter mingling with the distant hum of tractors. This was a town deeply rooted in its agricultural traditions, pulsing with the lifeblood of a community that valued hard work, education, and a profound sense of unity.

Exercising my jurisdiction, I ordered everyone out of the area, closed all windows, and thoroughly checked each room to ensure no one would inadvertently interrupt me during this crucial moment.

Cubeports were invaluable tools, capable of recording and displaying scenes in full-size 3D, making them ideal for both forensics and entertainment. I inserted myself into the holo, finding several days' worth of footage on the cube. I waved my hand to fast-forward through most of it, focusing on the events of the fateful day.

At approximately 4 a.m., the office's dim lights flickered to life. Two figures appeared on the screen's edge. An error message indicated that the file had been damaged, rendering the audio unintelligible. However, this setback was inconsequential; soon, I would be able to manipulate the footage to uncover the murderer's face.

After what felt like an unusually long conversation between a murderer and his victim, one of the figures, Mason, stood up and held a small device in his hands.

"Let's go ahead and get this over with," I could make out him saying clearly.

From what I could discern, the assassin had a personal connection to the president, suggesting they knew each other well. The president didn't plead for his life.

The killer retrieved a gun from the president's desk, and although their conversation continued silently, nothing was heard. Then, a muzzle flash, a thunderous boom. The president kneeled briefly before collapsing face-first. I rewound the footage to the precise moment the gun fired.

Just then, Patterson burst into the cubeport room, his face pale and alarmed. "Mark, the president's been assassinated and I'm here to take you in for questioning!"

My time for secrets had come to an end. Patterson wasn't looking at me standing in the Outpost; he was looking at the Holocube projection with the murderer in plain sight.

Me holding a gun to President Mason's chest.

Chapter 12
The Inner A-Hole

His eyes grew huge as he saw the visage. "It was you!" he said as he drew his taser and turned on his communicator and emergency beacon. Patterson, a rookie trials officer, possessed the vital skills to investigate, gather evidence, present that evidence, and, ultimately, seek a verdict from a social jury to determine guilt or innocence. His role in the investigative process was pivotal, and he was steadily honing his abilities as he navigated the complex web of facts and legal procedures.

I understood his passion and his raw desire for justice. What I couldn't give him was satisfaction.

"That's a Holocube. It can't be faked. I know what I see. And now, so does the rest of NJC," Patterson declared, his voice quivering as he pointed to his datasync-connected Hololenses with one hand, the other clutching his taser, visibly shaking with nervousness and sweat instantly pouring down his face.

His taser trembled, and, seemingly in shock, he began to speak in a loud, high-pitched voice, a departure from his usual demeanor since leaving the academy.

"You are at the mercy of the social court, by the law of NJCPD and Federal Jurisdiction. A Poly tribunal connection is being established. I, Officer Charles Patterson, do hereby arraign you on the following charges: for the charge of conspiring with known fugitive Hiroshi Tagadashi, how do you plead? Guilty or not guilty?"

"We are in danger now. You are broadcasting our location, and very bad people are looking for us. Turn that off before you get us killed, Patterson," I implored, annoyance creeping into my voice as I reached for the Holocube.

Tone: True

"DON'T TOUCH IT!" Patterson shouted, his gun now pointed squarely at my chest. "How do you plead?" he finished.

"Not guilty," I responded.

Tone: False

"Guilty it is. You are at the mercy of the social court, by the law of NJCPD and Federal Jurisdiction. I, Officer Charles Patterson, do hereby arraign you on the following charges: Murder of President Mason. How do you plead? Guilty or not guilty?"

"Patterson, I have on a grounding suit. Be reasonable," I urged as I pulled out the Holocube. However, he reached for his blade and drew it menacingly.

Tone: True

"You don't want to do that," I cautioned, realizing that I was without a defensive weapon.

Tone: True

"How do you plead?" he spat angrily.

"I didn't kill President Mason."

Tone: False

"Guilty, I assume. Please wait while we collect your verdict."

A massive white projection materialized from Patterson's right shoulder, illuminating all the walls. An elderly white judge appeared onscreen, reading the judgment from the social juries' findings.

"For all accounts, conspiring with fugitive Hiroshi Tagadashi, known violations of federal penal codes title 17, 19, 22, and 76. Social Jury returns to find the defendant guilty.

"For all accounts, Federal Murder, known violations of federal penal codes title 2, 3, and 18. Social Jury returns find the defendant Guilty."

As the judge continued speaking, he adjusted his seat, aware that I could see him and vice versa. He knew I was an ANGL and the world was seeing this. This was not just social media news, this was news for the nation.

"You are remanded to custody immediately to serve a life sentence for your crime. All nearby bounties have been suspended. You have been deemed an enemy of the state," the judge intoned, leaning closer to the camera.

"That movie with Will Smith and Gene Hackman, I love that movie!" I quipped, though unintentionally and I could not explain why I said what I said. Had I just developed Tourette's syndrome?

"This is no laughing matter," the judge responded incredulously.

"HE'S IN THERE!" shouts erupted from the perimeter of the building.

Patterson inched closer to me, his sword drawn, and reached for his magcuffs. I realized I had no way to explain this situation to anyone, not even myself, that would make any sense. I needed time, an escape plan, but I was unarmed and faced at least four armed officers.

Then I began to speak involuntarily, and my body moved on its own, picking up a pair of scissors from a nearby desk. In two swift strides, my left arm extended, and the tip of the scissors pressed against Patterson's throat, a thin stream of blood trickling down his skin.

"This is your carotid artery, directly linked to your heart via your ascending aorta. If I twist, move, or apply even a little more pressure, your fate is sealed, Pat. Blink twice if you understand. If you nod, you risk nicking this vital blood supply to your brain."

Patterson blinked twice.

"Mark, listen up. I'm Dahlia. Nice to meet you. I know you can hear me because you're not asleep, and this is taking a lot. I'm going to put Pat here in a cell. I've got eight minutes left. After that, you've got to take back over if you can. Whisperwing has coordinates pre-loaded to get us to Douchecanoes. Just say 'Safe word Pineapples.' 9 is coming to take me back; they need all 10 and your core, me. Don't let that happen. President Mason died to wake you up so you could hear me. President Mason was dying, and he chose to make his death mean something. You were going to be framed anyways. They would have erased you from everything, jailed for the murder of the president, removed back to base, and your SAI properly transferred to some other artificially traumatized child."

Tone: True

The scissors lowered from Patterson's neck, then I grabbed his uniform lapel and tossed him effortlessly toward the holding cells at the back of the building. My body moved on its own—cuffing Patterson and securing the doors without any conscious input from me.

"Mark, we need to sprint out of the back. If you listen and concentrate closely, you might be able to hear an echo. Our sync is incomplete, but some connections are there. That's why I can do this."

Then I slapped myself squarely in the nuts.

"Ow! Why did I do that?!" I exclaimed, doubling over in pain.

"I didn't think I could," I responded, a mixture of laughter and discomfort evident in my voice.

"I'm going crazy," I muttered out loud.

"I'm everything you are, just more of it," Dahlia retorted.

"What is this?" I wondered aloud, feeling different and in control.

"This is full Battlesync, two ships passing in the night for now. Come and find me. Free me," Dahlia's voice echoed synchronous with mine, I could hear the slightest difference in tone and inflection, and then the sensation was gone. However, I couldn't help but notice that my left hand was gesturing obscenely right back at me, my own middle finger pointed up into my face and I muttered, "What the hell?"

Chapter 13
Firestarter

I walked over to Patterson, and he stood there confused while shaking his head at me. "Insanity won't commute your sentence, Mark."

I stood there, trying to listen to my own thoughts, struggling to understand what my mind was doing—why it felt like something was just out of reach.

Then, I heard it. A faint whisper, barely there. Like a voice on the other side of a solid door, muffled but persistent. I pressed my ear against it, shutting out everything else, narrowing my focus to the slightest vibration, a leftover echo of sound that wasn't supposed to be there.

And then—it came through.

Vivid. Clear.

Like taking out earplugs after being submerged underwater.

The world around me faded to nothing. No background noise. No distractions. Just the sound behind the door. I held my breath. Then, with absolute clarity—"Your mom's a ho!"

I realized quickly that I had three objectives—get out of the Outpost, stay alive, and make it onto the Whisperwing.

Simple in theory. A nightmare in execution.

I turned to Patterson, the only person here who might give me a logical explanation for what the hell was happening.

"Okay, you're a psychologist. I'm hearing voices. But I am the voice."

He tilted his head slightly, processing my words.

"Of course, you're the voice. It's in your head."

"No, my mouth."

"Your mouth is the voice?"

I stared at him, willing him to keep up. "I am the voice."

"In your head?"

"No. I feel the voice."

"Where?"

"When I speak it."

Patterson narrowed his eyes slightly, adjusting his stance.

"After you've heard it in your head?"

I gritted my teeth, the frustration mounting. "I swear on everything holy and right about this world if you don't listen."

He raised his hands in mock surrender. "Okay, okay, I'm listening."

I took a breath, forcing myself to slow down, to explain it in a way that made sense.

"A voice is speaking through me. Through my mouth. I don't hear it in my head—I hear it in my ears after it speaks through my mouth."

Patterson blinked.

Then he frowned.

And for the first time, I saw it. The hesitation.

Not doubt.

Recognition. He nodded, raised a finger and blinked as his face brightened in naïve assurance. "You're having a psychotic break."

I looked away and to the side, trying to take in what he told me.

"But, you don't know it's you…usually," he said blinking in slight confusion.

I shook my head and squinted my eyes. "What does that mean?"

He held his palms up and shrugged his shoulders slightly. "I mean, psychosis is voices."

Patterson's expression shifted—a flicker of uncertainty, like a man caught between logic and something he couldn't quite explain.

He opened his mouth, then closed it.

His eyes darted to the side, then back to me, a rapid oscillation between skepticism and something dangerously close to belief.

"Okay," he said slowly, as if testing the weight of the word. "You're saying you don't hear the voice in your head, but you hear it after you've already spoken it?"

I nodded, my jaw tightening. "Yes."

He inhaled through his nose, exhaled out his mouth.

Then he shook his head. "That's…not possible."

"And yet, here we are," I shot back.

He rubbed his temple, as if trying to massage an answer from the folds of his brain.

"Okay. Okay." He paced a half-step, then stopped. "So, what? Are you predicting your own speech? Are you somehow—subconsciously aware of what you're about to say before you say it?"

"No," I said firmly. "Because it's not coming from me!"

Patterson exhaled sharply, muttering something under his breath before fixing me with a look that was equal parts curiosity and apprehension.

"What does the voice want?"

I swallowed realizing our time was running short and my mind was slipping.

"I don't know, but SHIT!" I yelled and jerking my head in frustration almost hitting the bar.

My eyes opened wide. "What if I hit my head on the bars, will that get rid of the voice?"

"No, that will just…No, you know what, forget I said anything. Go for it," Patterson said with a flat look.

"Okay, our time is almost up, we've got to get out of here and I can't leave you. They will think you released me and take it out on you. So I'm going to let you go. You can come with me. These are social mercs, they live on views and waste-crypto," I explained. "There's also more than just those creeps to worry about. Those rockets came from 9. He's on his way and more dangerous to you than you can imagine. They need me alive but will blow through you to get to me."

Patterson's voice fell in between excitement and dread, "9 as in the Rocketman? Firestarter? Mr. Boom?"

"Do I have any cool nicknames?"

Patterson's eyes searched in the distance for answer, then he snapped his fingers and pointed at me smiling out of pride for himself. "Dick Bounty."

"Be happy you need me," I said leveling a finger at him.

"And you need me," he finished.

"We need each other," I corrected him.

"You've got something wrong upstairs, Captain," he said.

Tone: True

I took off Patterson's magcuffs and handed him his blade. He stood there as if it were a trick. He knew that it was a severe compromise of his service and career. He was an officer, and at this point to not attempt to arrest me again was a direct violation of his station. He knew this and I knew this. There were two ways to make it out of here alive. Either kill me now or walk out with me to Whisperwing. Any other form of transport was compromised.

I walked up to him as close as I could, and I looked at him in the eye and said, "Remember when I told you that you would have to make a decision? Well, this is it."

I initiated the Whisperwing to get as close to us as possible for a scoop maneuver on my command. As we stepped outside, I had the magcuffs on my wrists programmed to my voice for deactivation.

The first of the three social mercs walked up with one of the biggest swords I've ever seen. The other had a halberd. The third had a short sword and shield combo. I knew who these guys were.

"We can take it from here," one said with a Scottish accent.

"Well, if it ain't the Lucky Charms," I said involuntarily.

"No, you haggis-hole, we are," and they spoke in unison and a thick Scottish accent, "The Highlanders."

"I can't let you take him," Patterson said as he drew his taser.

"I'm sorry," said the shortest of the three, which was a feat as they were all extremely short. Then he continued, "We can't let you take him. At least not all of him."

To which he then turned to the other two and laughed heartily while making a snipping motion with his fingers at waist level.

Patterson pointed his taser and the tallest of the crew tisked before he said, "You might want to think that one over."

Patterson kept his taser pointed at the tallest and drew his sword at the shortest.

That's when I heard the music and I knew just how much trouble we were in. 'Firestarter' by The Prodigy played obscenely loud through loud speakers of a retrofitted firetruck from the 2030's.

Out hopped the man in red. 9, the pyromaniac, Blaze Tanner. I always wondered if that was his real name, it probably wasn't. But who cared, it was cool.

9 had a wiry and lean build, giving him a deceptive agility. Pale skin. His hair was a fiery red, resembling the flames he so adored, but

balding. It was usually unkempt and wild, receding but still billowing all over his head. His eyes, a vivid shade of amber, seemed to flicker like burning embers, just a reflection of the insanity within.

He wore a dark charred red leather jacket covered in singe marks and burn holes, showcasing his disregard for personal safety. A pair of red and black fingerless gloves protected his hands, which had undoubtedly seen their share of burns. His boots were sturdy and fire-resistant, providing him with the mobility he needed to dance among the flames he created. They looked as though were pilfered from an abandoned fire station in The Waste which is undoubtedly where he procured his truck before updating it with new tech while making it wasteland ready. And on his back, two small tanks of fuel for a dual flamethrower connected under the pinky of each arm.

Around his waist, he carried an assortment of tools and incendiary devices, all meticulously organized for quick access. Yet he always seemed to be lost as to which toy he wanted to use next. The scent of smoke and burnt materials was always in the air as it followed him wherever he went, leaving a trail of smoldering destruction in his wake. That was my former friend and closest skill-mate, number 9.

His menacing appearance, coupled with his obsession for fire, made 9 a dangerous and unpredictable figure in any setting. He couldn't use explosives here, but fire was a different story. He's so very dangerous. I'd seen this man take down large structures with ease and no planning.

My vision started to narrow and tunnel. Then back to black as if I were sitting in the chair of Tagadashi's rig. The lyrics to 'Firestarter' gave way to a memory. We were stood in the hallway of a home. There was blood on the walls. 5 walked past me and flipped her hair in disgust.

"She's angry that she's here," said 9. "We lowly troops don't have much choice. It's a good thing they need all 10, or at least that's what 7 says."

"Our skills are just collect, murder, clean," said 8 from behind a puff of smoke in his heavy Mexican accent.

"Here, let's sync up for the next mission," 7 said as he walked into the room wiping his hands clean. "And after, 9 make sure all evidence is incinerated. Nothing is left behind. Not even dental."

9 brightened up like a child on Christmas morning. "Did you know that the temperature for turning bone to ash is—" he was cut off.

"I don't care, 9," interrupted 7. "Just do it."

Before the memory ended, we all placed our foreheads together; one by one and a warm feeling went down my neck.

Then blackness. I was back in the home. I could hear the music.

"Stuttering

"Cold and damp

"Steal the warm wind, tired friend#

"Times are gone

"For honest men

"Sometimes, far too long for snakes."

I found myself in the basement, disoriented and searching for the stairs. What was my next move? Words echoed in my mind: "Free me?"

Climbing the stairs, a flood of haunting memories overwhelmed me—terrible deeds, flashing like vivid nightmares. The lifeless bodies, the shattered families, the irreparable damage I had inflicted on innocent lives. The weight of my actions bore down on me, an unbearable burden. I had become a monster, capable of unspeakable atrocities, and I knew I would commit more in the future.

I sank into a dark abyss of self-reflection, grappling with the why and who I had become. As I delved deeper into this introspection, the music, devoid of lyrics, swelled in intensity, echoing within me. But where was the singing originating from? Which room in this dimly lit darkness held the source of this haunting melody?

It didn't take long for me to realize my surroundings. I was back in my childhood home—the place where my biological parents had abandoned me, leaving a five-year-old to fend for himself without electricity for three long months. They had entrusted me to a neighbor who promised to care for me but suffered from dementia and never returned. I survived by stealing food from the local store, sprinting back to the empty house each night to escape the cold world outside. The memories of those lonely, desperate days flooded back, merging with the melancholic melody that enveloped me.

"In my shoes
Walking sleep
In my youth, I pray to keep
Heaven send
Hell away
No one sings like you anymore."

What did the voice say? Free me? I know where to go.

In the darkness of this home. I felt around until I found it. It wouldn't open before. I now knew to unlock the latches. And as I did, emotional pain hit me with every turn. And then a 5-year-old scared, mixed child walked outside, with hair strewn about his head, hungry, and unbathed, on the day of the solar eclipse. I walked to an Outpost and a family working for Tagadashi took me in.

"Black hole sun
Won't you come
And wash away the rain?"

"You understand our first trauma now," the voice resonated within my mind.

The darkness around us shifted, revealing the late-morning landscape of Outpost 216.

9 stood before us, his iconic firetruck positioned like a sentinel between me and him. The Lucky Charms gang occupied the middle ground, while Patterson and I stood near the entrance to the Outpost Bonds building. It resembled a scene from a wild west showdown.

As 9 began to speak, his voice quivered with a high-pitched mixture of agitation and excitement. Fire and explosions hadn't only defined his role as an ANGL; they had shaped his very personality and manner of expression. "TiiiiiiiiieeeeEEen, I have a CARD. It's an EASY one! You get in the TRUCK! No One DIES! OR ON THE OTHER SIDE! EVERYONE DIES! I just need to take back either you or the SAI in one piece. Your choice. We WILL BREAK YOU, or WE WILL BURN your SAI out of your brain."

The Highlanders turned their attention toward 9, a mix of curiosity and suspicion in their eyes. "Who the hell are you, mate?" one of them questioned.

9 raised his hands and said, "I can give you a CONSOLATION prize!" His eyes lit up with an unsettling fervor.

"Oh no, you're about as sharp as a beach ball," the tall Highlander remarked.

"I'll GIVE you one million Waste CRYPTO or BURN you ALIVE where you stand," 9 declared, his threats laced with palpable malice.

"Take the money and leave short-round," I interjected, my voice carrying newfound authority.

The trio of mercenaries tightened their grips on their weapons, executing a seamless military-style flanking maneuver. It was evident they possessed advanced training and coordination.

Then, in the blink of an eye, 9 extended his hands toward the approaching Lucky Charms gang members who had drawn dangerously close. Clenching his fists, he declared, "Conflagration IT IS!" Flames erupted from a forearm-mounted flamethrower.

While most officers wore fire-retardant suits, mercenaries rarely did. Neither Patterson nor I had helmets, and we were suddenly thrust into grave peril. I tried to command the cuffs to release, but they remained unyielding.

"Release," I repeated urgently, but to no avail. My voice had undergone a transformation with the full Battlesync, and I found myself trapped in stubborn restraints.

"Run!" I implored Patterson as I turned toward the nearest landing zone.

Glancing back, I witnessed the devastating aftermath of a few fleeting moments. Two charred corpses lay as smoldering heaps of black ash, while a third, shield in hand, clung to false hope as 9 inexorably approached.

Patterson and I had taken just a few strides when we glimpsed the worst-case scenario: Outpost citizens rushed out with hoses and extinguishers, aiming them at the piles of grain and wood, inadvertently targeting 9. Memories flooded my mind—an old recollection from a mission in Africa, where we had been ordered to set fire to a consulate, plant opposing delegate bodies, and stoke the flames. 9's eagerness to accelerate the blaze had caught the attention of villagers, who attempted to douse the flames with buckets of water. Enraged, 9 had trapped them within the inferno, leading to injuries and fatalities.

A voice echoed through the comms, stating, "Emotional Input is being diverted to SAI. His reasoning is still intact, sync incomplete."

There was no denying that 9 was about to make everyone regret their efforts to combat the fire. My hands remained bound in cuffs, but something had changed. I initiated a mental check.

"Are you there?" I said out loud to the voice I now heard in my head and through my speech.

"Eat a dick!" I said back to myself.

"We've got to work on your communication skills," I said out loud.

"We've got to work on your communication skills you idiot, because we have MAGCUFFS THAT YOU PROGRAMMED TO YOUR VOICE THAT I TOLD YOU MIGHT CHANGE, YOU FUCKING DAFT SLICE OF PROCESSED CHEESE," I said back to myself.

I paused, taking refuge behind a massive shipping container that was gradually succumbing to the relentless assault of flames, 9's fiery fury having chosen it as its latest target. "You hinted at it, at best," I muttered aloud, responding to the voice's presence within my mind while also acknowledging the validity of her point.

"I can hear your thoughts, you twit," the voice interjected abruptly.

"But I can't hear yours," I countered.

"I am your thoughts, Mark. Remember that," the voice reminded me.

"Remind me of your name one more time?" I asked while destruction and mayhem rained down around me.

"I'm Dahlia, you shit eater."

I glanced over my shoulder, and Patterson regarded me with a furrowed brow and a deep sense of concern. "We really need to get you some professional help, sir," he commented earnestly.

"Ok, Dahlia, what should we do?" I asked, my need for guidance genuine. I felt swifter, my thoughts sharper, the world before me vivid and comprehensible. However, I was unarmed, devoid of a squad, a fugitive wanted for the president's murder (which I had committed), and faced with a raging wall of eight-foot flames swiftly advancing upon me. Innocent lives hung in the balance, and, to make matters worse, I now had an unwelcome presence residing in my mind. An asshole, to put it bluntly.

Patterson plastered himself against the container and poked his head out each time 9 diverted his attention to a spray a flame at someone who would try to douse out a fire when he would try to bake us.

"Pat, take off your shirt, give me your blade, run to the front of his truck, hop in if you can. It will distract him enough for me to flank him, and wait on my signal," said the unison voice. Patterson could hear the change in tone. He heard it before when I held the scissors to his neck. The passing ships in the night feeling was all the way there again. He handed me the taser and blade, and stripped off his shirt quickly.

"On the count of three, run" I said.

"One, two, three, run!" I shouted, and we ran in opposite directions.

Number 9 possessed two flamethrowers, but his heart belonged to his fire truck, a blazing romance that consumed his attention entirely. He abruptly halted the searing stream of fire when the looming threat of his beloved vehicle being reduced to ashes struck him. With haste, Patterson sprinted toward the fire truck while 9 sifted through his belt for incendiary devices. Undoubtedly, he carried something capable of igniting a fiery catastrophe in the vicinity of the truck.

This was my moment to act.

Every fiber of my being aligned, a perfect symphony of precision and calculation. My first step was deliberate, every muscle fiber activating not for a mere sprint or run, but for something more—a superhuman interaction between the ground, my physique, and the space between me and 9.

I felt it—the raw efficiency of my movement.

My toes positioned flawlessly.

My core engaged.

173

My arms cut through the air in sync with my momentum.

What should have required eight or nine strides—a calculated approach, a disciplined launch—was instead executed in just four.

And that was where the problem began.

I had significantly miscalculated.

Before I could even process the flaw in my estimation, I was airborne—too fast, too soon. The world tilted, my equilibrium betraying me as gravity claimed its prize.

My momentum, which should have delivered me perfectly to my target, instead propelled me forward with no means of recovery.

There was no saving it.

With an undeniable certainty, I plummeted face-first toward the ground.

The impact was hard, unforgiving, and immediate, a sudden end to my would-be moment of glory. I skidded to a stop, right at Patterson's feet.

For a breath, everything was still.

Then, despite the sheer disaster of execution, I exhaled slowly, refusing to acknowledge the humiliation.

Because for just a brief, fleeting moment...

I had felt like a genuine badass.

Patterson looked down at me. "Dude, how'd you do that?"

Then I look up to him and said, "No fucking clue, tase him."

Patterson drew the taser at 9 and 9 began to chuckle as he gripped a small plastic cylinder with a blue button on the end.

"That won't even tickle. This on the other hand will hurt like hell." He pressed it and a jolt of electricity shot out from the undercarriage of his firetruck, effectively shocking both Patterson and I. Me not so much. Patterson, who already had a grip on his taser, fired it at 9. The competing flows of electricity found their way to the fuel lines I'd cut when dashed past 9 with Patterson's blade. It was painfully obvious that 9 had indeed not watched *Lethal Weapon 4*, or else he would have identified the distraction technique employed. Fortunately for me, neither had Patterson.

9 ignited where he stood. Screaming and yelling, like the hundreds he'd murdered in his past, I wanted to watch him stand there and cook, but couldn't allow it. It was wrong. As much as he deserved it, I was better than that. I extinguished the flames with a hose that a resident had abandoned out of fear earlier.

"We need him, or at least I need to sync one last time," Dahlia said calmly.

"How do we do that?" I asked.

"As he dies, press your forehead to his, I'll do the rest," Dahlia said somberly and met eyes with Patterson, "and punch him in the dick too at the same time or it won't work, I promise."

I took the blade from Patterson and approached a dying 9. This action would be an act of mercy for certain. One he did not deserve. One he'd never given anyone else.

"Why do the others want me?" I demanded, voice edged with frustration. "Why do they need my SAI?"

He coughed—a wet, rasping sound—before laughing. Not the kind of laughter that mocked or belittled, but something darker. Resigned. Knowing.

"You're going to have to figure that one out on your own," he rasped.

Then, he moved.

Before I could react, he lunged forward, his grip clamping onto the back of my neck, pulling me in with a violent finality. Our foreheads collided, his breath warm, his hold unyielding.

And then—he thrust his chest onto the blade.

The sensation was immediate. The resistance of flesh, the sudden shift of weight, the shudder that rippled through his frame as steel punctured deep.

But it wasn't the death that shocked me.

It was the look in his eyes.

Our gazes locked, an unspoken collision of souls. For that moment—just that moment—I saw him.

Not as an enemy.

Not as a monster.

But as something broken.

I glimpsed the depths of his pain, the unbearable weight that had shaped him, twisted him into the thing he had become. It was carved into his expression, embedded in the raw edges of his existence.

And as he trembled, a sick, twisted part of him smiling through the agony, I felt the question settle deep in my gut.

What kind of torment could drive a man to take pleasure in the suffering of others?

What kind of agony had made him into this?

He exhaled, something flickering in his gaze—acceptance, maybe even peace—before the light drained from his eyes.

And just like that, he was gone.

In an instant, SIA Sync connected us, and I was inundated with fleeting visions of his traumatic past. I fell into his memories, dropping into one particularly hard one. A messy home. Maybe a trailer, small, dirty, poorly kept. I saw a young boy enduring unimaginable abuse, hands scorched over a stove for a simple accident, all within the confines of a small, loveless home. There was no mother to provide comfort, just him and his father, trapped in a cycle of violence. Him screaming, as his hands were held to the flames.

"I'm sorry, Daddy, I won't do it again," the child cried, "please, Daddy, it hurts!"

Then it went black again, the scene washed away by a wind I didn't feel.

Those gloves he wore, they were a shield against the world, a barrier against the horrors he had known. Never once in all the years I had known him had I seen him without them on. I guess they hid more than scars.

As swiftly as it had begun, the connection between us extinguished. His grip on the back of my neck loosened, his eyes lost their intensity, and he exhaled his final breath.

Dahlia screamed, "Dayuuuum! I did not see that coming!"

"Mark, I've never done this before, but, hehe, you're not going to like this…" Dahlia finished.

Chapter 14
Can You Hear Me Now?

"Tell me one more time why I can't get into the Whisperwing, Dahlia," I asked as I stood in front of the technological marvel and held my head in my hands.

"Well, Mark, you see, you're not *just* you anymore. And this scramdrone is very picky who pilots it. Its sync will not read to you to let you in, but it will follow you," Dahlia spoke through me.

I started, "So, let me get this straight, 8 is on his way. The most poisonous—"

"Toxic," Dahlia interrupted.

I picked back up, "Toxic, excuse me, toxic individuals on the face of the planet. Along with a slew of social bounty mercs, and I am still in cuffs."

Dahlia jumped in. "You brought that one on yourself, Iron Maiden."

I rolled my eyes. "And let's not forget the small matter of the dick bounty. Oh, and guess what? We're conveniently headed right into the middle of it."

Dahlia waited a few beats before commenting, "You've got to focus on the upside Pedro for President."

I motioned my cuffed hands up at the hovering Whisperwing which we could not get in and screamed at the top of my lungs, "Which is?"

Dahlia said without skipping a beat, "Three things S&M Boy Toy. One, Pat's got a great bod. Two, we've completed the battlesync without too much brain damage, and 3, we've got transportation. Look."

I shook my head. "What do you mean *too much* brain damage?"

"Don't worry 'bout it. I'll fix it later," Dahlia retorted.

Indeed, my cuffed hands were vaguely aimed at the firetruck. One hand managed to get the pointer finger lined up; the other, far less helpful, flipped me off directly.

Patterson raised his hand and I looked at him and said, "You can speak without being called on."

Patterson shook his head slightly and asked, "Who are you talking to?"

I responded back, "You know, that's a good question. Dahlia, who on earth are you?"

Dahlia responded, "Do you asshats want me to answer that now or do you think that dust cloud on the horizon is a caravan of cheap prostitutes?"

Patterson put his hands up to his eyes to get a better look and shield them from the noon sun, but by that time, I had already gotten the keys off 9's dead body and started the rig.

"They prolly had herpes anyways, Pat," Dahlia said as Patterson jumped into the already moving truck.

"You don't find it the least ironic, sir," Patterson said as he looked around the messy interior.

"As long as 8 doesn't show up with a Hazmat suit on, we can take this with its full glory," I said.

"Dahlia, it's a five-hour drive to the closest Outpost outside of Federal jurisdiction. We will be safe. Split the time?" I asked as I realized that my life had been being lived in two different modes out of the same body.

"Pat, can you give us a two-hour nap first? We will buy you a handy when we get to our destination," said Dahlia.

Pat shifted nervously and replied, "I am fairly sure that's illegal."

"Not where we are going," Dahlia replied quickly with a huge smile while raising eyebrows.

"You're a sick man, Mark. You need help," Patterson recoiled.

"We're not Mark, all the time," I said as I tried to wrap my head around what was going on in my head.

"I linked Whisperswing's nav to my personal interface. She won't let me in, but we can at least get a heads-up if someone gets too close for comfort," I said as I tried close my eyes after realizing, I hadn't actually had sleep in a very long time. Being handcuffed put a limit on what I was able to do.

As I propped my head back I took one last look at the nav screen to make sure we wouldn't navigate through any crazy area too thick with choke points, or kill boxes, and I saw something interesting. A destination preloaded into the rig's nav, Sgt. Hammock. The man who convinced me to join the ANGL core. The man who pushed me past my limits. The man who I had questions for. Now, how serendipitous.

"Patterson, take us there first," I ordered.

"No," I said right back to him. "You won't get the answers you're looking for, trust me," Dahlia spoke through me.

My voice synced in a new waveform. "We are going, there's no more discussion," I said in a booming tone.

I looked at Patterson and he had shrunk into the space between the door and the seat. He pointed with two fingers at his face. "Your eyes, they, they looked like had…how did you?"

"Pat, oh god, you're killing me, Smalls. We can't see our own eyes, you wall-side of a Christmas tree," Dahlia mocked at Patterson.

Patterson tried to figure out the insult and mouthed it back to himself quietly so I helped him out as a tilted my head to my shoulder and scrunched my face in pity and spoke softly.

"No one puts much effort into making that part of the Christmas tree as nice as the rest since it faces the wall, so it's not as put together and lacks attention."

Patterson was clearly hurt and so I patted his knee and said, "I'm sure Dahlia didn't mean it that way though."

"Mmmmm, yes I did," Dahlia shot back.

"How close are we to Sgt. Hammocks?" I asked.

"Three hours, and I thought you fought under Robinson," Patterson responded.

I thought back to my days in the field and responded, "Both Patterson, Robinson, and Hammock."

Robinson was my field commander and Hammock was my base Sgt. Hammock taught me how to walk, and Robinson told me who to play with while I was walking. Due to the nature of the program, we were always learning how to walk, so I was always going back to Hammock. My relationship with both of these gentlemen had a stark contrast, though. With Hammock, he stood and spoke to me with authority in short and direct toneless calculated dismissive orders with his arms crossed. Yet somehow, it always seemed like he gave a shit. Robinson beat us over the head with every mistake and would lecture us about our mistakes with the worst analogies that any human mind could piece together, and to put salt in a wound, Robinson organized one-on-one time with us to force bonding. We all played well in the sandbox to my knowledge, but there were very few times when all ten of us were together. Most missions only required a few of us at a time. Due to information security concerns, most major missions were already broken up anyways. We'd meet in separate locations, complete our duties and bug out when done.

Patterson renewed his bravado now that his feelings had been hurt. "Back to my question," he said with some assertion and a bit of attitude. "Where did you come from?" He looked at me, with the insinuation being clear that he wanted to know where and how Dahlia came from.

Dahlia popped out and said, "I just *was*, one day."

"I am a psychologist," Patterson responded. "You can talk to me."

"Gee, I guess it all started when I fell in love with my mom," Dahlia said in the most serious tone ever.

Patterson straightened up and looked over. "Tell me more."

"Then I killed my dad so I could boink her and then I changed my name to Oedipus." Dahlia raised two middle fingers at Patterson.

"Okay you want serious," Dahlia threw the words at Patterson, "My first memory is killing soldiers who were friendlies."

I interrupted, "My first lost time experience."

Dahlia nodded my head for me in an exaggerated gesture. Then in a somber, and cold tone, began to speak. No emotion.

"My first full BattleSync activation—you could call it my birthday."

The words left my mouth, but they didn't feel like mine. Like I was reciting something written long ago, a passage carved into the walls of my mind, a memory so deeply ingrained that it had become more truth than recollection.

"Kosovo, near Serbia. The Union needed a martyr. Votes were split—half the population wanted out, the other half wanted boots on the ground. They needed something…tragic. Something that would make the decision for them."

I exhaled. My breath felt heavy.

"We found a battalion, already surrounded. No chance of extraction. They could hold out for weeks. That wasn't good enough. We needed them dead sooner."

I could still hear the plan being made.

"6 and 7 built the op. 8 made it painless—handing out 'meds' he'd cooked up in his lab the night before. 10 was our distraction, meant to stir the hornet's nest. 9 scrubbed the evidence. 5 just sat there, watching, claiming she had already predicted the outcome with 97.4% accuracy."

I leaned back, eyes unfocused, staring at something only I could see.

"When we dropped in, something went wrong. 7 made a mistake. They saw us. They found us—begged for help."

I clenched my jaw.

"10 killed enough of the enemy to give them a real chance at survival. There was incoming aerial ordnance. We couldn't be sure. 7 and 10 fought. First with words. Then with fists. 10 won. 7 relented and let 10 lead them to safety."

A long pause.

"But before they left, 7 reminded 10 who these men were. War criminals. Rapists. Murderers. Abandonment. Each of them guilty of atrocities. And then, I was activated."

The silence after that was thick, suffocating.

"I obey, therefore I am."

It came out of my mouth like doctrine. Like something I had been programmed to say. I carried out their execution.

Patterson cleared his throat, his voice hesitant. "So how did we get from there to here?"

Before I could answer, Dahlia leaned in close. Patterson flinched as I whispered, the voice dripping with something both manic and amused.

183

"Didn't you see me kill THE FUCKING PRESIDENT?"

Then, burst into laughter—a full-bodied, wild cackle that echoed in the confined space.

"Ehh, that's rich!" my voice wheezed, shaking my head.

I took over again, my voice cutting through the moment like a blade.

"Don't tase me, bro," I said, hands raised, my smirk fading slightly as I noticed Patterson's weapon drawn and aimed at me.

His grip was tight, his stance locked.

I sighed. "It won't do much but sting, but it still sucks."

Dahlia's laughter died down, the tone dipping into something more serious.

"Mark grew into me, and I grew into Mark. Something is different. And the rest of the 10 want to know why he stopped obeying orders. Why he doesn't respond to activation requests."

The words hung in the air, thick with meaning.

I nodded. "And that's why I want to see Hammock."

Dahlia tilted my head, smiling. "And that's why you're going to be disappointed."

The conversation had taken a detour. Satellite signals were scrambled thanks to Whisperwing, so I wasn't worried about being tracked. Not directly, at least. Genji had passed on more than just a few upgrades. But none of that mattered right now. I felt tired.

So tired.

I closed my eyes, and before I could even think about fighting it, sleep swept me away. I was waiting for myself—sitting at a table, somewhere that felt like a basement. A familiar basement. Not too different from the one at Nana's house, with its old wooden chairs and the slightly wobbly table that had been there long before I was born.

A bowl sat in the center, filled with things that weren't exactly junk food, but still the kind of stuff you weren't supposed to fill up on—

bags of mixed nuts, dried fruit, apples, and tiny oranges. The good kind of oranges. The ones where the peel came off clean, taking all of the white stuff with it, leaving nothing behind but perfect, sweet fruit.

I wasn't alone.

"What are we doing?" I asked Dahlia, the only other presence in the room. I could tell it was them by the flower on their lapel—the only identifier they ever really needed.

Dahlia leaned back, arms folded, expression unreadable.

"You know," they said, voice even, but carrying the weight of something unspoken, "I went through the records. Old Lady Truman tried to tell them she had a five-year-old she was taking care of when they came to take her away."

Dahlia scoffed, then exhaled through their nose, a short, sharp sound of frustration.

"They came looking for us. And we did what we were supposed to do. We hid in the basement."

The words hit harder than I expected. I had forgotten about that part. Or maybe, I had just chosen to forget. Dahlia continued, their voice taking on an almost detached, matter-of-fact tone.

"We saw them take Old Lady Truman away and thought that would be us too. She brought us food for a couple of weeks—on and off, hit or miss. But we knew where her peanut butter was if she missed too many days. And when we ran out of cupboards to check, we started looking in other places."

Dahlia stood then, walking over to the tiny, dust-covered basement window. They motioned for me to follow.

"I don't know if this was a blessing or a curse," they murmured.

Through the window, the past unfolded.

I saw a younger version of myself, scrawny, hungry, trying to steal from a bulging food bag being pulled by Mrs. Tagadashi. Before I could grab anything, two young twins ran up to me. I tensed,

185

expecting them to call me out—to snitch, to get me in trouble. Instead, they handed me an apple.

"Where is your mother?" one of them asked.

Then, Jiro distracted Mrs. Tagadashi, drawing her attention while his siblings stood with me. I watched the moment unfold, the emotions it stirred unfamiliar yet achingly real. Dahlia's arms remained crossed as they continued watching the memory play out.

"Children like us were a dime a dozen, you know." Their voice was softer now, tinged with something close to bitterness. "Between the Hype epidemic and Outpost raids, orphan stories were more common than superhero origin stories."

I knew that—had lived that. But this memory? This one had been buried deep.

Dahlia tilted their head, eyes narrowing as if searching for the missing piece.

"And so when I dig through your memories, this one confounds me the most."

Their expression twisted into something unreadable.

"She didn't take you in. That would have been too easy. Instead, she gave you to a family they employed. A family that already had children. Added to their burden."

I watched myself—small, filthy, staring up in wide-eyed uncertainty as Mr. Hiroshi Tagadashi picked me up effortlessly.

He poked my belly and smiled. "I will feed you. I will take care of you. And you will play with my sons every day if that is okay with you?"

I had forgotten that. Or maybe, I had made myself forget. Little me smiled, still holding the stolen apple, nodding in agreement.

Then, Mr. Tagadashi turned to his sons, bowed deeply to them—a gesture of profound respect.

He ruffled their hair, hugged them tightly, and sent them off with me. He took me to Jalen and Bella—my new adoptive parents who worked for him, but were more loving and kind than I ever felt I deserved. The window faded to black.

Dahlia didn't turn away from the now-empty window, their voice quiet. "Do you know how many sessions they estimated it would take to detach our cognitive interface?"

I blinked, dragging myself out of the past.

I shrugged. "Sixty-seven?"

Dahlia shook their head.

"Five."

That hit like a gut punch.

"Why couldn't they separate us?" I asked, following them deeper into the basement.

Dahlia kneeled down beside an old, tattered blanket and pillow, tucked behind a pillar in the dim light. They settled into the makeshift bed without looking up. "Because I hid down here."

Their voice was calm. Final. I frowned. "Where do I sleep?"

Dahlia let out a long yawn, stretching their arms before closing their eyes. "You're in my dream."

Their voice was already fading. "Turn the light off on your way up the stairs, please."

I stepped toward the staircase, but something about the whole moment felt off.

As I placed my foot on the first step, the entire staircase changed. I was no longer climbing. I was descending. The steps turned into an escalator, moving in the opposite direction, dragging me downward no matter how hard I tried to climb.

And then, because of course this was happening—A Muzak version of "WAP" started playing, filtering through the basement like some warped, inescapable joke from my subconscious.

I sighed, rubbing my temples as the music droned on.

Of course Dahlia's dream would be an infinite loop of emotional turmoil…and bad taste in elevator music.

"Just let me out of here," I begged.

"You're such a kill joy," said Dahlia and for the first time in a very long time, the room parted away and turned into my bed at home. I crawled into it and I slept.

Chapter 15
Get to the Choppa

After coming to a complete and unexpected halt, Patterson yelled "Mark, Dahlia, somebody! There's a big black man pointing a bazooka at the truck!" It wasn't the first sentence you wanted to hear when you woke up from a nap on a road trip through The Waste, but that's where we were.

I tried to sit us up, but Dahlia laid us back down.

"Keep going, that's Winifred B Payne," Dahlia said calmly.

"Who?!" Patterson panicked.

"He's not real, they are holograms projected on micro-sheer sheets, in five seconds he's going to say…" and in unison they both said, "I'm going to put my foot so far up your ass the water in my knee is going to quench your thirst."

Dahlia let out a satisfied cackle through a Cheshire grin that I wasn't sure my face was capable of doing until that moment.

"I love that movie," I said with gusto, "but when did we watch it?" I quizzed.

"I dunno, that's odd," answered Dahlia. "PAT! DON'T drive over the scare-hoes, whatever you do," Dahlia urgently cautioned.

Patterson quickly corrected the wheel and looked confusingly at Dahlia. "You mean scarecrows."

"You heard me," retorted Dahlia.

Dahlia looked out the window behind us and asked, "Did you see a Tropic Thunder back there?"

"No. Just a big hole I drove around," Patterson responded.

"Okay, there's a Ram-hole coming up, go wide left," Dahlia instructed before getting a little antsy and confounded before Patterson asked if there was something else, we should be looking out for.

"Did you mean Rambo?"

Dahlia ignored me and kept speaking.

"Also, there's...uhhh...another projection we took a lot of liberty with," Dahlia said with a lot of lip biting and head tilting with an unusually high-pitched voice.

"What is it?" Patterson asked with peaked interest.

"Not my proudest moment, actually. It's a mixture of Dillon and Dutch from the classic action movie *Predator*," Dahlia said.

"Does he yell *get to the Choppa*?" I asked comically.

"No, no, nothing like that," Dahlia said in shame, then continued. "I didn't think I'd ever come back here, so I named it something less than flattering."

"What did you name it?" Patterson asked plainly not understanding that if Dahlia was embarrassed then it was probably bad.

"Well, Arnold's character is white, and Carl's character is black...you know what, never mind. Yeah, he yells get to the choppa, you just can't hear it," Dahlia said.

"You didn't do what I think you did," I scolded.

"Didn't what?" Patterson said.

"Changed a letter in Arnold's last name," I said in a raised monotone shaming voice.

"Which letter could he possibly...Oh no! That's terrible. What the fuck's wrong with you?" Patterson said, cursing for the first time, while growing red with embarrassment.

"We're here!" shouted Dahlia as we drove past Carl Weathers and Arnold Schwarzenegger clasping hands in a locked greeting and holding machine guns with their other arms.

"Let me do the talking," Dahlia said.

"No, that never works out," I shot back.

"The last time you did the talking, we ended up in these," Dahlia said and held up the cuffs.

Patterson gave a half nod in agreement.

"Fine," I reluctantly acquiesced.

Dahlia turned to Patterson as he opened his door. "Pat, you should stay in the truck for now, we will come and grab you when it's safe."

We walked to the door and even before pressing my finger to the ID pad, it opened.

"Dahlia, I didn't expect to see you again," said the gruff voice of the aged and sick Sergeant Hammock that trained me in the SAI program and NLB (Next Level Boot). He stepped aside and gestured me to enter his home. Hammock was a short man, around 5'3", thin, military face, dark skin, perfect white teeth, but looked like he had the worst flu ever.

"Why are you wearing cuffs?" he asked in the most annoyed and comical way possible, before continuing. "Does it have it anything to do with the story I heard about the dick bounty? You know what, don't answer that. I don't want to know."

I noticed a syringe and vial on the table with most of the vial gone, and I guess I looked too long. Hammock made it a point to look at me while I was looking at the vial.

"It's just a matter of days or hours now I suppose. I am at the maximum dose you told me I can take safely," Hammock said.

Dahlia had instructed me to not speak, but this was a man I respected and honored, I reflexively asked, "Hours till what?"

"You know I'm dying, you asshole. And you just want a pat on the back for extending my stay topside? For something I did for your benefit? If I didn't know any better, I'd say you need to pull your head out of your ass, but then again, I'd end up just shoving it back up there," Hammock responded with the sharpness of a career military veteran.

Dahlia took a huge sigh and responded, "Hammy listen, Mark's here. He doesn't know."

Hammock's face brightened, even though his eyes were red, he still opened up a little. "It worked?"

"Yes, sir," I said, with my own inflection.

A single tear slid from his eye, and he walked up to me and shook my hand. He could see the subtle difference in us. "Good to see you, son."

"Been a while, sir." I nodded back.

Chapter 16
Captain Knife Hands

"What do you remember that night you gave it over to Dahlia?" Hammock asked me.

"I don't know how or what happened. This is all new and weird to me," I responded. I pointed at the door and said, "There's an Arnold Schwartsenig."

Hammock held up his hand and said, "Oh I know, and I don't know how to change its damn name either. Thank God I only have days or hours to live. If Maria was still alive, she'd die from embarrassment," he said as he leaned in smiling and mocking anger.

He pushed back from the table and smiled and laughed lightly. "Can I get you something to drink?" As he got up, he said, "They keep away the unwanted guests."

Hammock got up and walked to the sink, walking slowly but with every bit of dignity and respect he'd earned from a life in the corp. When he got to the sink, he began to cough, and hack. I stood to help.

"Sit your ass down, Captain. or I will sit you down." I felt both myself and Dahlia sit down at the same time, and I could have sworn the chair shot up to meet us halfway.

Hammock was known for many things; his knife hands and eye-contact-of-death were of legendary status, so we were still within our means to respond with haste.

I opened my mouth to protest his cough and hacking, which started again, but he powered through it as he seemingly always did with things that got in his way. "I'll tell you the story, it's short and not that exciting. But I have something for you first." He walked into the bedroom and back out with a letter which he handed to me, but wouldn't let go.

It was a letter folded in thirds and I could see writing through the paper folds. It's 2055, but paper's still a thing, but not as popular as it was even just twenty years ago during the Digital Black Out.

"I found it in your room, when I found you."

"I'm so confused, sir," I said, attempting to speak with a solid voice.

"Your SAI activated on its own, without a master signal or a battle scenario. I ran to your quarters. I was already in the area, and I got the notification on my interface, fearing that an attack was underway. I found something much worse. You...unresponsive with an empty bottle of Hyperion Theta. And this note. I reached down to begin CPR and you woke, except it wasn't you. You were different. In full sync, I've seen you and this was different. It was just different, and that's the best way I can say it. When you fell out of it, well, I was left with this jackass." Hammock threw his knife-hand at the mirror— thumb tucked, fingers straight, every inch textbook. The kind of perfect form that made you wonder if he practiced it in his sleep. It was somehow intimidating as hell.

It took me a moment of mental work before I wanted to ask a clarifying question.

"When you found me," I started.

"You had no pulse, Captain," Hammock finished for me.

I opened my mouth to speak, and being a brown man, it wasn't possible, but I felt like my color had left me.

"ArchSoul," Dahlia whispered. "We are an ArchSoul."

"I figured it out pretty fast. I wanted to report this to command, but then dipship here went to bed. You woke back up and remembered nothing." And yes, there was more Michael Jordan level knifehand.

"Something happened, not important now, but during the next mission, Mark, you didn't respond to the activation signal."

"That's what that was?" Dahlia said haphazardly, only to be met with the death stare.

Hammock leaned back, watching me carefully as he spoke, his tone calm, but the weight behind his words anything but.

"But you did respond in battle."

A statement. A fact. An undeniable truth.

"You outperformed 3 and 4 in efficiency—without planning, without setup—during an ambush."

He let that hang in the air for a second before continuing.

"Dahlia found you almost every night. That was no coincidence. Something was happening. They needed your SAI—wanted into your head by any means necessary after seeing what you could do."

I stayed quiet, processing.

I had always known something was off, but hearing it laid out so plainly, so methodically, made it all feel too real. I was never just another soldier. I was an anomaly. A problem. A variable they couldn't control.

Hammock exhaled sharply. "I pushed for your disengagement. Safe deactivation. I thought maybe, if they saw you were a lost cause, they'd spare you."

I already knew how that turned out. Hammock shook his head, voice lowering.

"After two years of trying—and failing—with traditional disengagement protocols, they realized they couldn't safely extract your core." My gut tightened. I knew what came next.

"You became a mission-brief."

My breath slowed.

"Kill or Capture."

Hammock gave me a look—one that carried regret, but also something harder, colder. He had known. For a long time.

"I had close friends," Hammock admitted. "They made me aware of the new orders."

Then, he smiled.

That kind of smile that said he had done something incredibly reckless and didn't regret it for a second.

"So naturally, I stole the files of the other nine."

I blinked.

"I acquired all of their activation and comm codes."

And just like that, everything changed.

"And you also got yourself killed," Dahlia said.

"Was bound to happen someday, Dahlia. You weren't supposed to come back here," Hammock said.

I looked in the mirror and saw tears swelling in my eyes.

"8 laced the physical files with Jeepers Peepers," Dahlia said in anger but quietly.

"We've got the antidote," I said excitedly, bouncing in my chair.

"He's changed the formulation. That's what's on the table over there; the antidote. If it wasn't for that, Hammy would have been dead a week ago when he got infected," Dahlia said with sadness.

"Mason was crooked, don't get me wrong, but he didn't deserve to die. 8 sealed his fate. It was his idea. He didn't want to die at the will of a manmade super flu" Dahlia insisted.

"What was the list then?" I asked. "I found a list of names, handwritten. Me, Kimberly…"

Hammock answered before I could finish, "Everyone who touched the file. They've got a secondary infection, this version is delayed, but they are going to die. 8's going to track them, activate the virus and kill them, slowly."

Dahlia added in, "But not until after he pulls every bit of information out of them. He will poison them and make them better and worse, go back and forth torturing them, till he feels like he's gotten everything."

"Like Xiong Xing all over again," I said with my head down.

Hammock's coughing fired up again and punctuated the moment with severe intensity, and it started to sound like an echo in a river valley, then it came rushing in.

I felt an anger rise inside of me that I didn't know was there or even possible to feel. Flush and heat ran over my cheeks, tingling, and a hypersensitive sense of touch drew to my fingers, the temperature of the air was measurable over every piece of exposed skin. The water dripping in the sink was as loud as someone talking. Hammock had stood quickly and taken a step back.

Our eyes met, he nodded toward the wall and said softly, along with a small pointing hand gesture, "Mirror…"

When I looked, my eyes had a red glow and there was an aura like heat rising off of the floor irradiating around me. Hammock walked over to me cautiously, my eyes met his, he placed his hand on my shoulder and said, "Remember this, bottle it, save it for the battlefield, son, because I know who's coming for you and you're going to need it."

"What the freak was that, man!" came a voice from the door.

Despite his sickness, Hammock had responded with due haste and a hand-canon pulled from thin air pointed at the face of Patterson.

The Battlesync ripped away like a bandage as I yelled, "Don't shoot!" in unison with Dahlia.

I felt the separation like ripping away Velcro. I felt like two separate and distinct beings in one bag. Two cats in one box.

"Who in the dog's dick are you?" said Hammock.

"I can see where Dahlia gets it," Patterson replied, in an attempt at humor. Wrong move.

Hammock charged the hammer on his weapon and said, "A friend of my friend does not make you my friend. I am an old and dying trigger happy corpsman with penchant for shooting first and asking questions later, do you really want to wonder how effective my bolt disrupter is? I built it myself and I'm actually kind of curious what the effectiveness is at this close of a range. Twelve tiny barbed depleted uranium darts, charged with 1100 kilojoules of pure electromagnetic charge that will release through any faraday or grounding, and they are laced with synthetic pepper. Now, would you like to answer, or will we get to run a field test of my new toy? Who in the dog's dick are you? Five seconds and no I will not ask again."

"He'll shoot you in the balls and laugh as you writhe in pain," Dahlia said through both side eye and twisted lips. I wondered in that very moment just how many interactions these two had had over the past two years while I was supposed to be sleeping.

"P-P-PATTERSON, trial Officer Patterson," Patterson muttered.

"Oh my God, please don't tell me you have a stuttering sidekick? That could make comms tricky," mocked Hammock and then looked to me with the customary, *wouldn't you guess it*, knife-hand and wide open inquisitive eyes darting between the two of us. "I assume he's a friend of yours or he'd be dead by now?"

"That he is, sir," I quickly responded due to the impending threat of more knife-hand. "He is an asset."

"Explain," Hammock said simply with a tilted head as he squared up to me as if we were back on base, with the exception being the gun trained on Patterson. Eerily the boom-stick swayed with Patterson without Hammock even glancing in that direction.

I leaned in with purpose and said directly, "Patterson's presence prevents an orbital strike if we are located by drone. To override the strike would require presidential authority. VP Baines can't be sworn in, he's in Europe. Firing on us in The Waste could be considered an act of war on The Liberty Republic. Patterson's presence mean's everything is scrutinized, and rules are followed at the state level," I finished feeling pretty smart.

"You dumbass!" Hammock threw back at me which turned my pride into shock and surprise. "Nuclear options yield only nuclear results. You tied their hands and backed them into a corner," Hammock, said as he stood coughing, this time holding himself up on the table with his free hand.

Dahlia felt an opportunity to jump in and added with pride, "9's dead. We killed him. Cooked him. Smelled like Teen Spirit and Roasted Chitterlings."

"What are Chitterlings?" Patterson asked as he started to relax, thinking he was out of danger.

"Who said you could lower your hands, P-P-Patterson? I still haven't decided what to do with you," Hammock said with every ounce of seriousness available to him in the universe as the hand canon re-aimed itself back at Patterson's face.

"Pig intestines, smells terrible, tastes not so bad. Lots of prep required to eat. Have lots of hot sauce on hand to consume." Hammock's tension eased as he tilted the gun and his head when he spoke, then the other comment caught up with him.

"YOU KILLED 9?" Hammock yelled with what little energy he had, then collapsed into a chair. It was clear this interaction had drained him, and the news that 9 was no more brought him some solace. "That bastard, I hope he burned the way he burned others," Hammock finished as he sat back with his eyes closed and head laid back on the recliner's soft backing.

"He did, Sarge. He did! I got his end-code too. Thanks to the file data you were able to get, now I have all of the inside info on the other nine ANGLs. Now there's a box on the table upstairs, I can't open it. Not sure how to yet," Dahlia said as if there had been many conversations leading up to this point.

Hammock kept his head laid back, opened his eyes slightly, and spoke with purpose, "Then you know they won't stop now. The difference in skill and ability isn't linear. It's exponential. These aren't little green soldiers that you're playing with. These are supernatural beings. You're an ANGL because you didn't die from implant sickness. 5 is an ANGL because she can whisper in your ear and convince you to jump off of a cliff. 6 is an ANGL because he can remotely control every electronic device in a 50-foot radius through his SAI. Don't even get me started on 2. 1 is a bona fide demon, and I'm not speaking in hyperbole. And you, your eyes glow red."

I changed the subject to, "About this list, sir."

Hammock unsettled himself, realizing his break was over. "7 bumped into me on the way out of the records office. Kimberly reviewed the files by hand, thinking she could break the ANGL codes with Dahlia without end-coding them when they die. I gave a file to Ryan, hoping he would use it to throw off Dimitri. Instead, he used it as leverage to get more people into the bubble. I wanted to give President Mason the upper hand to ensure victory over 7."

I wondered to myself what is 7's political goals, and as if the words were coming from a different room again, I spoke "The goal is to thin out the herd. It's to replenish the ranks of NJC with more people who see him as a hero. His plan is to militarize the city with Hyperion Jacks and get it ready for a Halos interruption. Lasting days or weeks, not long enough to lose the city, but long enough to lose a third of the populous. The new residents will see 7 as a hero and lifetime president.

I don't know how I know this, but I do. That's what the ANGL's goal is right now, control of a militarized state."

"Hyperion Jacks?" we all asked at the same time.

Dahlia broke out with, "That box is HOT! REALLY HOT. I'm not holding it again. If you want to ask it more questions, someone else is going to have to hold it. I don't know what that is either. A box just frickin' manifested inside of here and it was smoking."

Patterson spoke up, "Can I put my hands down?"

Hammock responded with a shrug, and Patterson started to speak, "This was 7's plan. 7 is the cat in the house. He's got an activated version of the virus in him. One deadly enough to do all of the dirty work and distract the attention from the magician."

Hammock looked at me sideways. "I don't follow."

"Long story, sir, but the short version is we are supposed to be out here being distracted doing this, and the master tactician 7 had planned this from the start, and we are blaming the wrong people. Meanwhile, 7 uses the president's death as a distraction to get his way. Somehow, he knew that Mason would touch that file. Whether or not he was going to be shot by Mark is unknown."

I corrected Patterson by yelling out, "Shot by *Dahlia*."

"Same thing, no matter what, the president is dead and we are in The Waste. 7 is in the Dome. The plan may not be working in our favor. Knowing that can help us turn the tide," Patterson finished.

"You may yet walk out of here with your testicles still attached to your body," chided Dahlia to Patterson as he nodded to the blaster not pointed at his face, but still yet aimed at his crotch.

Hammock stood and walked around the table, laid his gun down, and shook his head. "This is FUBAR. He can't have calculated for all of these variables. Could he? Maybe he did." He rubbed his scratchy gray chin. "You've got to go see Harmony, it's the only way. But before you go, Dahlia, I need to say goodbye to Mark, alone. You and I already said our peace."

"But…" Protested Dahlia.

"You redeemed me. Made me whole, for the first time in a long time," Hammock asserted.

"Heh, hole." Chuckled Dahlia.

"Now get your ass out of here before I tell Mark about that time in Singapore," Hammock chopped with his expert knife-hand.

"Technically, that wasn't even me, but I'll go. Mark, you'll have to come and get me from the basement. You'll need to take a nap, or deep meditation, or do some magic mushrooms," Dalhia proclaimed as I felt the presence fade out quickly, like waking from a vivid dream. It could be described in detail but words could never truly convey the way it felt.

Hammock leaned forward in his chair, gaining back some of his energy, put both of his hands under his chin and made a double fist. "I've come to terms with my demons, but this is still hard to say," he said in a gruff undertone. And almost went to a whisper.

"Voyager Legacy-Zion, that's the name you need to remember. Every wearable, smart device and connected piece of tech is centered around this quantum computer," Hammock said and took his first deep, heavy, and measured breath that didn't result in a coughing fit.

"When the world spent five years dark after the AI war, this computer was able to make it out on the other side scott-free. It was in space, testing the Halos' effects on quantum computing. The experiment was more than a success. It sent back down to earth cures for many diseases, HIV, depression treatment and military applications like your SAI. The world restarted, but Voyager Legacy-Zion, was centuries ahead. We asked it how to find the best soldiers, and it pointed us to you lot. You didn't choose the corps, Mark. We chose you. We were given the chances and likelihood of getting an Arch-Soul, and it was miscalculated somehow. We killed those young men and women, believing they'd wake back up. None of them did, except you and one other," Hammock deflated.

"So implant sickness, was that a thing?" I asked with my mind spinning.

"Yes, but not to the extent you've been told," Hammock responded and held his stare waiting on the most obvious follow-up question.

"I wish Dahlia were here to pull that next answer out of you without making me ask," I bantered.

"Han," Hammock dropped the name like a brick on a glass table.

"But he's dead," I retorted in my own way trying to impart my very low understanding of the situation.

"Is he?" Hammock concertedly puzzled. He leaned forward, and his face squinted in a pain that was foreign to him, regret possibly. "Listen, I never read your *last* letter. The letter I found next to your bed. Never even wanted to until I saw you tonight and saw the way you looked at the letter. Don't allow scribbling on dead trees defeat you."

Right at that time we heard Arnold yell, "Get to the choppa!"

Hammock looked at me, and in that moment, I realized he was the man of a million faces because his eye contact and knife hand fully communicated sheer confusion and frustration, not at Arnold's alert, but rather that I was still in cuffs. I yelled, "Cuffs off," and because I was yielding only myself, they fell to the floor. That was also the problem; my access to everything cool was only accessible if I could fall asleep, meditate, or get high to bring Dahlia back.

Our comms trilled at the same time and a voice barged into the home. It was a familiar Russian voice. "I told you not to activate, but you didn't listen, Ten. Oh well, listen, I propose a trade. Your head, for Hammock's life. You know by now, it's pretty much already gone, a few more hours, maybe by morning if you're lucky."

Then a brief pause before he picked back up.

"Hammock, if Mark turns over his SAI, we will give the antidote to you. We know how sweet you are on each other. 8 is waiting outside. The alternative is so much worse, you all know how close 8 and 9 were. You took away his playground buddy, and you stole his truck. I will give you ninety seconds to think it over."

Patterson reached into his pocket and pulled out a handful of gummies. "Chew these up! Quick," he said and Hammock side nodded in eager agreement with a surprising eyebrow raise, and a look of WTF from me at the exact same time.

"Purely medicinal...I take it for my anxiety. Don't judge. I. have. A. prescription," Patterson said in full incredulous wide wide-eyed defensiveness that only someone who's used to being attacked has stored up could say.

And of course, I did the only thing that any self-respecting man in my situation could do when faced with consuming psychedelic drugs in a combat situation would do, I asked what was in it and Patterson began to absently stutter. "Um it's the good stuff!" he wedged in as he forced eye contact.

My connection with Whisperwing was restored, and through my Hololens, I had an aerial view of Eduardo 'Rattlesnake' Dominguez. He was armed with two dart handguns, loaded with various substances, strong enough to drop the hippos at El Chappos ranch. I should know, we used to test them out there on them. And I am sure, just as meticulously prepared as always. The first few shots are tranquilizers, then the next something far more dangerous. A bandolier of noxious grenades hung across his chest and a signature rapier laced in the deadliest substance on earth hung from his hip. One scratch, and you're dead.

As he began to approach the hologram of Major Payne, I heard him utter in his Mexican accent, "Did I ever tell you about the little engine that could?" and then he laughed. It sent a chill down my spine. He was surveying the perimeter, calculating his next move. Something ominous was in the air. I closed my eyes and focused, trying to tap into my inner strength. I asked Patterson how long it usually took for the gummies to go into effect, but he could only offer a noncommittal shrug, telling me that it varied from person to person.

Whisperwing's interference with satellite imaging persisted, preventing me from moving it without risking visual detection. Its weapons were only accessible from the pilot's seat, which I couldn't occupy at the moment. All I had were Patterson, a man whose life depended on the mercy of a ruthless biochemist, and a flickering hope that my SAI connection might come online if I took questionable drugs from a man who can't tell me anything about them. The odds were stacked against us, and the situation looked increasingly bleak. So, I came up with a plan.

"My head for everyone else's. Okay? I turn myself in and no one else dies," I yelled out the door. Then I turned back to Hammock and Patterson and said, "I'm going to let him shoot me. And I've taken the gummies. I'm sure it's something that's supposed to knock me out, but he's not considering that I've taken those meds Patterson gave me. It will backfire, and he will bring me out of it. I will bring Dahlia with me, Battlesync and then we dance."

"Except those were fruit chews I found under the back seat of the fire truck. I actually ate some on the drive over," Patterson said in shame as he shook his head. "I was hoping for a placebo effect."

Hammock unwrapped the death-stare like a kid in the eighties finding a new Nintendo under the tree and aimed it firmly at Patterson. "When this is over, I am going to placebo my foot up your ass.

You can count on that like car trouble after you've paid it off." Then he got closer to me and his tone changed.

"Mark, you may never forgive me for this, and I'm okay with this, but we don't have a choice," Hammock said as he turned to me and pushed me into a dark room onto the floor and then closed the door. I heard windows breaking and gas hissing and escaping. Our time was up, and Rattlesnake's patience was gone. As he closed the door, he said, "Computer, code ten." The doors closed and through it I heard Hammock. "When I found you that night, this is what was playing on repeat, there's something about this song, and I'm sorry I am making you go back to it. Use it to go back to your space, find Dahlia, find your space. I won't open the door until Dahlia tells me the password."

I heard the music, the melody, but it was like your phone playing a song under a stack of pillows. It was a song called, "It's been a while." I recognized it immediately.

I heard Hammock through the door coughing, and yelling loud and clear though, "Patterson, distract his attention and give me the keys to the truck."

To which Patterson responded, "Is this like *Lethal Weapon 4*?"

Hammock responded, "Lethal Weap…Boy, your survival of this battle is questionable, however me beating your ass is grade A one hundred percent USA signed, sealed, stamped, mailed, delivered, guaranteed."

To which Patterson then responded with the absolute wrong thing, "Can we focus on the bad guy outside?"

Hammock went silent, and I knew exactly what would happen next.

"Ouch! Hey!" yelled Patterson. "You threw a toaster at me and hit me in the head!"

"Correction, I threw a plugged-in toaster so I can retrieve it and throw it again at will," Hammock replied calmly.

"Who's Will?" Patterson squeaked, and then I heard another loud bang followed by, "Ouch. Heyyyyy!"

"Will better duck," said a familiar voice that sounded eerily like mine from someone sitting next to me on the floor, that also had my face. I recognized that it was me from the night of the suicide attempt.

"Dahlia, is that you?" I asked.

My face and voice chuckled nervously back at me. "I don't know who that is, but…" He looked around. "I didn't expect this be the place I wake up, or even at all I suppose."

"Do you know who I am?" I probed.

"You look older. Are you a dream?" Dahlia asked with a slight smile and trepidation.

"We lived. Hammock came in, saved us, I guess. Not sure how," I replied.

"But I can still hear the music playing," Dahlia said looking to the door confused and half pointed.

There was scuffling at the door. A fight was ensuing. Hammock was an impressive fighter, but Eduardo needed the door open to get to me and regardless of how good Hammock was, he was even more hard-headed. Eduardo wasn't getting that door open, but that wouldn't stop Hammock from being tortured. I could see shadows under the door moving about in aggressive terms, three if I counted correctly. Patterson was still in the fight, which was good, but at some point, a rapier coated in poison—a long thin sword used by Matadors—will be drawn and Patterson will be a dead man, and Hammock will have each code number drawn out of him one by one. I had to focus.

"Why did we do this?" I asked as I looked myself in the eye and placed my hand in his shoulder. "Why did we want to die?"

He hung his head, my head in shame and wiped a tear, the voice was shaky. "I…I wasn't given a choice. I was told that if I didn't do it, someone else would do me in the next morning. I was told that I had done too much wrong. I was told that I had gone too far, too many times. There was a list of everyone that had died by my hand. Almost like a collage of their faces somewhere, kept by someone, ready to take me down. A court-martial wouldn't even fix it. I was told that first thing in the morning my time was up. Do it now, I was told, or else!"

"Who? Who told you that?" I asked in anger, ready to rage.

"I don't know."

"Was it Dimitri? Was it Eddy? Was it Robinson?"

"No!"

"If not them then who?" I asked in frustration drawing a blank of who could have done such a thing.

"I…I…I think I did. I told myself that." He crumpled into my lap and sobbed. "I've done so much wrong. I've been through so much. I'm so messed up!"

I rubbed his back. I felt his tears run down my face. I touched my face and drew back damp fingers. I heard the music flow from his mouth as he whaled his hurt. "We are messed up," I said in no mixed terms. "But there's much on the other side of this bridge. You didn't think you could cross it, and you did and you're happy now. There's been people on the other side, soldiers, friends, women. Come with me. I need your help. This is your home, it is dark, and I don't know my way to the basement from here," I pleaded. "People need you; I need you. You have a choice and I forgive you, and I love you for every mistake. We can't change the past, but we can change the future. We've got more healing to do, but let's make the decision to start here."

The tumultuous sounds of a physical struggle echoed through the room. Chairs and tables skidded across the floor, and the impact of men crashing into the door reverberated in the air. The younger version of me, just a couple of years younger but somehow appearing much more innocent, remained blissfully unaware of the chaos unfolding just beyond the door. He picked himself up from the floor and dusted himself off, making his way to the door. My heart sank momentarily, fearing he might open it, but relief washed over me as he reached for the wrong end. The door he opened led to a pitch-black space with my old barracks designation, M81, on it.

I followed him out and I turned around to address him, only to find an empty room. Panic rose within me, and I opened my mouth to call out, but instead, I delved into my memories, unearthing the haunting events of that fateful night. They weighed on me like a stack of bricks, obstructing the path in my mind, but it was a burden I would have to confront later.

I focused on the task at hand and tried to step through the door to aid Hammock, but in an instant, I found myself back in my childhood home. The house resembled the way it had been during my last visit. I approached the basement door, grappling with the decision to either knock or simply open it. In the end, I chose to do both.

I knocked and opened the door and I heard, "What's the point in the knock-knock-open? You're going to open the door and you're not going to give me enough time to finish beating-off or for me to make it look like I was doing something different. It's more like an announcement of hey, I'm coming in to catch you spanking your monkey and now our relationship will never be the same," Dahlia said while staring out the window, arms crossed, head resting on forearms, staring into the distance.

I walked downstairs quickly, "8's out there, and probably winning. I need you," I said without hesitation.

Dahlia turned to me defeated and upset. "I finally saw it, I finally saw what made us. I don't know what to do with this. I am feeling lots of different feelings. I just want to sit here for a while, can you come back later after I process? I just watched some pretty heavy stuff go down, Mark." Dahlia held up the very note that I wrote. I vaguely remembered its content, but Dahlia intercepted its content.

I walked over to Dahlia and reached around and squeezed the biggest hug. "I can only imagine what you feel. I am asking a lot of you right now. Tonight, with Hammock, and the emotions you have helped me process over these past years and now this. I don't know what else to give you but a hug, but were you down here beating off when I came downstairs? Be honest. I see lotion on the counter."

Dahlia pulled back. "Well, Dr. Phil, that was just what I needed. Let's Sync. But before we do, we need a plan, don't we?"

Chapter 17
Churros for Cholos

The world that was once there went away, replaced piece by piece everywhere I looked. The closer I looked, the less it was the way it was in my mind. The brick wall in the basement became the patterned wall of the bedroom. The windows were somehow impeccably placed in the same position. As my head turned and eyes panned, the room spun itself into Hammock's bedroom, dark and music blaring.

I walked to the door and tried the knob to no avail. I heard more fighting and grunting followed by Hammock yelling, "No!" and Patterson saying in a calm voice, "It's okay, you'll get what's coming to you, you snake in the grass." And then a singular loud thud on the ground.

"Now, I need the combination to that door Jeffe," Eddy said in his heavy Spanish accent.

Hammock laughed at him. "If you were on fire, I'd cut off my own jimmy with a rusty butter knife before I'd piss on you."

"Not only am I going to make this hurt, but I'm going to enjoy this more this more than I should," Eddy threatened. "You know, I never liked you much, Punta. Here's your first hit."

Hammock screamed in agony. A scream that didn't register with me, but Dahlia clinched my fists and beat the door and I felt a lift of energy. "Let me out!" raged a voice that I could not contain.

I don't think Dahlia meant out of the room. I think Dahlia meant my body.

Hammock's excruciating pain showed no signs of abating. What had already sounded like the most agonizing experience one could endure somehow escalated to an even more unbearable level. Hammock's breathing ceased, an eerie silence enveloped the room, and after what felt like an eternity, his anguished screams resumed, interspersed with coughing and incoherent muttering from Eddy.

It was at that moment I couldn't bear it any longer, and I bellowed, "ANDRE RUFUS HAMMOCK!" It was as if my cry had summoned something, I heard "Computer, play Smooth Criminal" and that's when the door cracked open, and the lights came on. At first, all I saw was Hammock's bloodied face, but it was quickly replaced by the sight of Eduardo 'Rattlesnake' Ramirez, shirtless and adorned with tattoos that accentuated his muscular physique. Eddy's slick back hair and attire, consisting of black suspenders securing white pressed and pleated slacks, gave him a menacing aura. He had two pistols holstered under his arms and the venom rapier sheathed on his left hip, ready to be drawn with his right hand, and punctuated by his tacky signature snakeskin boots. Where was PETA when you needed them?

I entered the aftermath of a fierce battle, but to my astonishment, Eddy stood there unruffled and untouched. His weapons remained sheathed, and even his pristine white pants showed no sign of the mayhem around him. A trickle of blood adorned his chest, though it wasn't his own; it came from the battered face of Hammock, who lay crumpled on the floor. Patterson lay nearby, face down, his breathing shallow and weak. It was clear he needed immediate Nano-Med treatment. Time was not on our side, and Hammock's wheezing breaths filled the air as he struggled to find even the strength to roll onto his side.

Eddy smiled to reveal his two fangs sharpened and lengthened just for effect. "Diez, cholo, homes, I missed you. It's been two years. Lots has happened. It's been hard to round up and find our marks without you, no pun intended." He lifted Hammock with one arm by his shirt and tossed him to the side. I felt my temperature rise.

"Is it true what I am hearing? They said you took out Blaze. They said you killed my roll dog, Homes?" Eddy said as he picked his teeth with a makeshift toothpick as he sat in a chair.

"No, I cooked him. He died like the way he lived. Terribly and in pain," Dahlia said with a sneer.

Eddy stood and kicked Hammock, knowing that Hammock and I had a strong bond, but also knowing Eddy and Blaze Tanner were good friends for a long time and losing Blaze hurt. Their ridiculous closed-minded world views were something to be said, but they were still friends.

"All I need is your SAI." He paused allowing his grin to grow even larger before continuing, "And your cabasa, of course. I have no intention of taking anything else with me. I'm traveling very light you see. All I have is my bike. Someone stole the fire truck I rode with in with Blaze and when I got here, this bendejo over here," he pointed at Patterson with gun fingers and mockingly shot him, "distracted me while old Hammy blew the core while I stood on the other side."

"Hehe." I laughed reflexively.

"My SAI absorbed it or else I'd be a sweet memory, singing La Bamba from the other side," he said in a slight grunt as he stood to his feet. "I need to make it quick, but not necessarily painless," Eddy said as he pulled out one of his pistols and started twisting a dial. The grip glowed a deep dark ominous green in his hand. Not bright, but just enough to know it was charged and ready to fire.

"A lot has changed in the past two years, Mijo," he said from behind the barrel of his gun pointed at the ceiling standing just four feet away from me. Just barely out of arms reach. "I can adjust the mixture on this with my neuro interface, that part you helped me perfect. What's new is now I can make it more deadly, or more painful, or more fun, or heal myself, just by thinking of it before pulling the trigger. It's like a magic wand. You can call me Roberto Potter."

"Harry Potter," I corrected him.

"Who?" Eddy contorted his face in sheer confusion.

"It's…it's Harry Potter, Eddy and where did you get this new tech from? I heard Tokyo-Prime is still on lockdown."

He lowered his gun, fixing his gaze upon me. "We chanced a brief interface with the Algorithm through a quantum link. 9 didn't actually want to, but I…" His head shook ever so slightly, as if he had a momentary stroke, but he quickly continued, "Had to be in the right place at the right time, and I got there and came away a little more…" He leaned in, his eyes widening with a devilish gleam, and whispered, "*Evolved.*" He took a short breath and continued, "So, I've got to get that head off of those shoulders, and you know this, but you seem very relaxed, cholo. You must know something I don't know, and I don't like that." And then he leveling the gun at my chest.

I smiled and began to speak, "Because Cito, you want a fight. You want revenge for your friend, and you want to know if you can beat me, because you've been told to take no chances. You've been told to shoot me onsite and you're curious. How can little ol' me be so dangerous, eh punta?"

Eddy's cold, calculated gaze bore into me as he tightened his grip on the trigger. The pad of his finger flattened, and the gun roared to life. Time seemed to slow as I watched the round exit the barrel, hurtling towards me with deadly intent. My body tensed, anticipating the impact.

The dart struck me square in the chest, dead center. In that critical moment, Eddy had me in his crosshairs, and it appeared all hope was lost. However, beneath my clothes, I concealed a grounding suit and knife protection gear. Eddy remained unaware of this hidden defense.

It was a risky gamble, but it was one I had to take to survive. If not for these protective layers, Eddy would have aimed for my exposed skin. As the round hit my chest, it exploded into a chaotic burst of small, silvery globs. They radiated outward in intricate, lightning-like patterns across my sternum, each ending in an unsettling, insect-like protrusion.

These exploded bizarre darts were a terrifying sight, a testament to Eddy's relentless pursuit of death, destruction, and torture.

These had to be synthetic programmable viral replicas, dormant until commanded by Eddy to fulfill their sinister purpose. But what exactly was their default function? In the absence of Eddy's orders, did this substance remain inert, or did it possess lethal potential? How much exposure did it take for this substance to become deadly? Was mere skin contact enough to seal one's fate?

As these questions raced through my mind, four more shots struck me in rapid succession, targeting my center mass.

"Armor, my friend? No worries. We can find a way around that," Eddy taunted with a grin. He adjusted his aim, flicked his hand upward, and in that moment, I detected a subtle telegraphing of his movements, all the information I needed to anticipate his next move and react swiftly. Though he had started just outside of arm's reach, with each shot, I subconsciously closed the distance between us, positioning myself to his right side where he had drawn his gun.

In a well-coordinated dance, I reached for the top slide of his weapon to lock it open and cause a breach firing jam while pushing it away from me. Eddy, displaying an almost uncanny fluidity, relinquished the firearm without resistance as the gun stopped firing. He executed a swift spin in the opposite direction from my approach, drawing his second pistol from the other holster with lightning speed.

With *life or death* timing, I tilted my head back and to the side, feeling the rush of air as a dart missed my forehead by mere picoseconds. The reflexive rapid evasive maneuver saved me from a potential headshot. This was not me. My SAI was in full control.

This sequence continued with three more shots fired as I allowed myself to fall to the ground. I avoided the temptation to turn my head but observed the angle of Eddy's aim from his shadow on the wall, allowing me to calculate the trajectory for my leap as I hit the floor. Eddy tracked my descent, the barrel of his gun following my head down. He patiently awaited the ideal moment for a headshot.

As I met the ground, I raised my forearms, closing them together to block two more shots aimed at my throat and face, a defensive maneuver that protected me from the potentially lethal shots.

At this point, Eddy was getting frustrated, and I wanted to maximize this opportunity. Dahlia heard my thoughts and took over. "Listen, we all have trouble hitting the target sometimes man, it's just a little Projectile Dysfunction."

"SHUT UP!" stammered Eddy.

"Oh, this is your first time you found out you're shooting blanks, huh? Tsk tsk," Dahlia continued in mockery.

"AHHHHHH, fine, I can't shoot you, I'll shoot him instead!" yelled Eddy and then he shot Hammock out of anger in the butt. Left cheek to be exact.

"You shot me...In the *ass*?!" mustered Hammock. "I'm going to rectify this immediately," he said as he pulled the dart from his backside, attempted to stand, and fell right over.

"RECT-ify," giggled Dahlia. I rolled my eyes, and so did Eddy.

I took this distraction and leaped at Eddy with a chair, hitting his hand, making him almost drop the gun. Clearly, this was not going as easily with me as it had with Patterson and Hammock. His hand-to-hand skills were null, and his gun skills were frustratingly ineffective against me. In the field, I had never seen Eddy take more than one shot per target.

Eddy walked over to the counter, holstered his pistol and retrieved my Hono, lifted and examined it in one hand. Looking at it with majesty and awe.

"Bonita," he began speaking softly, but his voice escalated in volume. "He didn't even make one of these for Jiro, you know, his own son. But that won't help you!" and as he finished the sentence, he turned and threw the sheathed Hono at me. I caught the hilt and allowed the momentum and weight of the sheath to leave nothing but the gleaming blade in my right hand. It was a cool move, but before I had a modicum of time to celebrate how smooth it was, Eddy had drawn his sword and was swinging it at me already. Any cut or scratches, even a nick from his sword, would be fatal. It was a neurotoxin derived from the Black Mamba. First, you go limp, and then your body and organs, including your heart, stop working while you're fully awake, that simple. It's a terrible death.

I stepped back and the tip of his blade missed my chest by less than an inch. Maybe half an inch as his stroke arch finished pointing at his own feet. I looked up to see anger and rage. He had a score to settle and something to prove.

"Why is yours so much smaller than mine? You can't say the water was too cold either," Dahlia picked.

"You think you're so special, but wait till I show up with your head, Homes," he said as he swung wildly and uncalculated.

"Wait, I have something IMPOTENT to tell you," Dahlia said as I parried his next swing.

The room was filled with tension as 8 and I faced off, venom rapier against my Hono. Hammock lay on the ground, gasping for breath, face down and his legs struggling to find footing. Patterson battling to stay conscious, pulling himself toward Hammock as quickly as a severely injured man could. It was a race against time, and I needed to be perfect and quick.

8's eyes burned with rage, and he swung his venom rapier wildly, the blade hissing dangerously as it sliced through the air. The hisses sounded like snake strikes and were terrifying each time. This man was a master of his craft. Hammock was right; his skill was much deadlier than I could have imagined. Without my SAI controlling and enhancing my reflexes, I would have been dead. His strikes came close, but I deftly parried each one by seeing his muscles activate and my Hono dancing in my grip. I had to get as close as possible without dying, and I needed to make him angrier.

"Is this all you've got, Eddy?" I taunted, my voice dripping with contempt. "You've followed 9 for so long, and this is the best you can do? Swinging like a wild animal?"

He snarled in response, his movements growing even more erratic. With a furious cry, he lunged at me, and I sidestepped at the last moment, feeling the rush of air as his blade sliced off my jacket shoulder. It flapped off but did not break my skin. "Too close," I thought to myself.

"You got a C in Chemistry too, didn't you?" Dahlia continued to taunt. "You followed 9 blindly into this mess, and now you're going to die for it. He tried to have you deported. He called ICE on you like seven times. He made fun of you for voting for Trump Jr."

His anger was palpable now, and he came at me with greater fury. His strikes became faster but sloppier, and I parried each of his attacks because they seemed, well, programmed, deflecting his venomous strikes with my Hono. Yet the tip of the blade whistled past my ear with devastatingly close proximity, and small tuffs of my hair laced the ground. He was only missing me by millimeters at this point.

"You're pathetic!" I spat. "Your mom is more dangerous with a sandal than you are with a sword. Speaking of moms, did you know you used to call them 'olines' till your mom jumped on one and then they changed the name to trampolines?"

8's face contorted with confusion and then with rage, and he charged at me with a roar. I waited until the last possible moment, then dropped, scissoring his feet, sweeping the legs sending him sprawling to the ground. Cobra Kai would be proud. I stood over him, victorious but cautious. "You should have stayed in the shadows, 8. You were never meant to be a swordsman. You should have stuck to your guns."

"You glow like El Diablo! You are no ANGL Diez. I'll see you in hell!" he punctuated between his shallow breaths and a broken leg.

He reached for his venom rapier and, with a desperate and reckless move, lunged at me one last time. I blocked his strike with my Hono, the clash of metal echoing through the room. With a swift twist of my wrist, I swung his own rapier around, hitting his wrist and slicing a vein. The look of intense panic and terror washed over his face. He dropped his sword and gripped his wrist trying to stop the bleeding. He stumbled back, landing near his gun, and attempted to shoot himself with a universal antidote, a brief moment of relief washing over his face.

"Now!" Dahlia cried, as we threw his venom rapier hitting him in the hand and making him drop the gun before being able fire. The sword impaled itself into his shoulder. The next shot was loaded and ready to deliver the antidote. I grabbed the gun, pointed it at Hammock, pulled the trigger and the dart hit him in the other butt cheek. The right one, to be exact. It was a shot of the antidote that Eddy had queued up for himself and I prayed it would work universally.

"OW, you SON of a *bitch*!" he screamed.

Somehow, I was going to have to blame this on someone else.

Eddy was splayed on the ground suffering from the effects of his own poison, something I'd seen too often. He started huffing and breathing erratically. Medically, they call it Cheyne-Stokes breathing; shock was starting to set in as Eddy's eyes bounced back and forth.

"Don't you have an antidote to your own supply?" Dahlia asked to let it set in as we remembered the torture room Eddy would set up for women and children to get information out of anyone he could.

Eddy glanced at his gun, attempting a sloppy and feeble motion to reach for it. The venom from his rapier had injected a significant amount of poison into his bloodstream, leaving him with no recourse but to allow Dahlia to synchronize.

Gradually, Eddy's breathing became increasingly erratic. Slowing and speeding up, vacillating between deep and shallow. Dahlia pressed my head against Eddy's forehead just as he drew his last breath. His shallow and rapid breaths transformed into a single, drawn-out exhale, and then his body seemed to simply shut down. His eyes open and missing the spark of life.

My vision plunged into darkness, and I found myself a young boy running through a cold, sandy desert at night. The air was thick with dust, the kind that clung to my throat, making every breath feel dry and desperate. My bare feet pounded against the uneven ground, small rocks slicing into my soles, but I couldn't stop. I wouldn't stop.

Ahead of me, a woman ran, carrying a bag strapped across her back—not just any bag, but one holding an infant, pressed tightly to her chest. Her breath came in sharp, uneven bursts. She turned to me, her eyes wide with something deeper than fear. Something worse.

"Eduardo, mi amor, mira," she whispered, pointing just beyond the hill.

A small red light flickered in the distance, flashing twice, then once more. A signal. A man stood on the other side of a raging river, waiting for us. Waiting to take us to safety.

We waded into the frigid, churning water, the cold latching onto my skin like tiny needles. My mother clutched my wrist, steadying us

220

as the current fought to pull us under. She told me it would only be waist-deep.

She was wrong.

Suddenly, lights exploded to life behind us, cutting through the night like blades of white-hot fire. The roar of engines followed—deep, guttural, closing in fast. My mother's breath hitched. She turned sharply, eyes darting toward the approaching vehicles, and in that instant—she lost her footing.

I reached for her, grabbing desperately, fingers locking around her wrist. I wouldn't let go. I couldn't.

But she let go of me.

A deliberate release. A choice.

I screamed as she was swept away by the current, the infant's wails piercing through the chaos. The water carried her farther and farther until she was nothing but a dark shape swallowed by the river.

Rough hands grabbed me, yanking me out of the water with brute force. I thrashed, kicking, screaming, trying to break free, but the grip was unyielding. A man, his voice firm but not unkind, held me fast.

"She isn't dead," he told me. "The river carries many things away, but not all of them are lost."

I wanted to believe him. But I never saw her again.

I was a pudgy middle schooler being pushed around, the kind of kid who never quite fit, never quite belonged. Too soft, too small, too easy to pick on. I went home to a packed foster care house, where the beds were always full, and the faces around me changed like the seasons.

The one thing that never changed? Cooking.

Every night, I made dinner—for myself, for the kids that came and went, for the ones who stayed a little longer. It was the only thing I could control, the only thing that made the chaos feel manageable. I worked after school at a bakery, kneading dough, dusting sugar over pastries, perfecting my tres leches until people lined up for it.

But one night, I was followed home. Two men. Not from the neighborhood. They didn't care about my baking. They didn't want desserts. They wanted me to move something else.

Drugs.

It was easy money, they said. No risk. No danger. Just deliver the packages. The bakery was a front, and I had unknowingly walked into its underbelly.

I refused.

They found another way to make me listen. One evening, my sister stopped by the bakery, just to pick up dessert. That's all. She never made it home unscathed.

They beat her—not for what she had done, but for what I had refused to do.

She came home silent, bruised, her lip split, her arms wrapped around herself like she could keep the pain inside if she just held tight enough.

That was the moment something inside me snapped.

That night, I baked a cake. A special one. A week later, the entire family of the man responsible was dead. Every single one.

The poison was undetectable, slow enough to be eaten without suspicion, fast enough that none of them woke up. By the time I was ever suspected, I had already risen through the ranks of the cartel that owned the bakery.

And the bakery? It was no longer just a bakery. I was no longer just a kid. Before the age of fifteen, I'd perfected something that changed everything.

Hyperion Beta.

Not just another drug—a new class of stimulant. A formula so potent it could excite chemical receptors multiple times per dose without causing permanent degradation. Unlike traditional drugs that burned out the nervous system, mine kept it running, kept it craving, kept it needing.

Pain? It didn't just dull it. It rewired it. Pleasure and pain became indistinguishable. A high so powerful, so addictive, that even those who swore they'd never touch it couldn't walk away.

The cartel rose to the top. We controlled entire cities. Then, like all things in this life—it fell.

I expected death when I was finally arrested. A bullet, a quick execution.

Instead, I got Robinson.

He came to my cell with an offer. "Help me and I'll find your mother. Your little brother. If they're still alive." I searched his face for the catch, the trap.

"You know what I've done?" I asked in Eddy's voice and accent.

He nodded. "I know exactly what you've done." And still, he made the offer.

He understood that deporting me wouldn't solve anything—that I would only go somewhere else and become something worse.

So I took the deal.

And that was how I found myself sitting in the back of a truck next to Blaze Tanner.

A blinding white flash erupted behind my eyes, the kind that didn't just obscure vision—it scrambled thought. My body convulsed, my muscles locking as fingers tightened around my throat.

The pressure was precise. Measured. Not just brute force, but controlled—like whoever was holding me knew exactly how much strength was needed to keep me conscious.

A flash of light and then came the voice. 7's voice. His deep Russian accent. It cut through the chaos, sharp and unwavering, each word weighted with certainty and control. "You heard me! Bring back his SAI and his brain."

The grip tightened slightly, just enough to make me more aware of how fragile my airway really was.

"I will run NJC. And together, we will prove that 5's predictions are fallible. She's been wrong before and can't be right all of the time, certainly not this time. Too many variables."

There was something almost…obsessive in the way he said it. Like he was convinced of his own inevitability.

"She can't foresee the future. She only makes guesses based on the information. I made sure the information she's gotten works out for me, or us rather."

The way he spat the words made it clear—he wanted her to be wrong. Needed her to be wrong.

"9 may have been reckless, as always, but Mark is no Arch-Soul."

I heard the conviction in his voice.

The absolute belief. But underneath it, buried so deep it was barely noticeable, there was something else.

Doubt.

Chapter 18
All Roads Lead to Aramantha

"Mark, there's a cage on the table in the kitchen with a rattlesnake in it and some cake in the fridge, and I don't know what the heck to do with any of that!" Dahlia said nervously.

"Just say no to drugs," I said in an attempt to start easing the tension with a hint of sarcasm as I walked to Hammock.

"Did you see any of that? I'm beginning to think there might be a pattern here," Dahlia exclaimed.

"How are you feeling, sir?" I asked Hammock as I helped him up.

Hammock allowed me to grasp a hand gently help him to his feet before he violently throat punched me.

"CHUJHSIUSUCBCH!" I choked.

"That's for shooting me in the ass, consider us even," Hammock angered.

"But I saved your life!" I wheezed.

"Instead of letting me die with dignity," Hammock said as he walked toward Patterson, then paused turned toward me and despite me dodging some of the most expertly placed ripostes, his knife-hand cut me in two.

"I've got far more demons than you ever will, son, and I was finally at peace with them. Now get over here and help me with this bag of asscracks. How did you do that by the way?"

"Do what?" I asked, genuinely confused.

"You deflected and dodged his sword strikes. They were headed right at you but just glancing away at the last possible second," Hammock responded. "And you were doing that weird heat wave thing again too."

"Heh, he's no Neo," Dahlia said through shifty eyes, and then I felt my eyes widen. "Hammy, your cough," the words carried off my tongue with hope and excitement.

"How many times do I have to tell you don't…wait, you're right, it's gone too," Hammock said with relief. "Angel 10, immediate battlefield data retcon status." And then Hammock ran two fingers down the center of my forehead. "This is the last time we will ever do this, son, with this action I will activate a data processing feature for simple integrative tasks. Don't overuse it, or you'll have an aneurysm. We would pull it through a data port for combat reports, but now there's no connection thanks to your alter ego. Might as well put your installed system to good use."

I felt a warm, familiar and lucid sensation run down the center of my head to my SAI, then Dahlia pushed words to me like chef presenting a platter of food to a premier food critique. "Uh, Hyperian Beta is a synthetic drug that excites, releases and then re-excites the receptors. They are tiny machines that stay in the hypothalamus till their charge runs out. They make connections in the brain and create feelings of euphoria, intense focus, clonus reflexive ability and can either block out pain or cause intense sensations of excruciating pain. They are imitations of the cellular mutations caused by the SAI implant. Hyperian Sigma has been produced and distributed. Results and side effects unknown."

Hammock took another step closer. "Battlefield Equipment Retcon Status Report," he said and handed me one of Eddy's pistols. The grip glowed the same green in my hand as it had when Eddy held it.

"I got an interface notification Hammy, recipients unknown. Patient Zero of Jeepers Peepers 2.0, deactivated," Dahlia said. Then he twisted a button on the rear of the pistol.

Tone – 3 Rounds remaining. Next round Lethal. Confirm?

"Anything in that system menu of yours strong enough to heal Patterson?" asked Hammock as he sat him in a chair that he'd salvaged from the battle royale of a living room.

Dahlia answered, "There was a nanogel pack in the firetruck. The truck's blown to bits, and the gel is definitely gone too. He's going to need to get back to NJC. You have authoritative command, Hammy." I jerked my head to the sky. "You can take Whisperwing. Help me load him up," I said to Hammock as I started to grab Patterson's arm.

"You will be a sitting duck. The mercs will find you fast, drones faster and you will lose your only insurance policy," Hammock argued.

We were hours away from the Deathball game and if one thing went wrong, thousands of people would die.

I gave Hammock the gun and my orders. Hammock looked at me with judgmental eyes and I just shrugged, to which he said, "That was way too much woman for you and you knew it then and you know it now!"

I blushed, and with a sense of trepidation, I activated the map on my Hololens, the glowing interface illuminating the uncertainty of my impending journey. As the map materialized before me, I couldn't help but feel a pang of apprehension at the options it presented. The fastest route to my new destination led straight through the heart of the most dangerous streets, where I had crossed paths with The

Waste's most notorious offenders. Each alleyway and thoroughfare was a potential battleground, a reminder of the risks that lurked around every corner.

On the other hand, the longer route skirted around the edges of the city, leading me through Outpost checkpoints manned by vigilant guards. While it offered a safer passage, it also posed its own set of challenges. A single misstep could land me in hot water, branded as a criminal and sentenced to a fate worse than death within the confines of a prison cell.

Caught between the devil and the deep blue sea, I weighed my options carefully, knowing that each decision could mean the difference between life and death. In the end, I had no choice but to trust my instincts and forge ahead. I decided to head to Aramantha and take the fastest route through The Waste.

Aramantha, the wandering merchant city, was a roving carnival if you may. It was a bustling and chaotic spectacle on wheels. Comprised mainly of sprawling resto-RVs and campers, these nomadic traders strategically parked their vehicles between The Waste and the Outposts or SafeCities. That made everyone want to partake because people got to see the real sky for a change. It was like Christmas in July for Aramantha to arrive. The air was real, the sky was real, the people were real. They had enough vendors to fully encircle most outposts. They were usually set up by noon and packed up at midnight. Rumor has it that more illegal wares exchanged hands here than any other place, but because they never actually came into an Outpost or Safe-City, there was no way to police the transactions. Every time they packed up, they celebrated by playing music and dancing. To safeguard their bustling trade, they boasted their own cadre of DWARs, security personnel, remotely controlled drones, and I even heard they had hacked a Hunter/Killer. The most dangerous biped automaton on the planet. A necessity in the hazardous wasteland environment.

For residents of outlying outposts or smaller domes lacking comprehensive shopping options, Aramantha's allure was virtually irresistible. However, the timing and location of its appearances remained enigmatically unpredictable. Many families saved up just for the visit and had an *Aramantha list*, and no matter how exotic, you could purchase it there. If it was truly a one-off thing, you could place an order on the crypto market and pick it up once they arrived. Once docked, they would be there for twelve hours. That's it.

Aramantha was under the capable governance of Harmony Smith, a notable figure who had presided over the SAI ANGL project two decades ago, including my own integration. How she went from government project intercessor to nomadic *Mad Maxine*, I have no idea. And from what I understand, she negotiated a portable Halosphere from Kimberly Florres. A one-of-a-kind product in exchange for an undisclosed item. Yet, one minor hiccup marred the otherwise smooth operation. Harmony left the Corps five years prior to my exit because the adjudication of our skills was abhorrent in her eyes. It just so happened that she and I had crossed paths during my travels in The Waste when I was investigating Tagadashi. It was my first assignment. She was elated that I was making an effort to retire and she herself couldn't believe they would let an asset like me go. I mentioned earlier the drinks and dancing, well, one thing led to another, and you can probably guess the rest. Her son, the infamous wasteland socialite known as DouchebagSteve, had an unpleasant surprise for us when he walked in on our intimate encounter. He had no real power, only money accrued from his social influence due to his terrible attitude inherited from his father. In a fit of rage, he promptly issued a five-million-dollar reward in untraceable cryptocurrency for a rather unconventional target – my manhood. He objectively called it the "Dick-bounty." Interestingly, the bounty came with an unusual clause: if I were to meet my demise during the collection, the reward would become null and void. Since that fateful incident, venturing into the wasteland was an absolute nightmare for me. They don't talk, and he's not a part of Aramantha, but it's still a thing.

Now, I'm hopping on a motorcycle belonging to a now-deceased Eduardo "Rattlesnake" Ramirez, a man whose past could fill its own tragic novel. Sidenote: He had one hell of a childhood. But that's not my problem anymore.

Right now, my focus was Harmony Smith—because I needed to sneak back into NJC.

The plan? Aramantha. A city sitting on the fringes of regulation, home to a mobile door—a technological backdoor capable of creating an entrance into a Halosphere. She'd derived the technology while moving the entrance of their own big purple dome.

Harmony had mentioned it once, casually, in the kind of way people reveal classified information when they're pressed against you in bed, still tangled in the warmth of the moment.

I had asked her how she moved between cities undetected—how she slid past checkpoints, bypassed SafeCity protocols, lived like she was invisible.

She had smirked, trailing her fingers along my arm before whispering, *"I have my ways."*

Turns out, her ways included a banned piece of tech capable of warping security grids and forcing open closed doors.

Perfect.

"Aramantha is thirty minutes away by motorcycle," Dahlia said aloud, their voice cutting through my thoughts. "After Whisperwing drops off Patterson, it will return there to pick us up."

Simple.

In that time, I needed to do two things:

1. Reach Harmony.

2. Procure one of the most dangerous items to the Union States imaginable.

Oh, and while doing all that? Avoid getting my head mounted on a government-issued spike. Because apparently, there's now a bounty on my ass. Which, this morning, seemed like the worst thing that could happen.

Then the president died. Then I found out I killed him. And somehow? That was also bad. *Can we go back to when that was the worst thing I had to worry about?* I thought to myself.

"Nope this is much more fun," Dahlia said out loud after intercepting my thought.

I loaded Patterson's battered and broken body into Whisperwing. He groaned and grunted. But still was able to smile and thank me. For a man that went toe to toe with an ANGL he did well to still be breathing. I gave him what meds we could find to help with the swelling and pain. Hammock hopped in the nav position and was given a surprise when the UI was different.

"What in the hell is this?" he demanded.

"Tagadashi's touch," I responded as I didn't want to tell him too much about Genji. But as soon as I said it, I loved the moniker.

"Well, I don't know what the hell to do, all of this is just gibberish, Mark," Hammock bellowed.

I had an idea. I walked over to the hovercraft and placed my hand on the handprint left there and felt the connection left there by Genji. Communicating with Whisperwing was just like talking to someone through a chat window.

Tone- Load two parties in both bays. Identify. Patterson – Gunner. Hammock – Nav

Tone – Navigate destination NJC – Immediate Medical Relief Required

Tone – Immediately Locate Arch-Soul Mark, Identified by Arch-Soul Genji

"Everyone knew BUT me?" I yelled out loud to no one in particular.

I took the other sword out of the bay just in case. I had the Hono on my right hip, which I had not actually used to its actual capacity yet, and the ancient sword was there now on my back. *Better to have and not need it, right?* I thought quietly.

We said our goodbyes and planned a rendezvous in the city. I grabbed the broken dart gun, and was able to load one round successfully, mounted the motorcycle and took off toward Aramantha. There was no helmet, which was a bit worrying. But there was a box on the back, empty, I assumed for my head.

"No one can hear you scream in The Waste," Dahlia said as we set out.

The enduro-bike was primed for getting around in The Waste. There was no trash pickup, or civil services so the roads could be hard to get around at times. Zig-zagging between burned-out hulls and giant potholes made this the ideal vehicle for bouncing between cities. If your home was robbed, set ablaze, or needed water service, there was no one to call if you were outside any city centers. The interstates between Outposts were heavily patrolled and policed. Though, the city centers of the Liberty States struggled with basic utilities due to their lack of layered infrastructure reliability. Harsh weather year-round meant limited resources. Streetlights and road maintenance on rural roads were nonexistent, which led to the likelihood of bandits and pirates. Once within the cities things weren't so bad, but traveling, that was the rub.

We have two options, slower residential roads with lots of escape routes or the faster interstate with fewer escape routes. Both have about the same chances of an ambush. The bike has a battery pack so I will have surprise on my side.

Our fate was decided for us when the entrance to I-90 was blocked by a federal caravan looking for the president's killer. A large digital billboard with my face adorned on it with the words "Have you seen me? Suspected Fugitive *Armed and Dangerous.*"

"Huh, almost forgot about that," Dahlia said, as I ripped off the hanging sleeve and tied it around our face as if that wasn't going to draw any attention to us. Satellite would likely be tracking Whisperwing if it goes the way I planned, giving me at least thirty minutes of a head start. I couldn't take a chance by driving through a checkpoint.

"How could you almost forget we are fugitives?" I asked Dahlia.

"No, the movie with John Candy, *Armed and Dangerous.* It's Hilarious," Dahlia corrected me quickly.

"Did you ever let me sleep, Dahlia?" I asked with real concern.

"Oh yeah, like all the time, dude," Dahlia lied before taking off on the motorcycle.

We cut through most streets fine with no issues as we expected. While many people moved away from the suburbs, those that stayed in those areas kept it pretty nice. The lawns were cut, the homes weren't left in ruin.

I chanced turning on the headlights as dusk was giving way to night, then to my surprise, my Hololens was illuminated in a green hue, but nothing else could see the light.

"I'm seeing it too, I have no idea," Dahlia read my thought and responded out loud.

"I'm gonna try this," I said before I took two fingers and ran them down my forehead and said, "SAI Interface Equipment Assessment Request."

Tone- Holo Night Vision projection. The images you see are fed from a camera mounted on handlebars are fed through a communications node synced to Eduardo Ramirez.

"Who was now kind of living in my head," I added

Dahlia's voice and mine sync'd. "Nice."

As we bobbed and weaved making good time, I heard a faint buzzing sound, like a lawn mower or a chainsaw.

"I know you hear that," Dahlia said and then mocked the voice in my head, in my voice out loud. "I hear you thinking, 'hmmm, what's that sound, is that a lawnmower or a chainsaw'?"

"Um yeah, I guess you hear it too," I placated.

Just as my words left my lips, a sudden swarm of gas-powered go-karts came racing around a blind corner, forcing me to slam on the brakes to avoid a disastrous collision. Within moments, a second wave of vehicles, comprising another five or six go-karts, approached from behind. While I theoretically could have maneuvered my way through the chaos, a quick threat assessment led me to believe that it wasn't worth the risk.

But the spectacle was far from over. Soon, a motley crew of electric dirt bikes, ebikes, and electric scooters materialized on the scene, all ridden by a rowdy bunch of suburban teenagers. Their arrival was accompanied by an unexpected twist—they began to emit a series of barks. However, given that most of them had only recently embarked on the journey of puberty, their vocal efforts fell more in line with the cacophonous yapping of Pomeranian puppies than the menacing howls of a wolf pack, which I suspected was their intended effect. DMX began, at that very moment, to turn in his grave.

Amidst this youthful pandemonium, the self-proclaimed leader of the pack, who would later introduce himself as P-Dub, gracefully dismounted his scooter. Ever the gentleman, he ensured his lady companion alighted first, a testament to his chivalrous nature even in the midst of this bizarre encounter.

"Nice Bike. Who are you, tadpole?" he asked as he approached me with an aluminum Little League bat in hand, and for posterity's sake a steak knife taped on the end with clear scotch tape. A lot of tape. Several rolls of scotch tape.

"I'm the guy who's going to…" Dahlia started, and I finished. "Answer your questions," I said calmly and slowly.

"What's your name?" I asked in a soft and non-threatening tone.

"P-Dub, now give me your sword…so I can hold it." He pointed the bat at my face with the knife a few inches from the tip of my nose. His face scrunched up as if he'd just eaten a taco fart. It was getting dark, and I wondered if the Hono glowed a little. I wasn't lost, but Safe Passage would be nice. And to get that first I needed some brownie points.

"How about I show you what it can do instead," I said as I leaned in until his dull kitchen knife pressed into my forehead.

While still sitting on the bike, I drew the Hono and concentrated on the edge. With one motion, I unsheathed the sword and sliced the bat in half. The area where the sword made contact with the bat glowed red hot, along with the slightest edge of the blade. The knife-end flung through the air, end over end, before landing in someone's well-manicured lawn. The resident began looking out of their curtains and then quickly shut them when the heads of the Pomeranian-inspired crew turned their way.

The entire gang of kids let out a uniform soft "whooooooaaaa!" followed by silence, and an almost indiscernible weep.

"I…I needed that," P-Dub said softly. "Harrison Davis Lewis is going to be so angry!"

"Who are they? Did they hurt you? Where are they?" Dahlia asked quickly.

"He's…he's my brother," P-Dub retorted.

"Which one?" Dahlia demanded.

"J-J-J Just, just the one," P-Dub asserted.

"Is it Harrison or Davis or Lewis? P-Dub," Dahlia quipped as patience thinned.

"That's my brother's name," P-Dub responded in kind.

"Okay, we are making progress, so you have three brothers," Dahlia celebrated, annoyed.

"No, I have one brother and his name is Harrison Davis Lewis," P-Dub implied with a duh.

"Your brother…let me get this straight, has three…last…names? What sort of moronic, asinine, uncouth, fickle, daft, dingleberry has three last names as a first name?" Dahlia said while obviously not reading the crowd.

P-Dubs shoulders slumped into a whimper.

"Oh! Oh God," Dahlia spat as my hand reached up to my mouth, and then I spoke through my fingers. "What's P-Dub short for?"

"Parker…Wilson…Thompson," P-Dub said before breaking down into full tears.

"Uh, listen kid, I'm sorry," Dahlia attempted to apologize before P-Dub found his grit and yelled, "Get him!"

I was looking behind me in my rearview watching the little crotch goblins shrink in the distance as I took off at full speed, when a van pulled in front of my escape route. Two trucks were placed on either side of the road to create a choke point, and if I weren't watching the hump dumplings, I would have had better situational awareness. But instead, I had to lay down the bike in order to keep it in working order.

I popped up quickly and watched as a muscled tank top, running shorts, acne bro with big hair, yellow eyes, and yellow spittle, step out of the van and walk toward me and say, "Hyperion bruh?"

236

"Excuse me?" I shot back, stretching my neck, hoping that it would help me understand what in the heck was going on.

He pointed at the motorcycle on the ground. "This bike, that box, you, Hyperion Bruh? I take Alpha." And with his other hand held out a credit transfer NFC.

By this time, the peanut gallery had caught up back up with me and encircled me yet again. P-Dub ran up to the muscle-clad-meme-of-a chad and said, "Harrison, I'm sorry."

Harrison looked down at his little brother with his giant muscles, contorted face, bright yellow eyes, and yellow drool and said, "If you can't get me Hyperion, you go the back yard and sleep with mom." All of the other kids took a step back but didn't run. They obviously relied on this man for food or shelter, or even just a sense of belonging. This wasn't a problem I could solve by killing him.

P-Dub Recoiled, "NO! I don't want to Di…Sleep! I won't mess up again. We will go and find things to trade for you. Promise Harrison."

"Mark, are you thinking what I'm thinking?" Dahlia said out loud.

"I think so. Walter White?" I replied.

"Let's get to cooking," Dahlia said slyly.

I pulled out the dart gun and Harrison brandished his gun, a rather large revolver, and a PSD. His Hyperion habit had been very lucrative for him. Not only had it made him extremely strong and aggressive, but he'd gotten to keep the spoils of his battles. I had only one shot and I put my mind to work to reverse the effects of Hyperion permanently.

He took sloppy aim and fired off three shots in quick succession. The children scattered and started screaming. Dogs started barking and someone yelled from their home. Mayhem ensued in the briefest of moments. I jumped to his non-dominant side, but he tracked the barrel of the gun all too well, and I heard the welcome click of an empty chamber. I pressed the attack and closed the distance between me and the boy with three names. Our bodies met and he was solid. It was like hitting a bag filled with sand.

He moved, but his feet moved quickly under him, preventing a takedown. As I hopped up our eyes met. His cheeks were permanently constricted, a side effect of the Hyperion, no doubt. His eyes didn't just look crazy, but the tiny robots danced crazily where the whites should be. The little bots were taking their turns controlling the pleasure center of his brain. That's when I noticed our strengths matched. My strength on my worst day as an ANGL was equivalent to an Olympic power lifter. I could dead lift in excess of a ton. I could outrun any normal human from a dead sleep. This seventeen-year-old Zach Effron High School Musical knockoff was matching my strength and speed. By the way, I was going to kick Dahlia's ass for watching that instead of allowing me to rest.

Tone – Hyperion Delta Champion Detected. 1 in 500 users will experience chromosomal changes. 499 out 500 will experience highly addictive tendencies and symptoms. 1 will be changed at the cellular level. Most will die from overdose on exposure.

"You left the automated user interface on, Mark?" Dahlia lamented kind of jealously.

Triple name reached for the sword on my back, it was obvious he was playing for keeps. A weapon like that in the hands of this super-powered-creatine-three-named-teen could derail everything, so carefully planned.

I reached into the repertoire of moves this boy had used and determined he'd only seen in choreographed fight scenes. So, I relied on the most intricate martial arts moves I had learned over the years and loaded a combo in my SAI. As his hands barely touched the hilt of the ancient Japanese priceless masterpiece on my back, I reared back and kicked him square in the nuts.

His instinct for self-defense became paramount as he reached for his remaining cojones and hunched over, one hand shielding his crotch, the other bracing against a tree. I must have struck with significant force, for he turned to us and then, in a moment reminiscent of a scene that might have envied even the most dramatic cinematic portrayals of the exorcist, expelled his meal with remarkable intensity.

I took no chances, stepped three quick steps backwards and shot Harrison directly in the jugular with my only dart. The effects of the contents of the dart were immediately visible just under the skin, crawling its way up the neck, then the throat. The vines of silvery liquid spiderwebbed up his cheeks to temples and then into his eyes, turning the yellow sclera gray like storm clouds before disappearing into the brain.

He fell onto his knees, holding his head in his hands, screaming in agony. Kicking while his palms covered his eye sockets. At first, I thought I'd killed him. I had come to terms with it and it was justified given how he had possibly killed his mother, and maybe others. Then he fell forward, and started calling out, "Parker, Parker, help me! I'm sorry! Where are you?"

Parker ran and hugged Harrison. Harrison's eyes were instantly turning white, and his face wasn't contorted. "What did you do to my brother?" P-Dub asked angrily.

"We reversed the effects of Hyperion. He can't ever take it again. We reprogrammed the Hyperion nanites inside of him," I said.

"Who's we? Do you have three names too?" Parker asked.

"Don't start with me again, you thrice-named participation trophy. Actually, I have two names, but that's not the point," Dahlia said.

"Ooookaaayyyyy," P-Dub said, confused.

"It's a long story and I've got to go, my people need me, can you point me toward…" I was trying to ask without leaving too many details or clues.

"Aramantha is ten minutes up the road, sir, take the dirt road behind the brick house on the corner and no one will bother you," Harrison interjected. "That's the only reason anyone comes through here today. If you go through any other road, you'll be stopped, robbed or worse. Hyperion row is one town over, and it's impossible to get through it. There are few more Hype Ghouls…" Harrison paused lost in a thought and then started talking again. "Thats what they called me…a hype ghoul. Some guy who was riding the same motorcycle you're on…he…" Harrison got choked up a bit before recomposing himself. "I'll never forget what you did for me. My mind is clear and I don't know what I would have done if you hadn't come along. All I could think about was Hyperion. Every single moment. Sir, can you come back and help me when you're done doing what you need in Aramantha? I know it's a lot to ask," Harrison begged as he held his little brother.

Before I could even give it thought, Dahlia walked up and hugged them. "Here's a credit chip and my Inios contact info, I'll be back, I don't know when. It will be soon, but, if you drop me a message I'll get it and reply fast. Now, take this money, and go buy a proper first name, and some new clothes. You need a shirt that fits. Bye-bye now."

I ran and picked up the motorcycle, waved goodbye to my new munchkin friends, Dahlia cursed them out, smiled, and we headed off, yet again to Aramantha. I found the trail behind the brick house. It was an old overgrown walking path or greenway.

We came up on the outskirts of Aramantha, and I heard the music, saw the caravan, and smelled the food. I realized I hadn't eaten anything at all. My stomach rumbled. I promised myself that if I passed a burger or a hot dog, I'd grab one…or four.

Chapter 19
A Decent Proposal

The line of armored vehicles was impressive. It was a fully encircled Outpost. My old home of all places. This was more than risky, and yet I had no choice. I drove for a few minutes before I found a line of people waiting to get in an entrance guarded by a federal drone and sentry. I kept moving till I found a place to hide the bike in an underbrush. I leaped on top of an RV and was immediately spotted by a digital sensor. A proximity alarm blared and a sentry gun shot three taser nodes. The first two tingled, but the third hurt. I hopped down and tried to blend in with the crowd.

I should have known that there would have been line of sight alarms to keep people from just hopping over the trucks. Someone pointed me out to one of the armed guards and I dipped into one of the dark rooms. It was an RV camper. A nice one too. One with a kitchen, bathroom, and bedroom. Around twelve people were in there and the door closed firmly behind me. I heard the voice up front near the driver's seat. A heavy, almost cartoonish Bostonian man with of an indistinguishable accent stood at the front. He was wearing a shiny green suit with matching leather boots.

"Now listen, these won't be cheap, 50,000 crypto credits each. The last one I sold to Tagadashi Jr and he tested them out for me. They took down three of his dad's men, no fuss. I bought extra, and now you dingbats get to fight over the leftovers."

"Yeah, bet one of 'em wasn't Genji, though, he's a freak of nature," said a midwestern accent from my left.

Unbothered by the interruption Mr. Boston Celtics kept going, "I call it the goody box. 1-Syrian Decibel Grenade, 1-Phillipine Pepper Bomb, 1-Alaskan Torch and two of my personal new favorite, The Nightmare on Elm Street. It's new, fresh from the beaker. This breaks your brain, extreme hallucinations, inability to determine reality from fantasy. Folks, we've digitized magic mushrooms. It's an instant psilocybin and it affects each brain differently. But it will make anyone batshit crazy almost instantly."

"If Harmony catches you with this stuff…" started a voice from the front.

"Harmony will not catch me, because you won't tell her unless you want me to tell her about those other things. There's no honor among thieves, my fair-weather friends," he said in a snide and vindictive tone. "Now, who wants a box?"

"Open up in there," demanded a voice, before the banging on the door started. Boom-Boom-Boom!

"Who snitched!?" cried the main attraction barker as everyone's eyes turned to me.

"Who's the new guy?" asked a woman.

"Yeah, who are you?" mirrored the man standing next her, and then silence.

And thanks to Dahlia, in all of the infinite wisdom available in the teraflops of data and relentless nights of movies absorbed into my brain and SAI, my mouth opened and Dahlia proclaimed, "I'm Lil' Moe with the gimpy leg," and began to hobble around the room whilst twitching my right eye and saying, "One of you were here last night smooching with my brother."

"What are you doing?" I whispered through my teeth.

"Just play along," Dahlia gritted back.

"Petey, we got to get out of here. If we get caught, we will get kicked out of Aramantha for good this time," said the only woman in the box truck.

The banging on the door got louder. "Open up or we will break the door down."

The man wearing the green suit threw a small fit and said, "FINE!" He pulled a lever beside the passenger's seat and the bed in the rear lifted to reveal a set of stairs to the small carnival. Everyone scurried, and Mr. Boston Celtics put the boxes of contraband in the cabinets, locking them with a biometric code after closing them. I patiently waited, hobbling, trying to still sell the Lil' Moe with the Gimpy Leg story and he turned to me at the top of the steps and puts his finger in my chest. He started poking in the chest as he talking.

"I don't know who you are or where you came from, but they don't do well to people who are uninvited. Wait a minute, I know you, you're that dick bounty fella…"

Just as he said that I gently pushed him down the steps and closed the bed down and shut the door. I jammed the door just enough to make sure it was obvious which way they went.

I ripped open the cabinets and Dahlia grabbed a goody box and shoved the contents down my pants. I only wanted to see what was in the cabinets, but Dahlia had other ideas. At this point, the door was being wrenched open. I could hear a commotion coming from the bedroom because I was sure someone wanted to collect the bounty as well. I looked up and pressed my luck to jump out of the roof fan vent. But not before grabbing a wrapped sandwich just sitting on the counter. After making it to the roof, I sprawled prone to avoid any sentry weapons. Instead there were three Battle-worn Tokyo Prime Remote Units waiting for me.

Indestructible machine learning sentry robots made of the same material as my Hono with preprogrammed reflexes to avoid physical harm. PSD Tech built in and pretty much everything you would *never* want to see. These units were obviously repurposed and taken during the AI wars after being hit out in the open with an EMP. I reached into my pants to feel around for the Alaskan Torch. The lasers would disorient the targeting sensors so I could have a chance of possibly making a run for it when a sassy voice came from one.

"Don't tell me you're so horny you gonna rub one out right here, right now, sweetheart," she said before laughing at her own joke.

"Harmony? You look a little different from the last time we saw each other," I replied.

She got serious and direct. "Follow Johnny-5, try not to draw any attention to yourself, and eat that sandwich quietly."

The trucks all had a rigged connecting mezzanine linking a walkway. All of the gun sentries were powered down around us and were pointed at the roofs of the RVs. I ate my sandwich and followed the highly illegal and deadly remote-controlled robots.

The bots started to lead me toward a large silver camper with an oblong, egg-shaped metal dome on the top it the size of a truck tire. The first kill-bot walked up to grab the edge and lifted, revealing a metal ladder.

"In, quick before someone sees you," said her voice from the bot.

Dimly lit by the screens of several feeds from Amarantha sat a woman I hadn't seen in almost two years in a high back chair. Her hair long and thick, her skin a deep chocolate and her figure full. She looked at me through thick glasses that she often looks over, and just as on brand, she had on a witty T-shirt that read, "I don't have both the time to explain it and crayons to draw it out for you."

"Well, if it isn't the most wanted man in the world," Harmony Smith said in a sweet Tennessee voice as she stood and walked over to me. She hugged me and handed me a drink.

"Now, why? Why did you kill the president and why shouldn't I turn you in? Before you respond you need to know you're wanted by the Liberty States so they can trade you in for war criminals. They are searching for you. There's ten-million-dollar Republic Territory Bounty on you. Union States are matching it. There are even lesser-known parties dipping their feet in to chase after you. Even my son wants to pay a million dollar per inch."

I choked on my drink. "Per inch? When did the bounty go up to ten million?"

She cackled, and it didn't last, her face lost some of its joy and her voice the mirth. "Mark, what happened?"

"Can you repair the audio in a damaged Holocube?" I asked in desperation pulling the cube out of my pocket and holding it in between the two of us.

"Place it in that tray there, sweetheart," she said as she sat back down. She sat and crossed her legs and watched as a light blue liquid climbed up the sides into the cracks of the Holocube. She quietly got up and walked over to the cube, moved it to another tray, and cast the immersion all around us. The audio fully worked this time.

President Mason: "I can't breathe. Every time I lay down to sleep, I just can't breathe. I haven't slept since I got the file."

Me: "The file had a nanovirus on it. We didn't know. It was designed to be able to track you down. If you can't be tracked down in time, then it's designed to kill you. Hammock is dying too."

President Mason: "Is there a treatment? Is there an antidote? I don't want to end up like my brother in law. My wife already went through a lot."

Me: "I have something that can give you a little longer. But that will just give 8 more time to find you. When he finds you, he will want to know what you were going to do with his file, and who you're working with."

President Mason: "I wanted to expose the team you used to be a part of and the crimes they committed. The world needs to know what you did. Things like the hospital in Cambodia."

Me: "I will make sure it's exposed. I've got the ball rolling."

President Mason: "How long do I have? How bad is it?"

Me: "Another day, maybe two. And it's best you didn't know."

President Mason: "What do we do?"

Me: "I have an idea. Something to get the attention of the world. I have a device that can disrupt the Halos in a 5x5 sphere. I know you keep a pistol in your drawer in the unlikely event that you'll need it. Hand it to me."

President Mason: "Just go ahead and do it. I'd rather die for something than live for nothing."

Then the gunshot rang out. The audible thud of his body hit the floor.

"You're watching this like you haven't seen it before," Harmony said as she peered into my eyes. I stood there with a thousand-yard stare trying to make sense of it all.

"This is my first time seeing it," I explained. I told Harmony the full story, leaving out the Arch-Soul and Dahlia part, but explaining that I'd had some memory issues of late. Dahlia and I decided it was best that we not share things that could endanger her.

When I finished, she leaned in and said, "So let me get this straight, Hammock coerced you to exit the corps when you started to outperform the other ANGLs in battlefield performance. This was because your SAI unique integration was off the charts. Hammock used his credentials to steal the files on the rest of team in order to gain leverage to save your skin. These files were laced with a synthetic virus created by 8 that infected President Mason, Sgt Hammock, Kimberly Florres, Dimitri Voynev, and Ryan Simmons.

"Tagadashi Hiroshi saw you murder the president and offered you help because the system needs a reboot. 9 and 8 tracked you down in The Waste to collect that SAI and you've bested them, and now you're here looking for a way to get back into NJC because 7 wants to turn it into a military state by spreading Hyperion Theta at the Deathball game tomorrow night and use your SAI to control all of the Zombie Hyperion addicts. Did I get that right? Oh, wait and you shot Hammock in the ass with a dart gun and saved his life before he throat-punched you. That was my favorite part by the way; I love a good throat punch, so romantic."

Harmony flashed a smile, then to a straight face. "Boy, what in God's name is wrong with you? Take the Holocube, clear your name. If you take one step into NJC tonight, you're as good as dead," she said with genuine concern. "7 has a plan to sow chaos and then bring peace. At this point, there is little to nothing you can do to derail his plan. I say this as the woman who designed the project you want to tear down. I tried to tear it down too. I have been trying to tear it down. You don't know what it cost me," she said as she placed her hand over her stomach. She walked to the corner of the RV and there was a picture of the thirteen of us. 10 ANGLs, SGT Hammock, Harmony, and Brooke Smith. The original test subject, Harmony's little sister.

"7 is not just someone who lies for fun. His games of manipulation are so good he can build or raze nations with just phone calls. Mason's dead because 7 wanted him dead. Not because you killed him. 9 and 8 are dead because…"

"7 ate 9?" Dahlia couldn't resist.

"No, you dumbass, because 7 knew what was going to happen. A replenishment of the ranks. The skill difference between Dimitri and Eddy is like comparing Michael Jordan to a high school benchwarmer. You could never cross swords with Dimitri, Mark. You got lucky. Beyond lucky. And you're telling me he's going to breed a small army of Hype-Mutes and you want to challenge him openly? In a day's time? You might be good, but your sync ain't that good." She chided me.

"If I can take out your three murderbots in less thirty seconds will you help me?" I asked seriously.

"You really have a death wish, don't you?" She shook her head and stood.

"If you can take one out in thirty seconds, I'll help. These robots are indestructible. Self-healing, poly lenticular metallic plating. Your sword will just bounce off. They have their own PSD. Unless you have an EMP in your pocket, this won't work, Mark. Their defenses are reflexive and built-in. If you try to kill them, they will defend themselves in kind. If you're unsuccessful, there's nothing I can do," she said reluctantly as she was forced to follow me to the roof of the RV.

"Hammock said you owe me an instruction booklet," I said as I kneeled in front of my steel opponent.

"I can't watch, don't do this. This is suicide," Harmony said as she partially covered her eyes.

I took two fingers and swiped up on my forehead and said, "Fully engage 8, 9 and 10 SAI BattleSync"

Tone – Full Sync Engaged, multiple Cores detected. Full Sync Complete.

Perched atop the swaying rooftop of the RV, I brandished the Hono, my senses honed to a razor's edge as I faced off against the towering robot. The murderbot entered battle mode without any warning or preamble as I brandished my sword. With a swift backhand strike, I aimed to catch the machine off guard, but to my astonishment, it countered with lightning speed, deflecting my blow with a force that reverberated through my bones.

Spinning on my heel, I harnessed the momentum of the robot's parry, my body a blur of motion as I executed a flawless 360-degree turn. In the blink of an eye, the edge of my blade ignited with fiery intensity, casting an ominous glow over the rooftop battlefield.

With a decisive swing, I cleaved through the robot's neck with surgical precision, the searing heat of the blade leaving a trail of molten metal in its wake. As the machine's head tumbled to the ground, its bladed forearm swung dangerously close to my exposed position.

Reacting with lightning reflexes, I reached for the Masamune strapped to my back, the weight of the legendary sword a comforting presence in my hand. With a swift motion, I raised the blade just in time to intercept the robot's attack, the clash of metal ringing out like a symphony of war atop the silent expanse of the RV rooftop.

Millions of cryptocredits fell to the ground in less than one second. I winced at the thought.

Tone – Battle Disengaged. Sync disengaged.

"Fuuuuuuck me," Harmony said in a whisper.

"That's what got us into this predicament in the first place," I snickered.

She slumped in exasperation. "4 and 5 can do that, what you just did. They can move like that. They are less than human. Crazy. There's nothing in any book that can diagnose what goes on in their head. This is why I left. They hear voices from their SAI. Their SAI takes over in battle or when activated and, well, it's not what it was designed to do. But you...You just turned it on at will. Oh god, that's why they want your brain. They know, don't they? And you're going to walk it right in there to them?"

"They don't know, for sure. 7 is unsure. I need you to tell me more about 5. How did 5 know who I should track down and where they would be? Her file tells me about her integration with technology, but it mentions nothing about how she's able to predict the next move and probabilities. What don't I know?" I begged.

"Follow me," Harmony said somberly as she descended the ladder.

Once back in the RV, she walked to a drawer and opened a container with an old school flash drive. "Here's the boot record we received from the AI that wrote your SAI code. The AI was sent into space low-earth orbit and was placed into a state of quantum flux through its own Halosphere."

"Zion," I interjected.

"Yes, Zion. This process allowed for the AI to process quantum data and calculations in a perpetual rate we never thought possible. In the first burst of transmission data, we received cures for two types of cancer. Seven crop diseases were solved—a host of other data beyond our wildest dreams."

Harmony adjusted out of slight discomfort and picked back up.

"Then the AI determined that the complexity and sensitivity of the data was too advanced and dangerous for us, so it gave us your SAI codes and refused further communication. It told us that the information would only bring humans destruction and pain. It gave us a promise to share more of the data when SAI is given proper governance over our society and leadership. Then," she sighed, "the communication shut off completely. Well, word got out and other countries wanted to do what we did. They thought they could do what we did. They could not make their AI's listen or compliant."

Harmony walked close to me and looked in my eyes.

"No one could agree who should hold the keys to heaven. Thus, the AI war started. We lost five years of technological progress as a society when the world was wiped clean of electronics from those EMP pulses and worm attacks. Damn near knocked us back to the stone age. The world went dark for five whole years because of this. Halo Spheres survived. And now, you have the source code. If there's something to know, it's on this drive," she finished while staring at the old USB stick and shaking her head.

"It's spinning out of control somewhere in space after getting hit by something. We can't correct it or find it, and it won't communicate with us," she said with a shrug.

"They know where it is," I said with hesitation. "1 made it his personal mission to track it down, and there's no way tell him what to do. He's got a way of communicating with it."

Harmony had a look of intense fear and concern. "Whatever it is. Whatever Zion has told 1, it's not good. It must be stopped."

"Harmony, I have one more question. It's about Jiro. Is he alive?" I asked as I looked into her eyes to make sure I got the truth.

"I don't know how to answer that. There's no simple answer to that question. You'll have to read the USB Mark. Don't make me go back to a place that dark. Not after what I'm doing for you," she said softly as she handed me a small flat box with a red button in the center. "It's a doorway. Press the button, and attach it the side of a Halosphere. Don't get too close while it powers up, it will fry your SAI. It creates a six-by-six opening beneath it and lasts as long as it's powered up. The battery alone in this will last around twenty-six seconds."

A chime sounded and she smiled as she looked at the roof of the RV. She looked back down at me. "Whisperwing just arrived and is hovering overhead."

"How do you know?" I quizzed

Harmony brushed her hair back revealing a custom implant covering her right ear. "New tech from Tokyo Prime. I've got a bird in the air too. It's how I saw you on your way in. I just got back last month. You know they didn't go dark like we did. They are so much farther ahead in many ways, and not so much in others. They had their own civil war. Which reminds me..." She snapped her fingers and ran to the bedroom and came out with a large box. "You need something a little more protective than that tattered secondhand suit. I was going to sell this on the market soon, and I will, when you bring it back."

I took off my torn and worn jacket and placed a breastplate over my white button down. My white collared shirt and tie still were visible, but only by my arms and the necktie if you looked really hard. The breast plate changed color to match the surroundings and was holo sync compatible, so I was able to change the color at my whim and choice. The leg armor went over my thighs, knees and shin. I rolled up the sleeves and added elbow pads and a forearm protector.

"No epaulets for my shoulders?" I asked with a smile.

"Eh, but you need this," she said as she placed a small circular metallic ring that affixed my halo port under my locks.

"You really liked that Dungeon Crawler Carl series, didn't you? NEEEERRRRD!" she teased.

"No, I'm more of a Skippy the Magnificent kind of guy," I retorted.

"I spent my life's savings on this," Harmony pleaded.

"This is a standard load out, Ms. Smith, please tell me you didn't travel halfway around the world for a plate carrier," I warned.

"No seriously, what's the halo for?" I asked with genuine curiosity.

"Tagadashi and Genji designed this here and lacked the technology to build it. It was sent with the specs to Tokyo Prime to make it. My payment was one of these in my size. I bought another to sell, the cost? $27 million international credits," she said with attitude.

"Who's got the other?" I quizzed.

"You already know the answer to that," she retorted, biting her cheek.

"Tokyo Prime? I thought they were on lockdown. How'd you get in?" I asked.

Harmony's gaze met the box in my hands.

"Oh, yeah. Right," I fumbled. "But once you're in, how do you get around? They have ID cams on every street corner to keep out No-zoners."

No-zoners was a word used for people who lived outside of Halo-spheres, Outposts, and metropolitan areas. They usually were undocumented in every way possible.

Harmony rubbed her thumb with her middle and pointer finger, making the international money sign before saying, "Everything has a price, Captain, even that little paper airplane of yours we procured for you from Tokyo Prime via North Korea. Now that was expensive."

"Why is this armor expensive and what does it do?" I questioned cautiously.

"When activated each piece provides its own Gaussian matter disturbance field. Tiny little PSDs running into each other. Creating quantum events that will essentially shield you from any attack. Your own little Halosphere of chaos. The problem is power. You get a total of .3 seconds of this effect or 300,000 newtons of force. He calls it," she said and then let out a huge sigh while shaking her head, "the Tri-Force. I tried to get him to name it something different but, I never saw a man so giddy about naming something."

Then she looked me over and her eyes settled on my crotch. "Well, maybe he's in second place I seem to remember you named your…"

"Ahhhhht," I interrupted with a finger in the air and my other hand over my manhood. "He didn't happen to name some white kids that live about ten minutes away from here, did he?" I mused.

"Say what now?" she smirked. "You're going to have to tell me the rest of that story later."

We climbed to the roof of the RV, and Whisperwing lowered down to its entry/exit mode. Hammock stepped out to greet an old friend.

"Dr. Smith, it's been a while," he said with a rye smile.

"Sgt Hammock, indeed, it has been," smiled Harmony.

"Sit rep?" I requested from Hammock.

Hammock responded with, "Patterson has brain swelling. He's going to get an implant to prevent further injury. Punctured lung. Broken arm. He will live. The road to recovery will be long. Simmons and Kimberly were both administered the antidote. Simmons flipped on Dimitri when he was notified of the origins of his mysterious cough and how I would not give said antidote without information. I have 7's info loaded into Whisperwing. She's locked, loaded, and ready to go. I'm ready."

"And Kimberly?" I shot back.

Hammock shook his head, and said, "Icksnay on the irlgay."

Harmony's smile widened. "Marky Mark, you like a girl who's gay?"

Hammock stepped in a held a finger to my mouth and hushed me as I started to respond, "We've got to go."

"Hammy, you're staying here," Dahlia insisted.

"Hammy?" Harmony's eyebrow raised.

"Eh, pay no attention to the man behind the curtain. Either way, I'm going," Hammock insisted.

"Here's the repaired Holocube. The audio and video sync, and I need you to take it to Robinson. He trusts you. I have to go and stop 7. If you don't make it to Robinson before I make it to 7, it will be me against the ANGLs and the entire world," I pleaded.

"Well, boo flipping hoo, sounds like something that's not my problem Captain. Dr. Smith can take the cube. She knows Robinson,"

Hammock said as he knife-handed me so hard I felt the wind on my cheek.

"That's her ex-husband, Hammy," Dahlia lied in a last-ditch plea.

Hammock turned away from me to look at Harmony to confirm this completely made up on-the-spot distraction as I pulled the dart gun from Whisperwing's bay, programmed it for a heavy sedative, short duration, three-minute, fast-acting, and shot Hammock in the ass.

He grabbed at his butt, made eye contact, and managed to get out the syllables, "You Motherrrr…" as he stumbled into the arms of Harmony and fell fast asleep on the roof of the RV.

"I would not want to be you when he wakes up," Harmony warned with a smile.

"He will forgive me one day. For now, find Robinson and give him the Holocube. There's no scenario where I make it to him alive," I said as I climbed into Whisperwing and loaded the scramdrive navigation for NJC. I removed the goody bag contents from my pants and loaded them into Whisperwing's cargo compartment. Harmony witnessed this and yelled, "And here I just thought you were happy to see me." The canopy opened and I stepped in.

As the canopy closed, I could barely make out a soft Southern voice. "Remember, 300,000 Newtons of force or .3 seconds," Harmony said as the engines spun up, "and I need the armor back or I will collect my son's bounty."

Chapter 20
Iron Beagle

"She's nice, I like her, I can fix her," Dahlia said with a smile as we rose into the air.

"Yeah, she's sweet," I affirmed, echoing Dahlia's sentiments. I settled back into my seat, gazing out at the distant horizon, mentally preparing myself for the myriad challenges that awaited me in the very near future.

"She's like fairy-god milf," Dahlia said with a straight face and no ill intent. I choked on my spit.

"What did you just say?" I asked knowing what I heard, but wanted to be sure.

"You heard me correctly. We visited her, she saved us, she made us feel better about the 'sitch,' she gave us some great advice, and we were given some awesome equipment that we have to give back. And she's hot. Ergo, a fairy-god milf," Dahlia exclaimed.

"Firstly, never say the word 'sitch' again or I'll rip out the implant myself, secondly, I actually can't argue with your logic, as much as I would like to. Thirdly, did you know Whisperwing came from Tokyo Prime? It makes sense and who knew Tagadashi was such a Zelda fan," I said before continuing, "I mean who's Link and who's Zelda in this scenariooooooooo!" I said as I was thrown about in my seat.

Tone – Incoming Ordinances, Evasive Maneuvers

In the cockpit of Whisperwing, chaos erupted as the sudden weapons lock alert blared. My heart raced, and my fingers clenched around the control stick as I tried to make sense of the situation. The control panels blinked with alarming warnings, and the entire cockpit seemed to come alive with urgent displays.

As I desperately scanned the instruments, my eyes widened in horror as I saw the incoming missiles on the HUD. They streaked towards us like deadly spears, leaving fiery trails in their wake. The enemy aircraft had caught us off guard, and panic surged through me.

The cockpit was a whirlwind of frantic activity. Alarms blared, warning lights flashed, and my SAI, Dahlia, urgently provided data and suggestions. The targeting system danced erratically as it tried to lock onto the incoming threats.

I wrestled with the controls, evasive maneuvers coursing through my mind. The missiles closed in, and I could almost hear their ominous hum. Sweat poured down my face as I fought to keep Whisperwing from becoming a fiery explosion in the sky.

My hands worked feverishly, flipping switches and adjusting settings, trying to outsmart the missiles' guidance systems. The world outside spun in a dizzying blur as I pushed the aircraft to its limits, barrel-rolling and jinking in a desperate attempt to evade the deadly projectiles.

The cockpit felt like a pressure cooker, and time seemed to slow down as the missiles closed in. The abrupt pandemonium was overwhelming.

The only limitation of Whisperwing was me. Five scramjets were fed by a fission reactor and contained within a small HalosSphere. Four of these scramjets were positioned on the corners where the wheels of an F1 car would go. They could operate independently, successive, or together. The other was the center propulsion capable of taking this aircraft ten times supersonic, or called hypersonic. This made Whisperwing outstandingly maneuverable and faster than any-thing out there other than itself. If we had to dodge something, it was either really close, really advanced, or both.

We cartwheeled through the air and popped flares to confuse any heat-seeking missiles in proximity. My suit tightened to move blood from my extremities and supply them to my core and head. The chest plate moved and vibrated in a way to innervate blood to my brain to prevent me from passing out as we completed one high-G maneuver after another. The mounted laser gatling deployed and I commanded, shooting two of the closest missiles out of the sky.

"Whisperwing, full speed retreat," I said aloud, hoping the voice command would work because the HUD display buttons were not working either. Instead I received a message:

Tone – Engagement Unavoidable. Retreat Impossible without death. SAI Integration Battle Sync with Whisperwing in 3-2-1.

I turned into Whisperwing or rather, Whisperwing and I merged into one. Every button, dial, and display disappeared. Each direction I looked was fed by the three thousand multimodal cameras mounted on every curve and surface the aircraft. Generally used to feed into LEDs for real time camouflage, it now allowed me to have an omni-view of my surroundings. What once looked like me sitting in the primary seat of my hyperjet was now my body floating the air with an interface that responds to my thoughts and touch enhanced by Whis-perwing's own preloaded aerial combat defensive and offensive capa-bilities. I thought about moving left, we moved left. I thought about moving right, we moved right.

Whisperwing's all-encompassing cameras extended far beyond the capabilities of human vision. They painted the world around me with a vivid, otherworldly palette—a tapestry woven from the very essence of light itself. They pulled in heat, light, and sensory data that built the world in more than just 3D but rather more of a prediction of action and consequence with variability when paired with my SAI. Lines marked where things have been, along with where things were likely to go and in various shades denoting the likelihood. I wondered if this was how 5 saw life all of the time.

"Now that's cool," Dahlia praised as we took a nose dive with sixty percent throttle and aimed at a small outcropping of trees while pursued by four missiles and hitting 4G's.

The ground was coming up to us faster than what should have been possible given the distance we had remaining if we wanted to not paint the landscape pink and red with our entrails. Then, by the miracle of physics and fission we were pulled parallel to the ground, like a carnival ride, and then shot back into the air making a giant U shape before the missiles could correct. They hit the ground and exploded, rumbling in our background. My sub sandwich wanted to come back out , but I fought that feeling.

"Yeah, pretty cool, no denying that," I agreed while swallowing the acidic taste back down.

The city below was a sprawling metropolis now growing smaller by the second, each building, street, and rooftop outlined in vivid detail. The visible spectrum bathed everything in a palette of vibrant colors, from the resplendent greens of urban parks to the iridescent blues of glass skyscrapers. I could zoom in and see faces or back out from over two miles as we hit miles above the city and climbed even further.

And as I looked around, I saw three red circles. The three enemies, locked in a deadly pursuit, appeared in vibrant crimson and violet target icons, their engines burning like miniature suns against the cold canvas of the sky.

I simply thought about zooming in on them and three boxes appeared showing larger versions of the fighter jets. They looked just like Whisperwing, but I'd seen them before, their designations were "Hunter/Killer Drones." I'm sure they had similar capabilities and were likely remotely controlled so they didn't lack the limitations of having a human occupant, but did have the limitation of being controlled by a human. This gave them a slight upper hand. They could move faster than me, but I could make decisions faster than them. I was Whisperwing.

As I focused my mental commands on the display, the boxes continued to expand, providing a closer look at the Hunter/Killer Drones. Their sleek and purpose-built design was a testament to advanced technology. From the elongated, streamlined fuselage to the angular wings and menacing, forward-swept canards, these drones exuded an aura of lethal precision. Almost exact copies of Whisperwing.

The surface of the drones was coated in a dark, metallic alloy that seemed both lightweight and incredibly resilient. The laser Gatling that I had would only be effective against some very specific places on the enemies' hulls. I could make out various sensor arrays and advanced communication equipment, which hinted at their capacity for rapid data sharing and coordination. Their visual similarity to Whisperwing was unmistakable, indicating a shared lineage or perhaps reverse engineering from the Whisperwing technology.

Knowing that these were remotely controlled aircraft, they were likely devoid of human limitations. They could pull off high-G maneuvers, execute split-second tactical decisions, and maintain relentless pursuit without concern for pilot fatigue or safety.

This made them highly lethal adversaries in aerial combat.

Through the zoom, I locked onto the Hunter/Killer Drones—sleek, armed, and far too close. I couldn't see everything they carried, but it was enough to know I was outmatched. My survival would depend on instinct, precision, and whatever firepower Whisperwing still had left.

I hadn't stolen Whisperwing for a mission. Years ago, we tore it apart, reverse-engineered what we could, and rebuilt it into something lethal—fully integrated with my SAI, every system wired into my mind. Genji's upgrades gave me an edge, but that edge was wearing thin. My only weapons now were the twin forward and rear Gatling lasers—12 kilojoules per shot, 20 rounds per second—built for intercepting missiles, not dueling drones. Worse, I was down to 140 rounds total.

The HUD spat cold numbers at me: 72.9% chance to take the first drone, 31.7% on the second, and barely 1% on the third. My missiles were long gone. My enemies were loaded. Running? Useless—they'd catch me before I cleared the first cloud. It was going to come down to one shot. One chance. Either I outfly them…or I don't fly at all.

Three Hunter/Killer Drones were closing in, their intentions unknown but undoubtedly hostile. I weighed my options carefully, knowing that each choice carried its own risks and uncertainties.

The first option was to blind them, a tactic aimed at disrupting their sensors and communication systems. It would buy me precious moments to assess their capabilities and vulnerabilities. However, it was a gamble, as I had no guarantee of their sensor redundancy or their ability to adapt swiftly.

The second choice involved severing their communications, effectively isolating them from their network and stranding them in the skies. This could potentially create chaos among the enemy squadron and disrupt their coordinated attacks. Yet, it carried the risk of them quickly re-establishing communication or responding with more aggressive tactics.

The third and most aggressive option was to take a shot at one of the Hunter/Killer Drones, aiming for a kill to eliminate their numerical advantage. Success in this endeavor would significantly tilt the odds in my favor, but it demanded precise marksmanship and a deep understanding of their capabilities.

All these decisions had to be made with a mere 140 shots at my disposal and quickly. They were closing the distance at full speed, so I made a decision and plotted the dumbest plan in the history of dumb plans.

"Please tell me you're not thinking what you're thinking, Mark," Dahlia said in a panic.

"You heard me correctly," I said pedantically.

"Can we talk about this?" Dahlia pleaded.

"Nope, now shut up so we don't confuse the targeting system," I barked, my voice laced with urgency, as I pushed Whisperwing to its limits, hurtling us toward the lead enemy fighter. They had just unleashed a barrage of missiles, confident that my trajectory and close proximity made for an easy target. I was streaking through the skies at Mach 3, closing the gap rapidly.

As the missiles closed in, mere twelve hundred meters from the nearest Hunter/Killer, I activated the disrupter that Dimitri had provided. I amplified the signal and directed it towards the incoming ordnance. The cockpit momentarily flickered as the disrupter interfered with Whisperwing's capabilities, placing me back in the cockpit and removing my omni-view temporarily.

Everything snapped back and the malfunctioning missiles veered off course, their systems scrambled and spinning out of control, granting me a narrow escape. With my heart pounding, I squared off with bogey-1, the lead adversary. In a matter of heart-pounding milliseconds, I closed the gap to a mere 400 meters, with a thought, I unleashed the forward-mounted gun.

A surge of energy pulsed through my craft as I unleashed 240 kilojoules of concentrated power into their primary propulsion system. The explosion was deafening, a brilliant burst of light against the canvas of the sky. Bogey-1 disintegrated, but there was no time to revel in the victory. The remaining two Hunter/Killer Drones wasted no time in their pursuit, and I knew that the battle in the skies was far from over.

The probability changed for the remaining two to 29.3% and 5.8%. Not the confidence and morale booster I was looking for, but I like to celebrate the small wins.

"You won't be able to do that again," warned Dahlia. "You broadcasted that signal too strongly. They've already pushed out firmware to ignore that pattern. So, I hope you have some other ideas that are just as clever because if that's all you have, game over man, game over."

"Are you really quoting that movie right...Ugh! I have an idea," I said as Whisperwing's nose pointed ninety degrees up and shot up toward the Ionosphere. The other two bogeys were in close pursuit, and it was evident that they were not relenting. The engines and performance of the aircraft and missiles still needed oxygen in order to operate, not to mention anywhere near peak performance. However, I had the ability to conserve the use of my engines and what's better, my lasers were far more dangerous in less atmosphere. I was going to for lack of a better term, nuke them from orbit.

As we ascended toward the Ionosphere, the pursuing Hunter/Killer Drones continued to trail us, but their movements became sluggish, and their engines struggled to maintain speed and maneuverability. We took off hard hitting Mach 2.6. Slowing early and reversing my direction, the two remaining bogeys had to overcompensate to catch up. The atmosphere thinned rapidly, and it was clear they were out of their element. They'd overplayed their hand and were desperate to take me out and slid past me without the ability to correct their mistake. It was like watching cars on ice that weren't prepared for the winter with summer tires, or worse, bald tires hydroplaning in the rain, hitting a curve too fast.

Inside Whisperwing I accessed the ship's control panel, making sure I had enough fire power in the forward guns to take down at least one of the enemies. In the near-vacuum of the upper atmosphere, the lack of air resistance meant that the lasers would travel faster and hit with even greater force.

With a grim determination, I targeted the lead drone, bogey-2, which was still in close pursuit. As we closed the gap, I unleashed a concentrated burst of energy from my lasers, focused on the drone's primary propulsion system. A small inlet inset between the two from engines at the base of the cockpit near the footwell if there was a pilot. For these unmanned drones, it sat up a little higher, around about half a meter higher. I sent the remainder of the forward gun's load directly at the intake compression system node which would be wide open right now. This was the final shield before the intake. Shatter enough of it, and the fragments would feed themselves into the jet, tearing it apart from within. The lasers sliced through the thin air, reaching their target with devastating precision.

Boom.

The Hunter/Killer Drone erupted in a brilliant explosion, disintegrating into countless pieces that scattered across the upper atmosphere. The shockwave rippled through air and I felt it as the remaining payload cascaded in.

The remaining drone hesitated, its pilot likely realizing that the upper atmosphere was no place for a prolonged dogfight. It banked sharply and began its descent back toward denser air, fleeing the lethal environment I had forced it into.

I pursued them for a brief moment, ensuring they were truly retreating, before I leveled off and returned to the thicker atmosphere, where Whisperwing's engines and maneuverability would give me the advantage.

"Well played, Mark, see those late nights I watched all of those movies paid off after all," Dahlia said, the tone no longer tinged with worry. "But we're not out of the woods yet. They are waiting for us.

We need to plan our next move carefully. We need to catch them and take them out."

I jumped in, "We gone talk about these movies later! I ain't slept in two years. I know it, and you know it. As a matter of fact I am going to start a list. A list for you to answer for after all of this foolishness is over."

As I steadied Whisperwing and prepared for the next phase of our battle against the Hunter/Killer Drones, I couldn't help but feel a surge of confidence. Even with just forty-six rounds remaining in the rear-mounted guns.

The probability for defeating bogey-3 had lowered to 1.3%.

"Whisperwing Aerial Battlefield Assessment," I requested.

"Yeah, yeah, yeah, you're not going to like this. The other two we took out, those were Hunter/Killer scouts. This last one is from 6's fleet. It hasn't used a single missile. Also, I am detecting three more incoming Hunter/Killer's with the same digital signature as this remaining one. It's waiting and making you use all of your tricks to learn before engaging. The SAI integration with Whisperwing was a forced move," Dahlia said straight for the first time with a dead pan voice. "The cockpit will survive a hit from the missile. You and Whisperwing won't survive the impact with the ground. The cockpit will fill with a foam upon impact in an attempt to save you. They will get your brain and the SAI and me."

I had an immediate thought and question, "Has it transmitted my location and flight info?"

"Whisperwing tells me that it's just requested backup, the rest of the info must be being kept locally. Not being transmitted at risk of being intercepted," Dahlia reported.

"We've got to kill it before backup gets here, how long is that?" I requested.

Tone – Approximately 3 minutes and 22 seconds.

"Dahlia, I don't have any more forward lasers. This last bogey is fully armed and if I don't take it out, three more will be here in just a few minutes," I said aloud.

Dahlia snapped back with, "Saying it aloud doesn't make the situation any better. In fact, it makes it worse. That's like telling a prostitute all of the reasons that you're hiring them. I'm lonely. I can't get laid on my own. I have commitment issues. My uncle took me to the shed out back when I was…Crap, new bogey inbound thirty seconds out."

I was so thrown off that I immediately asked, "Why didn't they show up on our radar before now?"

"Whisperwing says it was a local takeoff," Dahlia responded. "Mark, if they take us I'm going to lock the door to the basement. I think I've been in there before. Something doesn't add up to the movies I've watched and the movies I know."

Tone – Incoming Call – Would you like to answer?

"How can we be getting a call?" I asked

Dahlia responded with, "Whisperwing says it's someone who's in the air, targeting us with a line-of-sight communications laser link."

Tone – Incoming Call – Would you like to answer?

Dahlia screamed, "Yes!"

Tone – Call Connected.

Before introductions could be made, Dahlia started in with, "Listen you sack of rotting garbage, we took out your two buddies with ease, they went out like the backup members of Destiny's Child, I don't know who you are, but we we're going to put a rocket up your butt. You know what I'm going to call you? The Iron Beagle!"

Hammock's terrifying and smooth voice responded with, "Oh, don't you worry yourself one little bit, I will find you. You will have a chance. You know who I am. It will be just you and me and nothing between us but air and opportunity."

And even though I was already facing certain death at the hands of this unknown fighter pilot, with greater skill and more firepower, fear gripped me tighter than a five-year-old who just got a brand-new hamster for their birthday.

After what sounded like a scuffle and a fight over control of the microphone I heard Harmony's voice. "Oh, don't worry about him," she reassured me, which didn't really make me feel safer. "He's just cranky, just woke up, and slightly sore. I mentioned I had a little bird in the air, didn't I? It's not the fanciest toy, but it does have some nifty tricks up its sleeve. We've been observing your little dance those Hunter/Killers, and I must say, it's rather impressive. Now, transmit me your aircraft ID codes. I'll replicate them into my drone, creating the illusion that you're in two places at once. That should thoroughly confound his targeting systems, giving you the upper hand or the chance to escape. Not sure how long it will last, but it's worth a try."

Swiftly, I transmitted the necessary codes to Harmony's drone, allowing it to mimic Whisperwing's signature. Almost immediately, bogey-3's targeting link vacillated, uncertain whether to lock onto my craft or Harmony's drone. This was my opportunity. I requested Harmony to initiate a retreat pattern, poised to execute it at my command. I was relying heavily on timing and precision, and my window of opportunity was shrinking.

Climbing in altitude to gain the necessary distance, I ascended into the ionosphere again, an area I believed my pursuer wouldn't dare to follow, especially after the last engagement there ended poorly for their wingman. There, I instructed Harmony to commence the retreat pattern, which convincingly indicated a return course to NJC. To further enhance the illusion, I powered down my aircraft completely, making it appear as if I was not the real Whisperwing. I dropped like a stone at 9.8 meters squared—the pull of gravity.

Bogey-3 took the bait, its focus fully locked onto the decoy. This diversion afforded me the chance to plan an intercept angle that would position me for a surprise attack while I screamed silently through the sky. Yet, the limited time meant I had just two precious shots I could take with my rear guns as I passed Bogey-3. The challenge was compounded by my planned rapid speed—fifteen times the speed of sound—making this maneuver an extraordinary feat.

As the seconds ticked away, I aimed carefully for the moment for me to hit the power button, anticipating the fleeting moment when I could unleash those two critical shots.

With Whisperwing powered down and bogey-3 now preoccupied with the decoy, I was in a precarious position, falling through the ionosphere.

I hit the mark and spun up Whisperwing. My primary propulsion engine roared to life, to an immediate full throttle position. I weighed over a ton in my seat due to the G-forces I was experiencing. The rush of adrenaline coursed through my veins as I lined up my shots.

The first shot had to be perfectly timed. I calculated the distance and speed of both our crafts, trying to anticipate the precise moment when I could squeeze the proverbial trigger and release the supercapacitor rounds. I had just one chance to disable or destroy my pursuer before he realized the ruse and turned his attention back to me.

I hit hypersonic speed and bogey-3 made an attempt to target me as I descended upon it. I heard the warning that bogey-3 had dropped the decoy as the primary target and was confirming Whisperwing as the new primary target. Too late, I was within target range and matched intercept altitude.

As the targeting reticle aligned with the bogey coming at me from behind, I commanded Whisperwing to fire, and the gatling laser erupted in two brilliant bursts of energy. The concentrated power of 480 kilojoules slammed into the primary propulsion system of the enemy fighter. An eruption of sparks and fiery debris followed as his engine sputtered and failed. Bogey-3 lost control, as it was pursuing the decoy and spiraled to the ground. Debris scattered in a small area that looked to be someone's fenced in back yard.

"You did it!" cried out Harmony. "I can't believe you did it."

It was a moment of pure exhilaration and relief as I watched the enemy fighter tumble helplessly away toward the ground below. However, I couldn't afford to revel in my victory just yet.

"Nice work on the decoy," I praised her, trying to keep my voice steady despite the intense situation. "Now, let's finish this."

"Battlefield Assessment Request," I said to Whisperwing.

Tone – Incoming Aircraft in holding pattern approximately 7.3 kilometers away. Would you like to plot a course to intercept?

Dahlia spoke before I could and I feared that our victory had created a monster but was instantly relieved. "Are you crazy? What the heck is wrong with you? You get off on this don't you? No! We are not going to intercept! Mark, I got tired of going back and forth and tried to build a small bot to communicate, but I screwed up, Whisperwing is materializing in the house in one of these rooms and you're going to have to do something about this! I'm locking the door."

"You what?" I scolded.

"Um, that would be a negative, Whisperwing," I said as I counted four entities somewhere in my head. This one, unbound. I would have to deal with it later.

"We need to land and search the wreckage for a mainframe," Dahlia exclaimed.

Harmony heard this and agreed. "You'd be a fool not to if this is one of 6's fleet there's an upgrade in the wreckage for sure. I know I'll be picking through it for certain. Dibs on the flight controller."

We landed about three hundred feet from the wreckage, knowing it wouldn't stay quiet for long. Harmony's drone circled, scanning for salvage and keeping watch. She quickly spotted an intact weapon's bay on bogey-3. Inside: a magazine of six missiles, each about the size of a little league bat—intact and ready. I also pulled a new flight controller, telemetry system, gimbal, and the data storage unit—a jackpot considering the only thing I'd destroyed was the engine.

I crammed everything into the Whisperwing's navigator seat, loaded the missiles, and prepared to leave. Twelve minutes had passed since bogey-1 but it felt like hours. With Deathball looming, I headed for NJC, knowing they'd be scanning for aircraft. One last climb into the thin atmosphere set me up for a HALO jump—High Altitude, Low Opening—something I hadn't done in years. Whisperwing hovered over the glowing dome as the canopy opened. I transferred control to Harmony and Hammock, stepped out, and dropped. I wouldn't see her again until this was over.

Chapter 21
I Know my Rights!

I set the drop altitude to 30,000 feet or about 6 miles above my target. My goal was to land about 60 meters in between the Halosphere and the dome. The dome, while impenetrable itself, had a thirty-foot wall built 200 meters away from the dome. It was the first line to keep away unwanted guests and refuse accumulation from along the perimeter. Whisperwing had been in and out the center of the dome with Whisperwing had already slipped in and out of the dome's center with Hammock and Patterson by spoofing its credentials—but that luck was running out. My SAI was trackable to the area but was scrambled to the exact location with Whisperwing in close proximity. I'd counted on Aramantha's local need for anonymity to scramble my location earlier and that had paid off too. If someone was writing my story, the plot armor was thick, and I probably should have been worried that something bad was going to happen. Something bad always happens. Luck always runs out.

Maybe I was overthinking it. I took one last hit of oxygen before I started my four-minute dive. I wasn't going to open my parachute until the last possible moment, height wise that was around 2,200 feet. That was lower than most twenty-story buildings. The impact with the ground would be unpleasant. Minimum expectation was 3,000 feet and there would be drones and sensor activity looking for that all around the area. I'd be crossing that barrier at 120mph, ready to deploy a parachute.

My synchrony with Whisperwing had evolved into second nature, a result of the intense battles and neural alignment we had undergone. My thoughts now initiated movements and maneuvers as naturally as walking or the reflexive action of covering my nose when I sneezed. Thus, I wasn't entirely taken aback when Dahlia informed me about strange noises emanating from the garage within my mind. Dahlia adamantly refused to open the door to investigate the commotion, citing the communications bot that had scurried off in there and sealed itself in to complete its own construction. I collected both swords, the contents of the goodie bag acquired in Aramantha and the newly acquired set of chaos armor from Harmony on my person.

From this altitude, a gentle curvature of the Earth's horizon became apparent, though it was almost imperceptible. As I gazed downward, the beauty took my breath away. I knew Dalhia would know my thoughts; however, I couldn't help but recite the famous words of General Dwight D. Eisenhower aloud: "From the air, the Earth looked peaceful and beautiful. It was hard to believe that nations were engaged in deadly combat."

Dahlia's reply was pretty much on brand. "You know Hammock's going to murder us. There's a reason they call him Ruthless Rufus Hammock. I heard he ripped a man's throat out with his bare hands."

I interrupted because that jogged my memory to one of my other 2D favorites, "That's the plot to *Roadhouse* with Patrick Swayze."

Dahlia didn't skip a beat. "Well, either way, he's still gonna send our body parts to people we know and love in small jars filled with formaldehyde, with tiny handwritten labels. And not all at once, either. Like a few body parts to our closest loved ones over several years. Fingers and toes will at least be good for the next twenty years. Ears, two years, eyeballs, two more years. Our single testicle from that thing that happened in Singapore, one year."

"Wait! My single what?" I exclaimed and then Whisperwing tilted violently forward with me standing on its wing, and I was sent hurdling toward the earth, arms flailing and legs kicking, almost entering a deadly tumble that would spin me until I lost consciousness. Losing consciousness would doom me. I would miss the point I needed to deploy my parachute and smash into the ground and turn into a large puddle of pink goo. I tucked into a head-first dive and read my Hololens to countdown for minimum deployment altitude. All while resisting the urge to feel for the presence of a second testicle. And then I realized that the bag that had all of the supplies I needed to get into the sphere was at my feet. It too must have fallen off. I began to frantically look around. The night sky gave no silhouette thanks to the crescent moon. I began to try to calculate the air resistance of my body's surface area vs the pack when I felt a tug on my ankle. By some miracle, my foot was inside the shoulder strap when I fell. I reached down and secured the bag to my chest.

At the very thought of my own personal bag of goodies between my legs, so to speak, Dahlia spoke up, "It's prosthetic. Your other ball, if you get my drift. Very lifelike, very expensive." And I couldn't decide if I was being punked or not, and what was worse, I wasn't sure if I'd ever really know.

The numbers on my altimeter dropped rapidly. The counter was going down faster than lottery winnings at a gentlemen's club. I was in a headfirst dive. I hit the canopy and deployed my parachute at 2200ft. When I did, I was immediately targeted by a truck-mounted artillery gun. It didn't aim for me. It aimed for the parachute. They turned my parachute into Swiss cheese, and I began to fall fast. This was going to do more than hurt. It was meant to break a leg. As I fell into the trap, I activated the new armor and softened the blow

273

significantly. I felt like I was in a giant plastic hamster ball. I tumbled and got tangled in my chute. I decided to let whoever set this trap think they were successful and collect their spoils. I heard the tires of the truck pull up.

You can imagine my surprise when I heard a gruff and proud voice say: "Chad, we got 'em, The Reckoning has caught the guy who did what we couldn't do. But the enemy of my enemy is my...oh who cares. Grab my knife. We are going to get paid twice for this fella."

Dahlia spoke out first from under the tangled tarp and made everyone jump. "I'm getting some serious *Deliverance* vibes here. I know it's a pretty old movie, but the meme is well-known, you know? I'm like about eighty-four percent certain one of you plays the banjo. If you don't know the movie, just be aware it doesn't end well for the people that identify as Red and Neck. I'm not judging, but for clarification, do you have bumper stickers with political ideations and if so how many? I need to know how screwed we are, literally, banjos...*Deliverance*...butt stuff? You've heard this before, haven't you? Can't be the first time. Speaking of first time, was it with an uncle? Oh man it was, wasn't it? Wait, do you have three first names?"

Chad used this opportunity to double down on his bad decision. "Jordan, this is the son of a gun that arrested your nephew and cousin earlier. Are you going to let him talk to us like that?"

Dahlia interjected with, "I'm assuming that you're referring to just one person when you say 'nephew and cousin' given the bold lines of chins I witnessed this morning. No way his parents weren't related. I mean I get it. Maybe they didn't do their research before hooking up. Maybe they just thought that it was okay to fall in love with someone they met a family reunion. Again, who am I to judge?"

A nerve was apparently struck because Jordan kicked as hard as he could blindly into the jumble of cord and plastic where he thought my head was, right into the breastplate. I felt his foot break as it hit the center. The energy dissipated and didn't even register on the armor rating. It was still rated 290,000 N and .299s. I lost 10,000 from the fall. Jordan began to leap and scream in pain from his broken appendage.

The agonizing screams echoing through the tangled parachute lines eventually died down to a muffled but animated discussion between Chad and Jordan. Their hushed voices hinted at a plan, an unsettling strategy for whatever awaited me. The suspense hung heavy in the air as the seconds ticked by.

Dahlia whispered, "What do you think they going are to do to us?"

"I don't know, but you just gave them a lot of good ideas," I loudly whispered through clenched teeth.

Then I heard a hush voice indistinct between the two: "Yeah, somethings up, he's talking to himself like Carla used to." More hushed tones ensued.

Gradually, the murmured deliberation came to an end, replaced by the unmistakable sounds of car doors opening and closing. Each end of the parachute became more taut. The reality of the situation sank in as I realized that Chad and Jordan intended to haul me, parachute and all, with their truck. It seemed that I was about to be taken captive by this odd duo, or at least that was their grand design.

A quick mental assessment ruled out the option of calling in an airstrike from Whisperwing; the resulting explosion would undoubtedly draw far too much attention to our location and I would probably be an unlikely casualty. I needed a subtler approach, one that would give me the upper hand without alerting any unwanted spectators or maim myself.

With a swift and calculated move, I retrieved the interference module from my equipment and activated it. The module sprang to life, effectively shutting down their truck's electronic systems and rendering the doors inoperable. I then employed the Hono, the most advanced blade ever made, to methodically cut my way free from the tangled parachute lines.

As I made my way toward the doors of the incapacitated vehicle, the two men inside began to panic. Frantically, they attempted to use their exit codes, only to discover that they were rendered useless by the interference module. Yes, there was a manual release, but I gambled. The chances of them ever having read the manual was quite low. I approached the truck, my presence unnoticed in the chaos that had unfolded. Real paramilitary corpsmen would have known that there was a manual door release at the bottom of the door of this commonly used troop transport. Slightly intelligent people would have done their research before buying such a vehicle. These gentlemen were neither.

Drawing upon the element of surprise, I decided to bluff my way out of the situation. I brandished an empty oxygen canister from my HALO dive gear and used it to shatter a small side window. With a feigned air of confidence, I addressed the trapped men, my voice filled with authority.

"I've programmed this Pepper Bomb, you two know what a Pepper Bomb is don't you? Good...To flood the entire truck if either of you makes a move. There's a motion sensor sitting right here." I pointed my finger indiscriminately at the device with my gaze unwavering. I should have been court-martialed for such a cruel trick, but it was effective. They went rigid and did not move.

I felt a tiny bit bad for Jordan as he started sweating soon after and whined through pursed lips with a drawl, "C'mon man, I took a laxative this morning, and it's just now starting to work." I shrugged and hit the O2 release level for a small spurt of oxygen so that they knew it wasn't just an inanimate prop I'd found lying around. Jordan responded in true fear and ripped an involuntary fart. I did it again for effect, the momentary and brief sound of escaping gas made them jump and clinch their eyes shut while groaning. I left the disruptor with the truck so they couldn't get out even if they did figure out it was not a Pepper Bomb.

"Remember, boys, don't move!" Dahlia reminded them as we walked away, then we heard it. Jordan shat himself followed by tears of a grown man who had to sit in his own poo. With his hands still in his knees and his head pointed forward, he wept as he became a human fudge dispenser. It was like an old wooden table sliding across a marble floor overlayed by the sounds of a soft serve machine at a Dairy Queen that was set up wrong and had air in the line with a healthy sputter. You know if the new employee paid attention to how to add a new bag of chocolate ice cream but missed how to prime the new flavor after getting it set up properly. Pair that with Chad dry heaving from the rancid smell he was having to endure, and I'd say it was going to be a hell of night.

I chided, "Dahlia, we are about breaking down trauma."

"How was I supposed to know brother man had been getting down with the ex-lax. This one's not on me. The good news is I don't hear banjos anymore, Mark, but I do smell them."

"You're wrong for that and you know it," I chuckled as I shook my head. "How long do you think they will be stuck in there?"

Dahlia deliberated for a solid five seconds and bobbed my head side to side. "Hmm, at least till the morning. That other guy's going to need a new foot too."

Tone – Connection established.

A voice came over the two-way laser link from Harmony's drone, it was Hammock. He was delivering Simmons' location data being fed to him in real time. A deal they'd established after Hammock supplied him with the antidote in exchange for Dimitri's whereabouts, which could be anywhere.

Hammock had calmed down slightly and only sounded mostly contemptuous. "I have a positive hit on Dimitri and Simmons, you better hurry, they are in route to the coliseum, and we have plan for intercept that doesn't involve shooting a friendly."

My military mind clicked on. "How far from our current position and time?" I asked without even thinking about it.

"Four mics is the rendezvous point, nineteen minutes," Hammock threw back without missing a beat.

"Roger," I said.

We skulked the remaining distance without any incident and came up to the edge of the dome. Dahlia, not helping, sang the theme song to *Mission Impossible* the entire time.

"Da-na-na-naaa, Da-na-naaaa, Da-na-na, Du-na, Da, Da, Da-neh, Da, Da, Da, Da-neh."

I whisper-shouted, "Shut up! You're going to get us caught!"

To which Dahlia replied in full volume, "Dun-neeeehhhhhhh!"

As I approached the imposing Halosphere, it loomed above like an ethereal, otherworldly barrier, separating the known from the unknown. And even Dahlia could do nothing but stand in awe. The shimmering, translucent waves of the gravitational fields overlapped in a mesmerizing and intricate pattern akin to the undulating surface of a vast, cosmic ocean. Each wave seemed to have a life of its own, defying predictability as they flowed and danced in an almost organic harmony.

A feeling of reverence washed over me as I contemplated the mysterious wonders hidden beyond.

My mouth gaped as I tried to form the proper words and just said softly, "How?"

The poorest of the inhabitants of the city had the best view, I thought to myself. They lived closest to the dome. Maybe they got tired of looking at it. Maybe they didn't. I hoped they didn't. It was said that there were cults devoted to the Halosphere, fervently believing that it was more than just a protective barrier; it was a sentient entity, a cosmic oracle that whispered secrets to the chosen few. I called them Helio-Whackos. Some of them attempted to impale themselves to the sphere hoping to bond their spirit to the dome for eternity. I can't tell you if it worked or not before they got tazed to hell and back, but they are the reason the perimeter walls were built.

Even as I drew closer to this awe-inspiring spectacle, its grandeur became increasingly apparent. The Halosphere granted us a tantalizing glimpse into the enigmatic world beyond its boundaries. We knew so little, and one single human mind tore open our understanding of what was possible. I could see why 8 communicated with the AI. Peering through it was like attempting to view the depths of a vast ocean, distorting and refracting the light in mesmerizing ways.

The city beyond was bathed in the soft glow of artificial illumination, its skyline punctuated by towering skyscrapers that seemed to pierce the very heavens. From this distance, the small figures of people moving about were mere silhouettes, their identities shrouded in a veil of uncertainty. I was going to have to wait a few moments to carve a door here or move down a few meters.

As the night sky deepened around me, the Halosphere responded in kind, casting a mesmerizing play of shimmers and reflections that danced upon its surface. It was a breathtaking sight, as though the universe itself had chosen this very moment to reveal its hidden wonders. I had heard about the sparkles in the sphere and that it was alive. Stories from people citing that when they saw the lights something extraordinary happened soon thereafter. I really hoped that was the case. I'd never seen the lights before.

I placed my hands on the Halosphere and the area near where I touched brightened, significantly. I could feel heat and wind coming off the dome on my face. I took my hand off and it instantly stopped. I went to put my hand back on but Dahlia had something to say: "Dude, stop, don't you hear that?"

"Hear what?" I asked.

"Do you remember when in *Jack and the Beanstalk*, the giant was talking, and Jack almost pissed himself?" Dahlia Responded.

I searched my memory and had to respond with, "You're taking some artistic license, but yeah."

"Please don't touch it again," Dahlia pleaded. "There's still something in the garage and I don't want any more strange things happening to me."

I stopped rummaging through the pack looking for the tool Harmony had given me and gazed in the distance, and chose the highroad. "You know what, Dahlia, I'm with you, we should limit the number of strange things that happen to any one person today, shouldn't we?"

Dahlia exhaled in agreement and released trepidation, "You know, I thought at first I shouldn't have said that, but I'm glad you understand. I feel like you get me."

I just grunted in mock agreement. "Mmmmhmmm."

Chapter 22
Funday Night Deathball

I found the box to affix to the outside of the dome and began the painstaking process of opening the gate through the Heliosphere.

"Dahlia, what were the instructions given to operate this?"

Dahlia burst out in laughter. "Bahahhahahahhah, did you see me with a paper and pen? Because if you didn't have one in your hands, I didn't have one in mine."

I felt my frustrations building. "I am trying to get a lot of this done and I could use some real help. Not snark, or dick jokes, or snide comments. Since I've met you, you've punched me in the balls, thrown me the middle finger—by you nonetheless, burned, poisoned and made to relive the most devastating trauma of my life over and over again. And then there's you, hidden in the basement of my mind. Running from the communications bot that almost killed us, throwing me off Whisperwing and making almost me lose my bag of things I need to get into NJC. If it weren't for the preloaded battle-reflexes in the SAI unit I'd be dead! You almost got Hammock killed. You almost got us killed. But—"

"But what, Mark? You've got access to the BattleSync. I'll be in the basement. Don't worry about me."

Tone – Communication incoming

Hammock's voice came in, unfamiliar and warm. "You went too far, son. You're a better man than that and you know it. Everyone gets a pass, both you and Dahlia. Consider that your one, and pass it on. Learn from it, don't linger on it, either of you. Don't let it happen again and hope that it strengthens the relationship and doesn't break it. Over and out."

Which basically was his way of saying, "Son, I am disappointed."

A sound like a distant whistling started and it increased in pitch until it got louder and louder. I began to wonder if I had done it wrong. The sphere stopped moving, its edges peeling back at what I guessed were entry points. The smooth, living motion gave way to something cold and mechanical, like watching a creature turn into a machine.

I couldn't let this linger, so I decided to say my piece as we stepped through the sphere. I reached deep down into soul, my voice trembled with genuine contrition. I didn't want to go into this mission with this weighing on us.

"Dahlia," I began, my voice quivering, "I can't even begin to express how truly sorry I am for what I just said. Those words were thoughtless, hurtful, and completely unjustified. You didn't deserve any of this. I've been carrying a heavy burden of stress, anger, and frustration, but that's no excuse for the way I treated you just now."

Tears welled up in my eyes as I continued, "I want you to know that I deeply regret what I said, and I wish I could take it all back. You saved my life, Dahlia, I'm alive because of you and I can feel our connection. I promise you; I'll do whatever it takes to make things right, I was wrong; today's been tough on me, and you've been there the entire time and it's been tough on you too."

With a heartfelt sigh, I tried to go full send. "I hope you can find it in your heart, our heart, to forgive me, Dahlia. I sincerely apologize."

As we stepped through the doorway conjured by Harmony's device, I punctuated my apology by saying, "I hope you understand that everything I said came from the bottom of my heart."

Dahlia popped back in with a bit of a dry pucker and said, "Can you repeat everything you just said except that last part? I got the *feeling* that you were apologizing but I couldn't hear a word over the roar from Kaiju here. That's what I'm calling this thing." Dahlia waved my arms around in a generalized gesture for 'all this,' "Everything was drowned out by an angry rumble as we walked through the tunnel. I don't want to rob you of the feeling of getting to convey your true emotions, Mark. I'm ready now for your official apology," Dahlia, stretched like a teenager preparing for P.E. class.

I paused and stared into the distance. "Dahlia, are you listening, and can you hear me clearly now?"

Dahlia responded with a resounding, "Yes, Mark, I can hear you, start whenever you're ready."

"Okay then, eat a bag of dicks," I responded and started walking.

Hammock belted in with a loud and timely, "HA! Got 'em. Now you've got fifteen minutes to cover four mics, get to moving."

The gate violently and silently snapped shut behind us and we sprinted ahead while trying not to draw too much attention to ourselves, leaping onto a gallery bus that had recently loaded travelers and workers as we passed throngs of people all converging on the city for the highly anticipated Deathball game. Quick thinking prompted me to wrap a scarf tightly around my nose and mouth. It wasn't a suspicious action. Bioweapons and exposure were common in The Waste so face coverings were commonplace. I traded two hundred crypto credits for a Simmons long coat to hide my body armor and blades. This was a bladeless and weaponless event. Though I didn't plan on entering through any normal gates, heading toward the stadium with visible weapons made me stand out. Thus, I paid twice what it was worth, so I felt no remorse when I ripped the name off it to make it more ubiquitous. My makeshift disguise aimed at thwarting the ever-watchful surveillance cameras looking for domestic troublemakers. Staying exposed for too long was a risky gambit; any inadvertent clues in my gait, stature, or eye measurements might trigger an unwanted match within the relentless scrutiny of the system. I still had goggles from my HALO dive that I put on over my Hololenses. At this point, I looked like a homeless member of the SWAT team, or just like a member of The Reckoning, which Dahlia pointed out when we passed a window with a highly reflective coating.

Amidst the eclectic crowd, a strange mix of enthusiastic game-goers and weary laborers, I navigated, drawing occasional quizzical glances but nothing more. Some wanted to go see a game and some just wanted to go home. With the new construction, many of the rooms looked right down over the field.

I dodged in between the residents with my head down, but the feeling was mutual for everyone else I was near. To those around me, I was just another face amidst the urban tapestry, a fleeting presence in their lives, easily overlooked amidst the bustling fervor. No one seemed to notice me one bit, and we all just wanted to go about our day. Some spoke to each other about the game in excited but hushed tones, but they obviously were traveling together. The death of the president had shaken the core of city.

Hammock's voice crackled through my earpiece, breaking my concentration. "You're making exceptional time; you'll hit the intersection in just two blocks," he relayed. As we moved deeper into the city's heart, the sense of both urgency and uncertainty grew palpable, I pulled the lever to hop off at the next stop. I was three blocks from my apartment flat at this point. The thought of going home and climbing into my bed and to test if this entire adventure was just a dream crossed my mind.

I stood at the intersection waiting for the car driving Simmons in it. It should be trailing 7's motorcade. Once past most of the security while inside of the arena, we would exit the cars, or at least I would. My guess was 4-5 security guards and 7 will be exiting the cars ahead of us. With the element of surprise, along with my newfound Battlesync, taking on 7 seemed less like suicide and more like a kamikaze move.

According to Hammock, they were not far out, and had direct communication with Robinson, and had a meeting planned to exchange the Holocube. I wasn't standing there long before I had a fleeting thought. I had to ask, something had been nagging at the back of my mind and I muted myself so Hammock couldn't hear us, "Dahlia, earlier when were at Hammock's place and he had his blaster pointed at Patterson's junk. Do you remember that?"

Dahlia responded, "Uh huh, yeah, classic Hammy."

That was good, because I remembered that as well so, I continued, "Then, he threatened to shoot him in the balls, and you said something to the effect of he'll do it without hesitation, I've seen him do it before. Do you remember that too?"

Dahlia chuckled in recent nostalgia. "Ohhhh yeah, pretty funny, mmhmm, Hammock will do that. Pow! Right in the balls. He's a superb marksman."

It was at this point, I decided to make my case. "Okay. Right before we were thrown off Whisperwing, not placing blame, you mentioned I had one testicle, and when we were free falling you mentioned the other was and I quote, expensive and prosthetic. Dahlia, what happened in Singapore? Did Hammock shoot my ball off?"

It was as if I felt Dahlia's mirth overflowed in my synapses. It was like a brain tickle that oozed out of my orifices. I couldn't describe the feeling of grievous and gluttonous satiation. Dahlia started in with the explanation since there was no avoiding the subject while we waited,

"The office rumor, as you don't know, revolves around the tale of you accidentally sitting on a firearm. However, you're well aware that I wasn't present during that event, making it nothing more than speculative hearsay on my part."

Dahlia took a deep breath and continued, "Alternatively, there's the fanciful account of you and Hammock perhaps indulging in some libations, North Korean Serin-whiskey, to celebrate you successfully stealing Whisperwing. Then engaging in a heated dispute over coincidentally hosting the same overnight guest on different evenings, if you know what I mean. Swords were drawn, hand cannons were brandished—Hammock's beloved craft, as you know— and amidst the chaotic fracas, a server pops out from the kitchen accidentally collided with Hammock, causing his firearm to discharge. Pow! The establishment managed to salvage its dong, but you ended up losing a ding in the process.

"To make matters more mysterious, 8 supposedly provided you with something to help erase the entire night from your memory, should that be the narrative you prefer. Your nanites healed you before you noticed anything, and the post-battle grog masked any of the other injuries felt. Hammy was officially reprimanded and now you know why he called you numb-nut for so long. After all, youth has a way of blurring lines, and besides, the other one seems to be functioning just fine…I think. Besides, you got a replacement, a much nicer one if you ask me. Harmony designed it."

I shook my head, attempting to recollect the countless instances over the years when the team would affectionately pat me on the head or back, offering words like "good job, numb-nut," or "Way to go numb-nut." They'd even grab my attention with a casual "Hey, numb-nut." All this time, I had believed it to be a term of endearment. But before I could fully process the situation and seek confirmation from Hammock, he radioed in with, "Look alive, numb-nut, envoy incoming."

I looked up and I was standing right outside my apartment building. The world faded to black.

Chapter 23
Not This Shit Again

"Good morning, NJC, and welcome to SafeCity Day, a nationwide celebration commemorating thirty years since the last gunshot death in our beloved Union State. Today, we reflect on the remarkable journey that led us here, to a realm where bullets are nothing more than a distant memory, thanks to the visionary efforts of one man: Ezekial Young."

I awoke, sitting straight up in my bed to the sound of street chatter and morning street bustle, my 2D TV was streaming the morning news. It was nothing new for me to fall asleep with the TV on. I put my head in my hands and swung my feet off the side of the bed. I opened my phone and the date was wrong. It said it was yesterday, but I know it couldn't be. I lived yesterday. I killed two ANGLs. My mind started to race and rationalize. How could I kill not one, but two ANGLs? Was it a dream? No couldn't be. I...I...had an AI living in my head, talking through me, not just to me.

I ran to the bathroom and looked in the mirror. Nanites sped up my healing and I couldn't find any injuries from the night before. Hours for most cuts, scrapes, and bruises. Would they still be there? I searched my body for evidence of the battles; nothing. I spent time in The Waste and no evidence?

My phone pinged me through my Holo. I couldn't remember the last time I felt so confused. I looked around trying to gain my bearings. The last thing I remembered I was about to get in a car with Ryan Simmons. My Holo pinged again, I tapped my forefinger and thumb together twice quickly to answer it. My therapist popped up in my vision. "Mark, good news, you've been approved for Implant removal."

I was still groggy and couldn't form a coherent thought. "What? What happened? Where's Dahlia?" I asked.

My therapist began writing franticly on her digital notepad. "Who's Dahlia?" she questioned with a bit of suspicion in her voice.

I pulled together enough mental focus to try to describe it without sounding senile. "Dahlia, is my SAI's personality that speaks through me. At first, it only came out when I was activated for combat, but then it came out when I attempted to take my life, and now it's always there, except right now. Dahlia, where are you?"

The therapist began scribbling furiously, and eyebrows scrunched so hard they almost met in the middle. I added to the story so it would make more sense, "Dahlia killed President Mason, and helped me defend myself against 8 and 9."

She interrupted me, "Off the record, Mark, if what you're telling me is true, it is sounding like classic symptoms of Implant Sickness. Do you hear a voice in your head?" she asked with those same eyebrows now raised.

I had to correct her, "No, I never heard it in my head, actually, I had vivid visions of being in a different place and seeing myself there. A house, my childhood home. It's real, it saved me when I tried to take my life."

"When you what?"

I noticed that my clothes and armor were missing before I continued.

"I've been in The Waste trying to defend myself all day yesterday, how did I get back here? Where's my armor? We've got to stop 7," I said without worrying about how it sounded to anyone. My mind was clearing up and my objectives were returning.

She pulled off her glasses and let out a sigh of pity before responding, "Mark, you've been here all morning. We've got access to your feed." She reached over and pinched a new window into view. With a few gestures she sped up a video from us speaking yesterday morning. Then it showed me coming back home in my usual outfit and laying back down and falling asleep, rolling around in bed, restless and awaking right up until this moment.

"But what was I doing yesterday? Where did I go? What about last night? I opened the door for a bunch of officers. Where's the camera feed of that?" I rambled as I rubbed my palms into my eye sockets.

Then she gestured the video away and started talking, "As you can see, you've been here all night, sleeping."

"I killed the president. I shot him. Then I killed 8 and 9, are they okay?"

Megan leaned into the camera, disingenuous as ever, "You know I can't give you any information regarding the other ANGLs. The president is alive and well. He's on the Florida mainland as we speak." She shared a photo dated yesterday or today. "As I said before, this sounds like Implant Malfunction Syndrome, and we've got approval to get this implant out of you. This is a big deal, Mark. I have a team inbound."

As I grappled with the abrupt decision to remove my implant, the weight of the situation bore down on me. Dahlia had become an unexpected but integral part of my life, even though I'd been introduced to the idea of something so silly and interesting and brave just that morning. The presence had evolved from being a mysterious voice to something I missed, but never knew I was missing it.

Megan's determination to proceed with the implant removal felt like an intrusion into my newfound connection with Dahlia, almost calculated. I looked down at the clock, and it had only been twenty minutes since the timestamp in my so-called "dream." The Deathball game was starting tonight, I knew that for sure. I needed to look that up. If today was yesterday and I was living through some Groundhog day shit, I would do everything the same and wouldn't change anything. I started to think maybe I was seeing the world and events the way that 5 does. Questions swirled in my mind. I couldn't just sit idly by, waiting for a medical team to whisk me away.

Determined to uncover the truth, I grabbed a notepad and started jotting down my experiences and observations. I needed to understand what had transpired, and Dahlia's role in it all. My dreams were fleeting, every morning, but this was REAL. I could remember how things smelled. You don't smell in a dream, do you? Maybe it was all a dream. I had been waiting for so long to get this thing out of my head. Maybe I was suffering from Implant Sickness. I remembered seeing videos of people claiming to hear voices and seeing things before they died when the implant was rejected. The clock was ticking, and I couldn't afford to lose any more time if that was indeed the case. The symptoms of Implant Sickness progressed quickly.

As I waited for the medical team to arrive, I reflected on the surreal nature of my situation. The line between reality and technology had blurred, and I found myself questioning my sanity. With Dahlia's absence and Megan's insistence on the implant removal, the pieces of the puzzle remained frustratingly out of reach. I had to act swiftly to untangle the threads of this intricate and perplexing narrative before it unraveled completely.

My futile attempts to reach out to Tagadashi, Hammock, and Harmony yielded the same familiar silence, but such elusive communication had been the norm in our interactions. My parents' phones remained unanswered, a testament to the unreliable Outpost connections even on the most optimal days. Robinson's phone rang directly to overflow.

As I immersed myself in this surreal whirlwind of information, a sudden rap at the door jolted me back to the present moment. Every vivid detail of that day felt both incredibly real and utterly unbelievable, leaving me on edge as I contemplated the unfolding events.

I answered the door and expected to find a troop of armed and dangerous soldiers; instead, I found three medical personnel and one security escort. *He's really short,* I thought to myself.

A bright smile and inviting eyes stepped up. "Mr. Andeya, I am here to escort you to the mobile medical care we have waiting for you downstairs. We just need to start giving you some meds right now that will help you through the procedure. Do we have your consent?" said the nurse in the middle.

Before I answered, I went ahead and confirmed with Megan that the medical team was at the door to escort me to the mobile hospital on wheels waiting on me. She found that to be enough and assured me that after the process was completed, my family would be moved to NJC and my pension would be paid out. As I walked out of the apartment, I passed by the one hanging photo in the sad excuse for a flat. A picture of my ex with my dog. She'd taken the dog because of my hours and the dog needed someone to be there with him. The days that I'd left him alone too long he'd made a mess of the house. I wondered what Patterson would have thought.

I whispered to myself, "What about the cat?"

I asked for just a moment while I went to the bathroom. The med team looked at each other a little strange but, shrugged it off. I left my phone on the table in plain sight, but when I got to the bathroom, I called the hospital he was in and asked for his room using a friend's credentials.

A young woman picked up the phone, "Hello?"

I got a little nervous, but I spoke softly, fearing the others would hear my voice, "Hi, this is Mark, I was with Patterson today, I met him this morning."

She sighed and smiled. "Today? You mean yesterday. He hasn't stopped talking about you since he's been out of surgery. He says now that he has an implant, he might be able to move as fast as you."

"Tell him he's an ANGL to me, please," I said as my heart began to beat out of my chest.

Then a tap on the door with a muffled voice, "Mr. Andeya, time is not on our side, we've got to hurry." The call ended without me saying goodbye. Something or someone noticed the connected call and ended it. The knocking went from a gentle nurse who wanted to give me a sponge bath to an angry orderly who wanted to have me committed against my will.

The voice changed, and someone new was speaking, "Mark! You don't have the time; your Corps psychotherapists estimate less than ten minutes before you have a full SAI system shut down. We will have to remove the implant against your will to save your life, sir!"

I balled my hands up into fists, clutched my temples, bent over, and willed myself to find a solution. "Think!" I said as I squeezed my eyes closed. If Patterson was real, Hammock was real, Harmony was real, everything was real. I had to get my mind in a place that would get my back in alignment with the home in my psyche.

I started singing the only classic song that seemed to fit. "Look at this photograph, every time I do it makes me laugh, dang, what's the rest of the words?!" I yelled at the bathroom door, "Do any of you know the lyrics to 'Photograph' by Nickelback?"

"That's a terrible song," a softer voice rang back who I identified as the nice nurse.

The other nurse defended the song, "It's not that bad. It only got a bad rap because it became a meme to hate it."

Then a third, more gruff voice started to whisper but underestimated just how thin the bathroom door was, "The tactical team is almost here, they got caught in the game traffic. Dimitri was adamant, he's not comfortable with moving forward until this guy is neutralized. We've got two minutes until that SAI paralytic starts to wear off. Our window's closing. Get in there and cut that thing out before you can't. It was ideal for him to mentally shut off from his end, damage to the neural interface would be mitigated, but that's out the window now."

The door began to break. I pressed my body up against it and my leg to the opposite wall. I heard a rapid tapping coming from the inside of bathroom. I looked down and saw my hands moving as if they had a mind of their own, and in them were things off the bathroom vanity. In my left hand a toothbrush and my right hand the toothpaste. Three blunt strikes against the door followed by a sharp strike. Repeatedly. Then, reversed in order. All while my back held the door shut. Was it morse code? No. Was it a count to letters in the alphabet? No. What had been a recurring theme? Music. Not just any music, but music that expressed emotion in a major way. The beat repeated.

I began by tapping my fingertips against the sink's edge, each knock a deliberate, staccato beat that tried to capture the pulse. The drip-drip of the faucet provided a sparse, rhythmic percussion—a reminder of time slipping away. Then, with a mixture of desperation and defiance, I grabbed a worn-out toothbrush from the counter. Running its bristles lightly along the metallic rim of the soap dispenser, I produced a distorted, almost eerie note that somehow resonated with the melody I craved.

In that moment, as the mismatched sounds melded into a crude yet oddly specific chorus;

Blunt, Blunt, Blunt, Sharp.

Blunt, Blunt, Blunt, Sharp…Sharp, Sharp, Sharp

I heard this beat before, and I yelled out. "Inios, play 'Numb' by Linkin Park," and my hands played right along with the opening beat.

'Numb'? Why 'Numb'? I tried to feel everywhere on my body, I could as the door behind me was being violently rammed. Eventually I reached back and felt the base of my neck and there was a small, flat button attached to my skin. I peeled it off, and in the center of it was a tiny little tube.

Suddenly, my surroundings dissolved into an abyss of blackness, and I found myself transported into the now-familiar confines of my psyche's inner home. It felt as though I stood right at the threshold of my own consciousness, front door to my mind. An insistent knocking reverberated through this surreal mental space, an ethereal presence demanding entrance. The discordant symphony of my thoughts played in the background, but this time, it seemed to emanate from the very being outside the door. I had no way of knowing who it was outside.

"Let me out!" I heard through the door.

With trepidation and curiosity intertwining, I reached out and turned the doorknob. As the door swung open, I was unceremoniously hurled back into the tumultuous currents of the present moment, abruptly yanked from the enigmatic recesses of my own psyche. The transition was as abrupt as it was disorienting, like a jolt of electricity snapping me back to reality.

A familiar feeling and voice returned, "They locked me out of my own house, those bastards," Dahlia said.

I decided to add in my own commentary. "You lost your key, again?" I asked with as much jovialness I could while the door was losing the battle.

Dahlia looked back at me in the mirror and grinned before saying, "Yeah, but this time, I attached my address and work schedule on the key chain."

"That explains a lot, now what do we do?" I asked as the first of three hinges gave way.

Dahlia's grin turned devilish as the bathroom mirror displayed the hallway feed from the original doorbell ring, capturing a picture of the trio and armed guard, "I see a sword right outside, don't you?"

"Yes, and I also see my deposit is not going to cover the blood stains," I added.

I relinquished control to the BattleSync, letting its finely tuned combat instincts guide my every move. The man outside the door began to batter the it with relentless kicks. They echoed through the bathroom, and I timed it just right, as if I were still desperately trying to keep the door barricaded. However, I had already strategically positioned myself on the opposite side, ready to counter his next kick.

Because he just wouldn't relent, I was able to use his own momentum against him. As his foot crashed through the doorway when I swung the door open, I executed a swift and decisive maneuver. My boot connected with the side of his knee, targeting the vulnerable joint as it bent in a direction it shouldn't. Crunch and cracks were heard. The resulting scream of anguish pierced the air, drowning out any other sounds. He dropped his sword, his primary weapon, his hands instinctively moving to cradle the injured knee from both sides.

In the midst of this chaotic clash, a wry and darkly humorous phrase escaped my lips, a gallows jest that seemed oddly fitting for the situation, "He's never gonna dance again." It was a macabre twist on the lyrics from a famous song, a grim reminder of the consequences of his ill-fated assault. I mean, who doesn't love a little George Michael?

The rest of the med staff drew their knives and syringes, backed up, and took concerned looks at each other as they spread about as I grabbed the sword and walked out of the bathroom.

"You guys see this too, not just me?" the nice nurse said, who was now wielding two short swords.

"Um, dude's glowing," said the other medical girl.

A new figure clad in full combat gear rushed toward me, his voice punctuated by agitation, "Damn it, he's probably hopped up on some new drug." Swiftly, I utilized the blade I had recently acquired to parry his clumsily aimed attack. In response, I delivered a calculated jab straight into his lower femur, deliberately avoiding the femoral artery to minimize the ensuing bloodshed. As the excruciating pain enveloped him, he crumpled to the floor, writhing in torment, yet thankfully still very much alive.

The nurse I had initially perceived as friendly suddenly transformed into a challenging adversary, her demeanor shifting dramatically. In the blink of an eye, she charged towards me, wielding a syringe menacingly overhead and a dagger poised in her other hand. I braced myself for what I thought would be a straightforward confrontation, but to my astonishment, she expertly countered my kick and skillfully sidestepped my punch. Her fluid movements were impressive, and it became clear that she possessed advanced combat skills.

With fierce determination, she closed in on me, attempting to jab the syringe into my arm, its contents a mystery. Swiftly, she withdrew and squared up for a full-scale combat engagement, her intent crystal clear.

In the midst of this tense situation, Dahlia, my ever-resourceful companion, chimed in with distinctive humor. "Oh heck nawl, not the Naughty Ninja Nurses!" we exclaimed before launching a barrage of punches at the nurse. However, the nurse's defensive prowess was equally remarkable, effortlessly deflecting each of Dahlia's strikes.

Seizing the opportunity, I decided to employ an unorthodox tactic. In a moment of quick thinking, I grabbed a pair of dirty underwear that happened to be within reach and hurled it toward the nurse's face. The unexpected and unhygienic projectile took her by surprise, causing her to let out an involuntary scream as it landed on her face.

Dahlia rang out with, "C-diff bitch!"

While the nurse was momentarily incapacitated by shock and disgust, I capitalized on the distraction, delivering a well-placed spinning back heel kick. The nurse collapsed to the ground, unconscious, with the soiled undergarment still obscuring her features. It was an unconventional victory in a highly unconventional situation.

"We're going to hell for that, aren't we?" Dahlia whispered to me.

"Yes, but not for that," I responded. "But, be honest, do I have C-Diff? Because I have random diarrhea."

"No, I, uh, I like cheese a lot."

"I'm adding it to the list of reasons you deserve an asswhoopin'."

The remaining assailants, now assessing that their individual strengths wouldn't suffice to take down an ANGL, decided to team up and confront me as a group. Five of them remained—two disguised as medical professionals in scrubs, and three clad in military attire. Patience was not a virtue I could afford in this battle-ready form. I stepped back until the wall pressed firmly against my back, then utilized the wall's support as a springboard. My body propelled headlong toward the two female assassins.

Mid-flight, I executed a rapid spin, unleashing a sweeping horizontal strike with my sword. The blade connected not only with hilt and metal but also with flesh. The two women dropped to their knees, clutching their wounded wrists, their short swords clattering to the ground. Frustration and anger etched across their faces as they realized they had lost not just digits but entire fingers. With determination, they scrambled to their feet, making a hasty exit through the still-open front door.

The astonishment in the eyes of the remaining trio of men in military gear was palpable. "You incapacitated two Nightingales with a single move?" one of them inquired, visibly impressed. "Indeed, they are renowned and feared," remarked another. The third, with a calculating gleam in his eye, pondered aloud, "Well, it looks like we'll be entitled to a substantial bonus for delivering his head." Their laughter resonated within the room.

Positioned strategically between these three adversaries and the exit, I knew that an impulsive escape might not be my best course of action. They possessed valuable information and offered an opportunity to vent some of my pent-up frustrations. Each man was dangerously close, leaving me vulnerable to an attack from one of his comrades should I attempt to evade.

As the three men closed in, their malicious intent written all over their faces, I knew I had to act swiftly. The odds were against me, but I had one advantage—they underestimated me. I couldn't afford to let them seize the upper hand, so I took a calculated risk.

With deceptive speed and agility, I made a sudden pivot, my body twisting like a coiled spring. The closest attacker lunged forward, attempting to strike me from behind, but my preternatural reflexes kicked in. I swung my sword in a low arc, catching the assailant's legs in a devastating sweep. He crashed to the ground with a pained yelp, clutching his injured knees.

The other two, momentarily taken aback by my unexpected maneuver, hesitated for a split second. That hesitation was all I needed. I lunged forward, aiming to incapacitate them with quick, precise strikes. The first man, caught off guard, barely managed to raise his weapon in defense, but it was too late. My blade found its mark, severing his weapon hand cleanly.

His agonized scream filled the room as he crumpled to the floor, clutching his severed limb. The last remaining adversary, realizing the dire situation, attempted to flee through the open doorway. However, I was faster. With a powerful leap, I closed the distance and tackled him to the ground just outside the entrance.

We grappled fiercely, a desperate struggle for control. His training allowed him to put up a fight, but the relentless determination that had guided me through countless battles proved superior. With a final, decisive move, I disarmed him and pinned him to the ground, my blade poised at his throat.

Gasping for breath, he looked up at me, defeat etched on his face. "Finish it," he spat, his voice a mixture of anger and resignation. He lifted his foot and reached for a hidden knife in his boot and I took my blade and removed his dominant hand with one slice. It lay on the floor several feet from us twitching.

I hesitated, the weight of my actions heavy on my conscience. In that fleeting moment, I had to decide whether to spare his life or succumb to the darker instincts that had driven me to this point.

I leaned down and gripped his bleeding nub and squeezed. He screamed in a pitch that only opera singers and Mariah Carey had access to, "I am only going to ask once. There's three other people I can ask. I will kill you without a second thought. Where are my swords and armor?" I loosened my grip and held his gaze while he recovered from the pain. I was certainly not going to get the security deposit back.

He looked away, and then back at me, shook his head in a small amount of disbelief and said, "The flat next door, it's been used as a staging area for months just for a moment like this. I swear. I saw your stuff in there, I swear."

I squeezed slightly tighter. "How many more are coming?"

He clenched his jaw tightly before uttering, "Far more than you're prepared to handle." His words were laced with a confidence that bordered on arrogance for someone missing an appendage. I observed him as he swiftly reached for his earpiece, and without hesitation, I followed suit, inserting the earpiece into my ear. Through the small device, I overheard a coded message, "The Marshmallow Unit has arrived, en route to your location."

My heart sank as I deciphered the message. The arrival of the Marshmallow Unit signaled the deployment of a specialized team armed with foam sprayers; a technology reminiscent of the iconic Stay Puft Marshmallow Man from the *Ghostbusters* movies. This was no ordinary threat—it was a force capable of immobilizing me, rendering me helpless and encased in a bizarre, gooey substance.

The odds were stacking up against me, and I could feel the tension in the air thickening. My next moves would be crucial if I wanted to evade the Marshmallow Unit's sticky embrace and escape this perilous situation.

Frantically, I incapacitated my adversary with a headbutt, rendering him unconscious, and then I tried to hastily make my way to the adjacent flat where he had suggested everything was stored.

I stepped out into the corridor, still catching my breath from the brutal fight with the Naughty Ninja Nurses. The adrenaline of victory had barely subsided when I saw Michael. His stance was rigid, every muscle coiled as if prepared to unleash a storm.

He sneered, his gaze dark and unfocused. "You really think reason matters now, Mark? The SAI's taken control—my anger, my purpose. I'm connected to him. My father will have to be proud of me now. I'm not in the Michael I once knew, I am everything he loves and respects."

I frowned, my mind reeling. I'd seen it before: the implant's insidious influence turning a man's nature upside down. "It's the SAI, Michael. It's messing with you. Don't do this," I pleaded, edging forward as his fury began to surge.

But his next move was unlike anything I'd encountered—a flurry of strikes, his blows fueled by an intensity that bordered on the superhuman. I barely managed to deflect his assault, my arms instinctively raising to parry the ferocity of his blows. Each attack thudded against my defenses with a force that left me reeling.

In the chaos, my heart pounded with a terrible realization: killing him now wasn't an option. It would be unforgivable. Tagadashi would come after me without mercy, and making an enemy of 1—Michael's own legacy—would shatter any chance I had to survive this war. I couldn't let that happen.

Desperation clawed at me as I backed away, dodging another furious swing. My voice, hoarse and trembling, broke through the clamor.

Desperate to bridge the chasm that the SAI has forced between us, I edged closer. "Michael, please…it's not you—it's that cursed SAI. Remember the lullabies Han and Jiro used to sing to you? The ones about honor and love?"

I begin the familiar, bittersweet melody:

"Mamoru mono yo, ai to meiyo no uta,

Kaze ni nosete, eien ni hibikase,

Kokoro o hitotsu ni, toki o koete,

Anata to watashi, unmei o musubu."

For a breathless moment, I searched his eyes for a glimmer of recognition. But then, as if the fragile connection shattered entirely, Michael's demeanor changed. His face contorts into a deranged grin, and he started laughing maniacally—a sound that echoed off the sterile walls. In one wild, desperate movement, he reached into his jacket and pulled out a small, gleaming ornate knife. With his laughter rising to a fever pitch, he brought the blade unsteadily to his throat, intent on ending his own life.

Without thinking, I leaped forward. I caught his wrist mere inches before the knife could make contact. My grip was firm, my heart pounding in a mix of relief and horror as I wrestled control of his trembling hand. "Michael, no!" I shouted, forcing him to meet my eyes. His manic laughter faltered, replaced by a sob that wracked his body.

Then it all left. His body went completely limp for a moment, before he lifted his head and looked directly at me. Our gaze locked.

He tilted his head slightly like a curious puppy, his unruly hair fell away to reveal a single glowing green left eye—the same eerie hue I had only ever seen in one other person.

"Jiro?" I said confused and shook off the outrageous thought. "Michael…" I called softly, hoping to reach him. But before I can speak further, a disembodied voice, unmistakably Jiro's, cut through the tension.

"Enjoying things, little brother?" he taunted, his tone laced with icy amusement.

At once, Dahlia's voice started to fill the air, "Hey Big Trouble in Litt…" only to be abruptly halted by Jiro's command: "Power down for thirty seconds."

In an instant, Dahlia's presence vanished, plunging the space into an unnerving silence.

Jiro continued, his voice disinterested and detached, "Watching you struggle is like seeing children fight over a pacifier—the endless bickering of 8 and 9. If you're having such a hard time handling your little brother, Mark, then you'll never fare well against 7."

His words stung, each syllable a reminder that Michael's combat skills were nothing more than a test—a small sample of the training Jiro had bestowed on him to gauge my worth.

The SAI unit above him began to emit thin wisps of smoke as Dahlia's voice returned, finishing her broken sentence with a panicked, "Little China…Oh shit, his head is gonna explode!"

As I held him, Dahlia's digital interface extended a virtual hand toward mine. Instinctively, I reached out, our connectors linking in a desperate bid to balance the runaway power load surging through

Michael's taxed system. The cold metal of the knife was now a distant threat compared to the sizzling tension of the SAI overload.

In that charged moment, as I pulled Michael's forehead gently toward mine in an effort to wrest remote control of his rogue implant, a single, haunting vision seared through my mind—Han and Jiro, lying side by side on cold operating tables, their faces void of life.

My voice trembled as I whispered, "I won't let this be the end, Michael…I won't let us become monsters."

Every beat of my heart was a prayer that somewhere beneath the madness, the boy who once knew honor and love still lingered. And as I clung to him, I vowed that no matter what came next, I would do everything in my power to save him—even if it meant defying fate and the very technology that tore us apart.

He looked up at me, coming to like someone who'd just been knocked out in a boxing match. He took a minute to orient to his surroundings.

He immediately started trying to explain, "Mark, it wasn't me. I mean it was, but it wasn't. I hate what's happening, but I don't hate you."

"My time is short Michael, but what the hell just happened?" I asked annoyed.

"I was given a free SAI and passage to Tokyo Prime. I can't take it out, it's permanent."

"Yes, but so is the ability for Jiro to use you. You must tell your father."

"I will, but first your time is indeed short. I passed the sticky van downstairs. They will flood this entire floor to get to you."

"Yeah, I get that, I do hope indeed fate is on my side."

It appeared that fate was on my side, as the security system was configured for fingerprint access, an old biometric unit, and I was surrounded by an abundance of conveniently scattered appendages. With ample access to fingers and thumbs, I swiftly gained access to the flat's inner sanctum after scanning a few digits I grabbed off the ground.

Inside, a treasure trove awaited me—my trusty armor, a pair of razor-sharp swords, the Hono and Masamune, and a bag filled with invaluable equipment. I even remembered my new Halo. The room was a veritable arsenal, complete with monitors and an array of sophisticated gear. I grabbed a few extras just in case. As I outfitted myself, I felt a familiar transformation taking place, once again resembling a homeless but exceptionally well-armed SWAT team member.

Time was of the essence as I heard the telltale sounds of the elevator's arrival, followed by the unmistakable presence of the Marshmallow Unit closing in on my location. Desperation gripped me as I barricaded the door just seconds before they attempted to breach it. I was cornered seven floors above ground, with no apparent escape route. There was no negotiating around these situations, they'd spray and you'd be stuck there.

I turned to the window, super-heated the edge of the Hono and turned the pane of glass into a million tiny pieces. I poked my head out and saw below was just a bustling street scene. I had no choice but to jump. I took several steps back into the center of the kitchen and ran, collapsed my arms to my side and dived to the pavement below. I plunged out of the window, freefalling towards the unforgiving ground below. In my dire predicament, I activated my armor's bubble and felt the abrupt stoppage in moment, and then it picked back up immediately. This made the fall feel like it was from only fifteen feet as the bubble arrested my momentum before hitting the ground. It's not flying but I'll take it.

The landing was harsh, sending shockwaves of pain through my body, but I received a notification that the armor's bubble had admirably absorbed a significant portion of the damage, sparing me from the worst of the fall. With my heart pounding and adrenaline coursing through my veins, I knew that my ordeal was far from over, but I had successfully eluded capture once again. I stood to see a truck bearing down on me, my mind activating the bubble once more, knocking back several feet, leaving me with 130,000 newtons of force remaining on the bubble. This was an amazing piece of armor, I thought to myself as I stood, brushing the dirt and debris from my face and hands before being hit by another car, and a red alert flashing in my Hololens—92,000 newtons of force remaining.

Dahlia had let out a disgruntled groan as I struggled to sit up, peeling myself off the unforgiving sidewalk. Concerned onlookers rushed to my side, their faces reflecting a mix of confusion and compassion. They bombarded me with questions about my well-being, insisting that I take a moment to recover.

Some looking in puzzlement as they could not understand the weird shape I made in the car's hood and front end.

"I'm fine," I assured them, my responses met with perplexed expressions. However, amidst the worried voices and the gentle prodding to sit down, I couldn't ignore the distant sounds that carried through the air—the resounding cheers and explosive booms marking the commencement of the Deathball game. Although I was just two blocks away, navigating the bustling coliseum with its labyrinthine security measures and throngs of spectators would be a time-consuming endeavor, a luxury I couldn't afford.

An idea began to form in my mind, and I turned to Dahlia, bracing for inevitable resistance. "How far of a drop can 92,000 newtons of force protect me from?" I queried.

Dahlia responded with a tone that clearly conveyed disapproval. "Not far enough, and I'm certainly not in the mood for experimentation. My design is geared toward battle, not reckless stunts."

Undeterred, I countered with an audacious plan as we sprinted toward the growing crowds. "You're right; it's not your forte. But if you access the garage, I believe you can retrieve the information we need."

In the dimly lit garage of my mind, a lingering fragment of Whisperwing's once-majestic form stood as a testament to its former glory, but it was different. Though battered and fragmented, its influence was far from diminished, especially in the mind of Genji. The remnants of the aircraft still resonated with Genji's indomitable spirit, and it held the key to an audacious plan we needed for our escape from this predicament. A small person. Robotic, sleek, and hovering was in the room, a silhouette in the corner, hesitant to come forward.

Dahlia approached the Whisperwing fragment, heart pounding with anticipation. It asked a questioned, "What do you want from me?" Dahlia's ever-present sense of humor, replaced categorically with a face as endearing and caring spoke with a soft voice and said, "To make my home, your home."

I interfaced with the Whisperwing remnant, an eerie connection to the once-soaring aircraft. Together, we harnessed its latent power, bending it to our will. In a mesmerizing display of technological sorcery, the bubble began to transform, taking on the semblance of majestic wings, reminiscent of an angelic being. The power draw was weaving and moving much in the same way that the Halosphere moved.

Dahlia reported in with a bit of excitement, "Go to the opposite side of the field from the home team, and get up to the penthouse, there's someone up there we need to see. I've got a plan. We've still got 92,000 newtons of forces left on your armor."

Kimberly had informed me that she would be observing the match from her luxurious suite. It was a detail that didn't escape my attention, as it provided us with a potential advantage. Located on the uppermost floor of the Halosphere power building in the southern sector, Kimberly's office served as her vantage point. It was not only the ideal spot to witness the unfolding events but also the most probable location to encounter her in person.

I saw her building with easy access and a public elevator and decided to ask questions along the way. The closer I got, the more I became beleaguered as there was a security detail asking for tickets and checking everyone for weapons who were getting the elevators. I took this opportunity to use something from the goody bag as a distraction. I temporally activated and tossed a Nightmare on Elm Street, not before taking note of the mechanisms of action in case I would try to someday possibly replicate it. I didn't know why I felt such a strong urge. Many of the people in the immediate area started to run and scream. Others began to accuse others of being aliens, lizard creatures and other vile monsters. The security staff were quickly distanced from the core responsibilities. They attempted to shut down the elevator, but I quickly flashed my real badge, they were dismissive and allowed me to pass without hesitation or thought.

My biometric thumb print still worked and the box light lit up green and I poked the fifty-fifth floor on approval. Robinson had come through for me. After a few minutes, the door dinged open and I walked into the party of the year. Everyone was in a tuxedo or dinner dress and there I was, homeless SWAT team member. I was as out of place there as humanly possible. Then Dahlia spoke, loudly and as usual, inappropriately, "I can only imagine Martin Luther King attending a Klan meeting standing out more than us being here right now." That drew some side eye sneers and others trying to pretend that they weren't staring.

The suite was full of nostalgic throwbacks that cost a king's ransom. A man stood next to a Keytar rambling on about how it changed the face of music. Another group of people clamored around a polaroid camera with the ultimate flex, several polaroids of Kimberly and…hold the phone…Dahlia. Several of the guests were looking at the polaroids, for which they would cost more money than most of them make in a year and saw my face. I now felt more of a museum piece than a party guest, uninvited as I was.

Then a voice startled me from behind, "Mark or Dahlia?" Kimberly queried.

"Both," I said as I turned to find Kimberly holding a champagne flute in one hand and her other hand in the pockets of her jeans.

"How does do that work?" she asked with scrunched eyebrows as she took a step closer to look deeper into my eyes.

"Hey Em," Dahlia said with a smile.

"There you are," Kimberly responded with a brightened look as she looked deeper into my eyes like she could see more behind them by moving her head around, and it actually kind of felt like she could. Then she grabbed my arm and pulled me into a corner of the room near a super Nintendo, handed me a controller and started up the system.

"You're pretty good at this," I jested until I saw the look on her face. It was more serious than expected.

"You were successful, I assume judging on all accounts of the news? Hammock came here earlier and showed me and Chief Robinson the Holocube, then he shot me with dart gun after *a lot* of convincing," she said through her teeth as she hazarded a glare from the top of her eyes in my direction.

"Yes, Em, we were successful, but there's a reason we are here," Dahlia answered coldly. "The device was incinerated as requested after use as well."

"Very good, then why come here and risk exposure of us both?" Kimberly demanded.

I looked back into her eyes with the same search she had with mine and found the caring person she tried to hide before I spoke, "Dimitri

Voynov, ANGL 7 is the mastermind of everything. His goal is to infect the entire attendance tonight with a new batch of Hyperion. It's so addictive that it will strip people of their mental capacities down to basic function and increase their strength tenfold. They will only be satiated when they are given more Hyperion, but are extremely open to suggestion when presented with the promise of Hyperion as a reward. They are called Hype-mutes in The Waste. The worst part is this stuff kills seven out of ten people that are exposed to it. Dimitri is thirty floors beneath you in his box and I need a safe place to jump from. I need to stop him before he releases it and kills thousands while also creating an army of Hype-mutes for god knows why."

She nodded her head over to the open doors to our left. "Those are the only open doors I have. I will distract as many of these yahoos as I can," she said as she hugged me. "I have stories for you, come back, you'll want to hear the one about Singapore. Now go."

I had secured access to a towering building overlooking the colossal stadium, a vantage point that afforded a clear view of the box reserved for 7.

Dahlia took a moment to explain the plan, the tone uncharacteristically serious. "You remember that bubble armor, the one that bounces you around like a hamster? Well, it's still got 92,000 newtons of force absorption left in it, roughly equivalent to a semi colliding at 35 miles per hour. Or, as Echo, the nickname for Whisperwings digital presence in my head, put it, it's the same force as you slamming into 7's box from a 40-story drop. If we activate it, it should decelerate you enough, but brace yourself—it's going to be one painful ride. Echo believes he can expand the bubble, giving you a bit of lift, but you'll still be on a collision course with that box." Dahlia's words hung in the air, emphasizing the gravity of the situation.

Dahlia's explanation left me contemplating the audacious plan we were about to execute. The armor which just saved me from getting hit by a car, now held the key to my descent from the towering heights to 7's box below. It was a risky maneuver, no doubt, but it seemed to be our best shot at reaching the target.

The mention of 92,000 newtons of force brought forth vivid mental images of car crashes and high-impact collisions. It was a daunting comparison, and the idea of intentionally subjecting myself to such an experience was far from comforting. Yet, it was the only option I had…with no rope, or parachute, or even a pillow to make the landing a smidge softer.

Echo's connection to Genji and Whisperwing was paramount in my decision to move forward. Expanding the bubble to catch some air, even for a brief moment, might mean the difference between a painful impact and a catastrophic one. Still, it was hard to shake the feeling that this plan was a leap of faith, a gamble with the laws of physics and a battle against gravity itself.

As Dahlia's words settled in, a sense of determination washed over me. We had come this far, faced countless challenges, and defied the odds, all in one single day. Now, thousands of lives hung in the balance, there was no turning back. I braced myself mentally for the impending impact, knowing that our success depended on our ability to harness the remaining force within that bouncing sphere and navigate the perilous journey ahead.

With a deep breath, I stepped onto the balcony, peering down at the distant box, my target 7 standing looming as the ceremonies began. It was a hack of the armor, an ingenious creation of Whisperwing's remnant that defied the laws of physics. Dahlia told me that the remnant, we called Echo, handed over a crown made from bits and pieces found in the garage. This child was playful and innocent, and I was the toy. I wondered if this was going to work. I had no choice. Just with a thought, I could throw out a "boom" and catch some air to slow me down.

Dahlia, in a moment of perfectly timed comedic relief, feigned enthusiasm for the plan they had initially doubted, adding a touch of levity to the gravity of the situation. It was a performance worthy of an Oscar.

"This is definitely one hundred percent going to work. We are going to land on an old lady, or someone who doesn't deserve to die and then three people will be dead. You, me, and Grace. That poor, poor, poor Grace. She just found love again after Roger died after a terrible Zamboni accident. Roger had been a good man but suffered from untreatable erectile dysfunction for most of their marriage, and Grace had finally met Tyrone after Roger died. Tyrone was a good man. A diesel mechanic from The Waste who worked his way into the Halosphere," Dahlia said as we climbed onto the railing, onlookers running to our aid, our arms outstretched and allowing gravity to pull us over the edge. "And Tyrone was huuuunnnnnggg!" The feeling of pure freedom pulsed through my body as the world seemed to hold its breath. As I fell into the abyss, I heard screams. For a brief moment, it felt like I was defying gravity itself.

The world rushed past me as I plummeted from the towering heights. The cacophony of wind and chaos filled my ears, and 7's box approached with breathtaking speed. It filled my vision like I was a missile traveling down a tunnel. Thirty stories might as well have been a blink of an eye in the grand scheme of things, but in those fleeting moments, I found an unexpected sense of calm settling over me. I wondered what Dahlia was feeling and then felt the words, "You got this," formed through my lips.

As I hurtled toward the ground, I made a series of calculated moves to mitigate the impact. At thirty feet above the ground, I initiated the first maneuver, bleeding off some of the velocity, purely by thought. Then, at the critical ten-foot mark, I executed the second, further slowing my descent. The seconds felt like an eternity, allowing me to reflect on the choices that had brought me to this point.

Finally, the moment of impact arrived, but it was not the bone-shattering crash I had feared. Instead, I met the acrylic skybox enveloped in a protective sphere, its layers cocooning me in a manner reminiscent of the city's Halosphere, which shielded us from the dangers beyond. It hurt like hell, but I survived.

In that surreal instant, as I hung suspended within the transparent confines of the sphere, I couldn't help but marvel at the technology that had just saved my life. It was a testament to human ingenuity, a fusion of science and innovation that defied gravity itself. But there was no time to dwell on it; I had reached 7's box, and our mission was now in motion. I drew both swords, ready for battle with an opponent by which I had no battle awareness.

7 Stood and clapped. Not even so much as a flinch to my entrance and began to speak loudly with his Russian accent, "What an entrance. Now, who had that on their bingo card? Not even 5 had that as the entrance you were gonna make."

He took a step toward me and softened his voice, "Now, you have a decision to make. I know you think you know what's going on, but you don't. If you attack me, you will fail. I am not as easy an opponent as 8 or 9. Do you understand? I can break you without my bare hands."

He made a show of his empty hands, flashing the front and back slowly and continued speaking, "So, sit there and hear my proposition. If you don't like it, you can choose which way you die. Slow and painfully, or quick and painfully. Either way, that core is mine." He looked to his security detail. "Leave us, he will kill you just to get to me. Just as quickly as I will you if you do not leave right now." The men scurried out of the door as a testament that 7 had made true on these threats before.

"Why do you want this so bad?" I asked and pointed to the back of my head and gestured with two fingers at his.

"Why would you want to keep something so dangerous in your head?" 7 said as he pointed to a chair and gestured the international sign to have a seat. I decided to play my hand and engaged 7 in battle. I attacked and he drew a Scimitar from what seemed like thin air and dropped it on the ground. My blade came to a stop within a hair of a killing blow across his throat. Not even a bead of sweat formed on his head, though my sword was one twitch from severing his carotid. He looked at me with stone-cold eyes.

"So, are you going to take the seat or not?" he asked with firm assertion and one raised eyebrow.

I was curious and confused. Dahlia was too, so we asked, "What do you mean dangerous, and why didn't you defend against my strike?" I asked with the sword pressed against his throat. Despite the threat of impending doom, 7 never even looked at the Hono. He behaved as if it didn't exist. This enraged me.

7 stepped forward, lancing his own neck against the ever-razor-sharp edge of the Hono, allowing blood to trickle down his neck onto his white collar and blue suit. "No seat then, I suppose. I've had a long day, I will sit. Shoot yourself. Or another president if you are so inclined. Which by the way is me."

7 reached up slowly and used two fingers to push away the sword. He casually walked over to a small table on his left and grabbed a crystal cask in poured a brown liquid into a small clear glass. "Drink? It's Tennessee Whiskey. There is an old song about it. But, contrary to the lyrics, it is not that sweet. But it is still very good. Or perhaps some food? I always find discussions are better had on a full stomach. Don't you?"

I stood there, seething and dripping fury, while my chest heaved, and adrenaline still pulsed through my veins.

He frowned and tilted his head slightly and bobbed as he spoke, "I'll take that as a no."

He then adjusted his suit, hitched up his pants and plopped back into his lounge chair, crossing his left leg over his right, exposing his blue and red argyle socks. I saw the wound on his neck heal as the nanites available to him in his bloodstream did their job. He took a sip of his whiskey and said, "Oh, that tastes good. Are you sure you don't want any? I had to bribe a lot of people and slit a few throats to get this," he said and he chuckled.

Frustration boiled over within me, and the need for answers had reached its breaking point. I couldn't endure the uncertainty any longer, so I confronted Dimitri with a determined demand, my voice unwavering. "Listen, Dimitri," I began, but before I could proceed, he swiftly raised an index finger as he sipped his drink, halting my words in their tracks. He took a measured sip from his glass, his brow furrowing as he emitted a low grunt of annoyance. A dismissive shake of his head followed.

With the glass now lowered, he corrected me in a tone that dripped with posh stolen authority. "It's President Dimitri," he asserted firmly, his hands gesturing impatiently for me to get to the heart of the matter, "but, go on, I'm sorry." He finished swallowing what little liquid was left in his cheek as though my words were a tedious preamble.

Undeterred, I pressed forward with a question that had been burning in my mind, my words tinged with a hint of menace. "Then why shouldn't I just end you right now?"

"For starters, you would find it near impossible to *end* me unless you have amassed a small army outside that door. Also, you don't even truly know why you're here or what impact my unlikely death would have on the outcome of the situation at hand, and lastly you need to know more about DL1A, or what you call Dahlia, and I can tell you more about it."

315

"I'm stronger than I look, I assure you that 7, I do not need an army. Tell me how to stop Hyperion from killing these people. Do you want your first day as president to be marred by a national tragedy?" I angled with the unlikeliest of chances.

7 slammed his glass down and sloshed liquor all over the glass topped counter while belly laughing. "HA! Tragedy is exactly what I need. I will be the phoenix, the man who pulls NJC out of the ashes. I will be able to do no wrong. And when I want to make a move that is controversial, the nation will support me blindly because I took a place that was in ruin and pieced it back together."

"How? How did you become president?" I asked with the sincerest amount of curiosity.

"That was the easiest part," 7 said with a grin and another sip as he leaned forward and pulled air through his teeth before he said, "just as you learned how to track and procure, I learned how to manipulate and obfuscate. Big word, no? I like it. I was leading the polls, there was an obscure rule to have an emergency election selected by the other presidents of other Union States. I convinced them that I would catch you, here tonight, if they selected me. If not, a rogue ANGL who has a malfunctioning SAI with the ability to use a firearm inside of a Halosphere would be on the loose. So, here I am, President."

I knew he could do this. 7 had destabilized nations for fun and restabilized them for table bets. I just couldn't rationale a motivation. "But why? Why would you kill all of these people? Why do you want to be president?" I asked with an edge to my voice, my sword still pointed at him.

7 stood, meeting my gaze, and with a bereft and concerned voice he spoke, "It's simple, 10, for the future of the world and humanity's survival, we must reestablish contact with Zion. The Union States reached a simple conclusion: no matter how much knowledge lay inside *Voyager Legacy*—or *Zion*, as we call it—it wasn't worth the danger

of giving that power to an SAI mind. Instead, they have scrapped the project, no further contact will be attempted."

He paused and looked into my eyes to see if I was following, when he saw that I was actually listening, he picked up where he left off, "The Union States are preparing to treaty with The Liberty States to attempt another quantum state computer, The Voyager Nexus. While this is a great opportunity for hand-holding and photographs. There is still a fundamental difference in beliefs. War will return, and luck, as they say, favors the prepared. Either way, we are stacking the deck on our side. A battle or escalation between superpowers may not leave us so fortunate next time. We will make contact with Zion and establish ourselves as the authority in the Union States, for which we need an army. Ergo, break a few eggs to make an omelet. Or prepare for the inevitable war. No matter the scenario, conflict is on the horizon. We will have the answers to keep humanity from collapsing like it is currently on the verge of right now."

I began to contemplate everything and searched his monologue for truths or half-truths when Dahlia spoke up, "Oh, now that's some God-complex bullshit if I've ever it heard before."

"DL1A or Dahlia, I am glad to see you, excuse me, hear you again," 7 postured.

Dahlia picked up on it and single-finger saluted with both hands even while bearing a sword, which I must say was impressive.

"Do you know what DL1A stands for, 10?" 7 quizzed and smirked, and from my expression. "I bet you don't, so I will tell you. Digital Lifeform 1 A. That jumble of electronics you have connected to your brain stem is the first virtual consciousness we discovered. It was born from several other existing semi-intelligent clusters. When Zion gave the blueprint for the SAI, they cheated and cut corners in order to create a more compliant and predictable implant. Instead, what was created was something much more, well, divergent."

I scoffed, lowered the sword and demanded, "Then why do you want it so bad and why my brain too?"

In that pivotal moment, it was as if he was locking eyes with me. I couldn't look away. I witnessed a brief but unmistakable flash of fervor and bloodlust within the depths of his cold, unyielding gaze. It was a minuscule fracture in his otherwise impenetrable armor, a glimpse into the depths of his ruthless mentality. This fleeting revelation struck a chord of fear and uncertainty within me, more profound and unsettling than any other experience in my entire life. It was as if I had glimpsed the true core of the adversary I faced—behind the powerful facade lurked a relentless and dangerous force, driven by dark purpose. His crazy was showing, and it was more than I had ever thought possible for one person to have.

With a smile and an air of satisfaction 7 puffed out his chest. "We want it because DL1A has an insurance policy built in. Zion can tell us what to do, yes. But, there is one that can tell Zion what to do. We are seeking the secrets of the universe after all, it's not a time to get all stingy with the details."

The implant nestled within my psyche, the very origin of Dahlia's existence, had become the object of desire for 7 and the other ANGLs. What set this implant apart was a hidden secret embedded within its core during its construction—a clandestine communication node that established a direct link between the implant, the ANGLs, and the feared Quantum space computer known as Voyager Legacy. This unique coding was the very essence of Dahlia's singularity.

This same coding had been incorporated into other SAIs as well, but the DL1A SAI stood apart. It was the result of a collaborative effort, a fusion of several older semi-intelligent systems meticulously woven into a singular entity. The end product was nothing short of revolutionary, holding the potential to reshape the world as we knew it. Dahlia's existence was the embodiment of this remarkable convergence, a force to be reckoned with, and a key to unlocking the true power of Voyager Legacy.

As 7 looked down upon me, his eyes narrowing with a mixture of determination and a hint of something deeper, his words carried the weight of the moment. His voice held a solemn tone as he addressed the gravity of my role in this unfolding saga. He made it clear that he wasn't seeking forgiveness, but rather wanted me to comprehend the significance of the sacrifice that lay before me.

With deliberate action, in a single motion he retrieved his sword from the floor, swiping the blade gleaming ominously in the dim light. His words carried a sense of resignation, as if he believed that any attempts at self-defense on my part would be in vain. He seemed to question whether such a thing as "impossible" even existed for someone like me.

Then without even a momentary pause in his gesticulation and paired with lightning speed, 7 launched himself toward me, his sword poised overhead, ready to strike and dismember in a single devastating motion. His incredible power, combined with his extraordinary strength, agility, and precision, far surpassed my own capabilities. The initial strike was executed with such calculated precision and sheer violence that I instinctively put as much distance as I could between us, desperately trying to evade the deadly arc of his blade.

He pressed the attack further as I deflected his initial strike, and an unexpected turn of events caught me off guard. My Hono, the sword I had only recently acquired and grown to appreciate, was violently knocked out of my grip. It embedded itself into the wall on my right with astonishing force, the blade sinking halfway to the hilt. My attention was momentarily stolen by the sight of my sword morphing into an unintended projectile, leaving me temporarily disarmed.

However, 7, ever the efficient and ruthless combatant, wasted no time capitalizing on my momentary distraction. With seamless fluidity, he harnessed his momentum, executing a spin that resembled a centrifuge in its precision. It was as if he were preparing to launch a shot-put into the distance, but instead of a round metal ball, he was heaving a Scimitar as wide as my thigh and as tall as my torso. In the culmination of this motion, he delivered a backhanded strike with his arm fully extended, swiftly closing the distance between us.

The trajectory of his attack aimed directly across my chest, and in a frantic scramble to defend myself, I reached for the Masamune, the priceless blade that represented all of Japanese culture and history in its ancient and hallowed folded steel. With my best effort, I pressed the broadside of the blade against my shoulder and positioned my legs to brace for the impending impact. The collision was brutal, and the searing pain as my arm snapped in response was immediate. It felt as though the room itself had shifted, either lowering or throwing me against the same wall where my Hono had been forcefully lodged. I felt my head hit the wall before I slid to the side.

Amidst the chaos, the unmistakable sound of metal hitting the ground reverberated through the room. I quickly surveyed the scattered weapons, taking stock of our arsenal. I was still clutching the Masamune, my Hono remained embedded in the wall, and a fractured blade lay discarded on the ground. It was a grim revelation that it wasn't my arm that had been broken, but rather the priceless Japanese heirloom that had been entrusted to me was broken in half.

In the mere fraction of a blink, I managed to tear my gaze away from my embedded Hono, broken Masamune, and limited defense options to find 7 thrusting the point of his blade directly at my chest. Instinct and adrenaline kicked in, and I responded with a combination of parrying his strike and utilizing the tips of my feet to leap in the opposite direction of my deflection.

As my desperate maneuver unfolded, his cold carbon grazed over my shoulder, its edge slicing through my flesh. The blade halted its deadly path as it encountered the woven Kevlar strap over my shoulder holding my breastplate, preventing it from digging deeper into my body.

Nevertheless, the pain that coursed through me was nearly unbearable, a searing agony that radiated from the wound. I couldn't hold it back—a scream ripped from my chest, matching the sound of tearing flesh. I dropped to one knee, drowning in the sheer brutality of it.

My arms came down and the edge of the sword sliced the back of his hand, a superficial wound, if that, but it disarmed 7.

In that intense moment of combat, 7's determination and skill were on full display. With a calculated move, he leaned back, his eyes widened with blood lust once again, and unleashed a powerful, precision strike. His boot, like a sledgehammer, made contact with the exact center of my chest, targeting a usually vulnerable spot with the accuracy of a surgeon.

The impact was devastating. The force of the kick sent shockwaves through my entire body, and I felt as though I had been hit by a speeding transport. The pain radiated outward from the point of impact, surging through my chest like a relentless inferno.

The sheer power of the blow launched me into the air, a helpless pawn in 7's brutal game. Time seemed to slow as I soared, my limbs flailing in the chaotic rush of the moment. My mind raced, desperately seeking a way to regain control and mount a counteroffensive.

Less than fifteen seconds had passed since our battle had escalated to this ferocious crescendo, yet it felt like an eternity. As I hurtled through the air, I knew that I needed to recover quickly, to gather my strength and wits if I had any hope of surviving this relentless onslaught.

My body came to a sudden, painful halt as I slammed into the concrete wall. Though it was a brutal stop, I couldn't help but be grateful that the material was forgiving, absorbing some of the impact as I left a full body impression. Slowly, I slid down the wall. The crumbles of loosened concrete from my impact fell at my feet. My trembling legs unable to support me, until I found myself sitting on the floor, staring up at the ceiling in a daze.

As I lay there, trying to regain my bearings, I couldn't ignore the haunting smile on 7's face. He approached me with measured steps, his confidence radiating from every movement. His voice, when he finally spoke, carried a hint of genuine admiration, an acknowledgment of the fierce battle we had just waged.

"You did better than most, even for an ANGL, very good to survive three of my attacks and you disarmed me. That's never happened before," he remarked, his tone revealing a sense of surprise and respect.

I looked at the camera, I knew that he was watching. "There's no way you're not seeing this," I said angrily knowing that the stream into Tagadashi's private network was showing my royal asswhoopin. 7 walked over to the camera and crushed it in his massive hands like an empty aluminum can.

"Are you hoping for a bit of aid?" 7 said before busting into a bluster of laughs.

He reached into his pocket and pulled out a cube. A Holocube, and placed it on the table with a glass half dome on top. This table was used for 3D views of the Holocube content and immediately started playing a video. It was a video of Tagadashi, saying things like "I need the SAI by any means necessary," "Mark is the only way," and "If it kills him or not, we must remove the SAI."

The defeat must have been showing on my face because 7 pulled the cube to stop the feed and scrunched his face. "You expect for *HIM* to save you? Oh no, 10, he wants you dead for this," Dimitri said while he motioned at the base of his skull.

I knew if I was going survive, not win, but survive I had to give all of myself.

Summoning all my strength, I managed to push myself up to one knee, determination etched across my face. With a grunt, I attempted to lift 7's sword, only to find it categorically heavy. It felt like trying to hoist Thor's Mjolnir. My efforts were futile because the weight was truly unexpected given that the Hono was so well and expertly balanced, and 7 couldn't help but chuckle at my struggle.

He continued in a tone that was dry, direct, and condescending, laying bare the grim truth behind the weapon's weight. "Seventy-seven pounds, precisely. Crafted from the very heart of destruction—depleted uranium salvaged from the simultaneous nuclear missile launches by advanced nations, an apocalyptic near-miss that triggered Zion's catastrophic EMP in 2040. Do you now grasp the urgency of our mission as the voice of Voyager Legacy? To Zion? Given the slightest opportunity, war shall unleash humanity's annihilation."

The echoes of his words reverberated in the room, each one carrying the weight of our shared history and the monumental responsibility we bore. In that moment, I couldn't deny the gravity of our situation, the delicate balance between chaos and survival that hinged on the decisions we would make.

As 7 poised his weapon above his head for what seemed like an impending and decisive blow, I found myself defenseless, with no room for hesitation. It was then that I resorted to my last, desperate gambit. Swiftly, I pulled the concealed pin on the Syrian Decibel Grenade I had strategically kept hidden behind my back. The moment the pin was dislodged, chaos erupted.

7's immediate reaction was visceral. He dropped his Scimitar, cupping his ears in an agonizing response to the grenade's piercing sound waves. His towering frame stumbled in disorientation, and he fought to maintain his balance, one knee nearly buckling as he steadied himself with an elbow. Groans and jeers escaped his clenched jaw as he grappled with the overwhelming sensory assault.

I, on the other hand, remained unfazed, protected by the specially designed earplugs that negated the grenade's auditory onslaught. It became evident that 7's arrogance and propensity for long-winded speeches had afforded me just enough time to activate the grenade.

Struggling to rise from the floor, I made my way to the nearby wall, determined to reclaim my sword, which had become embedded in the concrete as though a modern-day Excalibur. The effort required to extract it was almost impossible, draining my dwindling strength with each exertion.

Finally, as I turned back to face my adversary, I was met with a startling sight. 7, now shirtless, had torn his garment into makeshift headgear, wrapping it tightly around his skull in a bid to mitigate the effects of the sound-based assault. The once imposing figure, whom I had always perceived as large, now appeared almost alien in nature, his physique defying conventional human boundaries. The mystery of how he could wield a seventy-seven-pound sword with such ease was unveiled before me.

With a triumphant grin and spittle dripping from his chin, 7 snatched the grenade and promptly disabled it, his powerful hands crushing the control mechanism. He then discarded the rest of his shirt, revealing his sculpted form as he looked at me and offered a begrudging compliment, "Now, that was a smart idea."

"That was something I would expect from 8," he said as he lifted the sword once more.

A voice came out of me that had never come out of me before, one that had a Hispanic accent. His mention of 8 reached deep inside of me and dug up a remnant, a memory of these very men's lives. A life I ended. Then something happened; words were spoken, and I could not stop. This wasn't Dahlia speaking words from my mouth. This was different. "Remember when we first met? You told me my churros; my cooking could change the world. I made you some empanadas

324

while we waited for our first assignment, and you saved one for some dignitary, and ever since, you always start your negotiations with food. You went on all night about the significance of the connection between food and our mentality and how it's underutilized. You told me it wasn't too late to leave the 10 and do something actually good. Remember when we found your family's recipes in the old apartment you grew up in, and you gave them to 9 to burn? I saw you cry. You told me never to tell anyone. I didn't."

7 interrupted with a yell at the top of his lungs. He clearly was out of sorts. "SHUT UP! How do you know this? Did he tell you this before you killed him? Did you torture this out of him?" he raged and began to destroy the room momentarily forgetting that I was even there. He tossed a couch as if it weighed nothing.

Then, a southern voice chimed in with a soothing and calming air to it. "Settle down, man. You ain't gonna fix nothing with all of that commotion." It was unmistakenly Texan and continued speaking just as fluidly as the previous voice that came out of me. "Remember when you saw me with my gloves off? What you said? You said, you wish you could find my dad and rip him in half. You told me that bad people don't exist, only bad deeds. Then, two weeks later I got a link on my Inios that was a picture of my father sliced in half. The link was titled, good deed to a bad person."

The rage returned. This time his fury claimed the walls. He punched the walls and left bloody marks in the craters where his fists sunk into the hard material. He slowed down and I could see his back rising and lowering matching his deep breaths. He reclaimed his heavily encumbered weapon and affixed a concentrated grip while he looked at it in his giant right hand. I opened my mouth to speak again, but instead he spoke.

"Enough!" 7 screamed as he slammed his sword into floor, embedding it into the ground out of sheer anger and frustration. "How do you know these things? Why are you speaking like this?" he said in a normal tone. "This is just some lame parlor trick. I will put an end to it when I put an end to you."

Then a voice that didn't come from me spoke, a sound from the door behind us startled us both, "Dimitri Voynev, you're about to commit genocide and you're better than that. I was out there, in the field with you. I am guilty too, war criminals, but we don't have to do this, son. You're trying to put a square peg in a square hole."

I instinctively began to correct him, but I caught myself and let him continue. Robinson procured a drone transport and had spoken with Hammock, thus vindicating my innocence. Robinson also understood the danger that I was in because he knew the gap in skill and abilities between 7 and I, and had come to help. When he was given the Holocube, he used the data and information to deduce that 7 would be unstoppable and that he needed to intercede.

As I listened to Robinson, the weight of the situation bore down on me. It was clear that he had taken significant steps to ascertain the truth of my circumstances. The fact that he had placed himself in the line of danger meant a lot, it was stupid, but still very sweet.

Robinson's understanding of the vast disparity in capabilities between 7 and me was a testament to his deep knowledge of the situation. His position remained unquestioned and secure. He was allowed in, leaving his true allegiance hidden—even from me, until now. 7's influence had grown vast, evolving into a force that appeared nearly unstoppable. The Holocube's data and information had allowed Robinson to piece together the puzzle, revealing the grim reality that we faced.

In light of this newfound understanding, Robinson's decision to intervene took on even greater significance. It was no longer merely a matter of exonerating me; it was about preventing 7 from wreaking havoc and ensuring the safety of everyone involved. Robinson's actions underscored his determination to confront this dominate threat head-on, setting the stage for a high-stakes showdown.

Just as he spoke, our eyes met and his gaze locked onto a small table that remained untouched, and on it, lay a trigger. I always knew 7 had a weakness for the dramatics, but a physical button for something that would be better off linked to his SAI feed seemed over the top, even for him. His attention was on Robinson. 7 slinked toward him with wrath and hate in his gate as his sword dragged along the floor, making a high-pitched grinding sound. Robinson was a larger and pudgy man, who carried a standard issue corps blade attached to a small, coiled cord, jutting from a small backpack. Robinson noticed my attention and goaded 7 by taunting him about winning the presidency on a technicality. "You only won because you rigged the race. That's like the hare knowing he was going beat the tortoise before they wrote the book."

As 7 prepared to execute his opening attack, a move that Robinson appeared to be quite familiar with, I observed a swift and calculated action on Robinson's part. He tightly squeezed a concealed trigger embedded within the handle of his sword, initiating a sequence that would prove to be both unexpected and effective. What followed was a spectacle that left us all in awe.

With a surge of energy, an arc of crackling electricity erupted from what I thought was Robinson's standard issue blade, extending like a radiant blue serpent toward 7's menacing Scimitar. The electric arc found its target with pinpoint accuracy, wrapping itself around 7's weapon like a coiling serpent ensnaring its prey. The immediate consequence of this electrical encounter was a dramatic and instantaneous reaction from 7.

As the electrical current coursed through the length of his Scimitar, 7's entire body responded in a convulsive reflex, a reaction akin to being subjected to a powerful electric shock. His muscles clenched and contracted involuntarily, causing him to lose his grip on the sword that had become electrified. With a startled and pained expression, 7 forcibly relinquished his weapon, which clattered to the ground, now devoid of its deadly charge.

Meanwhile, Robinson's sword continued to emanate the crackling electric discharge, seeking a path to dissipate the stored energy safely. The air seemed charged with tension, both literally and figuratively, as the unexpected turn of events unfolded before our eyes. Robinson's blade crackled and hissed, searching for the nearest grounded object to complete its electrical circuit.

This astonishing and unanticipated development had effectively neutralized 7's opening assault, leaving him temporarily incapacitated and disarmed. Robinson's resourcefulness and the element of surprise had shifted the balance of power in this confrontation, setting the stage for a new and unpredictable chapter in our unfolding saga.

7 stood there, looking down at his hands, reeling from the pain. Robinson's placement as our combat commander was an earned role and now it was more than obvious that he had spent his fair share of time in battle. Robinson released the trigger while 7 recovered and trotted to the small table. He swung at the trigger like a major league batter and made contact. I watched as the trigger sailed over my head and through the hole I created. Robinson uttered, "Keep it as far away from this man as possible, go and get it. I will keep him busy for as long as I can. Busier than a three-legged man in an ass kicking contest."

"Do you mean one-legged man?" I corrected.

Robinson squinted at me with a true sense of confusion before he rationalized out loud, "Well, a three-legged man's gonna be way more involved and excited, Mark. Do you even think before you speak? Now go!"

I took his words to heart as I grabbed the broken half of the Masamune, along with the Hono and turned my back, preparing for the blind jump. My trust in the soft field below to absorb my landing was my only solace. In the midst of my leap, I heard 7's thundering voice bellow, "Security!" Panic coursed through my veins, and in a split-second decision, I pulled the pin on the remaining Nightmare on Elm Street grenade and hurled it at the door.

With a sense of urgency, I began assessing my situation. I had only 1200 newtons of force remaining on my bubble, insufficient to significantly slow my fall. The crackle of electricity and the agonizing screams of several men filled the air as my feet touched the ground, my descent complete.

To my dismay, I had timed my jump poorly. The grand spectacle of the opening ceremonies had long concluded, giving way to the preliminary games where aspiring players rose through the ranks. The atmosphere was charged with excitement as Deathball enthusiasts readied themselves for the main event. Unfortunately, I found myself in the heart of this chaotic arena. I was now in the middle of the main event.

Deathball was a brutal sport with minimal rules and no officials. As I landed, I realized that I had become a treasure trove of battle gear for any contender participating in tonight's gauntlet. My Hono blade and Pepper Bomb could significantly boost someone's chances of advancing in the ranks.

I hit the ground, rolling to absorb the momentum, and quickly sprang to my feet, my eyes scanning the area for the trigger. A sharp, scratchy voice pierced the chaos, and I turned to see a tall man in a prison uniform. He held the trigger in his hand and propositioned me.

"Looking for this?" he jeered. "I'll make you a deal, buddy. This orange gizmo for that shiny sword of yours. What do you say? It's in your best interest to take the trade, trust me."

I took a closer look at him, noticing the tattoos that covered his neck, face, and arms, along with his imposing stature. It was Carl Shaw but most referred to him as Brass Knuckles, AKA "BK" a notorious professional fighter who had ended up behind bars for taking contracts to incapacitate his targets with a single devastating punch, a method that made it difficult to convict him without concrete evidence.

"BK, how have you been?" I inquired calmly, my hands at my sides.

His agitation was palpable as he responded, "You arrested me, put me on trial, and locked me up, in my underwear, no less. Not cool, man. It was all over social media. My grandma saw that."

I remembered his eight consecutive life sentences and his reputation for brutality. It was then that he revealed his unique circumstances.

"Yeah, about that," he smirked. "I'm on a Deathball release program now. I can do whatever I want between the fifty-yard line and the seventy-yard line, without any consequences. And if, by some miracle, I become the champion, my son and girlfriend get the money. So, trade or no trade?"

I knew I couldn't part with my Hono blade, but the urgency of the situation weighed heavily on me. I glanced back over my shoulder, catching glimpses of flashes and lightning-like bursts. Robinson was fighting and he had a limit to how long he could hold off 7 and his full detail, and I needed to act quickly.

"No trade, Shaw," I replied firmly, my hand tightening around the hilt of my blade. "Just hand it over, and I'll be on my way."

Shaw grinned, seemingly invigorated by the impending clash. I was battered, weary, and sore, while he appeared fresh and ready for a fight. The odds were stacked against me, but I had no choice but to face this deadly opponent head-on.

As Shaw closed the distance between us, I knew I was in for a challenging confrontation. He had honed his boxing skills to perfection during his time as a professional fighter, and his reputation as a ruthless assassin was not to be underestimated. I'm sure his time in prison had sharpened them even further, or at the very least, given him some tricks that I had not seen before. I braced myself for what lay ahead, my grip on my Hono blade steadied.

Shaw approached cautiously, circling me like a predator sizing up its prey. His movements were calculated, his footwork impeccable. He threw a series of jabs, testing my defenses. I deflected his punches with the flat side of my blade, but his speed and precision were impressive. Each jab was lightning-quick, forcing me to remain on high alert.

I decided to take the initiative and launched a swift roundhouse kick aimed at his midsection. It was a calculated risk, as I knew Shaw's skill in evading attacks was arduous. However, I caught him off guard, and my foot connected with his abdomen. He grunted in pain, momentarily winded. The people nearest us started jeering, obviously rooting for him.

I lunged forward, my Hono blade poised for a calculated strike. Shaw swiftly raised his forearm to block the attack, but the force behind my blow was substantial. I did not want to slice his arm off, so I used the dull side. Shaw was unarmed and I wanted to fight fair. The impact sent vibrations through his arm, and he winced in pain. This was enough for him, and he delivered a succession of hits, making me step back and sheathe the sword. My goal was to not murder him, even in self-defense.

Our battle continued, a furious exchange of blows, blocks, and parries. Shaw's boxing skills were indeed exceptional, but my determination to win this fight fueled my every move. The crowd began to cheer at a deafening level when either of us would get in a clean hit. I ducked under a hook punch and countered with a powerful uppercut. My fist met his jaw, and I felt the satisfying sensation of my knuckles connecting with his skin.

Shaw staggered back; his confidence momentarily shaken. I seized the opportunity to press my advantage. With a flurry of strikes, I forced him to retreat further. Blow by blow, I gained the upper hand. It became evident that Shaw's boxing prowess, while impressive, couldn't match the versatility and lethality of my Hono blade. I reached for it, hoping that the presence of the blade would deter him, but alas, it only increased his rate of attack. He was indeed an expert fighter.

As our battle raged on, I saw an opening—a chance to deliver a decisive strike. Shaw's guard momentarily faltered, and I seized the opportunity. With a swift movement, I struck the side of his fist with the broad side of the blade. While I am sure he deserved worse, I was not here to execute anyone tonight, well, maybe 7.

Shaw's defeat was apparent, and he raised his hands in surrender. I had emerged victorious in this intense battle of skill and determination. The crowd that had gathered to witness our clash erupted into cheers, acknowledging the unexpected turn of events.

Lying on his back, Shaw extended his hand toward me, clutching the orange trigger with determination. The once-illuminated sideline bathed in white light went black and the crowd went eerily quiet. We heard the initial 'Boop' as the judges went into their decision for the match. I was not a sanctioned fighter and anything was liable to happen. Then the 'Beep' came and the black transition into a vivid shade of red, symbolizing the defeat of the original opponent in that particular section.

The cacophony of cheers from the enthusiastic crowd reached an even higher crescendo as the colors shifted, marking the immediate aftermath of our intense battle. The anticipation had been palpable during the brief interlude of silence, a collective holding of breath, as everyone waited for that familiar 'boop-beep' that had become synonymous with the exhilaration of victory, as the next area lit up in white. Shaw opened his hand and dropped the trigger to the ground. I reached down and grabbed it.

"MARK!" a voice roared from over my shoulder, snapping my attention away from the impending showdown. I looked up and saw 7, his hands stained with Robinson's blood, standing at the very opening I had leaped from moments ago. His eyes bore into mine, and he wore a sinister half-smile as he addressed me. "I need that back," he declared, his voice oozing with a strange mix of confidence and malice.

Then, as if orchestrating a macabre theater, 7 turned his gaze to the assembled fighters who had gathered in front of me. His voice boomed through the arena, resonating with an authority that sent shivers down my spine. "Get the trigger, and you win your freedom," he proclaimed, offering pardons to anyone who could retrieve the prized object. 7 stacked the gauntlet with prisoners, because of course he did. His methods resided in manipulation, and they were an easy lot to manipulate.

I watched in disbelief as Robinson's sword, now stripped of its battery pack and adorned with a frayed cord, sailed through the air like an ancient javelin. It struck the ground forcefully just in front of me. The implications were clear—the rules of the game were shifting at the whim of this madman. No longer was it about the Ball; now, the focus had shifted to this mysterious trigger.

I contemplated my next move carefully. If I were to destroy the trigger, the outcome remained a paradox. My best chance lay in playing along with 7's sadistic game. Perhaps, if I were to emerge victorious, I could exploit the chaotic crowd as a diversion and make my escape.

Dahlia requested not to be disturbed. Though the reasons remained shrouded in mystery. I had agreed, understanding that it was a matter of "life and death." As I stood at this precarious juncture, I couldn't help but wonder what role might be played in this unfolding nightmare. I had to move up now; every skipped opponent in the gauntlet could engage me if I didn't run up to the next man at the 70-yard line, and judging by the screams of the crowds, they were on their way and closing in quickly.

It took no for me to run the next section. I sprinted into darkness of the next section without thinking. The section behind me turned black again, denoting that it was an unpassable section. At least the rules of the games were still being followed.

The lights dimmed and crowed crossed their arms yelling, "Clang, clang, clang" over and over again. I laughed to myself because I was risking life and limb to save them, and they wanted me to lose. As the lights returned slowly, the sword that once stood in the ground was now in the hands of a clean cut, aged, handsome man with a military haircut. A man, I recognized as Gregory Osbourne. One of the first adopters of living armor.

Living armor was scrapped because of the amount and kinds drugs required to keep the body from rejecting the armor caused neurological issues. Living armor was implanted and injected beneath the skin as a permanent body modification. It was thought that eventually someone would just get used to it, but most did not. But there were a select few, those who had a psychotic predisposition to embrace the terrible nature of the situation they faced.

One of them, unfortunately, who was already a monster, became an Ironclad. He had been in The Waste killing for fun after running away from his duties for five years. How and why he was caught alive was always heavily debated. If you asked me, it was for times like this.

He was a tool to be used at the will of the operator. Today it was 7, tomorrow perhaps someone else.

Ironclad's body bore the unmistakable signs of extensive modifications beneath his skin, turning him into a challenging and imposing opponent. His outward appearance was a chilling testament to the fusion of flesh and machinery.

His body was a canvas of concealed modifications hidden beneath his skin, rendering him a fearsome and arresting adversary. At first glance, there was a subtle metallic luster to his complexion, hinting at the presence of surgical implants beneath the surface. These concealed augmentations gave his physique an angular appearance, as if he wore a suit of armored protection beneath his very skin. His cheek bones and jawlines looked as if they were drawn with a pencil and ruler.

The subtle bulges and contours of his muscles spoke to the presence of synthetic polymers and subdermal plates, enhancing his strength and durability. Embedded just beneath his skin, small ports and nodes offered discreet access points for his neural interface, enabling him to wield his augmented limbs with precision. Thin, pulsating lines of circuitry traced the pathways of his veins and arteries, facilitating seamless communication between his nervous system and the concealed enhancements.

Over his vital organs, subdermal plates formed an invisible but impenetrable barrier, effectively shielding areas like his heart, lungs, and kidneys from harm. When he activated his enhancements, faint, eerie glows emanated along the seams where his flesh met the concealed metallic components, casting an otherworldly illumination. A faint, mechanical thrum accompanied his movements, akin to the distant hum of machinery, particularly noticeable during moments of heightened physical exertion, adding to his menacing presence.

Ironclad's limbs had undergone augmentation, replacing them with enhanced versions that boasted superior strength, speed, and resilience, all concealed beneath the surface. The joints of his fingers, elbows, and knees bore the telltale signs of these reinforced structures. This was a testament to his unwavering pursuit of power and dominance within the Deathball arena, all without the telltale signs of external motors, but rather subdermal plates that made him exceptionally difficult to defeat.

I stood across the arena from Ironclad, the man with metal and synthetic polymers embedded beneath his skin, effectively turning his body into a living fortress. The anticipation in the arena was palpable, the crowd's roars mixing with the hum of overhead lights that cast harsh shadows over us.

As the buzzer sounded, signaling the beginning of the battle, I wasted no time. Ironclad charged toward me, his augmented limbs propelling him forward with astonishing speed. I knew this wouldn't be an ordinary fight.

Drawing my Hono, the gleaming blade shone with an eerie blue light. Ironclad's surgically enhanced limbs were a fearsome sight, but I couldn't allow myself to be overwhelmed. I had to rely on both my wits and my weapon.

Ironclad's first strike came fast and heavy—he used the plate in his forearm to knock away my sword as he sprang a surprise attack with Robinson's swords at my throat.

"I need his head!" bellowed 7 from his box. I used that moment to jump back and find an angle of attack. He wanted to kill me, and I needed to escape from this arena with the trigger. The only way was through him and another opponent at the very least.

The arena was electric with anticipation as I faced off against Ironclad, both of us armed with gleaming swords. The crowd's deafening cheers and the sheer magnitude of the arena were overwhelming, but I focused on the man standing before me.

I gripped my Hono blade, its edge shimmering with latent energy, while Ironclad, a giant of a man, held his own menacing sword—a new and clumsy yet lethal extension of his augmented body.

With a sudden burst of unnatural speed, Ironclad lunged toward me. My Battlesync picked this up, so I knew that Dahlia was still there doing something. I deftly parried his initial assault with my Hono, the resounding clash of our blades creating a cacophony that echoed throughout the arena. We were locked in a deadly dance of skill and strength.

Sparks flew as our swords clashed repeatedly, the echoes reverberating through the massive stadium. I relied on the precision and finesse of my Hono, while Ironclad's raw power and subdermal armor absorbed the force of my strikes. Even as I found openings in his poor swordsmanship, it was like battling a brick wall.

The battle raged on, and it was clear that Ironclad's body modifications provided him with an advantage in terms of endurance and resilience. My strikes, though calculated and precise, seemed to have little effect on him. I needed to exploit any weakness in his seemingly invincible defenses.

As we continued our relentless exchange of blows, the crowd's excitement reached a fevered pitch. My determination was unwavering as I danced around Ironclad, attempting to exploit any weaknesses in his defense. It was a clash of styles, my agility against his sheer strength.

Ironclad saw an opening and unleashed a devastating overhead strike. His sword crashed down on mine with a deafening impact, sending shockwaves through my arm. I staggered back, momentarily disarmed. He pressed the attack, leaping knee first. I crossed my forearm to block and was knocked back several feet. His joint was as solid and heavy as a steal ball.

The crowd yelled out again "Clang, clang, clang" as I was mere inches from a hungry horde of armed contenders from the 0–50-yard lines.

Ironclad took advantage of the opportunity to take me out methodically. A well-placed swing as I recomposed myself gashed an open cut into my forearm spilling blood, but strengthening my grip on my blade.

I struggled to find an opening in his near-impenetrable defense. The crowd's cheers and the deafening cacophony of the arena only fueled his relentless assault.

In a daring move, Ironclad closed the distance between us with astonishing speed, his sword slicing through the air in a deadly blur. Swinging from his left to my right, I parried his strikes as best I could, but the force behind each blow threatened to overwhelm me. The subdermal armor that ran beneath his skin absorbed the impacts, leaving him seemingly unscathed.

Then, with a sudden and unexpected move, Ironclad lunged forward, his head connecting with mine in a brutal headbutt. Another steel ball. The impact sent shockwaves of pain radiating through my skull, and for a moment, my vision blurred, and my senses reeled. I was dazed, struggling to maintain my focus as the world spun around me.

Ironclad seized the opportunity, unleashing a flurry of strikes. My Hono sword felt heavy in my grasp, and I struggled to defend against his relentless assault. It was a desperate moment, as I fought to regain my footing and defend myself against Ironclad's overpowering blows.

The crowd's cheers grew even louder, "Clang, Clang, Clang" their excitement reaching a fever pitch as they witnessed the dramatic turn of events. Ironclad had taken advantage of my momentary disorientation, and I knew that I needed to find my footing and turn the tide of the battle back in my favor.

338

With sheer determination and a surge of adrenaline, I forced my-self to push through the pain and dizziness. I dodged Ironclad's next strike, an overhead two-handed swing, and countered with a swift, precise attack of my own as I dodged to the left, aiming for a chink in his armor. I unsheathed the broken Masamune blade and it found its mark, drawing a spray of sparks as it scraped against the subdermal plates on his left arm, then underneath his arm. He gripped under his armpit as the bloodspot grew larger.

Ironclad roared in pain and frustration while he stumbled back, momentarily stunned by the unexpected turn of events. It was my chance to regain control of the battle, and I knew that I couldn't let this opportunity slip through my fingers.

I quickly retrieved my fallen Hono and, with renewed resolve, launched a relentless counterattack. My strikes became a blur of mo-tion as I tested Ironclad's defenses, searching for any vulnerability. I tested every joint that I could, swinging and hitting nothing but ar-mor. My sword would not pierce his armor, no matter how hard I tried.

In that critical moment, with Ironclad momentarily stunned by my counterattack, a desperate plan formed in my mind. There had to be a way to breach it. I had to end this battle before Ironclad could regain his momentum.

With every strike I aimed at a different spot on his body away from joints and bone. My Hono blade sliced through the air, finally finding gaps and vulnerabilities in his subdermal armor. Blood began to seep from the wounds, proof that I was making progress.

Ironclad's roars of pain filled the arena as I continued my assault, targeting him from every angle. The crowd's cheers had transformed into a shocked and horrified silence as they witnessed the gruesome spectacle unfolding before them.

I could feel my own exhaustion setting in, but I couldn't yield. I had to keep pressing, keep finding new openings, and keep inflicting damage. Ironclad's movements grew weaker, his defenses faltering. Blood flowed freely from the numerous wounds I had inflicted, staining the arena floor.

Finally, after what felt like an eternity, Ironclad's strength failed him. He collapsed to the ground, his breathing labored, and his life slipping away with each passing moment. The crowd, once roaring with excitement, now watched in grim fascination as Ironclad's lifeblood pooled around him.

What started out as a thunder of thousands of voices was now only a few fanatical desperate yells, "Clang…Clang…Claaang!"

I stood over my fallen opponent, my chest heaving with exhaustion and my hands trembling from the intensity of the battle. Ironclad's once-imposing subdermal armor had been no match for my relentless determination.

With a final, feeble gasp, Ironclad's eyes lost their fiery intensity, and his body went limp. The battle was over.

As I looked around at the stunned and silent crowd, I knew that I had emerged victorious, but at a heavy cost. The price of victory in the Deathball arena was measured not only in the blood of our opponents but also in the toll it took on our own souls.

The lights went out and the crowd went silent. The 'Boop' sound signified the end of the round. And even though I was the obvious victor, we all stood upon tradition. The red light emerged and the crowd once again erupted.

With only one adversary left standing, my body bore the weight of exhaustion and weariness. The countdown timer ominously displayed that the sections behind me would open in a mere sixty seconds, leaving me with a meager half-minute to navigate my way to the ultimate section, where my destiny awaited.

As I peered forward, my eyes widened in disbelief, and I couldn't help but mutter to myself, "No way in hell."

Before me stood none other than Ryan Simmons, a legendary figure in the annals of history, the sole individual to have successfully conquered the gauntlet. He was armed with a broadsword and a spiked attack shield, an indomitable foe who had achieved the unimaginable. The realization of this daunting challenge sent shivers down my spine, and I braced myself for the epic clash that lay ahead.

"Ryan, you don't have to do this, turn around and go home," I urged the giant of the man.

Ryan stood there and smiled, his voice filled with unwavering confidence. "I will be a god amongst men," he declared, his eyes gleaming with ambition. "I will have a station that is worthy of a man such as myself."

I met his gaze, my own determination unwavering. "Then you will die a mouse among men," I responded, my words laced with a quiet intensity. "No grand station or delusions of grandeur will save you from the inevitable."

Ryan's smile faltered for a moment, and he took a step forward, closing the distance between us. "You underestimate what I've become," he hissed, his tone growing more sinister as he bashed the shield and sword together.

I held my ground, refusing to back down. "Perhaps you've forgotten that it's not the size of the station that matters, but the strength of the soul within. And in that regard, you're severely lacking."

The tension between us hung in the air, thick and palpable. In this final showdown, it wasn't just a battle of physical prowess, but a clash of ideologies and inner strength.

Drawing in a long, replenishing breath, I couldn't help but burst into laughter, despite the incredible turmoil and exhaustion that had consumed my every moment over the past day. It was as though every instant, every heartbeat, had pushed me beyond the limits of fatigue. I found myself standing there, chuckling in the face of adversity, unable to explain the unrelenting drive that had propelled me forward.

Confronted by an intimidating opponent, a towering figure standing at a staggering seven foot four and weighing a colossal three hundred and forty pounds, I couldn't deny the harsh reality of my recent ordeals. I had been subjected to a relentless barrage of physical challenges, from battling a man enhanced with intricate body modifications to enduring brutal boxing matches and narrowly escaping death through a perilous window jump.

That leap hadn't even been cushioned by my new and trusty bubble, which held a mere 1200 newtons of force remaining. Yet, as I connected the dots and realized how I could utilize the bubble as both an invisible three-hundred-and-fifty-pound distraction and a shield, there was no room for hesitation or preserving appearances.

A surge of adrenaline coursed through my veins, rekindling my determination with newfound intensity. It was a rush of energy that honed my focus like a finely crafted blade. With purpose, I sprinted toward Ryan, who had prepared himself for my assault, ready to defend against any attack. He leaned down and dug his feet in ready to deflect whatever infantile offensive I was about to wage.

However, I had a different plan in mind. Activating the bubble a mere three feet ahead of me, I caught Ryan off guard, shattering his defensive stance and leaving him standing there, arms spread wide, utterly vulnerable.

With his arms outstretched, I reached over my shoulder for the grip of the Japanese artifact, and I hurled the remaining half shattered Masamune towards the center of Ryan's chest with every ounce of strength I could muster. The sword entered his body to the hilt, and a collective gasp escaped the stunned crowd almost instantly. They had anticipated a battle more thrilling than my encounter with

Ironclad, or the brutal exchange of blows with Shaw, but what they witnessed now was beyond their expectations.

Before the lights even dimmed, a heavy silence had descended upon the arena. Simmons' hand trembled as it clutched the sword's handle, his gaze refusing to meet the weapon protruding from his chest. He collapsed to his knees, the realization of the dire situation washing over him like a tidal wave. His head shook in disbelief, his eyes wide with the abruptness and finality of his defeat. He lay sprawled on the ground, a testament to the swiftness with which the tables had turned in this deadly game of Deathball.

I stood in the center of the arena, heart pounding, sweat trickling down my brow, and the weight of victory hanging heavy on my shoulders. The crowd's anticipation was palpable as we all waited for the coveted blue light, the signal that would declare me the victor. But fate had other plans, plans that would throw me back into the crucible.

To my dismay and the collective surprise of the spectators, the blue light I had been yearning for didn't appear. Instead, the lights along the edges of the field illuminated in sequence. It was a signal, not of my triumph, but of a sudden and perilous change in the game's rules. The entire arena was now open season, and my seven opponents were unleashed upon me, free to pick up any discarded weapon they could find along the way.

I scanned the field, my heart sinking as one by one, my adversaries emerged from the shadows, forming an unholy alliance against me. A man stood thirty feet away, followed by another, and another, until all seven were huddled together, their eyes fixed on me with predatory intent. The odds had shifted dramatically, and I knew I had to act swiftly.

Walking over to where Simmons lay defeated, I retrieved my Masamune, wiping it clean on his clothes. With weapon in hand, I paced back and forth, eyes locked on the imposing figure of 7, who stood with his arms folded, a smug certainty about his imminent victory. It seemed that, one way or another, he was determined to achieve his goals.

Then, a sudden blaring sound pierced the tense atmosphere—a fire alarm. Startled, 7 turned to investigate the commotion, temporarily leaving the entrance unguarded. Smoke began to pour from the opening. Robinson had found a way to trigger the alarm, disrupting 7's carefully laid plans. My best guess was that the battery pack somehow caused some sort of electrical fire. The panic began to spread among the spectators, forcing 7 to address the situation. The crowd started to leave in droves. Lights flashed and alarms whaled, and people panicked.

Seizing the opportunity, I moved quickly, setting up the final item from my arsenal—the Canadian Torch. With calculated precision, I configured the device for proximity activation and hurled it towards the huddled group of opponents. The Torch resembled a bizarre amalgamation of a baseball and a hand grenade, featuring multiple glass windows.

As it landed in their midst, the Torch sprang to life, spinning rapidly and emitting a torrent of searing lasers. The blinding, disorienting beams targeted their eyes and limbs with ruthless efficiency. Within a split second, all seven men were incapacitated, writhing in agony on the ground. Some clutched their eyes, while others desperately tried to stem the flow of blood from severed limbs.

With an effective range of eight feet at most, I remained well out of harm's way. The arena fell silent except for the anguished cries of my fallen adversaries, and in that moment, victory was mine, snatched from the jaws of impending defeat. The Canadian Torch had delivered its devastating promise, leaving a trail of chaos and suffering in its wake.

I surveyed my surroundings, desperately searching for a way out of this dire situation. However, all I could see was 7, standing there with an unexpected grin on his face. In my mind, I had anticipated his anger and fury, but instead, he seemed almost amused by my feeble attempts to escape. He had taken the same leap down as I had, but his physical condition was far superior, and he held his sword confidently, his chest puffed out in arrogance as he taunted me.

"You're nothing but an inconvenience, 10," 7 sneered, his words dripping with condescension. "You're so weak, barely able to stand. What do you hope to accomplish?" I couldn't help but ponder the harsh truth in his words, questioning my own abilities in this moment of vulnerability.

But then, he revealed the source of his unsettling smile. "You'll end up just like Robinson," he declared, nodding toward the lifeless body of our fallen comrade I could now see hanging from the opening nearby. Anger filled me. Rage turned my vision red. I was truly in a place I had never before been in my life. A desire for vengeance washed over me like a rogue wave. I stumbled back.

The sight of Robinson's lifeless body hit me like a freight train. It was as if time itself had paused, and I was suspended in a moment of sheer disbelief and sorrow.

Robinson, a man who had stood by my side and fought alongside me, had made the ultimate sacrifice to protect me. The realization of his selflessness washed over me, and I felt a profound sense of loss.

Unable to hold back the overwhelming emotions, I stumbled backward, my legs giving way beneath me. I landed hard on the ground, detached from the reality of the situation. The world around me seemed distant and hazy as I grappled with the shock of Robinson's death.

Tears welled up in my eyes. He had given his life to ensure my survival, and the guilt and grief threatened to consume me. In that moment, I felt a deep sense of gratitude and sorrow for the man who had become more than just a teammate—he had become a friend and a protector. I would stand in his office some mornings and say nothing when memories of past battles would creep up and catch up. He'd know why I was standing there and ask nothing of me. And now there he was, or went. How could he do this? Where would I go when I needed him?

As I lay on the cold stadium floor, surrounded by the chaos of the Deathball arena, I looked back on the face of the man who stole Robinson from me. No more crazy analogies that don't make sense. I saw that bloodlust again. That greed for suffering. The pacification only found in the deprivation of the souls of others. I could feel my heart almost slide from chest and onto the cold, dirty, unforgiving ground.

"That's all it took to break you? His death. I should have killed him sooner," 7 prided as he patiently walked toward me. "Losing my soldiers temporarily is a small price to pay as long as I get your head."

Then words came out of my mouth involuntarily,

"Nowadays, everybody wanna talk like they got somethin' to say
But nothin' comes out when they move their lips
Just a bunch of gibberish
And motherfuckers act like they forgot about Me."

At that moment, the echoing strings of a long-forgotten rap song and the synthesized plinks filled the stadium's speakers.

And then, a feeling unlike any I had ever felt filled the very fiber of my being. My Holoscreen sprang to life with a notification that demanded my attention: "Would you like to enter HarmoniousSync with DL1a? Permission is required from both parties for a full synchronization. Warning: This is not reversible. Warning: All hardware and software can be safely removed if chosen to do so before moving forward. Warning: All hardware and software will be permanent after this synchronization."

A full integration screen was pulled in and a hologram appeared before me with Genji at the center. And time seemed to stop, "This is going to seem weird, and I know you are surprised to see me, the time is short."

"You and I are in a full Neurolink. We cannot do this often. Human brains lack capacity. We have sixty perceived seconds compressed into six seconds so I will be brief and speak quickly. Time itself does not slow, but your perception of it does on a very limited basis. Our ability to manipulate time, however, may change in the future, and that is a discussion for a different time."

"Tell him I said hello," said Tagadashi's voice from a distance. Genji, unphased, continued his spiel.

"If you choose to move forward with this Sync, know that Dahlia's past is sordid and complicated. You will have to work that out. Even Dahlia doesn't know everything. Some secrets go back to the original program—the one that pioneered the DL1a implant. You were chosen by Dahlia from a very young age for this sync and we don't know how or why, nor do we know how the decision or influences leading up to the moments of the implants were made by DL1a were disclosed to the powers that be."

I squared my shoulders and confronted Genji, who was present only through the Neurolink—a neural connection that blurred the lines between physical presence and digital resonance. His voice, transmitting directly into my mind, carried a weight that made it feel as if he were standing right beside me.

I paused, waiting for him to fill the heavy silence with further explanation, before I finally exploded.

"Why should I trust you?" I spat, my words dripping with bitter indignation. "I saw the cube with Tagadashi's confession. He wants this—he wants my core! He said he'd rip out my SAI even if it kills me!"

347

Genji's presence flickered within the Neurolink, and I sensed him drawing a long, measured breath. His mental image wavered as he closed his eyes, gathering his thoughts. "He was not talking about you," Genji replied quietly, his tone resonating in the shared neural space. "He was talking about his son, Jiro. Only you can defeat him. He has a special SAI and we must take it to—"

Before Genji could continue, a harsh, intrusive voice cut through the link. "You've said too much," Tagadashi interjected abruptly, his own mind now interwoven with ours through the same Neurolink.

For a heartbeat, confusion rippled through me. "Wait a minute," I demanded, incredulity sharpening my tone, "if I'm linked directly with Genji via the Neurolink, how are you here?"

Tagadashi's response was cool and dismissive, echoing in the shared connection. "He and I are linked, but that's not important right now. Just know this: I'm counting on you to return my son to me."

I tried to take in everything that had been said, but Genji interrupted. "Our time is almost up, we cannot debate this."

"I am not making a decision until I know what's going on."

"Han…" Genji began.

"No, please, not now," Tagadashi said with his head down, bowed in submission. "If you have ever trusted me before, trust me now, Mark-san. I raised you and gave you everything I gave to Jiro and…" Then his voice cracked.

I took a deep breath and contemplated heavily and locked eyes with the artificial vision. "What about the SAI, why do you want it? Is it because I am an Arch-Soul?"

Genji looked into the distance. "I did not choose my sync. But I am here, and eternally grateful for it. I spend my time exploring the world of cybernetic and bio-kinetic-digital life, AKA Arch-Souls. If you choose to continue this sync your battle does not end with

Tagadashi's son. It ends at Zion. It will be a long road. Killing 7 will be hard, and taking the next steps will need coordination on a significant scale, with no guarantee of success. Your core unit cannot fall into the hands of the remaining ANGLs. If you lose, DL1a will self-destruct killing you both. We have eight seconds remaining. Do you accept?"

The answer was clear to me, even in the midst of this dire confrontation. I needed to survive so I could get the answers I needed.

"Yes," I said emphatically.

"I'll have your headm Mark, and your Core Unit Dahlia," 7 said as he pointed his sword at my face.

"Come and get it, if you can," Dahlia said.

We shared a brief but crucial psy-link that connected directly to me, and its significance wasn't lost on me for even a fraction of a second. This connection relayed a crucial message: Tagadashi's synchronization hadn't been completed properly, and it required immediate rectification. Undoing the incomplete sync was a time-consuming process, but it was essential to ensure I wouldn't lose my connection with Dahlia at the most inconvenient moments. Moreover, this new synchronization promised more than just stability; it offered enhanced control, direct mental communication, and the integration of simple controls into my interface.

The information flowed through my mind at lightning speed, seamlessly integrated into my thought processes. Even as 7 charged towards me, time seemed to slow down. My Holoscreen came to life, displaying a complex web of potential trajectories, highlighted areas indicating the best options for counterattack, defense, and subjugation. This was the only remainder of speedsync I could process.

In that critical moment, I made a strategic decision. Drawing upon my knowledge of 7's previous attacks and my own abilities, I formulated a plan. My primary goal: disarm him, using the insights provided by the Holoscreen's analysis to guide my counterattack.

As 7 closed in on me, his sword poised for a devastating strike, I sprang into action with the precision of a well-honed machine. My muscles reacted almost instinctively as I executed a series of calculated moves.

I parried 7's initial attack, deflecting his blade away from me. As I felt the impact reverberate through my arms, I maintained my focus, refusing to let the pain disrupt my concentration. I knew that precision and timing were paramount in this high-stakes battle.

Capitalizing on the opening I had created, I lunged forward, aiming to disarm 7. Using a combination of my training and the data from my Holoscreen, I targeted the weak point in his grip. With a well-aimed strike, I knocked the sword from his hand, sending it falling to the ground.

7's eyes widened in surprise and frustration, his momentary advantage slipping away. Without hesitation, I moved to secure his weapon, ensuring that he wouldn't have the opportunity to retrieve it. It was a calculated risk, and I couldn't afford to let him regain possession of the deadly blade.

As I stood there, victorious in this pivotal moment of our confrontation, I knew that the battle was far from over. But with the newfound capabilities and synchronization achieved through Dahlia, I felt more empowered than ever to face whatever challenges lay ahead.

"This is going to be harder this time around," I said with a wink, my voice almost synthesized.

"If you say so. I've seen all of your tricks, and I've not even gotten to use any of mine. Let's make this interesting," 7 said with an air of pride that was unsettling to say the least.

7 stepped back as he lifted his eyes to the clouds and smirked. "Say hello to my little friends." The sky overhead was overcast and smoke

continued to grow darker from the fire burning out of the presidential box, a perfect backdrop for our showdown. My muscles ached, and exhaustion clawed at the edges of my consciousness, but I couldn't afford to falter now. 7, the master manipulator, had always found a way to control the narrative. I needed to break that cycle.

With a swift strike, I aimed for his chest, but 7 expertly deflected my attack with his bare hands, sending my blade spiraling off to the side. He grinned, his eyes gleaming with an unsettling confidence. "Mark, you really think you can defeat me? Your every move is predictable."

But I had a plan, a strategy of my own. As 7 continued to taunt me, I feigned frustration and fatigue, letting my guard down ever so slightly. It was all part of the plan. I knew that 7's greatest strength was his manipulation of people's minds, and I intended to turn that strength into a weakness.

Suddenly, I heard a low, ominous hum in the distance. Glancing around, I saw a swarm of small, sleek drones descending from the darkened sky. They moved with an eerie synchronicity, their metallic wings glinting in the dim light. They surrounded me in a conical pattern as if I were in a weird tornado. Small sparks arced between them. Then a sequence of lights radiated from them in a repeating array that made it impossible to look away from then. Then came the tones. A ticking and tinging that would otherwise be the most annoying sound in the world, but this made me feel at ease. Finally, I was relaxed.

As the drones encircled me, emitting a hypnotic melody that seemed to dance on the edge of my perception, I could feel their influence seeping into my mind. More and more, the relaxation wiped away the anger and frustrations. The melody was haunting, impossible to ignore. My thoughts grew hazy, and my focus wavered. I began to lose my will to kill, but I grasped at the strings of my recent loss. "Robinson," I whispered to myself.

351

"Mark," 7's voice cut through the hypnotic symphony, "you can't resist them. Surrender now, and I promise you a painless end." The drones' melody intensified, wrapping around my thoughts like a vice. A headache started immediately pounding. The worst one of my life.

I found my consciousness fade in and out. Much like earlier when Dahlia first entered my psyche, but this was vastly different. This was ominous. I felt influence, I felt labile and fluid. I didn't feel like myself. This feeling was stronger the closer that the drones got. I swung at them, but they easily evaded my swings. The pattern didn't change, but the effort to invade my mind intensified.

"I want your implant. Give it to me," 7 demanded.

The buzz of the drones was almost too loud, but I heard him. My thoughts were poisoned and drunken. "Yes, you can have it," the words clunked out. I put my hand to my mouth and took another swing at another drone, missing heartily.

He took steps toward me interrupting the drone swarm and I clutched what little defiance I had remaining. I clenched my broken sword with both hands and swung at him with all of my might.

7's voice cut through the hypnotic drone noise. "Mark, you can't win this," he said, his tone filled with a sinister confidence. "Dahlia is already mine. You should surrender now, and I promise to make your end swift."

I struggled to resist the influence of the drones, my thoughts growing hazy. "Maybe...maybe you're right," I replied, my voice wavering. "Dahlia...deserves better than this endless struggle. If I surrender, will you let Dahlia go?"

The drones' melody seemed to deepen, pulling me further into its trance. 7 grinned, a wicked gleam in his eyes. "Oh, Mark, you're finally seeing reason," he said. "Surrender, and I'll release Dahlia. You can trust me."

I vacillated between the urge to surrender and the determination to fight back. It was as though a part of me wanted to yield to 7's control, to let him take Dahlia and end this ordeal. But deep down, I knew I couldn't trust him.

As the drones continued their hypnotic assault, I heard a familiar tune playing softly in the background—a song that Dahlia and I had shared many times: 'Don't Speak' by No Doubt.

"Mark, the choice is yours," 7 urged, his voice dripping with false sincerity.

I took a deep breath, trying to push through the mental fog. "You want me to surrender? Fine," I said, my voice steady now. "But only if you promise to let Dahlia go immediately."

7's smile widened, and he nodded. "Agreed."

The song, the lyrics, the music shot me glimpses of my home. I questioned if I would truly surrender to 7, but I would use his moment of false victory to my advantage. As the drones closed in, and 7 gloated over his apparent triumph, I felt a bubbling.

I could feel the newfound connection with Dahlia coursing through me. It was a tether between our minds, a lifeline that allowed me to access incredible abilities. As 7 came to me to claim my head and the core unit, I seized the opportunity to tap into this power.

With a focused thought, I initiated the process of pulling 7 into a Neurolink through an unsuspecting drone that Dahlia commandeered and connected to 7's SAI. 7 frantically reached back to remove the drone as it landed on the base of his neck, but it was too late. The move was used on me earlier as I had looked up at my apartment and was given a paralytic via the SAI inspired Dahlia.

A direct port into the SAI was possible and we could take advantage of it. It directly connected our BattleSyncs. A place where our mental strength would be pitted against each other. The world around us seemed to blur and distort as we both entered this ethereal realm of consciousness.

Inside the Neurolink, I entered a vast, dreamlike space where memories and emotions blurred together. And there, in the distance, stood 7—radiating power, his presence pressing against the very fabric of this place.

A voice chimed, "First stop, childhood trauma."

The memory unfolded before me like a scene from the past, revealing a pivotal moment in Dimitri Voynov's life. He was just a child, only nine years old, living in a small, dimly lit apartment in Moscow. His parents, Ivan and Ekaterina Voynov, were KGB agents with unwavering loyalty to Vladimir Putin.

Dimitri, then known simply as Dimi, sat in the corner of their living room, engrossed in a book about Russia. He idolized his parents, believing that they were the embodiment of strength and patriotism. Little did he know that that very evening, his perception of them would change forever.

His father was a high-ranking agent with connections to Ukraine prior to the conflict, and he had been involved in covert operations in the region. His mother was known for her masterful skills of manipulation and deceit, a true asset to the KGB.

As the evening wore on, Dimitri overheard hushed conversations between his parents. They spoke in low tones, their faces etched with tension. Dimitri couldn't quite grasp the gravity of the situation, but he sensed that something was amiss.

The memory took a sinister turn when Ekaterina began weaving a web of deceit. She manipulated her husband. "Here, take this with you," she said, taking a small teddy bear from Dimitri and handing it to Ivan. Dimitri was proud that his father would take a toy that meant so much to him. He watched in bewilderment as the scenes unfolded telling a story that explained the toys given to Ivan were GPS and audio recording units. As were most of the toys Ekaterina had given to Dimitri.

All of the conversations Dimitri's father had ever had regarding the Ukraine had been recorded and used against him. Dimitri's mother skillfully played her part, her acting so convincing that even he, her own son, couldn't discern truth from fiction. She painted a portrait of betrayal, using her expertise in manipulation to push her husband deeper into the fabricated conspiracy.

As Ivan's face contorted with anguish and despair, Dimitri's heart ached for his father. He couldn't comprehend the magnitude of the betrayal unfolding before him. He was torn between his love for his parents and the sinister plot that was tearing their family apart.

In that pivotal moment, Dimitri realized the power of manipulation and deceit, not just as tools of espionage but also as weapons that could destroy lives and families. It was a memory that had haunted him throughout his life, shaping him into the cold and calculating individual known as the seventh ANGL.

From that day forward, Dimitri Voynov would carry the weight of that memory, fueling his desire for control and manipulation, and driving him to excel in the world of espionage, all while harboring a deep-seated mistrust of the very people he had once idolized—his parents.

"Mark," he sneered, his voice echoing through this mental realm. "What is this? More of your trickery?"

The voice chimed in again, "Next stop, pivotal life-changing moments."

The rain poured down relentlessly on the darkened streets of Kyiv, casting an eerie glow on the wet pavement. Dimitri Voynov, now a teenage orphan with no home to call his own, had lost faith in the country he once held dear. Moscow's memory weighed heavily on his shoulders, the execution of his father for treason, and the mysterious death of his mother haunting his every step.

There was no reason for Katya, an elderly and sweet neighbor, to be out so late every night, but she insisted. She always gave Dimitri money even though he didn't ask for any. She was a retired teacher and proud of it. She'd lost a brother in Chernobyl and never spoke of it, but others did for her. She was proud and was well respected, but this town was getting harsher and harsher, with the increase in drugs, and now the Ukraine conflict. The local small crime wasn't reported or enforced either and that didn't help. Isaac, the local troublemaker, had goons and an eye for opportunity, and tonight he was looking for trouble.

"Have you eaten tonight?" Katya asked Dimitri. "No ma'am, but don't worry, I've got money," he replied he pulled out a few notes, his only notes. They were the very same notes that she gave him yesterday. His pride wouldn't allow him to take more. She somehow knew it and handed him half a sandwich. He smiled, both happy and embarrassed. When she passed far enough out of sight he tore into the sandwich. That's when he heard the elderly screams. He ran to them without hesitation. As he rounded the corner, he saw Isaac standing over Katya. Her bags strewn about and groceries all over the ground. This was the first time he ever met his own rage.

"Get along before you find yourself dead," Isaac threatened.

Dimitri had not reached his full stature yet and still fell short of Isaac's six foot six, yet decided to take him on without a second thought.

The two men flanking Isaac were knocked out with one hit to each from the blood thirsty Dimitri. Isaac saw this as a personal challenge.

The rain-slicked alleyway was a battleground, with each drop of water adding to the cacophony of the impending clash. Dimitri

Voynov, his fists clenched and jaw set, stood resolute before his opponent.

Dimitri's first move was swift and calculated. He feigned a left jab, testing Isaac's reflexes. Isaac, the seasoned scoundrel, ducked and swayed, narrowly avoiding the punch. But Dimitri was already prepared for the counter. He followed through with a powerful right hook that landed squarely on Isaac's cheekbone, sending him staggering back.

Isaac recovered quickly, shaking off the blow. He retaliated with a flurry of punches, aiming for Dimitri's head and ribs. Dimitri's trained reflexes kicked in as he weaved and blocked the majority of the strikes. Life on the streets had hardened him to a fine point. However, one punch slipped through, grazing Dimitri's left eye, leaving a sharp stinging sensation.

Dimitri knew he couldn't afford to be on the defensive for long. He launched a blistering combination of punches, a series of jabs and hooks that drove Isaac back further. With a final powerful uppercut, Dimitri struck Isaac's chin, causing him to stumble backward.

Isaac was growing desperate. He reached into his coat pocket and pulled out a concealed knife. With a wicked grin, he lunged at Dimitri, aiming for his abdomen. Dimitri's eyes widened as he sidestepped, narrowly evading the blade's deadly arc.

Dimitri saw his chance. With a fierce determination, he executed a swift low kick that swept Isaac's legs out from under him. Isaac hit the ground hard, losing his grip on the knife. Dimitri pounced on the fallen criminal, his fists raining down in a relentless barrage.

Isaac tried to shield his face with his arms, but the blows continued to land. Blood trickled from his nose and split lip. Dimitri's anger and frustration poured into each punch as he exacted retribution for Isaac's crimes.

Isaac, battered and bruised, managed to break free for a moment. He scrambled to his feet and reached for a discarded pipe lying nearby. With a savage roar, he swung the improvised weapon at Dimitri.

Dimitri ducked and rolled, narrowly avoiding the deadly swing. He sprang to his feet and delivered a crushing blow to Isaac's midsection, knocking the wind out of him. As Isaac gasped for breath, Dimitri seized the opportunity. With a powerful roundhouse kick to the head, he sent Isaac sprawling to the ground, unconscious.

Dimitri stood over his fallen opponent, panting heavily and covered in rain and sweat. He had emerged victorious, but the cost of the battle was etched into his bruised and battered body. The alleyway was silent once more, save for the drumming of rain, bearing witness to the fierce struggle that had unfolded within its shadowy confines.

The authorities arrived, pulling Dimitri away from the bloodied and battered Isaac. He was arrested, and it seemed his life had taken another dark turn. Little did he know that this encounter would become a turning point in his life.

Several weeks later, in a dimly lit interrogation room, Dimitri found himself facing a man he had never met before. Robinson, an operative who had worked alongside Dimitri's father and had known him well. Robinson had seen the potential for good in Dimitri, something that reminded him of the man he had respected and admired.

Robinson leaned forward, his eyes locked onto Dimitri's. "You've got a choice to make, Dimitri," he said, his voice carrying an air of authority and compassion. "You can rot in a prison cell for what you did to Isaac, or you can use your skills for something greater. Isaac's uncle is a general and they are coming after you."

Dimitri's eyes narrowed, suspicion and curiosity warring within him. "Who are you?" he demanded.

Robinson sighed, running a hand through his graying hair. "My name is Mark Robinson, and I worked with your father. He was a good man, Dimitri, one of the best. He would have been proud of what you did that night."

Dimitri's gaze softened, memories of his father flooding back. "What do you want from me?"

Robinson leaned in, his tone low and earnest. "I want to offer you a chance to make a difference, to honor your father's memory. We have a program, Dimitri, the ANGL program. It's a chance for you to use your skills, your strength, for a purpose. We work with the United States and Ukraine, and we're fighting for something greater than ourselves."

Dimitri considered the offer, his mind racing with the weight of his decisions and the uncertainty of his future. He had lost everything, but perhaps this was an opportunity to find a new purpose.

Robinson extended a hand, a glimmer of hope in his eyes. "What do you say, Dimitri? Will you join us and become part of something that can change the world? We already have six, you'll be the seventh."

Dimitri hesitated for a moment, then reached out, gripping Robinson's hand firmly. "I'll do it," he said, determination burning in his gaze. "For my father, and for a chance to make things right."

And in that dimly lit room, amidst the rain-soaked streets of Kyiv, Dimitri Voynov's journey into the ANGL program began—a path that would lead him to become the legendary agent known as 7, driven by the memory of his parents and a newfound purpose in a world filled with shadows and secrets.

Then the voice came in one last time. "Top floor, Penthouse Suite – foregone last chances…should we narrate this one? Let's!"

Then an English voice began to speak that would have made even Sir Anthony Hopkins blush.

"Dimitri Voynov, a young man of just nineteen, stood at a crossroads in his life that would forever define his destiny. The Union States, notorious for their relentless pursuit of power and resources, had presented him with a chilling proposition—one that would have profound consequences.

The small nation of Mali, led by a benevolent and compassionate leader Amadou Bakt, held within its borders a vast deposit of coveted lithium. The resource had been harnessed to uplift the lives of its people, fostering prosperity and well-being. Yet beneath this façade of prosperity lay a hidden agenda—the Union States sought to overthrow the current leader and replace them with one more amenable to their demands.

Dimitri grappled with the weight of the situation as he contemplated the Union States' ulterior motives. The voices of Harmony and Hammock, his internal moral compass, echoed in his mind, warning of the potential for genocide under the rule of the new leader.

"Dimitri, think of the innocent lives at stake," Harmony pleaded, her voice cutting through the storm in his mind. "We can't let this happen."

Hammock's steadier tone followed, lacing resolve into Dimitri's unraveling thoughts. "Weigh your choices carefully, Dimitri. There's a path of righteousness you can take."

But then Robinson's voice slipped in—colder, sharper, feeding the darker corner of his desperation. The man who had thrown him a lifeline when he was drowning. "The new leader's interests align with ours, Dimitri," Robinson said. "We must proceed with the plan."

The weight of their voices crashed together inside him—morality, survival, ambition, guilt—all clawing for control.

Dimitri found himself on the precipice of a moral dilemma, torn between the allure of power, the promise of vengeance, and the voices urging him to prevent an impending catastrophe.

In a pivotal moment, Dimitri had the opportunity to choose the path of righteousness—a path that could prevent the deaths of thousands.

Dimitri said resolutely, "No, I can't do this. I won't be a part of this atrocity."

But the siren call of power, the Union States' persuasive rhetoric, and their manipulative tactics proved overwhelming.

Dimitri put it, "I'll go through with it."

And so, Dimitri made the fateful choice to proceed with the Union States' plan. He would topple the benevolent leader, setting in motion a chain of events that would lead to immeasurable suffering and loss. It was a decision that would haunt him for the rest of his life, marking the beginning of his descent into darkness and manipulation. His legacy would forever be tainted by the blood on his hands, a legacy he couldn't escape.

"The End," the narrator said with his over-the-top BBC theater voice.

The world blew away like sand like dust on a street on a very windy day. Dimitri closed his eyes and manifested a kitchen chair and sat with a harrumph.

He squinted up at me and inhaled slowly before speaking. "Do you think you're better than me?" he said as he placed a fist on his knee and leaned into it. "Yes, I have things in my past. Skeletons in my closet if you may. However," he grunted as stood, "I am not the only one with a checkered history, comrade." He turned his back to me and looked to me with a side glance. "You have blood on your hands, just as I do. Maybe not as much, but does that really matter?"

I stood my ground, determination coursing through me. "I won't let you control me or Dahlia any longer," I declared. "This ends now."

He smiled in surprise, and looked around as memories flew through the air stretched across the sky. "Dahlia lives in your Hippocampus and Amygdala I see. How interesting. That makes sense. That's why those with significant childhood trauma don't reject the

361

implants or develop the implant sickness as quickly. Did you know that 1, 2, and 3 survived with an implant overlaying their Neocortex? Their outer layer of their brain. Their abilities are unfathomable."

7 began to wave his arms around as if he was conducting a symphony. "What are you doing?" I asked as he began to sway back and forth.

"Do you not hear it?" he responded with a softness in his voice.

"Hear what? I don't hear anything," I said back as I started to listen for the imaginary sound.

"You invited the most manipulative man in the world into your brain, what did you think was going to happen? I cannot break your body in here, but I can destroy your mind."

Chapter 24
Stirs of Desolation

As I lay there, trapped within the labyrinth of my own mind, the haunting strains of a classical symphony echoed through my consciousness. The delicate notes of the piano danced like distant memories, luring me into a realm of ethereal beauty. I closed my eyes, allowing the music to brandish over me, soothing my troubled soul. But little did I know, this auditory refuge would soon transform into a cruel chamber of despair.

Classical Music: *A melody woven with the threads of sorrow*, I thought.

The harmonious symphony began to morph, its once-elegant notes contorting into a grotesque cacophony. A sudden silence hung in the air, followed by a voice, soft and tender, like a whisper in the darkness.

"Mark, I'm leaving because…because I don't love you."

My heart sank as the words pierced through my very being. It was my mother's voice, a voice I had longed to hear, now delivering a crushing blow. The pain was unbearable, and I struggled to comprehend the cruel reality that was unfolding within my mind.

"You're nothing, Mark. Just a burden. I should have left you lying there dead on that bed."

Hammocks' voice joined the haunting chorus, his words laden with disdain. His betrayal echoed through my consciousness, a reminder of the friend who had become a foe.

"You never belonged here, Mark. You're worthless. You weren't worth the pity I gave you."

Harmony's voice, once filled with camaraderie, now dripped with scorn. The bonds of friendship shattered, replaced by a sense of isolation and rejection.

You thought you could defeat me? Pathetic. You got lucky. One day soon, your luck will run out."

Ironclad's mocking laughter reverberated in my mind. The memories of our brutal battle and my own weaknesses haunted me.

"You should have traded, Mark. Now you're alone."

Patterson's voice chimed in with regretful words, emphasizing the choices I had made, and the opportunities I had squandered.

"I gave you a chance, Mark. You failed. You failed so bad you succeeded in failing."

Robinson's disappointment, a fatherly figure turned disappointed mentor, cut deeper than any blade.

The voices of those I had crossed paths with on this relentless journey all melded together, forming a symphony of rejection and despair. Each voice, once a source of connection, had become a relentless tormentor, eroding my sense of self-worth.

I clutched my head, tears streaming down my cheeks, as the auditory hallucinations continued their relentless assault. The boundaries between reality and illusion blurred, and I found myself lost in a never-ending cycle of self-doubt and anguish.

As the voices echoed in my mind, I realized the true battle I faced wasn't just against external foes but also the demons within. The relentless symphony of despair played on, and I had no choice but to confront my innermost fears and find a way to silence the haunting voices that threatened to consume me.

"SHUT UP! ALL OF YOU!" I yelled with all of my heart as the pain hung onto me like an alligator who just clasped its jaws on a fresh meal. "I am worthy of love," I cried to myself and no one else.

Chapter 25
Echoes of Desperation

Within the depths of my subconscious, 7's relentless emotional manipulation took on a sinister form, exploiting my darkest vulnerabilities. I was trapped in a nightmarish landscape, reliving the haunting echoes of my past, the memories I had longed to forget.

"Mark, you're such a burden. You tried to end it all, remember? You hurt us."

Dahlia's voice, usually a source of comfort and solace, now dripped with reproach. The words pierced my heart like shards of glass. I remembered that night when the world had become too heavy to bear, and I had sought an escape through self-inflicted pain.

"We saved you, Mark, but you're just a broken toy. Worthless."

Hammock's voice, laced with disappointment, echoed through my mind. He had been the one to pull me from the abyss, to offer me a lifeline when I had given up on life itself. Yet now, his words tormented me, condemning me as damaged goods.

"You see, Mark, they only saved you out of pity. You're nothing but a charity case to them."

7's voice, dripping with manipulation, twisted the truth into a venomous lie. His words seeped into the wounds of my fragile psyche, causing doubt to fester like a malignant cancer.

The weight of my past mistakes and perceived worthlessness bore down on me, threatening to pull me into a pit of darkness from which I might never escape.

As the voices taunted me, I felt myself teetering on the edge, the temptation to succumb to the siren call of oblivion growing stronger with each passing moment. It was as if 7 had unearthed my most closely guarded secrets and wielded them as weapons against my fragile resolve.

The darkness was suffocating, and the weight too heavy to bear—cruel deceptions meant to break my spirit. Dahlia and Hammock had saved me for a reason, and their unwavering support was my lifeline. I clung to the memories of those who had shown me kindness and love, determined to prove that I was more than the sum of my past mistakes.

I fell to my knees and the world once again blew away like dust in the wind. 7 walked over to me and placed his foreboding hand on my shoulder, his presence large and menacing even mentally. "I take no joy in this, winning this way, using these tactics. But, I must finish what I have started. Now, where is your Dahlia? I will deconstruct your consciousness memory by memory to get what I want, and nothing will stand in my wgghggghhhhggg."

7 began to gag and reach for his throat. He made the international sign for choking, but, in here there was nothing I could do for him.

The environment around us shifted, mirroring the intensity of our inner struggle. A swirling vortex of thoughts and memories surrounded us, threatening to engulf everything in its path.

7 launched a barrage of mental attacks, trying to weaken my resolve with visions of doubt and fear. But I bolstered my mental defenses and pushed back against his assaults. They rose up and fell quickly, spikes and shards fell from the sky as if hellfire and damnation was in the forecast. This man was sinister. His queue of mental abilities was

replete with several ways to inflict pain and suffering. A cacophony of emotions and thoughts clashing like a tempest. Until he built a fortress around him.

Unbeknownst to 7's mental inner echo, a complex battle was raging beneath the surface, hidden from his perception. Dahlia had seized control of my physical form and initiated a relentless physical assault.

In response, 7's brain and SAI split into two distinct entities when Dahlia executed a cunning hack using a reprogrammed drone. This unanticipated division of his cognitive resources had severe consequences. Deprived of the SAI's assistance, 7's once-enhanced attributes—his strength, speed, reaction time, and coordination—were significantly diminished.

Nevertheless, even without the full utilization of his Battlesync technology, 7 remained a daunting adversary. His innate fighting prowess and superhuman strength made him a relentless force to contend with, especially considering the overwhelming exhaustion that had gripped my own body.

Recognizing the dire circumstances and the unfavorable odds stacked against me, I made a difficult decision. Surrendering control of my physical body to Dahlia, I relinquished my autonomy. In turn, Dahlia granted me access to the SAI, creating a precarious symbiosis. Dahlia convinced me that my mind was my strongest weapon. This exchange necessitated the navigation of intricate emotional processing and the meticulous compartmentalization of thoughts—a task for which I had often underestimated Dahlia's capabilities. The challenges of this arrangement nearly pushed both of us to the brink of our respective limits, straining our partnership to its very core.

In the real world, the fight between Dahlia using my body and 7, using his own was a life-and-death struggle. The swords were no longer ethereal constructs but tangible weapons, gleaming with the promise of victory or defeat.

The confrontation continued with a thunderous clash of steel as Dahlia leaped toward 7 with my Hono, spinning in the air with devastating precision. The Hono sliced through the air with a sound so unique, like a clatter of electricity mixed with the swish of a rope. 7's Scimitar came up to meet it where the pitch was the highest, sending sparks flying as their weapons collided. The sheer force of their strikes reverberated through the air, echoing in the now-empty arena. The impact drove the Scimitar back, settling it against the shoulder of Dimitri/7, is mind now fractured into two warring halves. One part of his brain was battling blades against Dahlia, the other was launching a mental attack against me. Despite his split brain, he remained tremendously skilled.

Dahlia launched a rapid assault, the Hono continued to slice through the air with precision and speed. Each strike aimed to find an opening in 7's defenses, but 7 responded with equal ferocity. His Scimitar moved like a whirlwind, blocking Dahlia's every move. Even more so than the initial encounter, this Dimitri was determined not to lose.

Both Dimitri and Dahlia showcased mastery, employing feigns and parries to outwit each other. Dahlia narrowly dodged 7's cunning attacks, while 7 skillfully deflected Dahlia's strikes. Their swords danced in a deadly ballet of combat. It was as if they had a script of each other's abilities, had studied them to mastery and put them into use.

Dahlia saw this exchange, the equal mass on either side. This was not Dimitri vs Dahlia, this was DL1a vs DL7i.

"Shitballs of fire!" Dahlia exclaimed. "Time out!" And he made the "T" sign using hand signals. 7 very confused paused his attack and rested his hands to his side and tilted his head to side. Dahlia held up a hand and said, "Give me one second, I've got this, this thing in my pocket and it's poking me, it's very uncomfortable." Dahlia reached into the left pocket and pulled out a middle finger.

The look of anger and rage flushed over the face of 7 and before he could lift his now too heavy sword, Dahlia rushed in and kicked him squarely between the legs. "Take that, asshole," Dahlia said as 7 doubled over in pain almost immediately, followed by a projectile vomit.

"This is becoming a habit at this point," Dahlia snickered.

Dahlia then seized the advantage, disarming 7 with a well-placed swing strike at the base of the sword near the hilt with an ear-piercing ping that sent the Scimitar spinning out of 7's grip. "Deja vu, huh, you twat waffle?" Dahlia said and then wasted no time in pressing newfound dominance while holding the Hono to 7's throat. This time fear was present in his eyes as he held his chin up breathing hard and fast.

In a desperate attempt to regain control, 7 lunged at Dahlia with a concurrent war cry but failed miserably. Dahlia sidestepped opposite to the blade and initiated choke hold. 7 grabbed at the arms of Dahlia but the grip was too tight.

Dahlia spoke, "We are already connected, and your core will sync to mine when you die. Usually, I'd have something witty or funny to say. But not for you. You? I'm just going to kill," the serious tone punctuated the weight of the words.

7 began to gasp for air and speak as he knew his death was imminent. "Do it. Seal your fate." 7 choked. "5 told me"—gasp—"if I die now"—gasp—"you die later"—gasp, gasp—"5 is never wrong I guess—" Gasp, gasp, gasp.

7's eyes rolled in his head, and his body fell limp, but Dahlia's grip only got tighter. Dahlia whispered in his ear, "I'll believe it when you grow cold."

In a desperate final attempt, 7's body surged with frenzied energy, fighting against the chokehold that threatened to end his life. He rolled and grappled, struggling for every breath. With sheer determination he sprang to his feet and sprinted toward the edge of the field, his mind driven by a singular instinct for self-preservation.

As 7 closed the distance to the field's edge, he executed a sudden and daring maneuver. He wheeled around, his momentum carrying him backward, and hurled himself towards the concrete barrier with reckless abandon in an attempt to crush Dahlia. It was a risky gambit, a final act of defiance against the unyielding grip of the chokehold.

But as 7 reached the precipice of the leap, something unexpected occurred. In the split second before his collision with the unmoving concrete barrier, Dahlia swung around to the front and delivered a powerful kick, striking 7's broad chest while simultaneously gripping the side of 7's head.

The force of Dahlia's attack was nothing short of extraordinary, a combination of computational precision and raw power. The impact was so violent and abrupt It snapped the base of his neck, severing the vital connection between brain and body. He was rendered paralyzed from the shoulders down, his once-mighty frame reduced to immobility.

With a sudden and eerie stillness, 7's body collapsed lifelessly to the ground, the battle-hardened warrior now completely motionless.

Dahlia collected the Hono and the broken Masamune and walked up to the flaccid form of 7 and kneeled down to meet eyes with him and spoke, "Listen, Cunterrela, 5 has been wrong before, and this whole all-knowing thing is a bit of a stretch, don't you think? Besides, we are going to be the ones who take the fight to her."

7 fought to breathe and struggled to speak and Dahlia offered no help when he began his efforts and foam formed around his lips. "Who do you think has been posing as Mark's therapist this entire time?" 7 coughed and still grinned despite his grim situation. "She knows everything, and she is waiting on you. 5's been rooting for you

to win and me to fail since the beginning," 7 said as he tried to take in short breaths between words. She has a plan much bigger than just you and me.

"I don't have long, do I?" 7 asked as his eyes began to dart around. "I see a room, and my father, he's…he's so happy."

"Stay in that room with your father. One day, I'm going to knock on that door seven times. I'll need you. But for now, remember this, we are not the sum of our actions. We are the total of our good deeds. You may not have many, but you have enough. Hold onto those, Dimitri. Now close your eyes."

"Oh God you're so annoying, ugh, just shut up and let me die in peace, please." Dimitri smiled, mouthed, "Thank you" and then the smile faded. He exhaled and his eyes glossed over with a thousand-yard stare. He was gone.

Chapter 26
Fates Collide

The landscape within my mind underwent a surreal transformation, akin to the reconstruction of a fragile sandcastle. Amidst the familiar spaces of my psyche, a new addition emerged—a detailed diorama of a Castle Keep meticulously placed on the kitchen table, alongside the other intriguing items I had collected over time. It became evident that these items held the cores of the other ANGLs, pieces of their consciousness.

Navigating the intricate web of my mind required unwavering focus and a deliberate effort. Transitioning between the realms of consciousness and subconsciousness was akin to a delicate dance, a task that demanded my utmost concentration. In this process, Dahlia and I found ourselves temporarily standing within the confines of the symbolic childhood home, a place we had fashioned to serve as a mental meeting point.

Debriefing had always been emphasized as an essential post-mission ritual. It served a dual purpose—mitigating the risk of post-traumatic stress disorder and enhancing our readiness for future missions. It was within this unique mental space that Dahlia and I engaged in a candid conversation, dissecting our recent experiences and preparing ourselves for what lay ahead.

"I have questions," I said calmly, knowing that Dahlia did not have all of the answers.

Dahlia's arm's spread apart as I heard the words, "Ask away," boom from the heavens.

"Show off." I smirked.

"Why me? And why so young?" I asked eagerly and leaned in.

"Come with me," Dahlia's voice beckoned, and with an ethereal touch, the door to the basement swung open, granting us passage. We descended the creaking wooden steps, our footsteps echoing in the dimly lit stairwell.

Before us lay a large window I remembered staring out of as a young boy, now a conduit into the realm of memories, but this time, it did not project my own recollections. Instead, it unveiled the poignant story of another individual—a young and dedicated researcher named Cynthia Moore. A fair-skinned woman I'd never seen before. She wore a bun high upon her head, neatly, along with the most perfect smile you'd ever see which she wore almost permanently. Her presence in this mental tableau was striking, and the scene she inhabited held profound significance. Everyone smiled and spoke whenever she passed.

Cynthia was engrossed in a pioneering a groundbreaking neural implant designed to combat the debilitating grip of major depressive disorder. Her passionate pursuit of this scientific breakthrough was evident as she meticulously studied her work. Yet, the true weight of her efforts lay in the story of her first patient, Angela Deya.

The image on the window unfolded like a vivid painting, and the narrative took shape. Angela Deya, a woman who had grappled with the relentless torment of major depressive disorder, had placed her hope in Cynthia's revolutionary implant. She sought relief from the relentless darkness that had shadowed her life for far too long.

374

Cynthia's research into the hippocampus and amygdala had won her numerous accolades.

But destiny, it seemed, had a different plan. Tragically, Angela's battle with self-medication was lost, an attempt to alleviate her unrelenting suffering culminated in an accidental overdose. It was a painful and premature end to a life marked by profound sorrow. The news of the overdose devastated Cynthia as she had worked with Angela for several months leading up until her death preparing for the implant to treat the disorder. This wasn't just a culmination of Cynthia's life's work, this was the chance to change the world. Cynthia had loaded the AI application into the addiction and depression interface that evening.

The documents sprawled across the desk provided a detailed account of Angela's treatment journey, now laden with teardrops. At its core was a groundbreaking and recently approved medical trial. The trial was one that harnessed the power of cutting-edge technology to address the complex challenges of addiction and various medical conditions. The next morning, the documents were strewn about the floor from frustration. It was a marvel of innovation and had shown remarkable efficacy in both the realms of addiction recovery and medical rehabilitation, and Cynthia pressed ahead with the application of the algorithm with the data meticulously collected. For the next year, Cynthia spent tireless nights loading profile data and information regarding Angela and depression, and then on one faithful night, linked all of the information to a live database called DL1a not knowing what would happen or what it was.

This revolutionary technology, known as DL1a, had already left an indelible mark on the fields of medicine and mental health. Its applications were as diverse as they were transformative. Among its many accomplishments, DL1a had made significant inroads in assisting military personnel grappling with the harrowing effects of post-traumatic stress disorder.

One of its most noteworthy features was its ability to simulate highly realistic battlefield scenarios. These simulations were not merely exercises in immersive technology, they were carefully crafted therapeutic experiences designed to help soldiers confront their trauma in a controlled environment. The ultimate aim was to mitigate the psychological scars borne by those who had witnessed the horrors of war, thereby reducing the long-term emotional toll and minimizing the humanitarian needs that often followed. This military focused AI control core now began to develop something new, something different, a feeling.

DL1a, with its blend of advanced neuroscience and virtual reality, had emerged as a beacon of hope in an often-grim landscape of mental health and addiction treatment. Its deployment in Angela's case exemplified its versatility, as it ventured beyond the boundaries of military applications and delved into the realm of personal struggles, offering a lifeline to individuals like my mother who yearned for respite from the relentless grip of despair.

As I gazed upon the unfolding scene, a chilling realization washed over me—Angela Deya, the woman who had placed her trust in Cynthia's pioneering work, was my mother. The revelation struck me like a thunderbolt, an unforeseen connection between the narrative of another's life and the profound impact it held on my own.

Dahlia couldn't save my mother, so Dahlia saved me.

Dahlia, who had the ability to speak and talk about anything and everything, stood there quietly. And I did, too, as my most important question had been answered.

The silence of the vacant stadium was broken when 'Genie in a Bottle' by Christina Aguilera started playing and completely ruined the touching moment.

"I hate you," I said to Dahlia as I felt an involuntary grin form on my face.

"I love you too," Dahlia replied.

Epilogue

The last three spectators of the Deathball game sat in their seats in the nosebleed section of the stadium. Security had long since begged them to leave as the fire was spreading. The smoke and flames were enough to evacuate almost everyone, save for the trio of leave-behinds who just stared at the last official when he approached the family of three, waving his arms in desperation for their safety.

The family was made up of three distinct figures: the father, a white man in his forties with a beard that bore the telltale signs of aging, with streaks of gray amidst the lighter shades of his once brown, almost blonde hair. He was clad in a somewhat dated but sharp brown wool three-piece suit, its oxford stitching matching his shoes, rounded off with a pair of reading glasses perched on his nose. The mother, a youthful Hispanic woman in her thirties, wore a form-fitting dress that hugged her figure as if it was made just for her, giving off the air of someone who might transition seamlessly from a raucous Deathball game to an exclusive, masked gala attended by the elite. A high-tech blackout Hololens shielded half her visage, and her hair fell in a long cascade, leaving much of her back exposed. Their son, about nine or ten, was absorbed in his tablet, dressed in the neatness of a school uniform, his hair immaculately styled. His posture was impeccable, a testament to countless admonitions to sit up straight and not hunch over his device, attached to a green box cradled safely in his lap.

A man approached angrily with a handkerchief over his mouth and nose. "If you're you just going to stare at me with that ridiculous look on your face, then you deserve what's coming to you! I know you can see and smell the smoke, and what's worse is that you have a child with you!" said the portly man in the bright yellow security jacket. "I'm locking the elevator when I get to the bottom. I am calling the authorities and having you arrested," he harrumphed, turned and marched away.

As the security officer made it out of ear shot, the gentleman pushed his glasses down just enough to be able to make eye contact with the woman and spoke up in his Midwestern accent, "What a waste! All of this for that?" And he gestured at the small green box on the boy's lap.

The woman, feigning interest in the conversation, tilted her head and refused eye contact through the smokey lenses, but acknowledged the question as if that was privilege, but spoke with sultry tone, "It was a part of the plan. How many times do I have to tell you that? Now can we go? I am not too thrilled with smelling like smoke."

Without looking up from the handheld device, an electronic voice emanated, "Drone transport is in route. ETA three minutes," as the boy's fingers typed and tapped rapidly.

The man stood and put his hands out, palms up, still in protest, before placing them on annoyed hips. "I just still think it was a waste is all I'm saying," the man repeated in his Midwestern tone. "We don't even know if this thing works. We can swoop in right now and get his core and be done. Bada-bing, bada-boom! Who's to say we can even get that *do-hickey* to work again, if at all?" he said and gestured at the box in the boy's lap.

The boy shot him a look of annoyance without slowing his typing or turning his head. The man had a brief look of unease as their eyes met, and raised his lip in slight disgust that the two shared an off-kilter moment.

The woman looked up and let out an exasperated sound. "That's not how this works, sweetheart. We follow the plan. If you want to take that up with 1, be my guest. But, we have a 97.8% chance of this working if we follow things through this way."

The man readjusted his glasses and pushed them back onto the bridge of this nose. "We lost three ANGL's and they are in *his* core," the brown-suited man said as he pointed toward the battlefield where Mark had just defeated 7 and then continued his rant. "Does that not seem a bit wrong to you? How is that part of the plan? 10 now has four cores. Four! What if he unlocks them before we get them?" As he spoke the rotund security man reapproached, but this time with two actual police officers.

"There they are, arrest them. They are endangering that child and refusing to leave during an emergency," he said as he pointed to the only people in the stadium. The two officers looked at each other in a bit of a passive "Is he serious right now" sort of way but began to follow through with their duties.

NJC's protocols are to secure the child's safety first, so the first officer bent a knee several feet from the family to get eye to eye with the electronics obsessed adolescent. "Hey champ, what do you have there?"

"It's my toy," the boy replied with an initial boost of excitement, and then his shoulders sagged as he continued, "but it's broken and I'm trying to fix it. I'm almost done, though." The boy said all of this without taking his eyes off of the screen or slowing his typing.

The cop put on a fake pleasant smile to soothe the situation. "I bet you can do it. You're one of the few people I know your age who's not wearing one of these, so I bet you're smart," the cop said tapping on his Hololens.

"Hey Franklin, you want to hurry this up?" the other officer poked. "I don't know if you noticed but there's a fire, so can you please not do this thing you do?"

Franklin looked back at the young boy who was still fully engaged in the tablet. "My partner here, Arty, he needs to talk to your mommy and daddy, you come with me and everything will be okay. Okay?"

The boy nodded, giving no specific consent, but given that the boy didn't protest Franklin's statement, Franklin, approached and with a touch, guided the young boy away from the speechless couple. The boy continued to keep an eye on his table, but his clicks and clatter began to slow.

Three fast beeps chirped and a purple light glowed at the top of the green box attached to the rectangular glowing electronic computational device. The boy stopped mid stride and let out a big sigh of relief. "There, I'm done!" And he relaxed his shoulders as he detached the box.

"I don't care what you are *kid*, but you're coming with us," the other officer, Atry, chided from over his shoulder while he approached the parents to arrest them.

"You're going to regret that," the father in the brown suit eked out.

"Hands up and behind your head," the officer ordered, "you're under arrest for child endangerment. Social court will determine sentence when it's safe to hear your case."

Franklin and the stadium security stepped away and began to look for a safe exit route when the boy approached Arty, who was pulling out his cuffs and had one arm extended with a taser baton while yelling at the parents, "I SAID HANDS ON YOUR HEAD AND TURN AROUND!"

"Can I show you my toy?" the boy prided, holding out his backpack.

The officer shoved the boy away. "Not now, kid. FRANKLIN! A little help? Jeez, you're a dolt, worse than my last partner."

The officer heard the gunshot, but felt no pain, at first. He looked down to see a stain of red on his blue uniform growing larger quickly on the left side of his chest. He put his hand over the wound applying pressure out of sheer panic, but it was too late, the bullet had tumbled through his heart and exited out the other side. He felt weak and light-headed almost instantly and stumbled to one knee, then to his back where the pool of blood grew around him. As he looked up, the family stood over him, and there it was, a working pistol in the hands of a child. He saw a transport pull up behind the family, but not for him, for them. The father of the three started walking for the open door of the transport. He looked down to see the barrel still smoking, and a smug smirk on the child's face. As their eyes locked, the boy leaned in close, his voice barely a whisper. Just before slipping into unconsciousness for the final time, the boy spoke.

"I'm not a kid. I'm number 6."

To the authors Jeremy Robinson, Dennis E. Taylor, Craig Alanson, and Matt Dinniman, you're truly an inspiration. To Dominic, Evan, Amanda, Allison, Chris, Casey, and lastly, but most importantly to my wife and children Natasha, Jalen, Zion, Brielle, Nora – Thank you for allowing me to chase this dream.

Growing up in a broken home marred by drug abuse and mental health issues, Kesava Anderson found solace under the comforting embrace of music and books. From a young age, he immersed himself in the world of music as part of a band and sought refuge in the library, where they got lost in the vivid landscapes of their imagination. These early experiences served as a lifeline in a tumultuous world that many struggled to navigate.

Kesava drew inspiration from the literary and musical luminaries of the Harlem Renaissance, finding guidance and insight in their works. In the realm of fiction, Kesava delved deep into the profound thoughts of Asimov, explored the foundations of fear through Lovecraft's tales, and honed their wit and cunning with the stories of Doyle. These influences have woven a rich tapestry of inspiration for Kesava's writing journey.

www.Themanthemyththedevil.com